PRAIRIE SPRINGS

THE UNRAVELING OF A SMALL TOWN

PRAIRIE SPRINGS

BOOK ONE

LANCE R. WILLIAMSON

Edited by:
Jennifer Lawyer-Wilson
redfernrebel@gmail.com

Gregory J. Hodges
editorgreg@mac.com

Cover/Book Design:
Lance Williamson & Greg Hodges

Dedicated to those who try to make the world a better place.

Special thanks to:
Gregory J. Hodges
Laynie Humphrey
Jennifer Lawyer-Wilson

Thank you for reading! It means the world to me.
    —Lance

Character Guide

Anna Aron: Jewish teacher who moved from New York
Kyle Brickey: Anna's friend from New York
Edwina "Winnie" Collins: the old lady
Rose Welsh: the landlady
Flo: the waitress at the 36 Diner
Maxine Burke: checker at the Save-All

Constance Faye Barker: *The Herald* reporter
Dorcas Bledsoe: overeater and Constance's sister
Ted Bledsoe: Dorcas' husband
Trey Stewart: the mayor and preacher's son
Stacy Stewart: Trey's wife

Ivory Black: Rose's sister who disappeared
Ronald Black: Ivory Black's husband
Louise Burke: Maxine's mother, also a Save-All checker
Mark Craven: high-school music teacher
Violet White: cereal-box diva from New York

Humphrey: Winnie's gentleman friend
Abigail Aron: Anna's mother
Officer Dick Richards: police officer
Ricky Richards: Officer Richards' son
Vivian Richards: Officer Richards' wife and Ricky's mother
Judy Jane Johnson: bank teller with half-paralyzed face
Ed Stewart: pastor at the Third Baptist Church
Crystal Stewart: pastor's wife

Mae Pearl Fisher: nursing home resident
Agnes: nursing home resident
Dr. Arthur Waxman: nursing home resident
Dr. Kimball: plastic surgeon
Chuck Dickson: police officer in East Texas, Chawli's son
Chawli Dickson: drives the taxi, raises black-eyed peas

Randy: Anna's hook-up
Frank: overeater
Roberto: gas station attendant
Sylvia: Stacy and Trey's housekeeper
Luciano: Argentinean visitor
Wilbur: "attorney-at-law"

April Something, Way Back When

"**M**ove in one!"

Edwina Collins was thrilled. Her plan was working. Standing five feet, five inches tall, she barely qualified to be a Rockette. Being the shortest of the high-kickers, Edwina, or "Winnie," as her dance mates nicknamed her, was placed on the outer edge of the line while the tallest girls stood in the middle. Feeling inadequate and simple, yet wanting to be the center of attention, Winnie was determined to come up with a way to grow taller. She installed a trapeze in her West Village apartment and hung by her legs, but all it did was make her head hurt. Miracle vitamin pills claiming to "add inches to your height" only made her nauseated. Finally, one evening after a show, a solution came to her. That night she rummaged the garbage bins throughout the Village until she found a pair of high heels similar to her dancing shoes. She took them back to her apartment, sawed the heels into layers, and each week glued a quarter-inch onto her height.

After four weeks, she was standing an inch taller and had passed three girls in line. The way she figured it, she would be front and center within two months. Unfortunately, standing became awkward. Using more discarded shoes, she added on the half soles. This relieved some of the discomfort, but it made her shoes way too heavy, as she found out one night when one of them flew off and hit a man on the head in the fifth row. That was the last time Winnie danced, but she was grateful for the experience and even more grateful for her nickname. Soon afterwards, she took the money she'd saved, packed her bags, and headed home.

CHAPTER ONE

At 1914 Harper Valley Lane, Rose Welsh was enjoying a rerun of *Three's Company* when the phone rang. She nearly jumped through her skin, fearing it was her pastor or Jesus himself condemning her for watching repugnant smut. She turned down the volume and reached for the phone. "Hello?"

"The tenants have arrived."

"Tenants? I thought there was just one."

"Two. Male and a female."

"What should I do?"

"Not my problem." The caller hung up.

Rose went back to the show. "What are they trying to pull, Bitsy?" she asked her four-year-old dachshund.

Years ago, Rose's house was a three-story Victorian showplace. But since her only income came from renting one of the three apartments in the backyard and from meager government checks, she couldn't afford to splurge on aesthetics. The once-desired house was now an eyesore, and Rose had fallen into a yearslong depression. When the school district asked if she'd be willing to rent a place to the new teacher moving in from out of state, she jumped at the chance.

After a sip of water, Rose settled into the reclining wingback she picked up at one of her many impulsive garage sale purchases. It matched the 1920s wallpaper that barely clung to the walls and flaked off every time someone sneezed—not that she had a lot of company.

She carefully rested her glass on *The Herald*, the biweekly eight-page local newspaper resting on the lamp table. Aside from the Bible and the occasional *Southern Living*, she needed no other reading material. When *Three's Company* ended, she continued her discussion with Bitsy about a potential extra tenant. "The school district told me she was single. Do you think she's married?"

Rose fetched the keys hidden on a hook inside the cereal cabinet, stepped onto the screened-in back porch that doubled as the laundry room, and reached for the bottle of insect repellant hanging snugly in a crocheted pouch.

The fenced-in yard behind the house was a mess of tall weeds. Hidden amongst them was a fountain that hadn't worked in years and was appreciated only by the mosquitoes after a rain. To each side of it were the cottages. On the left was the occupied one-story unit, and across from it stood the two-story cabin, divided into an upstairs and downstairs apartment with an external stairway. In the rear of the yard, a gate led to an open field.

Using the glow from the utility pole light, Rose made her way to the first-floor apartment. Bitsy followed closely behind, stopping only to raise his leg and tinkle.

Rose flipped on the lights and a cockroach skittered across the kitchen floor. After several failed attempts, she eventually stomped it and grabbed the innards with a wad of toilet paper. As she flushed it and watched to make sure it went down, she tried not to notice where the hard water had left a ring in the commode. Comforted there was one less roach in the world, she picked up the phone to verify there was a dial tone and glanced around a final time. When she turned out the lights, Bitsy ran to her side.

Rose prepared for bed. It was a quarter after eleven and there was still no sign of the new tenant (or tenants). She crawled under the covers and began her nightly prayer. Like clockwork, shortly after midnight, Bitsy came to attention and looked out the window. The long-term resident of the one-story cabin had arrived home. Rose slept through the slam of the pickup door and the motor that wanted to keep running even after the ignition was off. Once the noise of footsteps ceased and the engine finally died, Bitsy rested his head back down on the afghan at his mistress' feet.

THE PREVIOUS NIGHT

"Arkadelphia?"

The flickering lights in the distance broke the night sky like lighters being held up at a concert. "Doesn't look like there's much to it," Anna Aron commented.

Her friend and traveling companion, Kyle Brickey, didn't care what there was to the town as long as it had a motel. He spotted a green neon VACANCY sign and pleaded with Anna to stop for the night. She pulled the U-Haul truck into the parking lot.

Kyle sighed with relief. "I'll go check us in."

The next morning, showered, rested, and ready for the six hours that remained of their trip, Kyle set his suitcase on the second floor walkway, double-checked he had the room key, and latched the motel room door.

"Uh, Kyle? Where did I park the truck?"

Kyle turned around. "Whadaya mean? You parked it right down—"

Instead of being back on the road, they were waiting for the police to arrive. Anna's belongings, having been reduced to the luggage beside her, caused her to question leaving New York to accept a teaching position in the middle of Texas.

Once the policeman arrived and filed a report, they rented a car and continued their journey. The sense of relief they felt as they crossed the state line into Texas dissipated with the reflection of red-and-blue lights in the mirrors.

"Crap!" Anna pounded the steering wheel. "Could this trip get any worse?!"

When the officer asked for her license and registration, Anna fumbled for the papers from the rental car agency and dug in her purse for her license, pausing twice to unbutton her blouse. "My, sir, I didn't realize how hot it was until I rolled down the window. We had the air conditioner running, and—"

Kyle tried to keep from laughing.

The cop bent down and looked beyond Anna's breasts, the right one eager to expose some detail, and over at Kyle. "This your husband?"

"No, sir. Here's my license, uh...Officer Dickson. It's not a good picture," she defended, while running the tip of her fingernail seductively down her neck.

"Good grief," Kyle bit his bottom lip, but it wasn't enough to restrain the grin.

Officer Dickson winked at Kyle. "Where are y'all headed?"

"Prairie Springs, Texas," Anna answered.

"Of all places! I grew up there...My folks still live there...Y'all are free to go, but slower this time...And button your blouse, lady!"

"Thank you, Officer. We will." She quickly raised the window. "What a coincidence! Right, Kyle? You think my boobs helped?"

"Sure, Cupcake."

Hours later, with bladders at the overflow level and the cruise control set precisely at 65 MPH, the headlights shone on the sign they'd been waiting for: WELCOME TO PRAIRIE SPRINGS. They pulled into the first place certain to have a bathroom.

The 36 Diner and Roadside Palace motel sat side by side on Highway 36. As they entered, a waitress with platinum blond, cotton-candy hair approached. "Dinner for two?" She grabbed a couple of menus from the wooden box attached to the hostess stand.

Anna exhaled an exhausted, "Yes, please."

The waitress smiled briefly and led them to a table in the middle of the restaurant.

"Could we get a booth?" Kyle asked.

The waitress raised her painted-on, over-arched eyebrows, "You're the customers; you can sit wherever you'd like."

"We wanna keep an eye on the car," Kyle added as they scooted on the vinyl upholstery.

"Y'all ain't from 'round here, are y'all? You think someone's gonna steal your car? If anyone gets near your car, just yell out *Flo!* —that's my name—and I'll blow their brains out. I keep a 12-gauge under the counter."

Anna nervously adjusted her position in the springy booth bench. "Fantastic."

"I'll be back to take y'all's order and bring y'all some water. Just sit tight."

They waited until Flo walked away before hurrying to the restrooms and met back at the booth where two glasses of ice water awaited them.

"What are you going to order?" Anna asked.

"Geez, I don't know." Kyle looked around to see what the others had on their plates. He couldn't see what the woman sitting alone and wearing a loud turquoise dress was eating, but an overweight lady and her husband a few tables closer were having some type of battered steak. Kyle noticed a resemblance between the two women and briefly pondered why the obvious relatives weren't sitting together. The only other customer was a police officer. Kyle was more concerned with his intense stare than he was with the food on the man's plate.

"Kyle, why do I get the feeling we're not very welcome here?"

"I dunno, but I hope that changes since you've just taken a job in this town."

Anna looked up from the menu and glanced around the restaurant, "I do too, Kyle. I do too."

After an uneventful dinner of burgers and fries, they heeded the waitress' advice and went next door to the two-story Roadside Palace motel, agreeing it was safer to call it a night instead of venturing into unknown areas of town after dark. As they had noticed with other small towns, the designated city limits were premature and distant from any signs of life, as if the founders had envisioned a much larger city. Prairie Springs appeared to be in that same category. Aside from the diner, the motel and a few scattered farmhouses, there wasn't much around.

As soon as they left the diner, the woman in turquoise jumped up and ran to the payphone. "The tenants have arrived."

Kyle drew back the curtain of their motel room, making sure the car was still parked under the security light.

"You coming to bed?" Anna asked.

"I don't think so. Not yet." He released the curtain. "I think I'll go out for a smoke."

"Want me to come with you?" she offered.

"Get your beauty rest. I'll be back in a few."

Anna watched as he closed the door.

Kyle stopped to light a cigarette and spotted a picnic table next to a thicket of trees at the far edge of the parking lot. He quietly approached the stairs, looking into the different rooms as he passed. Most were vacant. The only room with a light on was next to the stairwell. He tried to sneak by quietly, but someone must have caught glimpse of him. When he looked back, a man was peeking out. Kyle turned away quickly and walked nonchalantly towards the picnic table.

As he sat smoking, he thought of Anna and the fated way they'd met in Central Park. He had propped his foot up on a bench to tie his shoe. Anna was reading the same David Sedaris book he'd recently finished. The two hit it off, spent the rest of the day together, and talked well into the night over a bottle of wine. They had been inseparable since. He wasn't sure how he was going to handle her not living in New York anymore. Why she accepted a teaching job so far away was beyond him.

"Got a light?"

The raspy voice startled him until he noticed it was coming from a woman he was certain wasn't far from death. "Um...sure."

"Bless your heart. I was in the room and couldn't sleep. My man snores like a hog in heat."

Kyle chuckled as he handed her his lighter.

"What's *your* excuse for being out here at this time a night, sonny?"

"Just wasn't ready for bed yet."

"Mind if I sit with ya?"

Kyle would have felt more comfortable if she'd taken the opposite side of the table.

"Surely you don't expect me to sit with my back to the trees, do you?" the lady barked as she urged Kyle to scoot over with a wave of her hand.

Kyle could tell after her first drag that her cigarette didn't come in a red-and-white box.

"Wanna puff? uh—"

"Kyle."

"Kyle? Get outta here! That was the name of one of my husbands."

"No kidding."

"Sure as shit. Did you wanna puff of my cigarette? It's special, if you know what I mean."

"I had that feeling," Kyle said.

"That's why I have to smoke while my man's asleep. He don't approve."

Kyle was intrigued by the old lady. How she applied her lipstick in a big circle around her mouth like a child who couldn't stay in the lines. The careless way she wore her coppery wig, not concerned with the tufts of white hair that escaped from underneath. Her presence that belied her size.

"You don't mind, do you, sonny?"

"Oh no. I don't mind."

"You married, uh...what'd you say your name was?"

"Kyle."

"Kyle—Kyle? I had a husband by that same name."

"You told me."

She took a drag, "My mind slips sometimes. I can tell you the weather in 1953, but I can't remember what I did five minutes ago—'specially when I smoke this stuff. It brings everything to life but the present. You know what I'm saying, uh—"

"Kyle."

"Kyle. Right. You's a fine-looking boy. You got yourself a girl?"

"No ma'am."

"You queer?"

"I guess you could say that."

"Ain't nothing wrong with liking men. I tend to lean that way myself. I got me a man now—Humphrey. I don't want him to catch me smoking my weed 'cause he's liable to leave me, and ain't nobody else want my worn-out hoo-ha."

"He's *got* to smell it."

"It's wrinkled, sonny, but it don't stink."

"Not your—the weed! He's bound to know you smoke."

"He's too dumb. I told him it's a new perfume I got at the Save-All. Say, sonny, what're you doing here, anyway? I can tell you ain't from Prairie Springs."

"No, ma'am, I'm from New York."

"Get out! I used to live there, many moons ago."

"Really?"

"Lived in the West Village when I was a Rockette," she answered, dreamily.

"I live in the East Village, and my friend Anna lives—lived—in the West. Wait! You were a Rockette?" He gave her a once-over.

"Whatcha lookin' at? I used to be taller."

Kyle grinned.

"I miss it so." She took a deep breath and exhaled, trying to avoid any vivid recollections "I left it all behind for this piss-ant town and my loser family."

"You regret marrying, um, Humphrey, was it?"

"Shucks! Humphrey and me, we ain't married. After I lost my last husband, I swore I'd never marry again."

"I see."

"Ain't nobody taught you no manners? You haven't even asked my name."

Kyle took the final drag on his cigarette, "I'm sorry. I didn't want to pry."

"Hell, that ain't pryin'. People call me Winnie."

"Winnie." Kyle acknowledged, but doubted he would ever see her again.

"You gonna be here a while...at the Roadside Palace?"

"No, we're only here for the night. I'm with my friend and she'll be—"

A light came on in one of the rooms on the bottom floor. "Slap me silly! Humphrey's up. I gotta get." Winnie stood and tugged at her nightgown. "Thanks for the light. Be careful out here, sonny."

Kyle watched as Winnie walked towards her room. He, too, decided to call it a night and headed back. When he opened the door, Anna shuffled her legs under the covers but never woke. He placed the key by the television, undressed down to his underwear and crawled beneath the covers.

CHAPTER TWO

On a hill at the northeastern edge of town stood the Third Baptist Church, a huge windowless aluminum contraption. The only feature distinguishing it from an airplane hangar or document storage facility was a small metal cross perched on the apex of the pointy roof. Even *it* appeared to be more an afterthought than a planned detail.

Despite its commercial appearance, the Third Baptist Church was home to the town's largest congregation, beating out both the First and Second Baptist churches in attendance and revenue. Most of the female members of the church belonged to the Third Base Ladies League, and they were pulling into the parking lot one after another to prepare for the annual fundraiser, which was to begin sharply at noon on the front lawn. Each car had at least one woman, most with kids in tow, and an occasional husband, every one of whom looked like they'd rather be bathing the cat.

It was a sure sign of summer when the grass looked like hay. Around the church, the only thing green was a potted plant by the front doors and what was placed into the offering plates each Sunday. A stark contrast to the pastor's church-owned home lawn, which was on a secluded piece of land just out of town, and manicured to golf-course standards.

The temperature was already in the nineties and it was as dry as a bone. Even the flies were thirsty and tried desperately to get some of the iced tea Maxine Burke was mixing in a keg-sized container. "These gawl-darn flies!" she huffed with a controlled tongue.

"I know it. Aren't they something this year?" Constance Faye Barker appeared, wearing a turquoise t-shirt with a turtle embroidered on the front and matching turquoise slacks. "I've even been thinkin' 'bout getting a screen door for my front porch. I've never seen them so bad, Maxine. You know, I was talking the other night—we need to have a prayer meeting about 'em don't you think?"

"Oh, Constance, I dunno. Pray for the flies to go away?"

"It couldn't hurt."

"I guess not. What you got under that foil?"

"The best baked beans you ever tasted."

"Yum, I can't wait," Maxine feigned enthusiasm. "I think the baked-bean table is over yonder." She pointed with the handle of the wooden spoon she was using to mix the tea. No sooner had Constance gone did Dorcas Bledsoe come over with a Pyrex dish. "I hope them ain't beans," Maxine said. "Any more beans and we're liable to blow the whole town clear off the map."

Dorcas, as big around as she was tall, cackled at what she was about to say, "I didn't even know we were on the map." Her laugh tapered off like a music box winding down. Just when you thought it was over, another chirp came out.

"Lord," Dorcas looked up to the sky and spoke to Him directly, "You got me a-sweatin'!" She turned back to Maxine in a snit and pushed up her glasses. "I'm gonna be a mess by day's end unless I get me a shower. Can you believe this heat? If you ask me, it's Jesus' way of reminding us what hell would be like. If I can't take the heat here, I don't *even*—Let's just put it this way: I hope there's an air conditioner in heaven!"

Dorcas grabbed a wasteful wad of napkins and dabbed at her neck and forehead, gesturing to Maxine. "At least *you're* leaning over cold ice!" She walked away with her baked beans and attempted to strategically situate them on the table under the canopy.

Maxine watched as the two sisters fought for the best place, preferably one of the corners where a line was sure to form.

"Good morning, Sister Maxine," a voice said from behind. Out of all the people on the church lawn, Maxine was by far the least eager to be there and would have preferred to work an extra shift at the grocery store. Usually having weekends off was a blessing, a well-deserved one after ten years of rotating shifts, but when she got suckered into events like this, she was beginning to think otherwise. Her manager at the Save-All grocery store thought it would be good for business to have a representative show support at such a large event. "...And no one is more charming than you, Maxine," he'd told her. She had lived in Prairie Springs all of her life, which wasn't uncommon in this town where the fruit didn't fall far from the tree—sometimes it didn't fall at all—and she was walking in her mother's footsteps. Her mother worked Lane 2 while Maxine checked in Lane 1, the express lane. She was the prettiest girl in town and also the quickest checker. Some said she was quicker than Judy Jane Johnson, the teller at the First National Bank, but they had yet to have an official showdown. Unlike most local women in their mid-thirties, Maxine wore only a touch of eye makeup and a light stroke of lipstick. Ever since she was a kid, her mother had encouraged her to be her own self and not fall victim to fashion, claiming it was "evil." It wasn't until Maxine was older that she realized it wasn't evil so much as it was expensive, and her family didn't have the money to spare.

"I said, 'Good morning, Sister Maxine.'"

Maxine knew it wasn't faith that was keeping most of the women sitting on the hard pews fanning themselves with the church bulletin each week; it was Ed Stewart and his distinguished good looks and irresistible, curly, salt-and-pepper hair.

"Good morning, Reverend Stewart."

"If the amount of food is to judge the turnout, we'll have another success on our hands. Praise the Lord."

"Uh-huh," she responded, disinterested. "Would you like some tea?"

"That'd hit the spot. Thank you."

About that time, the barbecue man came driving up to the church lawn pulling his trailer pit.

"The meat's here!" Dorcas yelled. "The meat's here!"

She continued cheerleading its arrival until Constance finally snapped, "Simmer down! It's brisket and sausage, not the Messiah."

Several of the women chuckled.

Dorcas tried to connive the barbecue man out of a piece of sausage. "If we don't start soon, we're gonna run out of food," Ed Stewart muttered as he came to stand beside Maxine.

"Let her eat," Maxine defended. "Who knows what she's dealing with? We all have our crutches."

The pastor lowered his head in penitence, taking the opportunity to admire her firm tush. "You're a good lady, Maxine."

She let the patronizing tone slide.

"I have to run into town for a few minutes. But first I'm going into my office where it's cool. Why don't you join me?"

"I'll deal with the heat," Maxine answered with detectible attitude. She looked at her watch after the preacher walked away, and sighed. 11:05. *Fifty-five more minutes. We're gonna need more ice!*

Kyle got the time from the clock radio on the bedside table. "You about ready?" he called into the bathroom. "Checkout is at eleven —we're five minutes late."

"I'm almost ready. Wait outside, will ya?"

"I'll take the luggage down."

When she came out, Kyle had the car loaded and met her at the stairwell. "Where'd you get the coffee?" Anna asked.

"In the office. I already checked us out. We just have to leave your key, plus I thought you'd want some free caffeine before we leave."

"Yeah, thanks. How much do I owe you?"

"For what?"

"The room, silly."

"It's on me."

Anna paused in her steps and cocked her head to the side. "You're the best, Kyle."

Kyle opened the door to the manager's office and pointed out the coffee pot. "Hello again," he said to the man behind the desk. "Here's the key."

As Anna shook creamer into her cup, several brochures caught her eye. She picked up one about the Cotton Festival and another on the history of Prairie Springs.

Winnie emerged from her room as Kyle was backing out the car. He honked and waved. Winnie held up her hand for them to wait and walked over to his window.

"You fellows get into any trouble 'round these parts, you know where to find me. Don't let 'em mess with you!"

Anna looked back as they pulled away. "What was *that* about?"

"I'm not sure. I met her last night when I went out to smoke. You'll never guess what she was smoking."

"You're kidding me. That frail old lady?"

"Yep. And get this: she used to be a Rockette and lived in the Village."

"No way!" Anna chuckled. "She doesn't look tall enough."

As they made their way into town, Anna perused the brochures. "This looks like fun. They celebrate cotton here—says they have a big celebration with food and dancing."

"For cotton?"

"That's what it says."

Anna looked out the window and spotted an old windmill. "This place looks a lot less scary than it did at night."

"I was thinking the same thing, but I'm still glad we waited until morning."

The two followed Highway 36 a mile into town. At the lone traffic light, they took a right, thinking it looked to be the most commercial, and found the town square. In the center was a three-story limestone courthouse with a fountain in front. Anna read trivial bits in an exaggerated schoolteacher voice. "Prairie Springs is the county seat of Milam County...The town was settled in the 1840s by a diverse group of pioneers..."

"Sorry, Anna, I just can't understand why you'd want to give up Manhattan for this. You have it *all* up there, and look where you're moving. I mean, it just doesn't make sense."

"I wanted a change, Kyle. Being a teacher was my first choice anyway. You know that. Plus, if I'm ever going to fall in love with a man, I have to break off my relationship with New York City. I'm not too keen on the two of us not being together, but moving is a sacrifice I have to make if I'm ever going to be happy."

Kyle squeezed her leg. "That's all I want for you. Just make sure you find it on the inside, too."

"Do you think I made a mistake coming here?"

"We just got here! I think it's a bit too soon for regrets. It's a cute place...a bit dead, but cute—has potential!" Kyle slowed for a squirrel crossing the road. "I can't imagine New York without you. Even if I make new friends, they won't be the same caliber."

"Aww, you'll meet new people. If not, you can always move here with me."

"I'll keep that in mind...Let's continue our tour of the lovely Prairie Springs, Texas," he said. "Up ahead—what do I see? Is that a Chevrolet dealership?"

"Hold up. Go this way." Anna directed Kyle to drive around the square once again. They observed each business as they passed, although there weren't many: *The Herald* newspaper office, a pharmacy on the corner, a barbershop, furniture store, and

JimBob's Hardware. The rest of the spaces were vacant, including an old movie theater with a wind-damaged marquee.

Kyle shook his head. "What a shame. Can't you imagine the parking lot full, the kids playing in the fountain, the people all dressed up waiting in line to see—I dunno—the latest Alfred Hitchcock movie?"

"*Rear Window*," Anna blurted. "Hey, you want to see the house first or get something to eat"?

"Let's eat."

Rose was pacing the floor. She wiped off the kitchen table a third time. Bitsy, tired from following her around, stretched out on the doormat. The lemon meringue pies she baked earlier that morning were on the counter, each topped with a cherry, but she couldn't risk taking them over to the church's Ladies League luncheon because she was certain she would miss her new tenant's —or tenants'—arrival. Bitsy lifted his head as Rose sat down to call Judy Jane Johnson, her next-door neighbor. There was no answer, so she stepped out on the front porch to see if maybe Judy Jane was working in the yard.

Judy Jane Johnson was consistently awarded Teller of the Month at the bank, and rightfully so. She was quick and friendly —so friendly that most didn't pay any attention to the fact that half of her face was paralyzed. It was divided right down the middle: the left half with wrinkles and the right half looked as if she slept on a Botox pillow. The doctors first thought it was some kind of stroke, but it turned out to be brought on by stress, a stress that most presumed had something to do with her mother.

Seeing that Judy Jane wasn't in her yard, Rose went back inside and phoned again.

This time Judy Jane answered. "...Give me a good fifteen minutes. I've just stepped out of the tub."

Anna and Kyle chose an outdoor table on the covered patio at the Dairy Queen.

"No wonder we are the only ones out here," Anna said as she shooed the flies.

"Wanna move inside?"

"No. It's nice to be outside, don't you think?" Anna caught Kyle with a mouthful of food.

Anna was more preoccupied with the teenagers than eating. It must be the place to go on a Saturday for lunch. They showed up in herds—each herd remarkably similar to the next—with both girls and boys wearing Wrangler jeans and cowboy boots. She wondered which ones would be her students?

"This burger is good," Kyle said.

"I'm glad you found *something* good here."

"Y'all going over to the big event?" a man interrupted.

Kyle turned. "I'm sorry. We're not from here."

"Well, don't apologize for that, for goodness' sake. Are you going to be in town for a while?"

"Uh, yes. Yes, *I* will be," Anna said, for the first time realizing her future.

"Well, we've got arts and crafts, food, and games over at the Third Baptist Church. Y'all should come."

"I dunno. I'm Jewish and—Kyle, what do you think?"

"Jewish, huh?" The man walked away.

Anna looked at Kyle and gulped. "I guess they don't like Jews here?"

"Don't worry; I'm sure you aren't the only one around. Anyway, you aren't a practicing Jew. This isn't called the Kosher Queen; it's the Dairy Queen—a double whammy."

Anna laughed, "I guess you're right. But it still hurts."

"I have a feeling if you're going to fit in here you'll have to be just like everyone else."

She grimaced and ate a french fry.

Judy Jane vocalized her knock and opened the screen door before Rose could get out of her chair.

"I can't see a thing," Judy Jane said. "It's so bright outside, coming inside is like walking into a cave."

"I'm sorry to have to ask you to do this, Judy Jane. I need you to take these pies to the church event. Doesn't look like I'll make it."

"It's not a problem. No problem at all."

"I've got that new tenant coming, or tenants. I'm not sure which—I thought whoever would have been here by now."

"Maybe they got lost. I wouldn't worry about—"

"No. Constance called from The 36 last night. She was right. She told me everybody stops at The 36 Diner, and sure enough, that's what happened."

"Leave it to Constance."

"Say, Judy Jane, when you go over to the church, if you see the mayor, could you mention that pothole in front of our house? That thing's big enough to fall into."

"I'll do that. By the way, Rose, any word on your sister?"

"No, but I'm not giving up. There's still hope."

Rose's sister, Ivory, who married local man Ronald Black, thus becoming Ivory Black—a dichotomy that fit her mercurial personality—had been missing for nearly two months. Ronald was a mess over her disappearance.

"I'm sorry. Keep praying. All we can do is 'Let go and let God.' That's what *my* preacher is always saying."

Rose took a shallow breath.

"I shouldn't have said anything, Rose. Let's change the subject."

"No, it's not your fault." Rose searched for a tissue.

Anna and Kyle were exiting the Dairy Queen parking lot when they heard the unmistakable sound of two vehicles colliding.

"Keep driving. I don't like to look at car wrecks," Anna said.

"It's just a fender bender."

"I don't care." Anna averted her head as they passed but couldn't resist the temptation. "Oh my gosh, Kyle! Isn't that the lady from the motel this morning?"

Looking to his right, Winnie stood in the street holding her wig at her hip. "It is. I can't believe she's still driving at her age. I'm going to stop and make sure she's all right."

Kyle pulled into the gas station. "We can fill up while we're here," he suggested.

They drove over a black hose in front of the pumps that chimed a bell, and a short and cheerful Hispanic guy ran over from the commotion. "Fill her up to the rim? Our gas is like the coffee: 'good to the last drop.'"

"Uh, yes please."

"Bet you think the old lady did it, huh? Nope. I saw it happen. Man pulled in front of her."

"I'll be right back," Kyle told him.

He and Anna walked over to the accident that had already attracted a photographer, an ambulance and fire truck, as well as the same police officer that Kyle had spotted eating at the diner the night before. "I hope I never get into a wreck here," Anna commented. "It would be too embarrassing."

"On the plus side," Kyle added, "The response is oddly swift...Winnie?" Kyle called.

Winnie turned around, slightly disoriented.

"Oh, you. Kyle, was it?" She walked over and grabbed him by the arm, pulled him aside and whispered something in his ear.

"Come here, uh, Winnie. Let me introduce you to my friend, Anna." While they greeted one another, Kyle casually walked over to Winnie's car.

"That's a fine feller you got there," Winnie said.

"We're not a—Can I ask you a question?"

"No, it wasn't my fault. Son-of-a-bitch pulled out right in front of me."

"No, I wasn't talking about the wreck. It's about what you said this morning at the motel. Remember? 'Don't let 'em mess with you.'"

"They ain't gone and done it already, have they?" She answered without taking her eyes off Kyle.

"That's just the thing. Who are you talking about?"

Kyle was by her car shrugging his shoulders. She made a circular motion with her hand, indicating for him to keep looking. "What is he, dumb?"

"What's he doing?" Anna asked.

Winnie leaned closer. "Fetchin' my stash. I keep it under my wig, but my wig flew right off—here he comes. Looks like he got it...Don't be waving it around like that, you birdbrain!" she hissed. Then she grabbed the baggie from his hand and stuck it in the secret pouch. "They never look here," she said as she straightened her wig—somewhat.

The guy at the gas station whistled at them. They were blocking the path for other cars. "Are you all right, Winnie?" Kyle asked, before leaving her to fend for herself.

"I am now." She patted her wig.

"What are you looking for?"

Flo stood naked behind her refrigerator door holding two Dr Poppers, the Save-All's store-brand version of the original. "Something to drink, of course."

"I can't, beautiful. I've got to get going. Who knows when my wife will get home from the festivities over at church?"

"Is that today?"

"Yeah. We got it fixed up good this year. I built a canopy for the food tables. I was going to put a mesh screen on there for the flies, but they said they couldn't afford to spend any more money on it."

"I'm glad you mentioned that," Flo said as she reached for her silk housecoat. "I wanted to check out the crafts. I collect anything with a moon on it. Plus, I've been looking all over for one of them wall blankets of the dogs playing poker. You know what I'm talking about?"

"I do, but I doubt they'd have that at the Baptist church. It's a sin, you know, to gamble."

"Speaking of sinning," Flo grinned. "Don't forget to pay me."

He tucked in his shirt, stuck his blue denim cap on his bald head, and left a twenty-dollar bill in exchange for one of the lollipops Flo kept in a crystal dish by the door. "The most expensive lollipop in town," he said.

Flo smiled. "They're *blow* pops."

He closed the door and snuck out the back gate where he kept his bicycle. In a small town, everyone knew what kind of car you drove, so he wasn't about to leave it parked on the side of the street.

Maxine Burke dispensed iced tea and kept guard on the sodas that Save-All had contributed. "Where's your mother?" she asked the little boy digging in the cooler for another Mighty Red. "How many of those have you had today?"

The kid flashed a soda-stained smile. "This is my first one."

"God's gonna get you for lying."

Constance ran up behind the kid and practically shoved him out of the way. She wore a giddy expression, suggestive of an inevitable climax, and Maxine knew she was about to hear some gossip. "Hi, Maxine. Be a dear and serve me up a refill of iced tea with lemon, would ya? So did you hear?"

"You'll have to be more specific than that," Maxine answered flatly.

"About the wreck."

"What wreck, Constance?" she sighed, uninterested.

"There's been a *major* accident at the light. Bound to be all over Monday's paper. And guess who was in it? Ronald Black. That's right. I heard they hauled him off in an ambulance, and..."

As she rambled on, Maxine's attention drifted. *Just get to the point. This is why you don't have any friends...God it's hot! I hate my life...What were they thinking having this in August? Outside! Jesus Christ, this woman could talk a cat off a liver wagon!* Constance's outstretched hand awaiting the plastic cup of iced tea jolted Maxine into the present.

"...Let's just pray he'll be okay. I can't understand why it's God's will for someone to have a car wreck."

Maxine handed her the cup of tea. "Honestly, Constance, I don't think God works like that."

"Aren't *we* blessed?" Pastor Ed Stewart walked up behind Maxine, observing her backside. "Look at the turnout."

"Brother Ed, where have you been?" Constance barked.

"I went into town to see if I could drum up some customers —even ran into a Jew at the Dairy Queen."

"Then I guess you heard about Ronald Black? He's been in a terrible car accident at the traffic light."

"No, I didn't know. Must've just missed it. I'm sorry to hear that. We'll keep him in our prayers then, won't we?"

"Yes sir," Constance replied.

"Is that Judy Jane Johnson I see over there?" Brother Ed asked.

"Sure is," Constance confirmed. "She brought over Rose's pies. Said Rose couldn't come 'cause she was waitin' on her new tenants."

"I was wondering where Rose was. Say, if you ladies'll excuse me, I'm going to see if I can get Judy Jane to make the switch from Second to Third."

"Oh, Brother Ed! You're a riot," Constance said as he walked away.

"What's he mean by that?" Maxine asked.

"Second Baptist to Third Baptist, of course. You know, I heard the preacher at the Second is thinking about quitting. Just can't compete. Just between you and me, he's on antidepressants. Proloft or some such..."

Anna and Kyle were amazed at how difficult it was to find Harper Valley Lane in such a small town. Not having a map, they circled the blocks to no avail. It wasn't all in vain, however. They spotted the school where Anna would be teaching, and the Save-All, the only grocery store they had seen so far. Anna also took note of a video rental store.

"Kyle, ask that man on the bike if he knows where the house is."

Kyle pulled up next to the man wearing a blue denim cap. "Excuse me. Have you ever heard of Harper Valley Lane?"

He looked into the car and over at Anna, who was craning her neck to see him, and pulled the blow pop from his mouth. "Uh, yes," he swallowed. "Why?"

"Could you tell us where it is?"

The man removed his cap and smiled, "Sure...I know that street well."

Kyle and Anna examined each house as they drove at a snail's pace down Harper Valley Lane. As they crept by, venetian blind slats were lifted, curtains were pulled, and porch swings came to a screeching halt to get a peek at the unfamiliar car. Anna read aloud the numbers on the mailboxes, "1907...1909. It'll be on the other side...1910...1912—Watch the pothole, Kyle!"

"I see it. Quit shouting like that while I'm driving."

"Sorry...1914. Oh gosh, it's huge...Don't block in the pickup —she must have company."

"It *is* big. I wonder if you'll have an entire floor."

"I doubt it. I probably only get a room, but it'll do until I can get my own place."

Bitsy alerted Rose to their arrival. After a quick peek out the screen door, Rose ran to check her hair.

"I hope my new landlady is nice. I tell you, though, she could use a lawn man! What's she growing, corn?"

"That's Johnson grass," Kyle replied. "What do you call *those* things? It looks like where a witch would sit." He pointed to the silo-shaped corner of the house with a balcony at the top.

"A turret."

"That's it."

Bitsy was so excited he turned in circles on the doormat. Since Rose wore house shoes she never noticed, but he leaked a few drops every time a guest arrived.

Anna knocked on the door.

"I'll be right there."

"Do you know her name?" Kyle asked quietly.

"I think it might be Daisy? Some flower. The school district lined it up for me."

They spotted movement inside and took a step backwards so as not to appear intrusive.

Bitsy stood at attention when Rose opened the screen door.

"Come in. I'm Rose. I've been expecting you."

Anna studied her new landlady as they passed through the doorway. "I'm sorry we're late. I know I said we would be here yesterday but we got in late and—"

"Don't be silly. They're having a big celebration at church I'd planned on going to—I generally do look so forward to it, but —Actually, I was under the impression there was just one of you."

"Yes. It's just me who will be living here. Kyle is a dear friend who was kind enough to make the trip with me."

"I see," Rose relaxed. "That's nice." Bitsy attempted to get Anna's attention. "Get down, Bitsy," Rose instructed.

"He's no bother. I love animals."

"Well then, we're off to a good start. I bet we have a lot of things in common—Anna, is it?"

"How thoughtless of me. Yes, I'm Anna Aron and this is Kyle Brickey."

"I'm Rose Welsh. Won't y'all be seated? I've made some iced tea and bought some salted peanuts if you'd like something to nibble on. You must be starved after such a long journey."

"We stopped and ate several times along the way," Kyle said.

"Of course you did," Rose let out an ephemeral chuckle, realizing how inane her comment was. "I don't know why I—I mean I knew y'all were at The 36 last night."

"The 36?" Anna questioned.

"The 36 Diner."

"Yes. Yes, we did eat there. How'd you know? Were *you* there?"

"You'll get used to it. Can't get away with anything in this town. So, would you like some of that tea?"

They were going to drink tea whether they wanted any or not.

"That'd be nice," Kyle succumbed.

Pastor Ed Stewart's son was returning from his weekly overnight trip to Austin, about an hour and a half away, where he visited the sick residents from his town who were being treated in the big-city hospitals. He honked from the highway in his recognizable shiny red pickup as he passed the Roadside Palace and then again next door at The 36 Diner. Honking was more often a greeting in a small town than it was a warning or an expression of rage.

When the preacher's son honked, however, he was mustering up votes for the next election. Mayor Trey was the youngest in the town's history, winning the last election by a landslide. During election years, women in town swooned at the posters hung on light poles and in shop windows. Judy Jane Johnson handed out *Trey A. Stewart: The Right Candidate for a Right Town* brochures to customers at the First National Bank. High school girls taped newspaper clippings to the insides of their locker doors. And the head cheerleader was suspended for two weeks when she was caught "behaving inappropriately" to Trey's publicity photo in the girls' bathroom. His Democratic opponent never had a chance and quit the campaign. The Democrat's name appeared on the ballot, but only for fun since he received only three percent of the town's votes, and those were said to have come from people suffering from cataracts who couldn't read who they were voting for.

Trey and his wife, Stacy, lived the 1960s sitcom life that made other families envious. Everything about their house was kempt and pristine, from the shrubbery to the picket fence to the three cars in the four-car garage. Of course, Trey hadn't made his fortune from being mayor; his pet food company was the town's largest employer. From the outside, life couldn't get any better.

Trey took his overnight bag from the truck and went in through the garage. "I'm home," he yelled.

"You're late. I've been waiting for you so we can go over to the church together. You know how they count on us to be there."

"I know. I'm sorry. I had to stop off at JimBob's Hardware to pick up some more nylon line for the weed trimmer." He held up the bag as proof and placed it on the washing machine by the garage door.

That was almost true. He did buy a spool of trimmer string, but he bought it before he went out of town. He always kept something as an excuse in case he arrived late.

"Can we go now?"

"You go on, honey. I'm going to take a quick shower."

"I told you. I'm not going without you."

"What's your problem?" he asked.

"*My* problem? I don't have a problem, Trey. The only problem around here is that you're late."

"I won't shave...I'll be quick," he called from upstairs looking over the balustrade.

When he was no longer in view, she gave him the finger.

He closed the bedroom door and emptied his travel bag. The main bath had separate walk-in closets on either side of the lavatory. He threw the dirty clothes from his trip into the shared laundry bin and hid the pack of cigarettes in the back of his sock drawer.

Rose, not wanting Anna and Kyle to know where she hid the keys, showed them out back and excused herself, retreating into the enclosed porch. "Sorry 'bout the yard. I know it's a mess." She emerged dangling the key from her fingers. "Seems like the only thing that survives the heat are the weeds and the bugs."

Kyle noticed the excitement and anticipation in Anna's eyes vanish as soon as they walked out the rear door to the neglected cabins amongst the Johnson grass. He wrapped his arm around her and squeezed encouragingly.

"I was thinking," Rose said as she led them to the cabin, "There's a motel out by the diner—you might have seen it..."

"The Roadside Palace?" Kyle asked.

"Yes. That's it."

"We stayed there last night."

"You don't say. I was going to suggest that might be a good place for you to stay, um, Kyle, while you're in town."

"I'm going to stick with Anna until she gets settled."

"The cabin isn't that big, you see."

"Ha!" Anna let out. "This is a mansion compared to my New York apartment." Rose stopped halfway to the cabin and turned around. "I just don't think it would be a good idea with you being a schoolteacher to shack up with a man. Who knows what the neighbors'll think!"

"Ms.—uh—Rose, I'm not sending the person who just traveled two thousand miles with me to stay in a motel by himself, and that's that."

Rose lowered her head. "Then maybe you should find somewhere else to live."

"I can't believe this! He's just a friend. We won't even sleep in the same bed if that'll make you happy. Of course we have to buy a bed first, since my stuff got stolen along with the U-Haul."

"No, there's a bed in there. It's furnished enough to live in, I just don't think—'Stolen,' you said?"

Anna nodded and was silent for a minute as she planned what to say next. "The school district told me they signed a lease with you because I told them it needed to be a sure thing. Right?"

"Well, yes."

"Then I think I have some leverage here, and unless you want to be sued, I suggest you show me—and Kyle—my new home."

Rose was stunned to be spoken to so harshly. She continued to the cabin and unlocked the door. Anna looked around while Kyle stayed beside Rose.

"She didn't have to get sassy," Rose said, injured.

"I don't think she meant to get sassy with you, Ms. Welsh. It's just that she's tired and nervous and, well, she does have a lease. She's really the best girl you'll ever know—good as gold."

Rose scratched her chin. "I *could* use the rent money."

"Now you're thinking."

Anna returned. "What do you think Kyle? It looks like it has everything I'll need...at least for the first few nights. I can always fix it up little by little."

"Just don't do anything major without checking with me first," Rose interjected.

Anna nodded. "I guess all I need is the key."

"Not so fast. There are some rules I need to tell you. This is where *I* live too, remember?"

"There's to be no wild parties, no drinking..."

Anna laughed. "I *will* be having wine so you'll need to get over it."

"No. No wine."

"I'm thirty-five years old and if I want to have wine, I'm having wine."

"You'd better keep it hidden, then. I don't want any neighbors finding out. I belong to a church here and have a reputation to uphold. Do you go to church?"

"No, I don't," Anna replied.

"Yeah, I didn't much figure you did." Rose shook her head, wondering what she had gotten herself into. "Here's your key."

The brown Ford Pinto backfired twice when Maxine turned off the ignition in front of her house. It had been doing it for so long the dogs in the neighborhood didn't bark anymore and trigger-happy residents no longer grabbed their shotguns.

Maxine reached for her purse and realized she had left it beneath the iced-tea table. She hurried back to the church and saw the activities were winding down. The only food left was some dishes of baked beans; one of them hadn't been touched. Several women held out hope of selling their latest crocheted animals, fashions and cozies. Maxine walked up to the empty space where her table had been when Dorcas, sipping a Diet Coke, threw her free arm up and yelled, "I've got your purse over here, honey!"

Maxine waved in acknowledgment, relieved that her faith in small-town honesty might prevail.

She thanked Dorcas and walked by the craft tables. Just as she was wondering who would buy a crocheted spoon holder, she spotted some dull, copper-colored hair she hadn't seen in a while. "You are much too classy to be buying knitted socks," Maxine said.

The lady turned around. "You think so? Holy shit!" Winnie

covered her mouth as quickly as she said it. "Oh, fuck it. I haven't seen you in a month of Sundays."

"I know it. You look great. What are you doing *here*, of all places?"

Winnie fluffed her wig, careful not to do too much adjusting. "I have to keep an eye on things, you know. And I thought I'd see what crap they had. I would've been here sooner, but I had a wreck this afternoon and had to catch a ride. Some jackass ran right out in front of me."

"Ronald Black? That was you?"

"You know him? Must be blind as a bat."

"Yeah. His wife has recently gone missing."

"Poor feller. He's probably distracted is all. I hope I didn't come down too hard on him."

"Where are you staying these days?"

Winnie looked around. "The owner at the Roadside Palace gave us a good deal paying by the month. Even got a little kitchen in the room."

"Really? I'll have to stop by and see you. How's Humphrey?"

"Hell, child, I don't think he's gonna last much longer, but thanks for asking."

"That bad?"

"All he does is sleep and pee...and sometimes he does that at the same time." She laughed, but painfully. "God bless him. I just couldn't stand to see him waste away in that home. We had to get out of there. It was a-killin' the both of us. Plus, you know, they caught me—you know—"

"Yeah, I know. I read it in the papers."

"Piddly town! Cain't nobody mind their own business? Say, Maxi, how's your mama?"

"She's doing fine, I guess. Been having some cramps, though."

"She ain't still having her monthly visitor is she?"

"No," Maxine laughed. "Not for a while now."

"Well, stop by and see me," Winnie said. She turned to look at the stockings, but immediately whipped around to face Maxine again. "Say, you wouldn't want to give me a ride would you? They took my car in to get fixed. I'll give you a present for your troubles." She pretended to hold an invisible cigarette to her mouth and arched what was left of her eyebrows.

"You don't have to do that, Winnie. I don't mind."

"We can enjoy it on the way over. Come on. Get me away from these darned knit socks. You're right. I'm much too fancy-shmancy to be sporting them boogers."

Everyone eyed them as they walked arm-in-arm to the Pinto and got inside.

"My stars, Maxi. Am I hallucinatin' again, or is there a giraffe in the back seat? I'm always seeing animals do the strangest things. The other day I swore I saw a unicorn twirling a hula hoop on his horn."

"You're not hallucinating today, Winnie. I won it earlier at the raffle."

"Looks like you did yourself good."

"You want it? Constance told me that Goodwill donated it because they got tired of looking at it."

Winnie turned in the seat to see it better. "Hot damn!"

"It's all yours then."

Winnie's face lit up like a child's.

Anna and Kyle spent the day examining the apartment's unfamiliar furniture and attempting to clean with water and a rag.

"We have to go to the store before they close and get some cleaning supplies. Want to go to with me?" Anna asked Kyle, who was busy wiping the dust from the ceiling fan.

"Sure. We can get some things to eat, too."

"That's true. Cooking a meal always turns a strange place into home, don't you think? That's what I did when I moved into my last apartment. I made spaghetti and meat, and burned the garlic bread...I never *did* get used to that oven."

Kyle jumped down from the chair he was standing on. "We should cook that same thing tonight and *not* burn the garlic bread. Whadaya say? We can make that your traditional new-apartment meal."

"Sounds good. Let's get some wine and cheese—oh, and candles. We'll do it up right. Do you think we should invite Rose over?"

"Maybe not on the first night."

Anna grabbed her wallet and met Kyle on the small cement slab in front of the cabin door. Above him were the stairs to the apartment on the second floor. "I was hoping for an upstairs place. Maybe I can switch someday," she said and tucked her arm into his as they walked to the car.

"That pickup is gone. Wonder who it belonged to?" Kyle commented.

"Maybe there's another tenant? But I didn't hear anyone upstairs, and the cabin across from us doesn't look lived in."

"How could you see it through all the weeds?"

Kyle drove. They stumbled upon the store before they even had time to get their bearings.

"Look, Cupcake. They have tomato sauce on sale." Kyle said.

Anna read the large paper displays in the windows blocking the view in or out of the store. "Green beans are also on sale. Should we get those to go with it?"

"Sure, why not?"

While they were discussing the evening's menu in front of the grocery carts lined up outside, a beautiful girl stopped them on her way out. "Y'all need help?"

"Hi. No. We're trying to decide what we're going to have for our first meal here in Prairie Springs," Anna replied.

"Did you just move here?"

"Yes. From New York."

"New York! Why on earth would you move here?"

"I'll be teaching at the high school this year."

"*You're* the girl who took the job?"

"Yes?" Anna was taken aback that everyone seemed to know her business. "That's me."

"I'm Maxine." She stuck out her hand.

"Nice to meet you. I'm Anna and this is my friend, Kyle."

"Kyle's cute," Maxine whispered in Anna's direction but not discreetly. She was feeling loose after sharing the joint with Winnie.

"Yes, he is," Anna agreed.

Kyle blushed slightly.

"Where are y'all staying?"

"The school rented a place for me behind, uh, Rose Welsh's house."

"Yikes."

"Why do you say that?" Anna asked.

"She's always complaining about something. Her latest is that we shouldn't put displays on the ends of the aisles because they block the view of others pushing their grocery baskets around the corner...says it's 'hazardous.'"

"I'm confused," Anna said.

"I work here during the week. I'm a cashier in the express lane, but I just stopped to get something for Mama."

"Okay. I gotcha. Say, what else do you know about Ms. Welsh?"

"I don't know her that well, really. She never seems overly happy when she comes into the store, but I think she's just a lonely old spinster—I shouldn't have said anything. It's always better when you judge for yourself."

Kyle watched as the two chatted. Anna was generally cautious at letting people in, so seeing them hit it off was a relief. The more friends she had, the better he would feel about leaving her in the town by herself.

"Would you like to come over and eat spaghetti with us?" Anna invited.

"Wow! This is my lucky day—a giraffe and now free spaghetti."

Anna chuckled, "A giraffe?"

"Yeah, I won it in a raffle they were having over at the Third Baptist Church. Of all things! I already gave it away."

"So...you want to come?" Kyle confirmed.

"Sounds good. What time?"

Anna looked to Kyle for confirmation, "In an hour?"

He shrugged.

"Fine. I'll see y'all then." Maxine got into her Pinto. Both Kyle and Anna feared for their lives when it backfired, but Maxine didn't pay it any mind and waved cheerfully as she revved the motor. A cloud of smoke shot out the back.

"She seems nice, don't you think?" Anna surveyed Kyle. "I hope you don't mind me inviting her over."

"Mind? Not only is she nice, she's stunning. Reminds me of Julia Roberts."

"I know...Sickening, isn't it?"

"Please. You're nothing to scoff at." Kyle ran his fingers through her hair as she grabbed a grocery cart. Twenty minutes later it was stuffed full of everything from cleaning supplies to cereal and ice cream. Shopping was definitely more fun than paying. Anna blinked several times at the total on the cash register, although had she bought the same amount in New York it would have cost twice as much. Nevertheless, she hoped the renters insurance would be quick sending a check to cover the loss from the stolen U-Haul.

They hurried home to get ready for company. Anna took an old blanket from the top of the bedroom closet, folded it and made a makeshift rug under the old coffee table. From the same closet, she used a sheet as a slipcover to conceal the sofa's damaged tweed cushions. When Maxine knocked on the door, the place was hospitable, to say the least.

Kyle greeted her with a kiss on the cheek. She handed him the lemon pie she'd bought at the church fundraiser.

"Can I take your purse?" he offered.

"Fine, but don't let me forget it."

Kyle took her purse and put it on the bed in the other room.

Anna rested the corkscrew on the counter and walked over to also greet her first guest with a kiss on the cheek. "Are you a lesbian?" Maxine asked.

"Uh, no...No, I'm not. Just being friendly...I'm going to open this wine and I've cut up some cheese...we have olives too. Do you like olives?" Anna asked.

"Not the black ones. I'm not racist, I just don't like them."

Anna poured the wine into water glasses. "Sorry about these. Obviously, Rose didn't stock the cabinets with any wine glasses. I'm not complaining though since our stuff was stolen on the trip down."

"That's horrible."

"Yes, it was. But we filed a police report and the insurance should pay."

Kyle rejoined them. "What were you sexy broads talking about? Is this my glass? How about a toast?"

"A toast," Anna repeated.

"Wow, I've never made a toast before. I've made toast—you know, in the toaster, but—"

"To a new home, new friends, a new job and a new town." Kyle held up his glass.

Their glasses clanged above the cheese.

They all sat back, Maxine in the chair and Anna and Kyle on the couch.

"Y'all sure you're not a couple? 'Cause you—"

"I'm sure," Kyle stopped her.

The conversation was dull until the wine kicked in and the tongues loosened considerably. Anna overcooked the pasta and scorched the sauce in the pan, but as Kyle pointed out, "At least you didn't burn the garlic bread."

"Let's eat," Anna announced.

The light above the dining table popped and burned out as Kyle flipped the switch. They all jumped. "Bulbs. The one thing we didn't buy," he said.

Maxine brought over the candles from the living room, and they ate dinner by candlelight and the fluorescent glow from the outside security light. After dinner they cut into the lemon pie.

It was approaching eleven when Maxine decided she'd better get home. "Hey. Do y'all wanna go to church tomorrow so you can see what it's like? I don't go, but I'd go if y'all would."

"I've never been to a Baptist church," Anna admitted to no one's surprise. "I'm sure it would be entertaining."

"I'm game," Kyle added.

Anna and Kyle walked Maxine to her car. The pickup truck was back at Rose's house. Maxine's Pinto backfired after several turns of the ignition. Bitsy barked. A few seconds later the light came on in what they assumed was Rose's bedroom, and Kyle and Anna darted back to the cabin like kids evading a mother's wrath.

Safely behind the locked door, they began the usual post-guest chatter. "She's nice, don't you think?" Anna searched for confirmation.

"She's great. Seems down to earth and sincere."

"She does, doesn't she?...Are you going to be a good boy and sleep on the couch, or risk it and hop into bed with me?"

"I'll risk it. Let's go make babies." He swatted Anna's rear towards the bedroom.

"...I couldn't have done this without you. I love you, Kyle."

"I know you do, Cupcake, I know you do." He pushed back a few wild strands of her hair and kissed her on the forehead.

Kyle got out of bed after what seemed an eternity of tossing and turning. He drank a glass of water and went outside to smoke. The thick moist air haloed the security light across the way. He stood in the shadow of the stairwell listening to the crickets chirp and watched the line of smoke he exhaled mix into the fog. A click, followed by the squeak of a door opening, interrupted the sounds of nature. His heart skipped a beat. He crouched down. The door that opened wasn't Rose's but the one from the cabin across the yard. All Kyle could see from his angle was a man and the arm of a woman adjusting his collar in the doorway. He quietly extinguished the cigarette and watched as the man left through the rear gate. Kyle stole back inside, locked the door, and crawled back into bed with Anna, this time drifting off to sleep.

SUNDAY, AUGUST 3, 2007

Early the next morning, Maxine awoke to groans of pain coming from the other room. She ran to find her mother curled up on the bed in a fetal position having more of her recurring cramps. "Stick a fork in me, I'm done," she cried to Maxine. She helped her mom to the car and drove her to the local emergency room.

They arrived at the same time as a high-strung woman and her son, who had sliced open his finger playing with a pocketknife. The jittery woman was more concerned with the blood already on her son's church clothes than she was with his finger.

"His aunt just gave him this shirt for his birthday. I do declare! What was he thinking?" the lady complained to Maxine and then continued to rant to her son. The nurse called Maxine's mom first, which further agitated the other woman. "We're going to be late for Sunday school!" she exclaimed. "You should take church-goers *first* on a Sunday, for heaven's sake."

The nurse brought a wheelchair. "We're going to take good care of your mother. Don't you worry," the nurse assured Maxine as she pushed her mother through the doors to the examining rooms. Maxine had been strong until that moment, but the wheelchair made her mother appear weak and helpless, two words she'd never associated with her mom.

A *Reader's Digest* was just big enough to conceal Maxine's face so she didn't have to look at the other woman and her son. She must have a big family, Maxine decided, because she had never seen her pass through the express lane. Most people who went to her lane were singles or young couples who picked up only an item or two, not those who shopped for a family.

When Anna got up, the movement of the bed woke Kyle. He slowly opened his eyes.

"Good morning, sexy," she yawned.

He folded the pillow over his face and rolled over until he realized he had to pee.

"Did you sleep well?" Anna asked, as she rummaged through the dresser drawer, wanting to change out of her nightshirt. "We've got to do laundry—at least I do. Shopping wouldn't hurt either, since most of my clothes were in the U-Haul."

"We have to take the car back, too," Kyle added, passing Anna in the hallway on the way to the bathroom.

"Yeah. We should do that today. What was that town called where we have to take it back?"

"Give it some thought, Yenta."

"What?"

"*Temple*. The town is Temple."

"Yeah. You'd think I'd remember that. Want to see if Maxine wants to follow us up there after church? We could ride back with her."

"That's fine, or we could take a bus back."

"Yeah. That's true, but I think I'll give her a call."

"Fine."

Kyle jumped in the shower. The tub was much cleaner after Ajax and some elbow grease, but he took extra care not to rub against the unfamiliar shower curtain.

"She's not there—or she just isn't answering," Anna informed through the bathroom door.

"Maybe she's hung over...or maybe she's already at church," Kyle yelled from the shower.

"Yeah. Maybe so...I'm going to put on some coffee. You want some?"

"That would be great." Kyle rinsed off and reached for the towel. He put on the same boxer shorts he had slept in and went into the kitchen. "Don't you think it would be better to keep the car for another week until we can get you your own? What are you going to drive if we take it back?"

Anna wasn't eager to spend the money for another week's rental. "You think that's what we should do?"

"Just something to consider."

"You're probably right. We'd just be stuck here...Or I could get a bicycle."

"This isn't Amsterdam, Cupcake."

"It was only a suggestion."

"Fine." After a brief pause, she admitted, "I can't believe I'm going to a Protestant church."

Kyle went into the bedroom to get a shirt. When he returned to the living room, Anna handed him a cup, prepared with sugar and a dash of milk.

"Hey Cupcake, I forgot to tell you, but last night I couldn't sleep and went out to smoke, and guess what I saw?...A woman opened the door to the cabin across the way and a man came out, walked through the weeds, and left through a gate in the fence out back. I didn't even know there was a gate back there."

"You don't think it was Rose, do you?"

"I couldn't see her. All I saw was an arm and part of a sleeve of what looked like a silk robe or something."

"How could you tell it was silk?"

"The way it shone in the light."

"I guess I have a neighbor, then," Anna said flatly.

"Sorry the story wasn't more exciting."

"You could have scooted over to see who the woman was...or followed the man to see where he went—"

"Or I could have just gone over and asked them their social security numbers and dates of birth. I didn't want them to see me, you snoop."

"You'd make a lousy private eye, you know that?"

As usual, the parking lot at the Third Baptist Church had overflowed onto the grass and cars lined the streets. The Sunday school crowd got the good parking places near the door while the latecomers, like Anna and Kyle, were left to burn a few calories. Maxine had given good directions—"follow the other cars"—but they still arrived late because Anna couldn't decide which of her two pairs of pants to wear.

Hyperactive Constance ran into Ronald Black at the water fountain. "It's a miracle!" she shouted, shocked to see him.

In his typical calm demeanor, Ronald replied, "What miracle? It was a fender bender."

Constance seemed disappointed, as if the Almighty had deceived her. "Well, I'm still praying for your wife," she confessed. "I refuse to think she's dead."

Ronald walked away and went into the sanctuary. Sanctuary was a stretch for a windowless, rectangular, drywalled room with fluorescent lights, but that's how the sign on the entrance read.

Dorcas sat as close as she could get to the pulpit, fanning herself with the church bulletin and nibbling on something crumbly and chocolate. Her purse rested next to her on the pew, saving a seat for her husband. After the opening prayer, she would be announcing the grand total from the Third Base Ladies' League fundraiser.

Most of the women anxiously kept an eye on the door waiting for the mayor and his wife to walk in. He would stroll down the aisle to the front and wave to his father before taking a seat. The entire time, the women would follow his every move whilst mentally fornicating. The wives would disguise their stares and lustful thoughts by commenting to their husbands about the mayor's wife: *What a lovely dress she has on this morning*, or *Her hair always looks so nice, don't you think?* Another trick the women had was to sit along the aisles leaving the only available seats towards the middle of the pews hoping that Mayor Trey would choose their row and be forced to scoot by. Often he would slide in facing them, giving a close-up view, a subtle wink, and occasional brush of what was inside his trousers. After all, he had to secure another term as mayor.

The Third Baptist Church was all about sex and money. Whether it was being preached or fantasized about, it was the reason Third had come in first in attendance and offerings. To the women's disappointment, Stacy showed up without the mayor at her side. His absence was becoming more and more common.

As Rose Welsh approached the microphone, an usher handed visitor cards to Anna and Kyle before they took a seat.

"Is this thing on?" Rose tapped the microphone sending a deafening hammer throughout the auditorium. "My dear sister, Ivory Black, was a great person. She disappeared over two months ago and for no reason. I don't know how it's possible someone could just disappear from this town and nobody saw anything. It breaks my heart she's no longer with us. The other day I was looking at old pictures of us when we were kids—If someone knows something, please let me know. At the very least pray for me."

"Did she say Ivory Black? Kyle, I know that name from some-where. I mean, how could you forget it?"

"Yeah, I was thinking the same thing. But from where? How is that even possible?"

"I'm not sure, but it's strangely familiar."

An eager young boy jumped up before everyone else when the choir director instructed them to stand for the popular hymn, "When the Roll is Called Up Yonder." After the last note was sung and all were quietly seated, Reverend Edward Stewart stood from the throne-like chair on the stage, walked to the center, rested his gilt-edged Bible, and gripped tightly to each side of the pulpit. "Let's talk about that song, shall we? But first I want to say what a terrific job y'all did with it. I wished you could have heard it from my seat up here." He turned around, "Choir, wouldn't you agree?"

The robed choir members let out a resounding *Amen*.

Anna looked around for Maxine, who had told them she'd wait by the front door. "I don't see her," she whispered to Kyle.

"Me neither."

"THAT SONG!—that song..." Reverend Stewart said it like a gunshot and repeated it in a whisper. "It's not easy to get on the Lord's roll-call sheet. This isn't simply a 'show up if you want to' list we're talking about. No, sir. You have to earn it."

Amen...Amen...Amen.

He lifted his finger and pointed, "You...and you...and you—"

Kyle leaned to Anna and, in a melodic whisper, added, "*You're gonna love me.*"

Anna snickered.

"...and you." The preacher continued by randomly pointing at members of the choir.

"Many are probably wondering what it is you have to do to make the cut. This life is one big rehearsal for qualifying for the round to come. It's like we're all athletes trying to make the Olympic team."

Kyle glanced around. "These people are hardly athletes."

Anna slapped the side of his leg.

A tinny, electronic and up-tempo ringtone of "Amazing Grace" interrupted the sermon. Constance dug in her purse and fiddled with the buttons before finally answering her cell phone. She hunched down in the pew to not be distracting. It was a little late, however. All eyes were on her.

"I'll tell you what the Lord wants—" the pastor continued. "It's all there in black and white...or red."

Throughout the service, he made several other dreadful jokes to keep the men awake, but nothing worked like a nudge in the ribs from a wife. Wrapping up the sermon, he reviewed: "I can tell you this. There won't be any homosexuals in heaven; there won't be any drunks in heaven; there won't be any sex-crazed people in heaven..."

"Heaven's not going to be very crowded," Anna remarked.

Kyle chuckled.

"...Won't be any non-churchgoers in heaven. A good start to make the 'roll up yonder' is to make the roll here at the Third Baptist Church. And for us to continue our ministry, it's important you remember to give your tithes and offerings. We can't do this for free."

That was apparently the cue for the deacons to stand and start passing the green-felt–lined wooden offering plates along each row. The man sitting next to Anna, who had been trying desperately to read her visitor's card, told her to drop it in the offering plate. Anna passed along that valuable information to Kyle.

"Are there any more prayer requests besides Ivory Black?" the preacher asked.

Constance stood and adjusted her turquoise polyester dress. "I've just been informed that Maxine, who helped us out with the iced tea yesterday, has taken her mother, Louise Burke, who we all know from the Save-All, to the emergency room. They fear she has *cancer*." Constance didn't handle the tone in her voice well, showing more enthusiasm for breaking the latest gossip than for any real sympathy for Maxine or Louise.

A gasp came from the congregation, but it wasn't loud enough to cover Anna's "Oh shit!" The man who had been overly eager to help with the visitor cards scooted away as if she had passed gas. Everyone in the nearby rows turned to see where the vulgar voice originated. Kyle held his hand over his face in chagrin.

Constance recognized the two thunder-stealers from the diner and cleared her throat, demanding the attention be returned to her. "I know Louise Burke isn't a member here," she continued, "but I think we should keep her in our prayers anyway."

There were some nods and a few subdued *amens*.

"Thank you for sharing that information," the reverend said. "We can always count on you to keep us informed of the latest goings-on in Prairie Springs, Constance." He scanned the audience for more raised hands. "Anyone else?"

With all heads bowed and all eyes closed, Kyle and Anna

snuck out during the lengthy benediction. Though they had left the church, they would not soon be forgotten. Children throughout the town would repeat Anna's crude outburst at every opportunity.

Maxine was biting her nails when Anna and Kyle arrived at the emergency room.

"How'd y'all know I was here? I'm sorry I didn't make it to church. I hope y'all survived without me. You just don't know—things happened so fast it—"

"Don't worry," Anna said and offered her hand in support.

"I'm scared. She was hurtin' so bad. I ain't never seen her like that."

"I'm sorry. It's hard, but you've got to be strong for her?"

"Yeah, I—I know. I'm trying, but this is the woman who picked cotton to put food on our table when times were tough. Can you believe they put her in a wheelchair?"

"I'm sure it was just procedure," Kyle reassured her.

"Have you heard anything yet? Do you know what's going on?" Anna asked.

"Not yet. The nurse just came out a while ago and told me the doctor was going to talk to me, but I haven't heard anything."

"Well, then, we'll wait here with you. Is there anything you need? Are you hungry?"

"No. I couldn't eat."

"Something to drink? How about a soda?"

"That would be nice. I left so quickly. I didn't bring a thing."

"I'll get it," Kyle offered.

Anna stood next to Maxine while Kyle went searching for a vending machine. "Some lady at church stood and told everyone your mother was here."

"Unbelievable! How'd someone find out? I swear, if I didn't live here, I'd—I'd move."

Anna clicked her tongue. "I try not to judge people—you know that—but that preacher is an ass. I just learned in church that I'm going to hell. I'm quite the sinner, apparently."

Maxine almost laughed. "Yeah, the only people that'll be in heaven are the ones you saw this morning. Just ask them."

Anna squeezed her hand. "Here comes Kyle."

He returned carrying a can of cold Diet Coke. "I hope you drink diet. I didn't know, but since you are so thin—"

"Diet's fine. Thanks."

A few swallows into the soda, the doctor came out. "Maxine?"

She recognized him from the grocery store, but didn't know he was a doctor.

"We're going to send your mother to the hospital in Temple for some more tests. Do you want to drive her or should we send her in an ambulance?"

Maxine nodded but wasn't quickly processing the information. "I'll—I—I can take her."

"Fine. I'm going to set everything up. I know a good doctor up there, but anything you need here, just call me. Understand?"

When the doctor walked back inside, Maxine fell into Anna's arms and cried.

"We'll go with you, Maxine. Don't you worry about anything. Kyle can drive and—we were talking about going to Temple, anyway. You can show us around up there," she suggested, trying to cheer her up. "Okay?"

Maxine nodded and wiped the tears from her eyes.

CHAPTER THREE

Sundays were Flo's favorite day to work because The 36 Diner filled to capacity ever since they implemented a policy to accept pre- or post-dated checks in order to "keep the Sabbath holy." It was the best thing that happened to the restaurant since they started serving homemade gravy instead of a mix. Flo's tips were a testament to the success.

The hardest part about moonlighting as a discount hooker was the occasional encounter with one of her clients.

"Dorcas...Ted. What can I get y'all?"

"We'll have the meatloaf special," Ted said.

"And an order of nachos to pick on while we wait," Dorcas added.

"Coming right up."

Flo had a tiny waist and long muscular legs from all the running back and forth she did, not to mention the aerobic exercise from her moonlighting job. Her fifty-something sagging boobs, however, plagued her. Unless Dr. Kimball, the town's plastic surgeon, got a craving for blow pops, she would need to keep saving her pennies. "Did y'all want baked or mashed?"

49

"Mashed—with lots of butter," Dorcas answered for them both.

"I'll be right back with those nachos."

Flo felt sorry for the wives—especially when they were as nice as Dorcas. The two had gone to school together many moons ago, but Dorcas was a year younger. She hadn't always been over-weight. A slender teen-age Dorcas had been elected homecoming queen. It broke Flo's heart to see her stuffing her face.

Most of the guilt from prostituting came from knowing what the wives didn't, like how unfulfilled their husbands were, or how their marriages were falling apart. She had to remind herself of what Winnie told her, "Flo," she said, "you're like a pharmacy, doll. You ain't the disease; you're the medicine."

Flo was skeptical.

"You're keeping all these people from getting a divorce."

Dorcas' husband Ted worked at the Canine Buffet dog food plant running the extruding machinery that adjusted the sizes and shapes of the pieces. He liked to think pet owners across the nation admired his work when they opened a bag of the Canine Buffet's Super Chow, or the less popular but equally tasty meal for cats, Feline Smörgåsbord.

Dorcas examined the plate of food in front of her with happy eyes. "Look at those potatoes, Ted! They're being generous today."

"Probably a Sunday thing."

A wife knows when her husband is cheating on her. It is an undeniable and agonizing sense that slowly gnaws away at self-respect. Nevertheless, Dorcas figured as long as Ted kept coming home at night, she couldn't ask for more. After so many years of marriage, their sex life was an obligatory holiday chore. It wasn't fun anymore and was often interrupted by Dorcas' tears after Ted would make an unsolicited comment about her weight. "Many a man would have left me already," she reminded herself.

Constance took a seat at the table next to them. "Hello, my

darling sister. Isn't that horrible about Maxine's mother? I just can't get over it. But wasn't that a great sermon?"

"It was...it was," Dorcas said between bites.

Flo handed Constance a menu and slowed her step long enough to ask Dorcas if she wanted more iced tea.

She shook her head, "But forget about those nachos."

"Oh, honey, I'm sorry. It's a madhouse in here and I forgot all about them."

The talk at the other tables centered on the same topic: the sermon. Flo heard it all but didn't voice an opinion. She learned long ago to let remarks slide with a grunt and a smile. Another trick she used was to distinguish the First, Second, and Third Baptist customers and answer accordingly whenever she was asked which church she attended.

If a patron said, "Wudn't Brother Ed on point today?"

Flo would respond, "Honey, I couldn't tell ya. I went to Second."

That would generally be followed by the customer trying to coerce her into switching congregations.

Flo knew the size of her tip depended upon her answers. It was amazing what people would believe. How they expected her to go to church and be waiting tables by the time they arrived was beyond her.

Louise Burke waited on the front porch as Maxine packed her a pair of sweatpants, knowing hospitals were generally colder than normal. She also threw in a toothbrush, hairbrush, and deodorant. No sooner had she closed the bag did Anna and Kyle pull into the driveway.

Kyle drove and Anna kept the conversation as cheerful as possible from the front seat, mainly by asking ignorant but valid questions about the scenery. "Look at that Dalmatian cow," Anna commented at one point, spotting a Holstein. Even Maxine's mother cackled at that one but was quickly interrupted by another cramp.

Maxine warned Kyle to watch his speed as they passed through Dustpan, a speck of a town on the highway. "These sons-of-bitches'll get you good. They like to hide up here on the left under a tree."

"Maxine! Don't let your mouth run loose like that in front of these church people."

"These people are from New York. They only went to church 'cause I told 'em I'd meet 'em there."

"But still—it's not very ladylike."

"Since when? I learned from you."

"Yeah, well."

As soon as they crossed the Temple city limits, Maxine pointed. "There's the bowling alley...And that gas station—See it to the right there?—that's where I bought my winning lottery ticket."

"You *what*?" Anna snapped.

"Bought my winning lottery ticket. I stopped to get gas after I came up here to go shopping. The pump cut off at nineteen dollars and I went inside to pay with a twenty-dollar bill. Instead of change, I asked for a lottery ticket. I forgot about it until one day I took it into the convenience store next to the Save-All, and you can imagine my excitement when I found out I won!"

"What'd you do with all the money?"

"I bought a bag of pretzels and a wine cooler. And then—get this—I had to pay twenty cents extra because I only won three dollars and the total came to three dollars and twenty cents with tax. You'd think the asshole would have knocked the cents off and let me celebrate. Now, every time he comes into the grocery store, I short him one penny in his change. He still hasn't figured it out. I'm three cents away from getting all twenty cents back."

"I didn't know you did that," her mother said.

"Oh please. It's no big deal. I've never stolen anything in my life, so I hardly think a few pennies are going to send me to Hell."

"Well, if it does, Kyle and I'll be seeing you there." Anna turned in her seat to face the back, obviously still hung up on the earlier sermon. "I can't believe some of the things that preacher said this morning. What gives him the right to—"

Maxine held up her hand. "You don't have to tell me. I can't stand that man, and I don't know why all the women lust over him. So he's got nice hair. Now, his son, the mayor—he *is* hot!"

"Maxine!" Louise reprimanded.

"What? He is."

Louise shook her head, but then broke into a grin.

"Maxine, did Anna tell you what happened this morning?" Kyle asked. "When that lady stood and told everyone you—uh, that you were over at the hospital?" He glanced in the rearview mirror. "She said, 'Oh shit,' real loud. Everyone stared."

"You didn't!" Maxine gasped.

"I did. It slipped out. The news caught me off guard."

"I'm surprised they didn't throw you out," Louise said.

Maxine leaned up to the front seat, "Was that lady who stood up wearing turquoise?"

"Yeah," Kyle answered.

Maxine looked at her mom and they simultaneously said, "*Constance.*"

Maxine continued, "That nosy bitch."

"I guess there are two nosy bitches because someone had to tell *her*," Anna pointed out.

A bit up the road, a gigantic hospital came into view.

Once parked and inside, Louise was checked into a semi-private room. While nurses milled about getting her settled, Maxine and Kyle went with Anna to buy clothes and supplies. Anna didn't find anything to her liking at the mall, but filled up two carts at Wal-Mart.

After the shopping spree, they went for a bite to eat. Maxine, not wanting her mother to solely rely on hospital food, bought a fast-food chicken sandwich near the car rental place...or what was left of it. A sign read: SORRY FOR THE INCONVENIENCE—

the nearest location is in austin, tx…"Jot down the address," Kyle instructed. "This is great. We get to see the capital of Texas."

Later that afternoon, Maxine left her mother in the hospital and returned with her two new friends to Prairie Springs. They spent the trip listening to 1980s country-and-western songs on the radio. The best was one Anna and Kyle had never heard before but Maxine knew well, "I'm Gonna Hire a Wino to Decorate Our Home." It was a good distraction from the matters at hand.

The wino trend continued well into the evening with Anna and Kyle finishing off a bottle of Cabernet. The recently acquired purchases inspired them to transform Anna's apartment from shabby-chic to downright quaint. Combining the antiques that were already in the apartment with the flattering accessories and strategically placed lamps changed the dull, humdrum quarters into a home. The same couldn't be said for the neglected yard, however. Kyle wondered if Rose even owned a mower.

Monday, August 4, 2007

On Monday afternoon, accompanied by the delightful hum of the window unit air conditioner, Anna relaxed on the sofa with an Anne Tyler book. "This Delia is a hoot!" she told Kyle. He ignored her, as he usually did, when she commented on books he'd yet to read. "I love these books with only one main character," she continued. "There's nothing worse than reading a book with a whole plethora of names and you have to look back every other page to remember who's who."

The next thing on the agenda was to watch back-to-back episodes of *Gilligan's Island* on the new television while nibbling on some cheese and ham bites to hold them over until dinner. A knock altered the mood. Anna turned off the TV. "Now we'll never know if they got off the island!…You think it's the thorny Rose?" Kyle whispered.

Anna opened the door, mentally scolding herself for not asking who it was first.

"You!" the woman said, holding a carrot cake.

"Please. Won't you come in, uh—"

"Flo."

"Flo. Gosh, how could I forget that?" Anna waved in Kyle's direction. "Kyle, look who's here. It's Flo, the, uh, waitress from the diner."

"How you doin' there, ya cute thang? I never thought this place could—Y'all did a nice job of fixing it up. Looks like a dream." She slowly turned in circles, gawking at the changes.

Anna reached for the cake. *Is she going to offer it, or simply carry it around?*

"I thought y'all might like this cake. I saw it there at the diner last night and knew they'd throw it out if no one took it, and I thought, 'I'll take it over to them new folks across the way.'"

"So, *you* live in the other cabin. That's very kind...It looks yummy."

She reached for the cake and Flo almost gave it to her. "Now, why didn't I ever think to put the couch like that?"

"Here. Let me take that." Anna had to pry the cake from her hands.

"I just can't get over it! I never thought it could look like this!" Flo followed Anna into the kitchen and proceeded to brew coffee as if she were in her own house. "I'm sorry, shoog. I don't see the filters."

Anna pointed to the cabinet where she kept them.

"Hell, that's not the least bit convenient with your coffee pot clear over here." Flo moved them to a more reasonable place. "You don't mind, do you, shoog?"

Anna smiled as if someone she didn't like was taking her picture.

"So, what have y'all been up to?"

"We were just hanging out enjoying the new TV," Anna said. "We were going to paint but decided to wait until tomorrow."

"Is that so? What color?"

"We were thinking of an olive green with an off-white trim, at least for the living room."

"Sounds nice. Where are your cups?" Flo asked, rummaging through the cabinets. "Oh, here they are. You moved them."

"Moved them?"

"Yeah, I guess I should tell you I used to live here before I moved across the way. I liked it here," Flo continued, "but I thought I'd better take the other one in case someone moved in upstairs. I could only imagine how it'd be with someone prancing across the wooden floors all hours of the night. The last thing I need is a neighbor making all sorts of strange noises, whooping and hollering. You can never really know what your neighbors are up to."

"The upstairs apartment has wooden floors? I love wooden floors." Anna's excitement was mixed with disappointment.

"Why the face? You got wooden floors in here, too."

Anna and Kyle both looked around.

"Under the linoleum."

"You're kidding me!" Anna said. "Who in their right mind would cover up wooden floors with linoleum?" She realized her mistake as soon as she said it.

Flo raised her hand. "That was me."

"I'm sorry...I didn't mean to—"

"Don't worry about it. But if you *do* take it out, paint first so you don't drip on the wood. It'll make things a lot easier."

"That's a good idea."

"So, tell me about y'allselves."

"Where should we start? Like Kyle and I told you at the diner, we're not from here. We're from New York, and—Hey, Flo, were you the one who snitched to Rose when we showed up at the diner?"

"Me? No. I wouldn't waste my nickel on her."

"Then who could it have been?"

"Constance. The only thing with a bigger mouth is a great

white shark. She was there that night when you came in. She's like a pimple—you never know where she'll pop up." Flo took a breath. "No, dear, Rose and I don't ride in the same boat, if you know what I mean."

Anna maintained a poker face, hoping she would clarify.

"We ain't got that much in common," Flo said bluntly.

"Did she tell you about the rules when *you* moved in?" Anna asked.

"Rules? What rules?"

"No drinking, parties...stuff like that."

Flo hissed. "*Tssk.* She needs a good romp in the hay is what she needs—*something* to ease her pent-up sexual frustration. It's my theory the world would be a much better place if we all got a little at least once a week."

The comment tickled Kyle.

"You okay over there?" Flo asked.

Kyle continued laughing. "I'm fine. My imagination often entertains me."

"Well, don't you pay any attention to them rules, hun. She doesn't get out much, so the only world she has is the one in that house of hers...and at that church she goes to."

Flo went for plates to serve the cake. Her familiarity with the apartment was borderline intrusive. Anna felt like a mother who had given birth and had the baby swept from her arms.

"*I'll* do that," Anna insisted as she jumped from her chair.

"I don't mind, really. I'm used to waiting on people."

"I know. I'd just rather—" Anna stopped when Flo cut into the cake. "Well, go ahead."

She cut a piece for each of them and then commenced to take coffee orders. "I wish y'all would've told me y'all were moving in here. I would've given you a ride instead of telling you to go to the Roadside Palace. I didn't even know Rose was renting this place." Flo walked over carrying three plates of cake. "Are we going to eat in here? Should I just put everything on the coffee table?"

Anna rushed to clear a place, forgetting Flo was accustomed to balancing multiple items up her forearms.

"Anyway, I figured it out when I saw the strange car out front all the time. I knew Rose never had company, at least none that stayed overnight, and I said to myself, 'I bet the old crone done went and rented out the place.' How'd you find out about it anyway? Hold that thought. I'll be right back with the coffee."

Anna waited for her to return to answer. "The school district set it up for me. I'm going to be the Spanish teacher at the high school. I can finally put my master's degree to use."

"Good for you. More and more, the world is becoming more bi-language. And Mister Kyle...what do you do?"

Kyle hated that question. He was a wannabe artist living off the rise in the stock market several years ago. He cashed out the day before it crashed after having a dream about rocks falling. "I'm, uh. Let's just say I'm currently unemployed."

"Maybe you could get a job at the dog food plant?"

"Unfortunately, I'm not staying."

"Well, that's too bad," she winked. "We are very welcoming here in Prairie Springs whether it's for a day or for a lifetime. This is a fine place to live. Good churches, good schools, good restaurants. We've got it all, wouldn't y'all say?"

Anna focused on the novel waiting for her on the arm of the couch. "Uh, yes. It seems nice." She paused. "But is everyone so religious?"

"*Tssk.* I'm not...but don't tell anyone," she said quietly. "And don't let 'em mess with you."

Kyle's forehead furrowed. "That's the second time someone's told us that. Who are you guys referring to?"

"The church folks, of course. They only want their own kind around. But like I said, just don't get 'em stirred up and y'all'll be fine. They're like snakes; they'll strike if you look at 'em wrong. You get into any trouble just holler, flick the light on and off, send up a flare—something. I keep me a loaded semi-automatic in the closet."

Where did she not keep a loaded gun? Anna and Kyle glanced at each other with the same thought.

"Well, I don't want to keep y'all..."

Kyle and Anna stood.

"...I just wanted to say 'welcome to the neighborhood.' Stop by The 36 anytime I'm working, and the coffee's on me, you hear?"

"That's kind...and thanks for the cake," Anna said.

"Yes, thank you," Kyle reiterated.

"Don't mention it," Flo waved off the comment.

They cordially watched as she walked to her cabin.

Kyle closed the door. "Interesting woman."

CHAPTER FOUR

TUESDAY, AUGUST 5, 2007

Anna woke early and went to the Save-All in search of a newspaper. When she returned, Kyle was not only awake but had made coffee and pancakes.

"Kyle, these are delicious." Anna sat at the table eager to thumb through the automobile classifieds. No thumbs were necessary, however, with only one column of items for sale. She scanned over a couple of fixer-uppers and a Jeep being sold for parts before one caught her eye. "Hey, Kyle, look at this:"

1976 PONTIAC BONNEVILLE. V. GOOD CONDITION, EXTRA LOW MIL. MUST SELL. $800

"Whadaya think? Sounds decent, huh?" Anna pressed.

"Sounds okay. Probably drinks a lot of gas."

"Yeah, but the car is so cheap I can buy a lot of gas...I'm going to call." Anna dialed the number. A woman answered on the second ring. "I'm calling about the car."

"Let me get my husband; he's getting ready for work. Hold

on...*Honey! Someone's calling 'bout the car! Hurry up! Could be long distance. Want me to ask?*"

"Are you calling long distance, ma'am?"

"No, take your time."

The woman put the phone down. It clicked loudly on Anna's end. A few seconds later she came back on, "He'll just be a minute. You caught him out in the garage doing something or another. So, tell me, are you from here?"

"No. Actually, I just moved here."

"Bless your heart. Welcome—oh, here he comes. He'll tell you all about the car. What did you say your name was?"

"I didn't. It's Anna."

"Anna. That's a lovely name."

A male's voice in the background interrupted. "Here I am, Dorcas. Hand me the phone!...Hello?"

"Hello. I was calling about the car."

"Oh yeah. It's a nice one. Pretty green color. Let's see..." he grunted, as if the cord wasn't long enough to have a good view of the vehicle. "What would you call that...*Honey, what kind of green would you say the car is?*" There was no answer from the wife. "I dunno. I'd say the color of a green tomato, or lettuce, maybe...It's got four new tires. I put 'em on last year around Christmas, but we haven't driven it much—to the grocery store and back is all, and church on Sundays, to the diner—'round town, you know. Occasionally, we go to Temple, but not more than once a month. As a matter of fact, that's where I got the new tires."

Anna listened. No need to say much since the man was carrying on a conversation with himself.

"And I'm good about the oil changes. Do you have a car now? If you do, you need to get your oil changed every five thousand miles or so. Keeps the car in good shape—'specially with all these gravel roads 'round here. *Honey!*" he called again. "*When's the last time you'd say we changed the oil?*"

"*What? You gotta speak up. I'm in the laundry room.*"

"*The oil!*"

"*What about it?*"

"*When's the last time we had it changed?*"

Anna tried to interrupt, "Sir? Sir?" She waited for him to return and told him she would come by for a test drive if that was okay. They agreed on five-thirty, and Anna wrote down the address.

That evening, she and Kyle found themselves in front of a small house with new, yellow, wood-grained vinyl siding. The siding company's sign was in the front yard. At first glance, Anna thought they were selling the house too. The car was in the driveway. Kyle tried to keep from laughing. Lettuce was too subdued of a description.

"He didn't mention it was as big as a boat," Anna remarked.

"Did he mention it would glow in the dark?"

Anna playfully slapped him on the arm. On a more positive note, upon inspecting the car, there wasn't a scratch or dent on it except for a small almost unnoticeable ding in the door. The front door to the house opened. "*P-shaw.* I forgot the keys," a man's voice called to them. "Be right back."

Anna and Kyle peered inside at the car's green velour interior.

The man came out and walked over to them. "How are y'all doing? It's a hot one today, huh? Don't y'all have any hats?" he asked as he adjusted his blue denim cap. Then he shook their hands. "I'm Ted Bledsoe, and that's my wife, Dorcas," pointing to the figure behind the screen door.

"Hi, y'all. I'm gonna close this door so it doesn't let all the air conditioning out. Nice to meet y'all," she hollered.

"My wife tells me y'all just moved to town. Is that right?"

"Yes, uh, we—well, I—just moved from New York."

"New York? Never been and don't care to go. But welcome to town."

Kyle grinned. "We've met before. We asked you for directions the first day we were here. You were riding a bike."

"That's right," Anna agreed.

He shrugged dismissively and handed the keys to Kyle.

"*She's* the one buying it."

Ted leaned into the car. "Pushbutton radio, AM and FM. Speakers in the back, too, but we always keep the sound in the front. Has electric windows and I can't say the back ones have ever been down. Air conditioner works real well."

Anna fastened the seatbelt hanging down from the ceiling and had to tuck it under her arm to keep it from choking her. It would take some getting used to.

"Why are you selling the car?" Kyle asked.

"The wife wants a new one. One day she just woke up and said, 'I want a new car.' I told her, I said, 'There's not a thing wrong with this one,' but she wouldn't hear of it. When she gets an idea in her head there's no sense arguing. Finally, I told her, 'Fine. Put an ad in the paper and we'll see what happens.' I wouldn't be selling it otherwise."

Anna turned the key; it started on the first try. A small cloud of sooty smoke shot out of the tailpipe.

"Take her for a ride," Ted said. "Enjoy."

They drove on the two-lane highway and then took the opportunity to pop into the Save-All—almost literally. The front of the car landed inches away from breaking the glass windows displaying the weekly specials. "I guess I'm not used to it yet," Anna confessed, slightly alarmed and extremely grateful for those yellow curbs at the head of each parking space.

"I'm going to run in and see if Maxine is working."

Kyle waited by the car, which stuck out like a big green tongue amongst the others.

Anna returned. "She already left for the day."

"Ya know, if you ever valet it, you can just say, 'the green one.'"

Anna was already attached to it and took offense. She sort of liked it. It was different—that counted for something—and it had personality...history. "Everyone will be *green* with envy," she said. "I might have to get a car cover for it since I don't have a garage."

TUESDAY/WEDNESDAY, AUGUST 5–6, 2007

Dorcas had eaten her last chili dog, her last chicken-fried steak with mashed potatoes, and her last 36 Diner meatloaf special. The change started Tuesday evening when she and Ted drove their pickup to go look at a new Japanese car in Temple. The dealership advertised on Prairie Springs' local AM radio station. It was an economical car about the size of a cracker box, but she wanted to downsize. When she got in it she couldn't easily operate the controls, and Ted told her, "Face it, honey, you're a heifer. We should have never sold your Bonneville." Wednesday, she did the unthinkable: she left Ted to move in with her sister.

Her sister's house was the last place on earth she wanted to be because all they did was bicker in an endless competition. Whether it was knitting, cooking, or being the most sinless, they inevitably wound up arguing.

Desperate, and with tears clinging to her eyelids, she rang the bell and filled her sister in on what was said.

"I'm sure you just heard him wrong. He probably said *clever*, not *heifer*."

"No, Constance. He said *heifer*...as in *cow*. Can I come inside, or not?"

"How long are you planning on staying?"

"I don't know. As long as it takes. For crying out loud, I thought you'd be thrilled with the news so you could go spread it around town. If you play your cards right, you might actually be able to make the front page in Monday's edition."

"You know I'm not one to gossip. It *would* make a good story...Well, come on in."

Wednesday night, Dorcas ate a boring but healthy bowl of Rise & Shine breakfast cereal for supper.

FRIDAY, AUGUST 8, 2007

Anna revved up the motor in her freshly washed Bonneville to make the trip to Austin. She and Maxine followed Kyle, who was driving the rental car. Maxine went along for the ride since the hospital in Temple was on the way. The nurses agreed to let her spend the night in her mother's room since she no longer had a roommate.

The aroma of the bacon-and-egg burritos Anna had made earlier that morning filled the car. It felt like poor manners not to offer one to Maxine, but truthfully, she'd made them with Kyle in mind, and the last thing she wanted on her green velour was bacon grease.

When they arrived at the hospital, all three went upstairs to say a quick hello to Louise, but Anna and Kyle excused themselves almost as soon as they entered because they were afraid of missing the return time on the rental car. They devoured the breakfast burritos in the parking lot before leaving.

Winnie got a ride into town from the manager of the motel to pick up her car at the body shop. After that, she stopped at the grocery store for a jar of pickles, a box of cereal, Milk of Magnesia and aspirin. When she got to the checkout line, she didn't see Maxine or Louise.

"Lord, these folks are slow. Where are all the normal people?" Winnie asked the person in front of her, who didn't pay her any attention.

Winnie tapped her shoulder. "I said, 'I wonder where the people who normally work here are?'"

The woman wearing a turquoise jogging suit turned around, "Didn't you hear? Maxine's mother is in the hospital in Temple with cancer. Room 634. She probably won't last much longer. She never did take good care of herself."

"Who the hell are you? Hedda-fuckin'-Hopper? I didn't ask you all of that."

Austin was closer than Anna imagined. It was like a subconscious Dramamine to know that civilization could be found only ninety minutes away. The traffic, however, was horrible, and Anna struggled to keep up with Kyle. Had they thought it through, Kyle should have been following Anna's car instead, since it stood out like a banana pepper. They followed the signs from the interstate to the airport where they dropped off the rental car.

Traveling in one car with Kyle behind the wheel allowed Anna to relax and enjoy the scenery as they searched for a place to eat. Each side of the highway was covered in quickly built chain restaurants sporting mass-produced replicas of vintage signage. They were both hoping for a place to dine that wasn't listed on the stock exchange. Noticing the capitol building from the interstate, Kyle exited to see how close they could get. Surprisingly, the capitol itself and the grounds were open to the public. Kyle stopped the car so Anna could pose beneath an oak tree. He stepped out of the car long enough to snap the picture.

Kyle had never driven such a large and powerful car. The gas gauge seemed to noticeably move towards the E every time he accelerated. "There's a gas station. We should get some while it's convenient."

With a full tank, they ended up near the newly renamed Lady Bird Lake (formerly Town Lake) and Anna suggested they park and walk over to it.

It was hotter than blue blazes. Shirtless men passed on bikes, rollerblades, and skateboards. Kyle took off his shirt and lay on top of it in the grass.

"It's nice here, don't you think?" Anna said.

He lit a cigarette and rested on one elbow facing her. "Have I ever told you how much you mean to me?"

Anna smiled and tilted her head.

"I mean it. The other night at the picnic table at the motel, I was remembering all of the fun times we've had together: the trip to Spain, walking on the streets of San Francisco...everything. What would my life have been like without you? We make a pretty good team, huh, Cupcake?"

"We do." Anna looked across the water. "Kyle?"

"Yeah?"

"Don't go."

"Don't go where?"

"Back to New York. Stay with me in Prairie Springs."

Kyle's eyes followed a Golden Retriever chasing a duck along the edge of Lady Bird Lake. "I can't. If I can't meet anyone in New York, how am I ever going to meet someone in Prairie Springs? At least in New York I have a chance."

Anna paused. "Couldn't we, you know—you and I? Geez, it's all so perfect between us."

"Except that I'm gay."

"I know, I know. But sometimes I don't care about that. Sometimes I think the sex isn't what matters."

"You'd miss it."

"I'd use a vibrator."

"You'd still miss it."

A tear formed in her eye. "Maybe I've made a mistake with this move and all. What was I thinking?"

Kyle reached over, took her hand, and reminded her of all the reasons she gave earlier. "More space...A new start...A chance to have a boyfriend..."

Anna's nod was subtle.

Kyle nudged her. "Come on. We still need to find a restaurant...and we definitely need a drink."

Maxine hurried to the cafeteria and bought the special advertised on the erasable whiteboard. She ordered it to go and took it back to the room in time to eat with her mother. Constance had been right: it was cancer. And Louise had had it for quite a while.

"Mama? You awake? I went and got some food to eat with you. They brought your food a few minutes ago."

"I'm not hungry."

"You've got to eat." Maxine encouraged her with a squeeze of the hand.

"Why *me*?" her mother asked. "What did *I* ever do?"

"You know it's not like that, Mama. It's not fair but—" Maxine realized she didn't know what to say next, so she lifted the lid to her mother's tray of food. "It looks like chicken and peas. Doesn't that sound good?"

Here she was talking to her mother the same way she'd talk to a three-year-old. One day all was good, and the next she was trying to keep her from the grave. Her mother was right; it wasn't fair. There was no time for preparation nor a proper transition. Cancer snuck up and changed life forever in the blink of an eye.

"Would you like some of my fried fish? It looks good."

"No. I told you I'm not hungry."

"Listen to me, Mama. I'm not up here for the fun of sleeping in a mechanical bed. And I'm not up here to waste my money on hospital food. You're going to eat your food, and I'm going to eat mine right here next to you. Then we are going to talk. Just because you're sick doesn't stop us from being mother and daughter."

Louise shot Maxine a piercing look she would never forget and then scooted up in bed and pulled the tray over. "Looks like these peas have been cooking since 1984."

"Want some of my cabbage?"

"Heavens, no! What kind of dump is this? You'd think you'd get a decent meal if you're dying."

"You're not dying, Mama."

"I am, too."

"You're not if I say you're not, okay?"

"You can't control that, dear."

Maxine threw the Styrofoam container of food across the room. It splattered against the wall next to the television. Her first instinct was to clean up the mess, but her legs failed her when she stood, and instead, she collapsed on the floor and sobbed.

Her mother watched in silence.

Winnie gave Humphrey a sleeping pill and waited until he was snoring before getting into her car and pulling out of the Roadside Palace. She lowered the front windows and stuffed her wig in between the seats so it wouldn't blow away. There was nothing more cathartic than an unpopular Texas highway in the night, especially when there was a full moon. It was powerful, and at the same time, lonely to be the only one for miles. The world was hers, if only for a minute. Sometimes, however, her mind wandered and occasionally played tricks, revealing things that weren't there. Winnie swore she saw a deer wearing a tutu standing by the railroad tracks.

It had been a while since she had taken a trip at night, but she didn't remember her vision being so bad. She turned up the volume on the radio. Frankie Valli played, and she relished the wind blowing through her natural hair. For a moment, she was young again. The sky was filled with a million stars, reminding her of her daddy.

Her father told her that if she connected the stars like dots in a certain way, she could see all of those who had passed on. Another time, he told her that each star represented a soul, and that's why there were always more and more of them. When it filled up, he said the sky would be one big white light and that would be the end of life on earth. Her daddy was the most creative man she ever knew, but he was also a rotten SOB. Even after all of these years, she missed him. Every time she caught glimpse of a falling star, she waved, figuring God had kicked him out.

The trip had become such a pleasure she almost regretted arriving to the bright streetlights of Temple. She reduced her speed, although she wasn't sure by how much since the dash panel was dark, apparently on the blink. At the hospital, she parked and reached to turn off her headlights. It was then she realized she had never turned them on.

Flo checked the living room clock as she stood waiting in her Wonder Woman outfit, complete with bracelets, lasso, and head-band. She charged this client an extra ten bucks because the wig messed up her hair, which meant an extra appointment at Henna's Hair Salon. When he became a regular on Fridays, she moved her hair appointment to Saturdays and came out ahead. She spied out the window to make sure there was no sign of Rose. As long as that dog of hers didn't start yapping, she was in the clear.

When her client arrived, he would exchange his real gun for a water pistol. Flo would run around the rooms of her cabin for a good twenty minutes, using her bracelets to block streams of wet bullets. Wonder Woman always won, and she'd tie him up with her golden Lasso of Truth, and they'd have sex.

Flo slipped on her robe and opened the door. He was right on time.

Since it was after visiting hours, Winnie waited until the nurses weren't paying any attention before she sneaked past their station. When the door opened, Maxine was lying in the extra bed watching television with her mom.

"Winnie?" Maxine said, surprised. "What are you doing here?"

Winnie put a finger to her lips, signaling Maxine to simmer down, and went over to cheer up the patient with a kiss hello. "How you doing, doll? I heard you was sick, so I made you some brownies, and I wanted to check on Maxi. That's a good kid you got."

"Yes, I know."

Winnie spoke softly, "I'd imagine you're tired from all the visitors, so I'm just gonna sit and watch TV with you-uns."

Winnie took a seat between the beds and patted Maxine's hand as she held it. Louise fell asleep after a few minutes. Not much was said, since Winnie knew sometimes you could say the most by being quiet. After an hour or so, she pushed a button on the side of her digital watch to light it up. "I need to get going. Maxi, girl, keep your head on straight, you hear? Your mama needs you to be strong even when she's not. When you wake up in the morning, go over and whisper in her ear that you love her. That's all she needs to keep her going. And don't be throwing any more friggin' food."

"How'd you know?"

"There's a piece of fish on the wall, and you have cabbage in your hair." She slapped Maxine's arm. "I brought you a little something..." She reached in her pocket. "Tuck this away, and when the pain gets too bad, this'll do the trick. This modern medicine is for the birds. But I tell you, if she sees any animals wearing ballet outfits, take it away from her."

Winnie squeezed Maxine's hands, which felt like silk compared to her own. Then she grabbed her purse and gently kissed Louise, so as not to wake her. Before leaving, Winnie whispered, "Them brownies ain't for the staff."

In Austin, Anna and Kyle rented a room at the Motel 5 to avoid patronizing a chain. Whenever possible, Kyle insisted on not contributing to the big corporations, and Anna was okay with it since it was three bucks cheaper than the competition next door. They left their bags in the room and went back downtown where they stumbled upon the Chug Wagon, a restaurant where beer, not iced tea, was the drink of choice. The wagon wheels and red-and-white-checkered tablecloths motif was highlighted by waitresses wearing ruffled tops and denim shorts. A large Ferris wagon-wheel next to the bar carried a draft beer on each spoke.

Kyle ordered the barbecue plate—brisket, potato salad, pinto beans and two obligatory pieces of white bread—while Anna opted for a salad topped with grilled chicken breast. When the food came, they shared off each other's plate, but Kyle was glad he ordered what he did.

Despite the rustic ambiance of the restaurant, the patrons dressed in more current fashions than the people in Prairie Springs, and for the first time since arriving in Texas, the two Yankees didn't feel like they stuck out like sore thumbs.

With full stomachs and a slight buzz from the beer, they walked along Sixth Street, which was blocked off on weekends when the pedestrians outnumbered the cars. It was packed with energetic college students checking out the various bars. Street entertainers worked the crowds, and artists displayed their creations.

Barkers attempted to lure passers-by with cheap drink specials or sexy female dancers. When Anna and Kyle could take no more, they ventured one block over to the less-crowded Fifth Street. They found a more artsy crowd and a number of cafés in converted warehouses with open garage-type doorways and live music. Despite the festiveness of the previous block, Fifth Street was more their style. Being in their mid-thirties, they were old enough to be the parents of the kids they were passing. "Should we have tattoos?" Anna asked facetiously.

"I know, right? When did that happen?"

"Stop it. You don't look any different than you did the first day I met you. If anything, you look better."

"Then why do I want to spank some of these kids? And why do my knees hurt when it's going to rain?"

"Quit being silly, Kyle; we fit right in!" She slipped her arm through his.

Just then a boy walked by with numerous facial piercings.

"Okay, so we *are* old," Anna conceded. "Who cares! It's not *all* bad, you know. We're wiser—"

"Let's try Fourth Street."

They walked another block away from the action to find mostly parking lots and the occasional business. "That bar looks nice, Kyle." Anna pointed across the street. "Let's go check it out. It seems a bit tamer than the others."

"Whoa!" Kyle said, "And did you see the guy who just went in?" He was referring to a man wearing khakis, cowboy boots and a white polo shirt with the alligator logo.

They crossed the street and opened the heavily tinted glass doors at Buster's. The doorman checked the IDs of the guys in front of them but motioned to Anna and Kyle to go ahead. Kyle was offended. It was true: he *was* getting old.

It took about ten seconds for Anna to realize what she had done, "Wouldn't you know, out of all the bars in this town, I'd pick a gay one."

"Damn, you're good." Kyle went directly to the bar, squeezing between pumped chests and firm buttocks, and ordered two margaritas. While he waited for the drinks, he looked for the man in the Izod shirt but didn't spot him.

After surveying the interior sections of the club, they opted for the more peaceful outdoor wooden deck with protruding live oak trees. There, the music was quieter and slower than the thumping rhythm pounding on the other side of the windows.

Anna enjoyed gay bars because she got more attention than she did in straight ones. Women could be ruthless when in search of the same prey, and straight men could be degrading in their methods of seduction.

"Gay men tell it like it is," Anna said to Kyle after a semi-butch linebacker type told her she had 'great boobs.' "A straight man would have said 'great tits'…You tell me which sounds better, 'great boobs' or 'great tits?' *Pshh*—and they wonder why we women are attracted to gay guys."

Kyle knew the alcohol was kicking in by the way she nudged closer and rambled.

"You know, Kyle, honey…if the government wants to maintain the 'holy sanctity' of marriage, then they need to have a mandatory class for straight men taught by gay men—oh, and then the straight guys could be assigned a lifetime gay mentor for emergencies. Just imagine—women everywhere would never have to hear the word pussy again. It would simply be *the vagina*," she added in a husky Kathleen Turner voice.

Kyle feigned attentiveness as he was more consumed by three guys checking him out. "Yeah, Cupcake, sounds good."

Anna pulled the cigarette from Kyle's mouth, took one puff and hacked up a lung. "Who in their right mind would smoke?"

"You get used to it."

"You know," Anna said, "I read an article that more gay men smoke than straight men. Why do you think that is?"

"I dunno. Where do you read this crap?"

While Kyle scanned the patrons for Mr. Izod, a different man walked over and talked to Anna. Kyle took advantage of the opportunity and asked the guy to keep an eye on her while he went to the restroom. Opening the door that led back inside, a blast of loud music and air conditioning greeted him. The place was packed, and he had the awful feeling he had missed something by being on the patio. After using the bathroom, he stood on the elevated platform near the dance floor. Mr. Izod was nowhere to be found.

He made a final trip around the different sections of the bar before giving up and going back outside to be with Anna and her new friend.

"Kyle, can you believe he's straight? He's here with a lesbian! Isn't that wonderful?"

"Yes, fantastic." He noticed her new sandy-haired friend had bought her another drink, something Kyle hadn't planned on doing. Leaning against a large oak tree the patio had been built around, he took out another cigarette. He was thinking about what Anna read about gay smokers when an arm came up from behind holding a lighter. The man lit Kyle's cigarette and then his own.

"Mr. Izod."

"Excuse me?"

Kyle laughed. "Nothing...Your shirt?"

The man looked down. "It's 'Lacoste' now."

"Really? I like Izod better."

An awkward pause followed, and was broken by them speaking at the same time.

"You first," the man chuckled.

"I was just going to say, I spotted you when you came in, but thought you'd left."

"I've been right behind you the whole time. Until you went to the bathroom, of course."

Kyle made a seductive glance down at Mr. *Lacoste's* crotch.

"Are you from around here?"

"Me? No. We're—I'm from New York. Just here visiting. You?"

"From near here. Let me buy another round."

"Fine. I'll letcha. Still in the closet, eh?"

Alex ignored the question. "Your friend doesn't want one?"

Kyle turned to find Anna in a deep kiss with her new acquaintance. "She's had enough."

Mr. Lacoste ordered two more margaritas. They sat on adjacent wooden barstools and watched as Anna and the blond guy continued their make-out session in the corner.

"Doesn't he look like that guy from *MacGyver*?" Kyle commented.

"I hadn't thought about it, but now that you mention it..."

They were rolling their eyes at the horny straight couple. They overheard one person crassly tell them, "Get a room!" Straight people could make out anywhere, so it didn't go over well when they occupied space in a gay bar with something that could be done on the front steps of the Vatican.

"You know, I don't even know your name," Mr. Lacoste said.

"I was wondering when we would get to the names. I'm Kyle."

The man put out his hand. "Nice to meet you...I'm Alex."

The night at the bar ended with Anna and MacGyver leaving for the Motel 5. Kyle tried to stop her, but she insisted she knew what she was doing. Kyle, consequently, accepted Alex's invitation for a night at the Four Seasons on Lady Bird Lake.

The Four Seasons was a showplace. Kyle and Alex kissed in the elevator and resumed behind the closed door of the room. Kyle took off his shirt, and Alex pressed him against the foyer wall, kissing his chest.

"Hold on, I gotta pee," Alex apologized.

Kyle removed his pants and waited on the edge of the bed in his underwear. When Alex emerged from the bathroom, he was shirtless. He was muscular enough to give him form and had the hairiest chest Kyle had ever seen. "Get over here you sexy ape." He growled and grabbed him at the waist. Kyle unfastened Alex's pants and they dropped to the floor...

While Anna and Kyle were finding love on Fourth Street, in Prairie Springs, Winnie was turning into the Roadside Palace—this time with her headlights on. A damp Flo was hanging her Wonder Woman outfit to dry on the shower rod. Constance was watching a show on cable that exposed celebrity secrets, while Dorcas was in the kitchen blowing her diet with a bag of buttery microwave popcorn. At Rose's, the lights were out and she was saying her bedtime prayers with Bitsy at her feet. Only God knew if she was actually praying for her sister to return.

SATURDAY, AUGUST 9, 2007

"Good morning. Going to be another hot one today." The nurse woke Maxine as she began checking vitals. She removed the blood pressure cuff from Louise's arm and hung it on the wall. "Oh! Looks like somebody brought you some tasty brownies."

Maxine smiled.

The nurse wrote a few notations on Louise's chart. "I'll see you late tonight," she said, gently, as she hung the chart back on the foot of the bed.

"Good morning, Mama."

Her mother looked over and smiled wanly.

"I love you," Maxine told her.

"Well, I love you too, honey. And don't you forget it."

"I'm going to run down and see what I can get for breakfast in the cafeteria. You want anything?"

"I'll wait for my tray."

Maxine slipped on her shoes and walked to the cafeteria. On the way back, she stopped at the gift shop and bought some lilies. It had been a week and no one from Prairie Springs had come to visit them other than Winnie, Anna, and Kyle. She wondered how many people had driven the thirty minutes into Temple to go shopping at the mall but hadn't taken the time to drive a few more blocks to the hospital. As she walked back to the room, she thought about all the things she and her mother had talked about doing but had never done. They were going to climb the Eiffel Tower, take pictures from the top of the Empire State Building, go whitewater rafting in Colorado, sit on the beach in Greece. There were smaller plans, too, like driving to Dallas and going to Six Flags, or going shopping in the Houston Galleria. Why did all the trips that seemed impossible a week ago suddenly seem as simple as buying the tickets or hopping in the car? She wondered how many other adventures she put off, taking for granted there would always be a tomorrow.

Later that morning Kyle woke and examined the human furball tangled in the white sheets.

A few minutes later, Alex rolled over, squinting and smiling.

"Good morning, *sasquatch*," Kyle said.

Alex muttered something undetectable through his smile.

"What?"

He muttered again, ran to the bathroom, and gargled a capful of mouthwash, something Kyle had already done. After he spit, he repeated what he had been trying to say, "I said, 'My breath stinks.'" He hurried back under the covers and kissed Kyle. "Want to order some breakfast? They make great *huevos rancheros* here."

"I don't know what that is, but it sounds good."

"Damn Yankees! What do y'all eat up there besides bagels and hotdogs?" Alex asked as he dialed room service. When he hung up, he asked Kyle, "Want to call your friend and make sure she's okay?"

"Yeah, I probably should." Kyle pulled the motel business card from his wallet and read Alex the number, "Room 246." He passed the phone over. After the sixth ring, Kyle started to worry and regretted having left her alone. Finally she answered.

"Hey, Cupcake. How was your night?"

"Don't ask."

"Were you asleep?"

"No. I was taking a shower. I'm standing here in a towel."

"You mean they don't have robes where *you* are staying?"

"No. Where the hell are you?"

"At the Four Seasons."

"I'm hanging up," Anna said.

"No, wait. I'm not calling to brag. I'm calling to see how

you're doing—hold on, Alex's telling me something...He's asking if you want to come to breakfast."

"No, thanks. I'm a bit hung over."

"We're having *huevos rancheros*."

"Thanks, but I'll pass. I'll swing by and pick you up in an hour or so."

"Fine—hold on..." He handed the phone back to Alex so he could give her directions.

As they waited for room service, the two men showered together.

Breakfast was eaten on the French-style balcony overlooking Lady Bird Lake. Kyle wished one of the birds singing in the trees could take their picture.

Once breakfast was finished, Alex took hold of Kyle's little finger and curled it around his as they watched the canoes go by on the lake.

It had been six hours since breakfast, and both Maxine and her mother were starving by lunchtime. Maxine wasn't about to blow her mom's appetite on hospital food, so she walked down the block for more chicken sandwiches and fries. When she returned, she found the hospital room full of Mexicans, flowers, plastic Virgins and prayer candles.

"Max-een-eh, Max-een-eh," they called, smothering her with hugs. "Berry, berry sorry."

She looked over to make sure her mother was alive. "I'll be right back." Maxine backed out of the room and returned with a Spanish-speaking nurse who provided the translation.

"They are from *La Iglesia de los Santos de la Virgen de Guadalupe de Prairie Springs*."

All Maxine understood was "Prairie Springs."

The nurse continued translating, "...One of these women's sons works at a gas station, and someone named Constancia bought gas there. They said she was wearing a turquoise dress. And this boy, Roberto, told his family, and they told their church, and now they are here to pray for her."

An already sensitive Maxine bawled at their kindness, and the Mexican ladies became hysterical.

"They think you are mad at them," the nurse explained.

"No, no. *Gracias...gracias...gracias...muy gracias.*" Maxine regretted not having continued her Spanish studies, or at least retained what she'd learned. And where were the First, Second and Third Baptist churches? It took a group of Catholic immigrants to give a damn?

One Mexican lady spoke to the nurse.

"She's telling me they took up a collection to buy flowers and gifts because your mother was always so nice to them at the grocery store. She says it was your mother who was responsible for getting them to stock prayer candles at the Save-All."

It was silly, but Maxine was proud of her mother. True, her mom, like any other, was far from perfect. She never made them pray before eating; she had, on several occasions, called the toll-free number on food packages and complained just so they would send her a coupon. And twice, she had filled up a zip-lock bag at an all-you-can-eat buffet. But when it mattered to others, even with something as trivial as insisting that Save-All stock prayer candles, she acted without hesitation.

The bilingual conversation went back and forth until the nurse was needed in another room. Maxine held up the bag of fast-food chicken sandwiches and gestured to share them with the visitors. They countered with an even better proposition—unwrapping a packet of aluminum foil with six dozen, warm homemade tamales. Lunch was served!

The fairy tale had come to an end in front of the Four Seasons. Kyle was left with only an empty feeling and an e-mail address.

It was silly to feel so let down since it was only a one-night stand, but he did. As Alex's shiny red pickup disappeared around the corner, Kyle wondered if he felt the same thing. Was it possible for two people to hit if off from the start and live happily ever after? As improbable as it was, Kyle kept his eye out for any signs of a red pickup screeching back into the hotel drive.

Anna slapped him back into reality tooting the horn and waving over the top of her green Bonneville. She came to such an abrupt and unexpected stop in the valet lane that her ponytail flew over her head. "I'm still getting used to the brakes."

"I see that, Cupcake. How are you?" Kyle went to the driver's side, but Anna, to his dismay, wanted to drive.

After traffic calmed outside of Austin, Kyle asked about her night. "How was your man? What was his name?"

"Randy Mann, if you can believe it. He showed me his driver's license as proof because I thought he was pulling my leg. Randolph G. Mann, it said. He told me the G stood for Great in bed."

"Well, was he?"

"I don't know. I passed out."

Kyle laughed, "You didn't!"

"I did. All I know is when I woke up, he was gone."

"He didn't steal anything did he?"

"No, 'he didn't steal anything.' He was a nice guy."

"And what happened to his lesbian friend?"

"That wasn't his friend; it was his ex-wife."

"Whoops. Happily married, and then one day, *poof!* 'I'm a lesbian?'"

"Don't ask me any specifics. I don't remember much."

Anna switched out of the fast lane to let a shiny red pickup go by. Kyle was busy tuning the radio dial in search of music. He let it rest on Juice Newton's "Queen of Hearts." When Anna cheerfully attempted to participate in the clapping parts, Kyle reminded her to keep her hands on the wheel.

"What a great song," she said. "I used to sit in my room and listen to her records for hours. What ever happened to her?"

"Got me."

When the song ended, Anna said, "So...tell me about your sexy man."

Kyle eagerly divulged the minutiae, starting with the bar and ending when she picked him up at the hotel.

"Does this mean you are going to stay in Prairie Springs so you can go to Austin every Friday for a tryst in a swanky hotel?"

"I don't know about moving here, but maybe I should see what happens. There was something between us, Anna. I could feel it."

"It's called a penis, Kyle, dear."

"No, seriously. There was a connection I haven't felt in a while."

Arriving to Temple, they made their way to the hospital. Anna, cautious about braking too hard as she parked, didn't brake enough and bumped the car in the space in front of them. "I'm still—"

"I know. You're still getting used to it."

As they approached the entrance, they met a group of Mexican women at the automatic doors and let them exit first. Upstairs, the scent of cumin lingered in the hallway and grew stronger as they approached Louise's room.

"Knock-knock," Kyle said as he opened the door. "Smells like a Mexican restaurant in here."

"We had visitors. There are some tamales left," Maxine offered.

Anna was starving. "I'll have one."

"How was your trip?" Louise asked.

"It was a trip. We'll just leave it at that," Kyle said.

"I can't wait to hear all about it...Would y'all like to stretch your legs a bit and go with me to take Mama downstairs?...Whadaya say, Mama, wanna go?"

"I'd love to get out of this room!" Louise answered.

They found a bench in the shade at the back of the hospital where the employees snuck out for cigarettes, which is exactly what Kyle did. Maxine offered Winnie's brownies.

"Winnie? A frail old lady with a sailor's mouth?" Kyle asked.

"Yeah, that's her," Maxine confirmed. "She told me she'd met you the other day. I gave her a ride home from the church fundraiser the day she had the wreck."

"Yeah, we saw the wreck. I'm glad she wasn't hurt. Is she playing with a full deck?"

"Her deck is full; it just includes the jokers. But she's really a good person...you just don't want to be on her bad side."

"I picked up on that," Kyle said.

The small patch of shade they found stretched and spread as the sun passed behind the building. One by one the brownies vanished. Pains were relieved and thoughts grew hilariously deep. After a nap in Louise's room, Anna, Kyle and Maxine headed back to Prairie Springs.

CHAPTER FIVE

E arlier in the week, Maxine suggested that Anna have a housewarming party. Anna suspected it had more to do with an excuse to temporarily forget about her sick mother than it did with warming the house. Nevertheless, Anna agreed, even though it was the last thing she wanted to worry about.

When Rose became aware of the gathering, Friday evening's party was almost canceled. She insisted it would keep her awake. To that, Kyle said, "Keep you awake? We were hoping you'd join us!" Far be it for Rose to show any excitement about a secular gathering, but if that slight raise of the eyebrow was any indication, she was thrilled. She accepted by insisting on bringing a dewberry cobbler. Kyle had never heard of it, "That'd be perfect!"

While Anna went shopping, Rose worked all Friday morning preparing the dessert, taking great care in the spacing of the lattice pattern of the top crust. At noon, she knocked on Anna's door to inform them the pie was made and suggested having the party in the garden.

"The garden? Are you talking about that field of weeds?" Kyle pointed.

The truth didn't appear to upset her. "All it needs is a good going-over with the lawnmower. I've got one in the shed."

"I'll do it!" Kyle responded in a heartbeat.

"Fine. I'll go and get the chigger spray. You're going to need it; the chiggers love this grass."

"Chiggers?"

Rose returned and sprayed Kyle's arms and legs with the insect repellant and led him to the shed, careful to not let him see which key she was using. The shed was full of gardening tools. "Say, Rose? If it's okay with you, I'd enjoy working in the yard if you'd let me. The garden tools look practically brand new—I could break them in for you. I enjoy that kind of thing."

"Oh, I don't know. I don't have enough money to fix it up nice." She turned to face him. "I guess you could keep it cut, though...If you do a nice job, I might be able to take five dollars off Anna's rent."

"It's a deal!" He had dreamed about what he would do with the overgrown bug-breeding playground every time he looked at it. "I'm going to make this the garden of your dreams. Just wait and see."

He put on a pair of pants so the Johnson grass didn't cut up his legs but took off his shirt to get a tan. He sprayed sunscreen and insect repellant on his chest and back and started the lawnmower. He was immediately drenched in sweat, and if it weren't for the partial shade from the pecan trees, he was sure he would have passed out. He caught Rose watching him from the window. *Does she think I'm going to steal the mower?*

When he finished both the front and back lawns, Rose took him a glass of lemonade. "It looks right nice," she said.

He glanced around to admire his work. It was hardly a show-place, but it was a start. He could almost hear everyone in town heave a collective sigh of relief. "I'm glad you like it."

Maxine was eager to get back to Prairie Springs. She left the hospital early so she'd have time to shower and get ready for the party. She couldn't recall the last time she went to any type of celebration, unless she counted Save-All's fiftieth anniversary extravaganza as a celebration. The housewarming party would be a welcome emotional break. She and her mother had been taking advantage of their time together to share stories from the past and express their love for one another. Maxine knew the end was near but held out hope for a miracle.

She hurried inside and immediately checked the answering machine. The light was blinking. She knew it was the hospital even before she pressed the button. She returned the call, and before she allowed her brain to process the news, she phoned Anna. Kyle answered on the fifth ring.

"I was afraid you weren't there," Maxine said.

"Anna's at the store and I just finished mowing the yard, front and back, if you can believe that. We decided to have—" He stopped when he heard Maxine whimpering. "What's wrong? Are you okay?"

"Mama's—Mama's...gone."

"Oh, Maxine." He could tell by the distant sounds that Maxine was no longer holding the phone. He hung up, threw on a shirt, and ran the four blocks to her house. He found her curled up on the floor beside the couch. After first resisting his embrace, she gave in and broke down.

As if the heavens shared in her pain, the sky grew dark in an instant and a clap of thunder announced the rain.

Anna was leaving the supermarket when the rain started. By the time she got behind the wheel, drops the size of elephant tears hammered the roof of the car. She flipped the windshield wipers on high, but they were no competition. Unable to see where she was going, she pulled into an empty space near the parking lot exit and waited until the downpour eased enough for her to get home safely.

With the dewberry pie made and resting on the counter underneath a cup towel, Rose, as she often did during a storm, went up to the porch of the turret. The access was via a narrow, spiral staircase hidden behind a door next to the pantry. The turret porch was big enough for a rocking chair and small wicker table. Bitsy loved to go up there and watch the birds. Rose usually went to escape and be alone. Today, she went to wait for Anna's reaction to the mowed yard.

She wasn't up there long before Anna drove right past. That tickled Rose to no end! Of course, some of her giddiness had to do with being invited to their little shindig that evening. She and Bitsy continued watching as Anna reversed and parked in front of the house. Rose giggled when Anna emerged with a grocery bag tied over her head and ran towards the backyard.

Once the hysterics of Anna's arrival abated, she and Bitsy slowly and carefully made their way back down the stairs.

Anna found the door to her cabin unlocked and presumed Kyle was at Rose's. She rested the bags she was carrying onto the kitchen table and went to take a shower to wash off the stickiness of the rain when the phone rang. It was Kyle. Anna grabbed the keys.

Kyle was holding Maxine tightly on the sofa when Anna took his place, and they both stayed until Maxine eventually fell asleep.

Saturday/Sunday, August 16–17, 2007

Saturday morning the storm had cleared, and Kyle, desperate to do something, knocked on Rose's door.

"Oh. It's you."

"Did I do something wrong? Did I cut the grass too short?"

"No...none of that...What do you want?" She avoided eye contact.

"I wanted to ask your permission to fix up the garden...I thought it could be a memorial garden."

"A memorial garden! For whom?"

"For Maxine's mother. Didn't you hear? She died late yesterday afternoon."

"That's awful...So, there was no party yesterday?"

"I'm sorry, Rose, I should've called, but in the commotion, I forgot all about it."

Rose breathed a sigh of relief. "I feel silly now. I stood in the rain for ten minutes holding the dewberry cobbler but never considered there was a reason nobody was there." Rose didn't share the part where she went home and cried, certain they were playing an evil joke on her.

"Oh Rose, I'm sorry."

"Don't worry, Kyle, dear. It's all good now...Let me get you the key to the shed."

Did she just call me dear? Kyle felt honored at the trust blooming between them. She wouldn't trust her hoes and shovels to just anybody!

He put his heart and soul into his gesture of sympathy, determined to give Maxine a magical place to be with her mother, if only in spirit. He went directly to rent a tiller and began digging up the yard.

Tilling after a storm usually wasn't the best idea, but it had been so dry, the ground soaked the rain right up.

The news of the death spread around town like wildfire. Flo was surprisingly upset; death affected her terribly. When she found out what Kyle was doing, she postponed her hair appointment and called in sick to the diner so she could help. She appeared wearing gardening gloves and holding a hand shovel. "What do I do?" she asked.

Rose popped out often with lemonade...lemonade and cookies...lemonade and hamburgers. Then she, too, got down on her knees and planted flowers, scattered bark and pebbles, and whatever else Kyle instructed that she was physically able to do.

One of the Mexican women who had visited Maxine's mother, co-owned the Casa Verde nursery and contributed plants and flowers. Anything else they wanted, she sold at wholesale prices.

Per Kyle's instructions, Anna stayed with Maxine until everything was finished. By mid-afternoon on Saturday, co-workers from the Save-All arrived and helped plant Saint Augustine grass, crape myrtles, azaleas, rosebushes, jasmine, climbing figs, and anything else that would withstand the Texas heat. Trellises were installed, as were winding paths of flagstone. People from all over town got wind and stopped to admire what was taking place, and many offered to lend a hand.

The backyard filled with neighbors. The fountain that hadn't worked in years was now flowing, and a lychgate separated the front and back yards. Winnie brought over one of her prized cultivations and suggested, with a wink, that it be put towards the rear. Dorcas and Ted happened to arrive at almost the same time and at first didn't speak. Eventually, Ted went over to Dorcas and begged her to come home. "I'm not coming back until I don't look like a farm animal!"

MONDAY, AUGUST 18, 2007

By mid-morning, Maxine had acquired enough resolve to finish arrangements for the Wednesday funeral. She and Anna went to the mortuary where caskets were on display like cars in a showroom. Maxine examined the choices with Anna close by her side. The names for the different models were garish: *Luxury, Classic, Deluxe...*

"Mom deserves this one." Maxine pointed to the Deluxe Steel Premium Primrose. "But I don't know how I could pay for it. How could anyone pay for it? I had no idea caskets were so expensive!"

"Me either. Geez! *Lose Your Loved One; Lose Your Life Savings* should be their slogan."

"Mom would want me to get the cheapest one they have because she was simple and unpretentious...but she deserves the best. Don't ya think?"

Anna stood back and kept quiet. It needed to be a decision that Maxine was comfortable with. After an hour of examining the different wood finishes, linings, and trims, she decided on the pine box.

Maxine was driven to tears again when she found out how much the burial plot cost.

"Maxine," Anna beckoned. "Have you thought about cremation? It would be a lot cheaper. Did your mom leave instructions in her will about her death?"

"Mama didn't have a will, and we never talked about it."

"Then it's definitely an option, and you could scatter her ashes wherever you choose."

"Really? That sounds so much happier than letting her rot in the ground...doesn't it?"

Anna offered an insecure smile. "It does to me."

Back at Maxine's house, neighbors brought food along with their condolences. The mayor's wife, a beautiful blonde, brought over fried chicken and potato salad. Others brought casseroles and soups, and the Mexican women brought over more tamales, beans, homemade salsa, and fresh tortillas.

WEDNESDAY, AUGUST 20, 2007

On the day of the memorial service, Maxine woke early and straightened up the house while nibbling on the assortment of foods. It wasn't until the house was tidy that she sat down and read the sympathy cards that had been stacking up on the dining room table. They were tough to read, especially the ones that included a cutout of the obituary. After the first ten cards or so, they all seemed the same. Then a pink envelope caught her eye.

I'm so fucking sorry, Maxi. I hope this eases the pain. There will always be more where that came from in the garden.
Love, Winnie.

The handwriting was shaky but legible, and carefully taped to the second page was a joint. Winnie's was the last sympathy card she would ever read.

The local AM radio station announced Louise's memorial service would be at the home of Rose Welsh. It was an impressive turnout, and everyone dressed in black—even Constance. It was a pleasure for Maxine to see how beloved her mom was, although she was aware that about a third of the people showed up to every funeral in town, regardless.

When it was her turn to speak, Maxine choked up talking about how her parents would finally be reunited. She regained her composure and observed those who had gathered. Winnie's tears traced the lines in her face and disappeared before they ever fell. The Mexican women dabbed their cheeks with cotton handkerchiefs. Sniffles, sobs, whimpering, blubbering. Her mother would have hated such a maudlin scene.

"If y'all keep crying, you're gonna kill the grass with your salty tears," Maxine blurted.

A church hymn was supposed to follow Maxine's remarks, but in her nervousness, she opened her mouth and out rolled "I'm Gonna Hire a Wino to Decorate Our Home."

A number of the attendees slipped quietly through the lychgate, offended by Maxine's non-traditional song choice. A small group stayed to show support or, more likely, to enjoy the garden they helped build. As they made their way along the newly installed flagstone paths, they were enveloped by a sense of calm. The mourners, scattered about on different stepping-stones and around the fountain, were a melancholy contrast to the oblivious perky hydrangeas and gay rhapsodies of the mockingbirds. Maxine was overwhelmed by the splendor and felt more comfortable knowing her mother would be where life was taking root. At eight in the evening, without giving it a second thought, she took the urn and scattered the ashes in the rear corner by Winnie's plant. "Mama always did love sunsets!"

Anna walked Maxine out and then joined Kyle, Flo and Rose by the screened back porch. Kyle flipped the switch, transforming the paradise into a wonderland. Strategically placed landscape lights illuminated the different paths, while others, nestled in the jasmine along the fence, created peripheral pleasure. The lights installed in the pond surrounding the fountain cast a waltzing glow as the water rippled in the breeze. The only other illumination that evening was from the waning crescent moon, which captured Flo's attention, and from the fireflies that were beginning to dance in the night air. The once-lifeless yard had suddenly come to life.

"Thank goodness, you took down that darn security light. I hated that thing...Who paid for this?" Flo asked.

"Kyle bought the stuff, and I'm paying the electric bill," Rose answered.

"Don't go raisin' the rent on us," Flo said jokingly.

"I wouldn't do such a thing."

THURSDAY, AUGUST 21, 2007

When Maxine returned to work, she wasn't prepared for the sign next to the entrance:

The population of Prairie Springs is one less, but losing one to the heavens is always a blessing. We at Save-All have lost one of our best cashiers. Louise Burke will be greatly missed.
–The Management–

Maxine could not bear to stand all day checking groceries while looking at the teenager they hired to replace her mother. She handed in her resignation along with her red apron and walked out.

The manager ran to catch her. "Maxine! I was afraid you were going to do this. How would you like a job as assistant manager?" He smiled, confident she would accept.

"No, thank you."

. . .

While Maxine was quitting her job, Constance was receiving the phone call of her dreams, a full-time position writing a gossip and advice column for *The Herald*. No more receptionist work and freelancing! She was going to be Walter Winchell, Ann Landers and Heloise rolled into one. First on her to-do list was to make an appointment with Henna. Next, she would need to get a decent headshot so they could print it with her byline. Maybe if she were lucky, Henna could squeeze her in before the dinner at the mayor's house.

CHAPTER SIX

FRIDAY, AUGUST 22, 2007

A nna and Kyle drove over to The Springs to enjoy the last of her summer break, knowing teacher meetings would occupy her time the next week. The Springs was the name of the park just outside the town's limit where a limestone-bedded, spring-fed creek cut through the pecan and oak trees. It was their first time going there, and it wasn't easy to find. Anna drove down the wrong gravel road and came to a dead end in front of a house with a plastic armadillo on the porch. They quickly sped off fearing a trigger-happy resident.

A bit down the road was where they found several parked cars in a field. When Anna turned off the engine, they could hear the water running and followed the sound until they came upon the brisk creek. The crystal-clear water fought its way over rocks and raced to the curve, where it had stripped the earth and left tree roots exposed. A couple of kids sat in the shallow water and let the current pound their backs as they watched their leaf boats float away. Anna and Kyle found it strange that more people weren't enjoying the creek's mystical serenity.

One of the kids got out of the water and ran over to his

mother and pointed. "That's the lady who said that bad word at church."

The mother turned to look. "Hush up. Go on and play some more."

The summer heat was persistent and snubbed the approaching autumn's attempt to cool the air. Anna and Kyle placed a blanket on the ground and set the bag of peanut butter and jelly sandwiches Anna had prepared on top of it. They undressed down to their swimsuits and relaxed in the sun a few minutes before heading to the stream where they played like children.

When they emerged, the hot air dried them off quickly. Anna lay face down and undid her top, careful not to expose her breasts, as she ate a sandwich. That didn't matter to the mother of the child, who ran over and insisted she refasten her top. Anna refused and told the woman to mind her own business and continued her discussion with Kyle.

Kyle took a deep breath before breaking the news. "I'll be going back to New York next week." The night with Alex at the Four Seasons was enough for him to realize how much he longed for steady companionship, but it wasn't enough for him to alter any plans.

"I wish you wouldn't," Anna replied without facing him.

"I know, Cupcake. But I have to. I'm getting to the age where if I don't meet somebody, I'll be the old man in a piano bar singing Streisand show tunes."

"Isn't that funny? I left New York for the same reason you want to go back. So, what about Alex?"

"I've worked too hard to come out of the closet to lock myself back in it."

"For the record, I don't want you to leave."

Kyle leaned and kissed her on the cheek. "I know, Cupcake. I'm gonna miss you, too."

"You *are* going with me to the mayor's house tomorrow night, aren't you? The mayor's wife hosts the dinner for all of the teachers—all my new coworkers will be there. I'll need you with me for support."

"Is that tomorrow? I don't know, Anna. I was looking forward to working in the garden."

"Come on. It might be fun. I heard there's a male choir teacher. You know what that means."

"There will be singing?" he said facetiously.

No sooner had the conversation ended did the police show up. Anna fastened her bikini top as the paunchy officer sporting a gray beard approached with a hand on his pistol. "You kids bathing naked?"

Anna glared at the uptight mother.

"Does it look like we're *naked*?" Kyle mocked, making fun of the cop's word choice, like they had been lying pubes to the sun.

"We got a report of some folks lying naked out here, and I suspect it's y'all. Ain't nobody else out here lying in the sun."

"Let's go, Anna," Kyle insisted.

They packed up their stuff under the watchful eye of the cop. "I'd better not get any more reports of y'all doing some indecent behavior."

Despite the interruption, and leaving sooner than they had anticipated, finding a natural retreat so close to town made the trip worth it.

SATURDAY, AUGUST 23, 2007

The Third Base Ladies League wasn't the only league in town. The Armadillos was an invitation-only group of men made up of members from all three Baptist churches. They met monthly at an old house not too far from The Springs, where they interpreted the Bible in their own way.

With the flip of a switch, the plastic armadillo on the front porch lit up, signaling a meeting was in session. One by one, pickup trucks lined the side of the gravel road, most in need of a wash, save for a shiny red one, and the members filed inside where they munched on snacks. A chant kicked off the meeting:

We do the work of our Lord Jesus Christ. Until we get to Heaven we'll fight for our rights. Sinners must pay; we'll take no more. There'll be none of them at Heaven's door.

The men headed to the field out back and gathered around a campfire to discuss issues at hand. The leader warned them not to fall prey to what was transpiring at Sister Rose's. "...The out-of-towners are already starting trouble by disguising their evil as good. What those of you did who ran to help with that garden was to contribute to non-believers...and the girl is a Jew! I read their visitor cards from church and they are from New York City. Yankees, I tell you. We can't let appearances fool us. We have to stay focused on the Lord's work, and the Lord doesn't want them Yankees around here destroying our town. They are trying to get people on their side, and it looks like they're already making progress with Rose. And the Jewish girl will be teaching at the high school this year. I'm sure some of y'all's kids will have her as a teacher. We've got to stop this! We need to start complaining to the school board, to the principal—whatever it takes to get rid of her. Imagine your child being taught by a woman living with a man out of wedlock!"

There were nods in accordance throughout. The police officer picked at his gray beard and said, "I caught them suntanning naked as jaybirds at The Springs earlier today."

"You look hunky," Anna said to Kyle as they walked up the sidewalk to the mayor's house.

"You don't look bad yourself, Cupcake."

The din of female voices grew louder as they approached the front door.

Anna rang the bell.

The mayor's wife answered and recognized Anna from Maxine's. "Anna! Finally someone with fashion sense. How are you? It's good to see you again. Please come in." She smiled to Kyle before closing the door behind them.

"This is my friend, Kyle Brickey."

"It's nice to meet you. I'm Stacy and this is our home, so please, make yourselves comfortable. We're going to be having something rather informal. Kind of a buffet-style dinner. It's all out back by the pool; iced tea and soft drinks are in the kitchen... That seems to be where everyone has congregated for the moment."

Kyle and Anna couldn't help but admire the décor, the architecture, the meticulous paint job and furnishings.

"Right this way." Stacy led them to the kitchen.

They had certainly overdressed. Anna wore a floral print maxi skirt accompanied with a white sleeveless top, and Kyle sported khakis and a white button-down with the sleeves rolled up. Aside from the always-elegant Stacy, the overwhelming fabric in the room was denim.

"Something to drink?" Stacy asked.

Anna took a Sprite; Kyle, a Coke. "Do you have anything to put in it?" he asked.

"Uh, no. We don't drink," another teacher interrupted derisively.

"It's gonna be one helluva party," Kyle whispered to Anna.

Anna motioned with her head towards a woman in a turquoise dress. "Isn't that the lady who stood in church and said Maxine's mom was sick?"

"Looks like it."

Constance was busy with a notebook and a feathery pen interviewing the different teachers when someone suggested they all move outside. Caterers were lighting burners under the serving pans but scattered as the vultures approached.

As people were lining up to get food, Constance asked, "Where is the mayor? I thought he always attended these events?"

"He should be here any minute," Stacy reassured her.

Some stood as they ate; others found places next to the pool or on lawn chairs under the vine-covered pergola. Anna and Kyle were both sitting on small boulders at the edge of the pool, wishing someone had told them it was BYOB. "This is the most boring party I've ever been to," Kyle vocalized.

"I can't argue with you there. Sorry I made you come."

"Don't be. I'm sure we can leave anytime. At least we showed."

When the French door leading out to the patio opened, Stacy stood. "I'm so glad you made it," she said as she rushed to greet her husband. All eyes followed her. She grabbed his hand and turned to face the ladies. "For the new teachers here—well, the one new teacher—this is my husband and the Mayor of Prairie Springs, Trey Stewart."

Kyle's mouth fell open.

"Not so boring anymore, huh?" Anna said.

Winnie and Humphrey sat on two different beds in their motel room as they ate and flipped through the television stations.

"Ain't nothing on," Winnie said. "They call this Saturday entertainment? What happened to the fuckin' *Carol Burnett Show*?"

"You say the same thing every Saturday."

"Yep. I know what I say—you don't have to tell me. Eat your eggs."

Winnie looked out the window.

"You alright, Winnie Pooh?"

"I'm fine. Don't mind me." She took a breath. "I just keep thinking about Maxi, with her mother dying and all. She was too young, you know—too dang young. I wish it would have been me."

"Don't be saying those things. It was her turn."

"Her turn? What'd she do, roll doubles? This ain't some game, Humph."

"What's really got you? It ain't that girl's mother, and you know it."

"We're running low on dough. We can't stay here much longer, and I ain't got no clue where we're gonna go."

"*All hail the pow'r of Jesus' name, let angels prostate fall,*" Humphrey sang.

"Stop it with that religious shit! I get enough of that from my son. And it's '*prostrate,*' not '*prostate,*' you jingle bell." She set her plate of eggs on the nightstand.

"What in Sam Hill is a prostrate?"

"Look it up!" Winnie snapped.

Here she was, ninety-one years young (according to her), and while she had pot, she didn't have a pot to piss in. It was not fun watching everyone else die around her. When she was young, she dreamed of being an actress. She wanted to be Katharine Hepburn so she could travel all over making movies. Living at the Roadside Palace had never been in her plans, but neither was living in Prairie Springs for most of her adult life. If she could have done it over, she would have stayed in New York, never married, and never had children. This life would have been hers and hers only.

"I'm only trying to help," Humphrey said. "Don't snap at me."

"It ain't you, baby...it ain't your fault," she sighed. "I'm going to get some fresh air."

Rose and Bitsy couldn't get enough of the garden and were constantly stepping outside to admire it. This particular night,

Rose turned on the lights and sat by the fountain. Ordinarily at this time, she would be getting ready for bed, but today was her sister's birthday. A creak from the gate at the rear of the yard frightened her. Her heart stuttered. The lights weren't bright enough to see who was there, but whoever it was ran off. Rose screamed and Flo ran out of her cabin to see what was going on.

"I saw someone coming in that back gate," Rose pointed. "We'd better call the police."

"I'm sure it was nobody," Flo assured her. "Probably just some kids playing. Maybe their ball came over the fence."

"You think? It's awfully late for kids to be playing ball."

"I'm sure of it. I'll keep my eye out for any strangers. You go and get some rest, you hear?"

"Yes, I suppose that's a good idea. Got church tomorrow."

Flo waved good night. "Dammit!" She searched for her client's cell phone number. "You can come back, but only if the garden lights are off!" He was her most generous tipper, and she loved running her fingers through his sexy graying hair.

Trey Stewart hadn't noticed Kyle and Anna sitting by the pool. He made the rounds visiting with the other guests before he came upon them. When he did, the whites of his eyes showed. "Hi. I'm Trey Stewart, Mayor of Prairie Springs."

"I'm Anna, and I think you know my friend, Kyle." She could barely control her grin.

"Please keep it quiet. I'm begging you," he said through his teeth.

"So, this is the small town that has you in the closet, *Alex*?"

Constance was getting too close for comfort.

Trey's eyes darted anxiously. "You could ruin me, you know that?"

Kyle lit a cigarette and offered one to Trey. "I don't smoke," he said.

"Wow! How many people are you? I know about Alex and Trey, but are there others?"

"Alexander is my middle name. I just use it when I go out."

Trey's wife approached. "Honey, have you met Anna...and Kyle?"

Kyle glanced at Trey and smiled at Stacy. "Yes, we've met."

"They'd like to see the house, Stace, so I'm going to show them around."

Stacy was flattered. "By all means, but I think Constance wants to do her interview with Anna now."

"You two go ahead," Anna insisted to Kyle and Trey with a discreet wink.

"Yoo-hoo! Constance!" Stacy called. "Anna's ready for you."

Trey and Kyle went inside and roamed the bottom floor, feigning an ordinary house tour before continuing upstairs. Kyle lagged nonchalantly a few steps behind.

Dorcas stood inside The 36 Diner holding her bus ticket and taking advantage of the air conditioning as she watched for the Greyhound to come around the corner. She had already paid for the Diet Coke in front of her so she could blithely sneak out and hop on the bus without too much commotion.

She scanned the diner, but the only person she knew was Judy Jane Johnson. Judy Jane looked over and halfway smiled, but that was as good as it got with her facial paralysis. Dorcas waved, hoping her suitcase wasn't in plain sight. It wasn't that she was hiding the fact that she was leaving, but she didn't want to reveal where she was going.

When the bus pulled in, some of the passengers got off to stretch their legs and use the restroom. Dorcas merged into the group as they re-boarded. She handed her ticket to the driver. "This is the bus to Houston, right?"

"Yep."

There were several vacant seats, so she took one towards the back, next to the window. As they rolled south down Highway 36, she watched the passing headlights going in the opposite direction and dreamed of taking the return bus back into town as a new, thinner Dorcas. Ted was going to give her some loving even if she had to sneak Viagra into his orange juice. It had been a while since the two had been intimate, and her self-esteem flagged along with the sex. She'd be so distraught wondering why he didn't want her anymore that she'd eat cheesecake to calm her nerves. She'd considered taking up smoking, but with her first cigarette she burned her dress and her leg, so that was the end of that. She tried diet pills, but those made her queasy, and since they were mostly diuretics, she had to pee if she so much as looked at water. Once she almost wet herself watching the aquariums at the Wal-Mart in Temple. She could imagine the announcement, *Clean-up in the pet department! Fat woman leaked near the fish display!* That was the end of the diet pills. Living with her sister had gotten even more difficult when Constance got the job at *The Herald*, because all she did was go around bragging about how *she* was making something of herself.

Well, Dorcas had had enough! She was off to Slimming Acres. Unfortunately, the confidence she had when she signed up had been replaced by a fear of the unknown. Would she be the fattest person at the camp? What would they eat? *Did* they eat? She considered asking the bus driver to stop and let her off—she would hitchhike her way back. But she stayed seated and wiped her glasses. After realizing the greasy smear wasn't on her lenses, she took a napkin from her purse and wiped the bus window. She continued staring outside.

At the Roadside Palace, Winnie sat at the picnic table pondering her financial woes. She had money twice in her life. Once, when she was a Rockette, and then again when she was married to her first husband. Since then, what little she received went up in smoke—sometimes literally—and there never seemed to be enough to make ends meet.

Humphrey, in a rare move, left the motel room and snuck up on her.

"What are you doing here?" she said guiltily, attempting to stub out her joint.

"You don't have to put it out. I came to keep you company."

Winnie attempted a smile. "You're feeling better, I see."

"I've been having a good day. Pooh, don't worry about the money. We'll figure something out."

"You sound sure of yourself. You plant a dad-gum money tree?"

"We can always go back to the home and let the government take care of us," Humphrey suggested.

"That's the last place I want to die." Winnie laughed. "But I don't think we'll ever die, Humph. We're gonna petrify into stones and be here forever."

Humphrey took hold of her hand. They sat and watched the stars. One fell, and Winnie said hello to her daddy.

"I love you, Win-Pooh."

"Yep," she replied. "I know ya do."

A scraggly mutt with a lolling tongue crept over to the table where they sat. He was rather large in size and looked to be part Lab. Winnie held out her hand so the dog could sniff it, but she knew what he wanted. "You're hungry, aren't ya boy?"

"Oh Lord," Humphrey declared. "A dog's the last thing we need."

"You can't expect me to leave him alone to starve to death. I'm going to make him some eggs. Come on, let's go inside." She patted her leg to get the mutt's attention. The dog followed closely, as did Humphrey.

"I hope the manager doesn't see you. He said, 'No pets.'" Humphrey rested on the bed.

"Screw the manager! The pooch is hungry." Winnie reached into the mini-refrigerator for the eggs.

"He's gonna get fleas everywhere, Winnie. Put him outside, will ya?" Humphrey got up and opened the door.

Winnie turned on the hot plate and cracked the eggs in a bowl to scramble. "He ain't gonna hurt nothing. Look at him."

As soon as the words came out of her mouth, the dog snarled at the giant stuffed giraffe Maxine had given them. He lunged at it, biting, and ripped it open. Winnie stomped her foot on the floor and clapped her hands. The dog spooked, ran out the door and into the trees. "Well, shit! Look what you did."

"I didn't do anything." Humphrey sat back down on the bed. Winnie stared at six eggs in the bowl.

"Well, I hope you're hungry for eggs. You want some SPAM with 'em?"

Humphrey didn't answer.

"I said, 'Do you want SPAM with your eggs?'"

Whenever he didn't respond, she feared his heart stopped. She turned to find him sitting on the edge of the bed with his mouth open. "You havin' a stroke?"

Humphrey pointed at the giraffe.

"Don't worry about it, Humph. It isn't real—it's stuffed."

He continued pointing. Winnie followed his finger to what looked like money sticking out of the giraffe's bottom. She tentatively approached it. She pulled a hundred-dollar bill from the hole and then stuck her hand inside. She could feel more paper and retrieved a handful of bills—all hundreds. Stuffed, it was! Humphrey stood to walk over but collapsed back onto the bed. Winnie kept reaching in and pulling out the bills. "Humphrey, we're rich! We're rich! We're rich! Are you hearin' me? I said we're rich. Our troubles are over!"

He didn't answer. She turned, and this time his heart really had stopped. The money she held fell to the floor, and she knelt beside the bed. "Don't leave me now, you son of a bitch! We've gotta travel! We can buy the Winnebago we wanted and go to Sin

City! And I want to show you Radio City Music Hall! Humph! Humph? Wake up! Wake up, dammit!" She slapped his face, but he didn't respond. She stepped away, frantically rubbing her crossed arms as she sobbed. "Why now?"

After she stuffed the money back inside the giraffe and stowed it in the closet, she called for an ambulance. Then she called Maxine.

Maxine showed up after Humphrey had already been taken away. She held Winnie in her arms while she cried. "Why don't you come over and stay with me tonight, Winnie? You can have Mama's room."

"Thank you, honey. That'd be right fine."

Upstairs in the mayor's house, Trey showed Kyle his closet.

"So, this is where you live?" Kyle asked cuttingly.

"No, smartass, this is where I hang my clothes," Trey said as he took Kyle's hand and placed it on his crotch.

"Well hung, I might add," Kyle said.

Trey leaned forward to kiss him.

"What are you doing? You can't just—You've got a wife, for God's sake."

"She doesn't have to know."

"I expected more from you. I'm not sure what, but married it wasn't. How can you do this?"

"What? Live two lives? I'm used to it. I've done it my whole life."

"Don't you think she suspects something? She's not stupid."

"She believes what she wants to believe. Isn't that how people are?" Trey attempted another kiss.

"Alex—Trey...I've got to go." Kyle backed away.

"Did I do something wrong?"

Kyle shook his head as he walked out. Trey grabbed his arm to pull him back inside the room. "Kyle, wait...I'm sorry. The only reason I didn't tell you the truth was because I didn't think I'd ever see you again. You said you were from New York."

"I am. But I'm staying here with Anna until she gets settled."

"I haven't been able to stop thinking about you."

"Yeah, right."

"I'm serious. Do you know I drove back to the hotel to look for you, but you had already gone?"

"You did?" Kyle whispered. It was all he could do not to give in, but having met Stacy, he couldn't. "I've got to get out of here." He turned to leave but stopped. "I'm staying at Rose Welsh's. You can find me there. I'll only be here for a few more days, though. I'm leaving next week." He went to find Anna.

"Are you ready, Cupcake?"

"Where have you been? Some friend *you* are leaving me here to mingle with these...these people I don't know...and they're nosy, too!"

"Can we go?"

"Yes, please!"

At 1914 Harper Valley Lane, Anna and Kyle walked to the cabins. Muffled voices coming from inside the main house caught their attention.

"Sounds like Rose has company. I imagined she'd be in bed by now with church in the morning," Anna remarked. "By the way, when we get inside, I want to know everything that happened upstairs with Trey."

"We'll need some wine first."

In the early hours of the morning, Ronald Black left Rose's and walked home. Rose had to celebrate her sister's birthday some-how, and that's exactly what she did. If Ivory wasn't going to have her husband, someone else might as well. Rose felt like a young hussy, but that was better than an old hag.

CHAPTER SEVEN

In her post-coital bliss, Rose woke early, made breakfast for all of her tenants, and set up a card table in the garden by the fountain. "Breakfast is served!" she called.

Flo peeked out the door, still in her nightgown. "Rose, shoog, aren't you going to church?"

"Not today...come eat!"

"Give me a minute."

When Rose knocked on Anna's door, Kyle answered in his underwear. "Let me throw on some clothes."

Rose waited at the table and drank a glass of orange juice.

Kyle walked over making sure his zipper was up. "What's the occasion?"

"Maybe I just wanted to be in the nice yard before the heat tortures us. Don't ask any more questions." When Flo and Anna showed, both in bathrobes, she asked Kyle to lead them in grace.

"Dear God—uh—Amen."

Arms crisscrossed the table reaching for the butter, syrup, salt and pepper. "We'll have to work on your prayer skills," Rose said.

Anna cleared her throat. "Kyle will be leaving us this week. He's going back to New York."

The news dampened Rose's jovial mood. "I don't know what to say."

"I do. Stay!" Flo blurted. "This town needs you. Look at all of the good you've done for this place."

"I'm sorry, but I have to. I think it's better for me to go back and leave Anna to her new life...and friends. I do like it here—especially *here*...but my life is in New York." He waited momentarily for the silence to break, but it didn't. "I'll be back to visit."

"You'd better," Flo insisted. "Could you pass the bacon?"

Rose handed her the plate with a few strips left. "I thought you and Anna were a couple. I know you told me he was your friend, but I assumed y'all were dating."

"Rose, um, Kyle is gay," Anna said.

Flo slapped the table. "I knew it!"

Rose, however, didn't know it. Nor did she suspect, or want to hear about it. "I never dreamed—that's the sin of all sins. I can't believe...Here? Here at *my* house?" She rested her fork and sat back in the chair.

"The sin of all sins?" Anna queried. "That's an awfully strong thing to say about someone."

"I've never considered my life to be a sin. And if it were, you were able to deal with the *sin* of Anna and me staying in the same apartment together. What's the difference?"

"The difference is—I don't want to talk about it anymore. This is what I get for not going to the Lord's house today. He's punishing me somehow."

"Get real, Rose," Flo let out. "Look at this garden! It's never looked so nice! These designs ain't the work of a straight man, I tell you. What matters here is the good he does and the good person he is, not what makes his heart flutter." She looked at Kyle, "But if your heart ever flutters in the other direction, I'm just across the way." She winked jokingly.

Kyle winked back and gave her a rascally smile before turning to Rose. "Honestly, Rose, I hadn't planned on telling you because I had a feeling you'd react this way. It's common when you have no experience—"

"Experience?" she interrupted. "The Bible gives me all of the experience I need about homosexuality."

"The term 'homosexual' wasn't even in the Bible until the 1940s," Anna informed.

"Really?" Rose questioned.

Kyle stood. "If you'll excuse me. I'm going inside."

"Look what you did, Rose. You scared him off. You gotta quit judging folks," Flo scorned.

A car door closed in front of the house. "Who could that be?" Rose wondered.

Trey had full intentions of waking early and going to Sunday school and church. Being the son of the preacher, there was rarely a valid reason to miss services. But that morning, when Stacy tried to drag him out of the bed he covered his head like a child.

"Are you sick?"

"No. Now, go on...Leave me alone. I'll go later."

Stacy slammed the door on the way out. A despondent Trey took a shower, but unlike most Sundays, he skipped shaving and opted for casual clothes.

As usual, he took Main Street to church, but as he moved into the left-turn lane, he had a sudden urge to turn right. With his directional light blinking left and no cars coming towards him, he hesitated. A car honked from behind. He glanced in the rearview mirror, waved apologetically, and flipped the blinker to turn right. Three blocks later, he pulled up along the curb behind a bright green Bonneville and turned off the engine. He got out, closed the door to the pickup, and walked towards the backyard.

It wasn't until he walked through the gate and everyone turned toward him, did reality slap him back into consciousness.

"Good morning," Trey said, as if addressing the local chamber of commerce.

"Well, Mayor Stewart, what are you doing here?" Rose asked. *Coming to condemn me to hell? I'm never skipping church again!*

"I, uh, I came—" He took a breath. "I came to see this garden. Everyone has been talking about it...and I see, with good reason. It's very nice."

"Trey?" Kyle emerged from the cabin.

"You two know one another?" Rose asked.

"I thought we did," Kyle answered.

Trey looked down. "We've met. Yes. At the teachers' dinner last night."

"Well, of course," Rose replied. "I forgot about that."

"Would you care for some breakfast?" Rose asked, but didn't receive an answer.

In the middle of Rose's backyard, Trey walked over to Kyle and kissed him.

Anna grinned so big her molars were showing.

"I knew it!" Flo applauded.

Rose tried to go inside but found the demonstration of emotions too entrancing and couldn't rise from her chair.

The kiss ended. "I'm, uh—well, um—I'd love some breakfast, Rose," he finally answered. "Room for one more?"

"Of course, shoog." Since Rose sat dumbfounded, Flo took over as hostess. "You just sit yourself down. Here—take my chair. I have to get ready to go to The 36 anyway." Flo fixed the mayor some food. "Sorry, but someone ate all the bacon," she said, glancing at Kyle as she handed Trey a pork-free plate. Flo took a seat on the edge of the fountain. "I'm gonna have me one more ciggy before I get dressed."

Rose continued to gaze about absentmindedly.

"Rose?" Trey said, "Are you okay?"

"I'm—I'm confused."

"I suppose I have some explaining to do."

"You don't have to explain nothin', shoog," Flo interjected, spouting two streams of smoke from her nostrils. "Well, maybe you *could* explain what you're going to do with your wife?"

Trey played with the scrambled eggs on his plate, starting to worry about the consequences of his actions. Behind his masculine façade were puerile ambiguities based on a need for approval and acceptance. He never wanted and would never intentionally hurt anyone, especially his wife, who was probably sitting next to an empty space on a pew, awaiting his arrival. Nevertheless, his struggle to please nibbled at his core and caused him to lie awake most nights. What remained was a vulnerable and sensitive man. Ironically, it was *this* man who was so well loved throughout town. "I haven't decided what to do. I'm hoping that what just happened doesn't have to leave this house until I can figure it out."

"The hell it doesn't," Rose said with a rare slip of a four-letter word. "I have every mind to call Constance and tell her what you're up to."

Flo chimed in, "I wouldn't act so fast, Rose. You're not the only one around here with a mouth..."

Rose scowled in her direction.

"...And eyes," she continued. Flo knew that birthday candles weren't the only things getting blown last night. "It will go no further—I assure you, Trey, honey. If people knew what went on behind closed doors in this town—including this house—y'all wouldn't have shit to be preaching on Sundays, pardon my French." Flo stood and dusted off her bottom. "Well, I've got to get ready. The 36 awaits me. I'll see you folks later...y'all too, lovebirds." She blew a kiss to Kyle and Trey. "This is the best day I've had in a while. Thanks for breakfast, Rose."

Winnie had already been awake for a couple of hours when she went to Maxine's room and nudged the bed. Maxine opened her eyes to the withered face looking down upon her. "I gotta show you somethin', child. I thought you'd never wake up." Winnie peeled back the sheet covering Maxine. "It's almost eleven o'clock. Come on!"

"What is it?"

"I'll give you a hint: it has a really long neck."

On the way over to the Roadside Palace, Maxine slapped her leg. "I got it. A beer!"

"A beer?"

"You know, a long-necked beer bottle."

"Just hold your horses. We're almost there."

Winnie parked and grabbed Maxine's hand. "Come on, slow poke!" Inside the room, she opened the closet door.

"The giraffe?"

"Yes'm. You remember, you gave this to me?"

"Of course."

"Don't go and get sassy with me."

"I'm not being sassy. What's this about?"

"Stick your hand up its butt," Winnie said, making a fist.

Maxine hesitated.

"Go on. Stick it up there and see what you pull out."

"Are you serious?"

"Trust me."

When she first touched a wad of bills, it scared her. "What's in there?"

"Money, honey."

This time Maxine grabbed the giraffe and shook it. A few bills fell out. Then she threw it on the bed and ripped it open. "Is this yours?"

"Ours, sunshine. That's why I wanted you to come out here. You gave me this thing. I can't rightfully take its guts. We have to split it."

"How much is in there?"

"I don't know. Humph—Lord, rest his soul—interrupted my count when he died."

"Let's count it now," Maxine demanded, but then second-guessed her enthusiasm. "I'm sorry, Winnie. I don't mean to make this money more important than Humphrey. You're bound to be upset and I'm—Let's just sit down, and we can worry about the money later."

"Forget sittin' down! Humphrey's dead, and sittin' down ain't gonna bring him back. I'm over it. I knew he was gonna die soon; he was dangling by a thread."

Winnie's words were tougher than she was, and as she spoke, she was overcome with flashes of recent memories. "You know, just last night he came out and caught me smoking. And you know what he said? He told me not to put it out. That was awfully sweet. He probably knew all along why I snuck out...He was a good man, but a cornered cockroach had more will power than he did. He just let himself rot away. I've never been like that. This life ain't been kind to me, but I just keep on truckin'. Ya know what I'm saying?"

Maxine nodded. "You're a strong lady, Winnie."

"Horse puckey! It's not about strength; it's about biting bullets. You don't think I'd still be in this gosh-awful dot-on-the-map of a town if my family wasn't here? They'll be disappointed to hear it wasn't *me* who kicked the bucket."

"What family are you talking about, Winnie?"

Winnie looked at Maxine and then back down. "That conversation is for another time."

Maxine's eyes danced back and forth as she considered the possibilities.

Winnie sat on the bed next to the giraffe. "Make sure there ain't no gaps in the drapes."

The two emptied the giraffe and double-checked to make sure there was nothing left inside. It was mostly hundreds with a few twenties. The total, after counting it three times, was $70,020.

"Holy cow!" Maxine said.

"You took the words right outta my mouth."

After breakfast, inside Anna's apartment, Trey called Stacy's cell phone knowing it would go straight to voicemail. "Hi, dear. I probably won't make it to church this morning after all. Um, someone complained that a bag of Canine Buffet made their dog sick. Trying to sort it all out. Catch you later."

Kyle came out of the bathroom as Trey hung up the phone.

"The Canine Buffet? That's *your* dog food company? I've seen that bag at Rose's back door—I even fed it to Bitsy once, but it never occurred to me it was your company. I could have ruined your life sooner had I known," he added jokingly.

"Last night at the teachers' party was soon enough, thank you very much."

"Bo! Luke! You boys want some coffee?" Anna tried her best at a Southern accent, as she came into the living room carrying a tray of coffee and wearing Daisy Dukes with a red bandana-like top tied around her breasts.

"Thanks, Cupcake."

"Thank you," Trey said. "Is that your teaching outfit?" He smirked, but couldn't help recalling the Armadillo meeting.

Protective of her best friend, Anna took a seat, and with a tone of maternal interrogation, set the record straight. "I might look like a good girl—well, not today," she glanced down at herself, "...but never mind that—I'll pull out your teeth one by one if you hurt Kyle. You understand me?"

"You don't have to worry," he attempted to reassure her, but his shaking voice was far from convincing.

"What's going to happen?" Anna asked. "Are you still going back to New York, Kyle?"

Kyle already had his ticket but didn't know how he could possibly ignore the man sitting next to him who demonstrated a very public mutual interest. "I have to at least go back and get a few things," he said.

"I'll buy you whatever you need. Just stay," Trey impetuously offered. "I don't want to face this alone."

"Thanks, but I'm not that impulsive. I need to have a plan—ya know, like a job, money so I can eat, a place to live. I don't want to be in debt to anyone. Plus, without me, you're Mayor Trey Stewart. With me, you're a vile homosexual who is getting plowed every night by yours truly."

"Sadly, he's right," Anna said.

Trey looked like a movie star as he sat on the sofa next to Kyle, but unlike a movie, there was no script. The townspeople's perception of him was more important than his own. He was unaware how invested he was in the character of a straight, Armadillo meeting, holier-than-thou, preacher's son until he was presented with a sudden twist in the role he had meticulously mastered. He never considered the tugging of the heartstrings. "I don't know what to do." He sat up to spoon sugar into his coffee. His breaths grew shorter, and he began to sweat profusely.

Anna fetched a wet towel. "Breathe in through your nose." She pushed the damp hair back from his brow and stroked his head.

His breathing returned to more normal. "I shouldn't have—I don't—I don't know what I was thinking coming over here. I'm really sorry, Kyle. I just can't—"

"Sit down, Trey," Anna said. "It'll be okay. There's no need to be rash."

"It's okay, Cupcake. Let him go if he wants."

Trey, still standing, said, "Anna, you're new in this town. Give it some time and you'll see why I'm afraid. There's a lot at stake here. It's not all about me, and I know that." He looked at Kyle, "That's why I'm telling you, I can't do this...not now."

Trey opened the door, glanced upwards as if seeking strength from above, turned and left.

"I'm sorry, Kyle," Anna said, scooting over to fill the void where Trey had been sitting. "These people here are crazy. Nobody in their right mind would—"

"If I had any doubt about going back to New York, it just flew out the window."

Trey arrived to church just before the closing-prayer. From the door, he looked over all the backs of heads for Stacy's unmistakable hair, the color of wood glue. Why did she always want to sit so close to the front? Wearing a feeble smile, he made his way down the aisle and took the seat in the pew next to his loving wife. She looked at him adoringly, rested her hand on top of his leg, and briefly admired her large diamond ring.

MONDAY–FRIDAY, AUGUST 25–29, 2007

The following day, Anna began the dreaded teacher in-service meetings. Full of nerves, she walked the two blocks to school. She received her very first tour of the campus and was finally able to step inside the classroom where she would be teaching.

The janitors were abuzz polishing the long tiled hallways, setting out chairs, and cleaning the windows. The teachers' aide was cranking away at an old mimeograph machine. The staff gathered in the cafeteria to welcome the newcomer, eat donuts, and discuss any changes in policy and teaching methods. But judging the dour faces, it served as nothing more than a reminder that summer was coming to a close. Anna, like most women in a room full of females, was trying to decide who amongst them would be friendly, who would be a good lunch buddy, and who wore what. Once she finished the analysis, she took inventory of the opposite sex by playing a mind game: *If I had to sleep with one, which one would it be?* To her surprise, there was one who wasn't too bad. His name tag read: Mark Craven—Choir.

The meeting ended by noon, and she declined a group lunch at Dairy Queen to go home and be with Kyle. With his departure looming only five days away, she wanted to spend as much time with him as possible.

Each day that week, after time-wasting meetings at school, Anna arrived to a home-cooked meal. Kyle's cooking was another reason she hated to see him go. On Wednesday, they went for a 2-for-1 special at Putter-About Mini Golf, but aside from that, they stayed in, talked, and continued working on Anna's apartment.

SATURDAY, AUGUST 30, 2007

Kyle packed his bags by pure inertia, not volition. He and Anna arrived at The 36 Diner to wait for the bus that would eventually get him to the Austin airport.

"I'm going to miss you, Cupcake." Anna took hold of his arm.

He kissed the top of her head. "I know. I don't know what I'm going to do in New York without you, but staying was never part of the plan."

"I know. It seems just yesterday we were sitting right over there and meeting Flo for the first time. Remember how we were frightened by her?"

"Yeah. Aside from you, I think I'll miss her the most."

"More than Trey?"

"I didn't really have a chance to miss him. I'll miss the thought of him, but I don't want anyone who's complicated."

"Is this it?" Anna nodded towards the bus pulling into the gravel parking lot.

"I'd say we can presume that it is." Kyle chuckled. He gave Anna a hug and picked up the two suitcases beside him.

Anna opened the door for him and fought the tears as he boarded. She waved as the bus pulled away.

On the way home, she passed the Dairy Queen, where only a little while ago they were eating their typical Saturday lunch at an outdoor table and observing the latest cowboy fashions. *Damn that Trey!*

With Kyle gone, Anna's little apartment felt empty and less quaint. The stillness of his absence amplified the flaws of the place: the ceiling had cracks in it; the kitchen faucet dripped every eleven seconds; the bathroom door sounded like a cat meowing. She put on a Maria McKee CD to drown out the eerie silence, and sat on the depressing, lumpy sofa. No sooner had she propped her feet onto the coffee table did her intestines need to let loose. Whether it was the cheese and pickles on her burger, or the nervousness about living alone in Prairie Springs, she barely made it to the toilet.

CHAPTER EIGHT

TUESDAY, SEPTEMBER 2, 2007

The day after Labor Day, Anna woke for her first day of school. She showered, put on a dab of makeup, and found herself standing in front of the mirror contemplating what to wear. Had she grown so accustomed to Kyle's fashion advice that she could no longer dress herself? She eventually went with her favorite outfit: a pair of khaki pants and a black, short-sleeved button-down top.

Anna was so nervous when the bell rang that she could barely function.

The students scampered about in search of their classes. With her brain and body not operating in sync, she stood likes a statue next to her doorway, underneath a colorful sign that read BIEN-VENIDOS.

After third period, she spent her break in the teachers' lounge. Halfway through a bag of M&M's, the principal popped in and pulled her aside. "We like for our teachers to wear dresses. We feel that it's important to set a nice, Christian example for the students."

"Absolutely," Anna sarcastically agreed. "As soon as the male teachers wear dresses, I'll wear one too," she said and took her M&M's to finish at her desk.

By the final class of the day, she was able to greet the students as they walked inside. When all were seated, she called attendance. Adams to Reed went without incident, but "Richard Richards" resulted in a giggle from one of the guys in the class.

"Ricky Richards," he quickly corrected. Anna jotted a note in her roster.

"Richard Richards," another male student repeated and giggled. Ricky stood, ready to fight. "Shut up, faggot!"

Anna was determined to not give detention on the first day of school. "Ricky, that's not appropriate language."

"Well, tell Brant it's not appropriate to make fun of someone's name."

"If you had told Brant what you just told me, we wouldn't be having this conversation. Think before you speak."

"Okay...J.A.P.," he mumbled.

My, word travels fast around here. Anna wasn't terribly offended by being called a Jewish American Princess, but she was upset he used it as an insult...and that he knew anything personal about her. She glared at him. "You're skating on thin ice, young man."

The girls in the class couldn't get their desks close enough to the smart-mouthed teen.

When the bell rang and the last student left the room, Anna couldn't refrain from spying between the white metal venetian blinds to see who picked up this "Ricky" fellow.

The surprise provoked a raise of her eyebrows. A police car. The sun's glare off the windshield was blinding, but as the car pulled away, she caught glimpse of the gray beard and realized it was the policeman from The Springs.

Chawli Dickson lived two doors down the street from Rose and cultivated black-eyed peas in his yard instead of grass. As an annual neighborly gesture, he brought her a bushel of his home-grown legumes. It was good timing since Rose had no other plans for her Tuesday, and while shelling peas wasn't the most exciting chore, it was a repetitive task that permitted her to wander into mental territories rarely visited. This year's black-eyed pea therapy prompted her to examine her recent behavior. After all, she was proof that even the most ritualistic of churchgoers wasn't perfect.

Sleeping with Ronald Black went against everything she had been taught. As far as sins were concerned, this one was so egregious Moses wrote it in stone, yet for some reason, she didn't feel guilty for what she had done. Whether Ivory was dead or had a late midlife crisis and ran off somewhere, Rose was angry at her absence, and sleeping with her husband made her feel perversely connected. If she twisted it that way, she could convince herself that she was doing her sister a favor by keeping her husband occupied.

The reality, however, had little to do with Ivory and a lot to do with Rose...the aging, lonely, and occasionally amorous Rose. While hormones hadn't played *much* of a part, she still craved a man, and it just so happened that Ronald craved a woman. Since she could so easily commit adultery, might she be able to accept other things? And was accepting others the key to accepting herself?

No sooner had she shelled the final pod did the phone ring and interrupt her cerebral inquisition. "Brother Stewart. What a surprise!"

A few minutes later, Rose hung up dejected and pensive. *Get rid of Anna?*

It didn't take long for the hungry husband to realize the mistake he had made. Ted pulled into his sister-in-law's driveway, ready to beg his wife to come home. Dorcas might have been plump, but she was also one hell of a cook, and he couldn't face another grilled-cheese sandwich—not even *those* tasted the same as when she made them. With flowers in hand, he stood at the front steps, rang the bell and pushed back the few strands of hair clinging to his scalp.

Constance opened the door wearing a turquoise apron.

"I'm here to see Dorcas."

"Dorcas? She's not here—hasn't been here for days. I assumed she went back home to you."

"No, she didn't come back home to me," he mocked. "You're her sister. You don't know where she is?"

"I told ya, I thought she went home to you. And don't start with me. *You're* her husband."

Ted backed off the porch and surveyed the sky. "Drats!"

"Should I call the police?" Constance asked from the door.

"No. Don't go making a big deal of it. She's probably just—I dunno."

"This is going to make a great story."

Ted glared at Constance for her selfish comment.

"I'm sorry. I didn't mean to say that out loud, but I bet it would make the front page. Come on, Ted, let's call the police and get this in the news. The quicker word gets out, the quicker we'll find her."

The only person in town who had seen Dorcas board the bus was Judy Jane Johnson, and she and her husband had gone to Port Aransas for an extended Labor Day vacation. Needless to say, all teller windows would be backed up without her speedy fingers.

It was the second time lately that a woman had gone missing in Prairie Springs. Women across Milam County tried not to let on how petrified they were that they might be next.

SATURDAY, SEPTEMBER 6, 2007

On Saturday morning, the townspeople gathered around the gazebo in the main park. It was constructed in the late 1800s when James Hogg campaigned for governor, and from the looks of it, it hadn't been repainted since. The grounds were equally as neglected.

Ted stood at the top of the gazebo steps informing the crowd, at least the ones that didn't blame him, of his wife's disappearance. He was too ashamed to mention that he had called her a heifer and she left him to stay with her sister. "One minute she was on the couch watching TV, and the next she was gone." Ted made it sound like she'd been the victim of a UFO abduction.

Anna suggested to Maxine that they go over to The Springs to search. A group was already there when they arrived. They sat in the car for a minute.

"See that cop?" Anna asked, pointing to the policeman standing amongst a group of searchers.

"Yeah. That's Officer Richards. He'll give you a speeding ticket for just thinking about speeding. He's an ass."

"He accused me of sunbathing in the nude and all I did was untie my top. I was on my stomach the entire time."

"I'm not surprised."

"And, his son is in my class."

"Lucky you...Look! Let's go see what the fuss is about. Maybe they found her."

Constance parked beside them and ran over to the scene carrying her notebook and pen.

The crowd was inching closer to a dog frantically digging next to a pecan tree. As Officer Richards instructed everyone to stand back, the dog reached into the hole and grabbed hold of a piece of fabric. He pulled and tugged, and as he did, an odor filled the air. Women turned their heads; several people gagged. Constance took pictures and wrote in her notepad so aggressively that her feathery pen nearly took flight. Rotting flesh appeared, and two of the searchers vomited.

"Oh shit!" Anna blurted. Momentarily, the corpse was forgotten and all eyes turned to her as if the vulgarity were more offensive than the putrid rot.

"Please keep your comments to yourself," Officer Richards said, making eye contact with Anna.

"What are *you* looking at?" Maxine snapped back.

Officer Richards turned and focused back on the shrouded body. "I've got to call the coroner. Everyone, step back. Step back!" he asserted.

"Let's go get something to eat," Anna suggested, squeezing Maxine's hand. "I don't care to see anymore."

"How can you eat after this?"

"Because I'm hungry."

Word of the body traveled fast. Winnie sat at the Dairy Queen holding a burger in her hands, wondering why everyone was rushing out. By the time Anna and Maxine walked through the door, Winnie was one of the few customers still eating. "What's all the fuss about?"

"Didn't you hear?" Maxine asked.

"Hear what? I just woke up half an hour ago."

Maxine looked at her watch. "It's almost one!"

Winnie rested the hand holding a french fry on the edge of the table. "Where would *I* need to be?"

"Anyway, Dorcas is missing."

"Who?"

"Dorcas, Ted's wife. And they just found a body at The Springs."

Winnie dropped her fry. "What kind of body?"

"A dead one," Maxine said. "Do you know my friend Anna?"

"Hiya," Winnie said. "Of course I know her."

"Do you want me to get you some extra napkins?" Anna offered.

"Do I have ketchup caught in my wrinkles? That happens sometimes."

"No. You're crying," Anna pointed out.

Winnie reached up and acted surprised at the tear rolling down alongside her nose. "Howdaya like that? Be a doll, would ya?"

Anna went to the counter.

Winnie beckoned Maxine closer with an arthritic finger.

"That ain't Dorcas they found out there."

"What?" Maxine gasped.

Anna returned carrying the napkins. "Here ya go."

"Then who is it?"

"We'll talk later," Winnie told her. "I need to talk to you, anyway."

"Anna," Maxine said. "Would you mind ordering for me—just a burger—while I talk to Winnie?"

"No...I mean, sure." She backed away slowly. Winnie hurried her with a go-on-along-now-dear smile and waited until she was out of listening range. "Maxine, honey, I buried Humphrey at The Springs under a big pecan tree."

"What?" Maxine said it loud enough that Anna turned around, curious. "You what?" she said again, this time in a whisper.

"I didn't want to put him in the cemetery, so I took him over to The Springs. He liked it there. He was always telling me stories of when he was a little boy. I thought, 'Screw the cemetery! I'm plantin' him where he'll be happy!' I guess we didn't go deep enough."

"We?"

"I paid that Mexican feller, Roberto, who pumps gas to help me dig a hole."

"Winnie, this is terrible! They're diggin' poor Humphrey up as we speak. We've got to stop them."

"No, you go ahead and eat your lunch. I'll drive over there

and explain." Winnie scooted out from her seat. "Dammit! The next time I bury a dead body I'm gonna have to rent a bulldozer."

"Catch you later," Winnie told Anna as she passed the order counter on the way out.

THURSDAY, SEPTEMBER 11, 2007

Thursday's edition of *The Herald* came out with the headline, "Missing Woman in Houston." The mystery was solved when Judy Jane Johnson got back to work at the First National Bank and saw the missing person poster. She called the police and reported having seen Dorcas catch a bus. The police were then able to obtain her final destination. Ted was in a state of chagrin. His wife had left him, and the people of Prairie Springs were wondering why. Constance was only too eager to follow up the article with another: "Wife Leaves: Husband Called Her A Heifer."

The disappearance was the hot topic in the teachers' lounge, where Anna looked forward to chatting with Mark. Because he was the choir teacher, she had presumed he was gay, but the more they talked, the more she became convinced that he was straight. Maybe that's why it bothered her that Ms. Biology was flirting with him by the soda machine.

"Excuse me," Anna interrupted. "I need to get a Coke. Oh. Hi, Mark."

Despite Mark's attempt to free himself of the garrulous co-worker, the woman remained determined to continue the tête-à-tête. Anna, sensing his distress, playfully and enticingly ate a banana at the table next to them. Mark left Ms. Biology mid-sentence.

"What's your take on all of this?" he asked Anna.

"On all of what?"

"The missing woman."

"I suppose she couldn't take any more of the small town and went to the big city."

Mark tilted his head, "Possibly. I doubt it's that simple."

"Haven't you ever thought about leaving this place?"

"Once or twice," he looked around, "...a day."

"My point exactly. They say that when you never leave home, the world seems small, but when you travel, you realize *you* are the one who's small." Anna paused to let her comment soak in before continuing. "Say, Mark, do you have Ricky Richards in your music class?"

"I have everyone in my music classes. Yes, including Ricky Richards."

"Is he a good student for you?"

"Kind of a bully—nice voice, though."

"Really?"

"Yeah. One of the best I've ever heard."

"Wow!"

"Why do you ask?"

"No reason."

"Just be careful with him. His dad's the law enforcement around here, and he's also friends with the county judge."

"What's that mean?"

"Let me put it this way. If you ever get a traffic ticket, you might as well go ahead and pay it, because it won't do any good to fight it."

She could tell he was speaking from experience.

The school bell beckoned them back to their classrooms.

SATURDAY, SEPTEMBER 13, 2007

At the house in the woods, the plastic armadillo was lit and the pickup trucks lined the gravel road once again.

Chili dogs were served, and while there was no alcohol at the meetings, the men were inebriated with the Holy Spirit, or as the wood-burned sign on the wall read, "...the Holey Spirit." The evening's agenda included the opening prayer, a vote on the food for the next meeting, the subsequent collection for that food, blessing of the food, and a speech entitled, "The Devil Personified." Afterwards, they gathered around the campfire and had to pronounce whom they considered to be the devil personified.

Despite Flo's extracurricular activities, her name hadn't made the list in years. The list was updated twice a year at each "Devil Personified" meeting and posted on the wall of the meetinghouse near the entrance. The names were tallied, and the person receiving the highest number of votes would be targeted until either joining a church and behaving in a Christian fashion...or leaving town.

While the Armadillos were downing chili dogs, Dorcas was dreaming of one as she stared at a plate of salad. "This is for rabbits," she told her new friend, Frank.

"Anorexic rabbits at that," he added.

"I've gotta get some food in me somehow," Dorcas said.

"Meet me tonight behind the shed by the pond."

"You have food there?"

"*Shh.* Just do it."

Dorcas finished touching up her makeup and sat on her twin bed. She felt stupid for fixing her face in the middle of the night. When the lights-out buzzer rang, she waited for silence before sneaking outside. "Lord, give me strength," she muttered as she opened the cabin door and looked around to make sure no one was watching. Approaching the pond, she spotted the moon's dull reflection on the tin roof of the shed tucked among the trees. Unfortunately, the moonlight wasn't strong enough to see where she was stepping, and her heart rate increased each time her foot hit the ground. She looked back towards her cabin, but it was out of sight. She took another step towards the shed.

Frank darted out from behind the tin structure and Dorcas nearly peed. "Mercy me!"

Frank stood in front of her.

"You're naked!" Dorcas said.

"No kidding. I just took a dip in the pond and am air drying."

Seeing a nude man made her forget all about food for a brief moment. She covered her eyes until he was dressed. "This is where they keep the food?" she asked, trying not to peek.

Frank smiled as he tugged on his belt. "I've got my pants on, you can look."

Dorcas cautiously spread open her fingers.

In a booth at the Dairy Queen, half an hour before closing, Winnie and Maxine discussed plans of what to do with the money. Winnie made one thing clear: they were *not* to go to a local bank because it would raise too many eyebrows. Judy Jane Johnson might be quick and friendly, but a mouth was a mouth —even if it was just half of one—and mouths tended to open in small towns. As they sat there sipping on sodas, Maxine suggested they invest it.

"Invest it?" Winnie slapped the table. "What, for Pete's sake, do you think we are? I don't know nothing about no investin'."

"I don't mean in the stock market, Winnie. I'm talking about *buying* something. We could open up a business."

"A business? What kind of business is you and me gonna open?"

"I don't know, but we could do *something*."

"The only business that seems to rake it in 'round here is the church...We could open up one of them!"

"*You* gonna preach...? And what about all the competition."

"I guess you're right. What about a Wal-Mart?"

Maxine shook her head. "I was thinking along the lines of a

coffee shop—you know, like they have on that sitcom where the friends meet to drink coffee."

"Must be a boring show," Winnie commented.

"No, I'm serious. This town needs a place like that. I remember all we did when I was young was come here to Dairy Queen and get fat on ice cream sandwiches. We could make a nice place and let people—I dunno—let them read a book or somethin'."

"You think people 'round here'll go for it?"

"Sure, why not." Maxine said confidently. "What's there not to go for?"

"Well, whatever you think is best. I'm so old it don't matter what I think 'cause by the time it gets open, I'll probably be closed for business for good. This body ain't got much left."

"You hush, Winnie."

Winnie sucked on her straw like there was still soda in the cup. "I'm gonna get a refill. Want some more?"

"No, I'm fine."

When she returned to the table, Winnie said, "You really think we could open up a coffee spot?"

"I don't see why not. What's there to it? A few cups, a coffee pot, and a cash register."

CHAPTER NINE

FRIDAY, OCTOBER 31, 2007

HALLOWEEN

Cooler and rainier days meant that cows no longer had to
take refuge from the sun under the shade of a tree. Dogs
had more energy to chase pickups. Tractors effortlessly plowed
softer fields. Snakes no longer hid in dewberry bushes, and the
slightest breeze knocked buckets of pecans from the trees. And for
those living along gravel roads, the rains meant housewives didn't
have to dust every time a vehicle passed.

The days remained warm enough to take a dip in the city pool
in the middle of the afternoon, but a windbreaker was needed
once evening came. Cold-natured Rose warmed herself with the
heat emanating from the oven, where she was toasting the seeds
from the pumpkin she'd carved for the front porch. As the sun
went down, carved creations were lit and porch lights were flipped
on to signal the imminent trick-or-treaters.

In the town square, there wasn't a pumpkin in sight, but there was one surprise: renovations had begun at the old movie theater that Winnie and Maxine bought to convert into a café.

Anna couldn't wait for the place to open, looking forward to a quiet spot to read a book and sip a latte, since she wasn't much on social interactions. She did, however, enjoy visiting with Mark at school during break time, which turned into sitting together at lunch. There had even been one kiss, albeit awkward, in the teachers' lounge when Anna leaned over to pick a cracker crumb from his cheek. Mark misread the situation and kissed her on the lips. Anna didn't mind but was so caught off guard she didn't respond. And when it came time for teachers to sign up to patrol the neighborhoods for Halloween, it was no surprise to the faculty that Anna and Mark chose the same route.

Before heading out on neighborhood patrol, Anna invited Maxine over to her cabin. When she knocked, Anna was putting on the Elvira makeup to match the costume she bought.

"Frightening," Maxine teased.

"Shush! I'm doing my best."

"What's Mark dressing as?"

Anna bit down on an erupting smile, "The Scarecrow from *The Wizard of Oz*."

Maxine laughed.

"He wanted me to be the Cowardly Lion, but the costume was too expensive. Want some happy punch? It's already made."

"Sure. What is it?"

Anna scooped from the crystalline plastic punch bowl on the counter. "Secret recipe...So, Maxine, how's the coffee shop coming?"

"It's more work than we expected, but overall, it should be open in another month or so. We are hoping for the day after Thanksgiving, but only time will tell."

"I'm excited for you and Winnie. I will definitely be a customer...Do you mind if we wait outside for Mark? I love this brisk weather."

"Enjoy it while you can."

Anna and Maxine had just lit the jack-o'-lantern when the phone rang. "Crap. Hold on a sec," Anna said as she ran inside.

"Happy Halloween, Cupcake! I'm getting ready for the parade."

"Hi, Kyle! Who are you going as?"

"Just as me."

"You're no fun...Hey, guess who's here? Maxine."

"Tell her hello for me. And how's Flo?"

"Happy-go-lucky as always. I saw her leaving for the diner dressed as Wonder Woman. So...do you know when you're coming back?"

"Oh, Anna, I don't know. Maybe next year I can come down for a visit. That's part of why I'm calling. I got a job."

"A job? You?" She tried to be thrilled but selfishly feared it would only tie him to New York forever.

"Yeah. Can you believe it? I got a job at a law firm as an administrative assistant. Get this—it's called Goldstein, Goldberg & Goldblatt."

"Good grief! Do you have to be circumcised to work there?"

"Yeah, they have a *bris* for the new employees."

"Well, congratulations, I guess..." Anna could see Mark through the window, dressed and ready to scare off birds all over the county. "...I hate to cut you short, Kyle, but Mark and I signed up for neighborhood patrol to make sure the kids don't get into trouble while trick-or-treating. He's here, so I've got to go."

"Fine. We can talk later. I've got something to tell you about Ivory Black."

"Yeah?" Anna responded, leaning back so she could wave at Mark through the open door.

"Go trick-or-treating. Call me when you get in."

Anna hung up the phone and carried a plastic cup of punch outside to Mark, interrupting the conversation he was having with Maxine. "You'll need this to get through the night."

He took a sip. "I'll need something stronger than this. Is it virgin?"

"No, it'll hit you like a ton of feathers. Just give it a few minutes."

Rose came out the back door and flipped the switch to light up the stone pathway. "What are y'all doing out here?" She looked around confused as to why she hadn't been invited to the party.

"Having some punch. Come on over. I'll serve you some," Anna offered, mischievously.

Maxine excused herself. "I'm supposed to pick up Winnie in half an hour." She looked over to where her mother's ashes were scattered, "We've, uh, got to run some errands for the café."

"Can't you stay?" Anna asked, politely.

"No, really, I've got to get going. Y'all have fun."

Maxine left and Anna handed Rose a glass of punch. "Do you know Mark?" Anna asked.

"Just from here and there," Rose answered. "Our paths rarely cross."

Anna took that to mean she hadn't seen Mark at church. "Drink up, Rose. I've got more inside."

"This is plenty. What flavor is it...Passion Punch? It tastes like real fruit juice."

"It's my special recipe."

About ten minutes later, Anna looked at her watch. "We'd better get going," she pointed out. "We've got children to protect from the evildoings of Satanists."

"Y'all stop by later," Rose offered. "And Anna, you've got to give me the recipe for this stuff. Could I get a refill before you go?" She handed Anna the almost-empty plastic cup.

"Certainly."

Left alone, Rose contemplated what seemed to be on her mind consistently these days: Baptist teachings versus what was transpiring in her life. If she followed the unsolicited advice Brother Stewart gave her on the phone the day she was shelling peas, she would isolate herself from the new people in her life, including Ronald. If she ignored the pastor, she might actually enjoy *herself* for a change. The one thing she knew for sure: sweet Anna wasn't going anywhere.

Throughout the neighborhoods, anxious children left their parents at the sidewalk and ran to the door to ask for candy. The residents looked to the curb to discern the disguised kids by their chaperones before dropping some candy into their plastic pumpkins and waving to the adults.

On their route, they walked by the mayor's house. Stacy had outdone herself. Spider webs dangled in trees, ghosts made from sheets hung from tree branches, carved pumpkins were scattered throughout the yard, and "Monster Mash" played from speakers on the front porch. It seemed quite excessive for the daughter-in-law of the preacher. "These people have too much money," Mark commented.

"Let's say hello," Anna tugged at his arm.

"We can't just—"

"Come on. They won't mind."

Anna knocked on the door. Stacy answered.

"Trick or treat!"

Stacy reached for the candy.

"It's me...Anna."

"Who? For crying out loud, I didn't recognize you."

Anna took note of Stacy's reaction and formally introduced the Scarecrow. "This is Mark. He teaches music at the high school."

"That's right. We were hoping you would come to the teachers' party, Mark. I don't believe you've ever come to one, have you?"

"I'm not a big party person."

Stacy smiled forgivingly, "I understand...Won't y'all come in? I have some pie inside."

"No, that's okay. I just wanted to say hello. We have to patrol the kids."

"What could happen in this town? They'll be all right. I insist —a quick cup of coffee and a slice of homemade pumpkin pie."

Stacy could have moved straight into Stepford. Her black stockings had spiders and webs sewn into them and she wore a black taffeta knee-length skirt with an orange, short-sleeved cashmere sweater. Her bobbed blond hair flipped upwards at the shoulder drawing attention to the pearl necklace Trey had given her for their second wedding anniversary.

"Is Trey, uh, Mr. Stewart, here?" Anna asked.

"No, he said he had some business to finish. You know he works like a horse," she defended, hoping it sounded credible. Stacy knew, and had for some time, that her picture-perfect marriage was painted with watercolors, and it was beginning to rain.

It didn't take Nancy Drew to know something was amiss when she got his work voicemail on nights when he claimed to be "stuck at the office." But as long as she didn't know the truth, she could continue pretending everything was all right.

"I'll serve you in the den," Stacy suggested, tugging lightly at the center pearl of her necklace. "How do you take your coffee?"

Meanwhile in Houston, Dorcas was having the worst Halloween of her life. She had always been an enthusiastic fan of the holiday because of the abundance of candy. It wasn't beyond her to simply turn off the porch light and sit in the dark drinking a Coke and devouring the bag of miniature Snickers she bought to hand out to the kids. This year, however, her Halloween treat consisted of a few, individual Tic Tac mints.

One-point-nine kilocalories was hardly reason to celebrate!

Slimming Acres resembled a scout camp with cabins, lodges, a nearby forest, a small pond, and other random structures. The cafeteria was the most popular building, and the most securely locked.

From time to time, a desperate hungry person would set off the alarm, which sounded like a civil defense siren.

Sitting in a circle around a plastic pumpkin, each person in the group was allowed to take one Tic Tac for every story told about how being overweight made a task difficult or caused embarrassment. To earn her first breath mint, she shared how she didn't fit in the Japanese car. Dorcas sat next to Frank, the man with guacamole eyes and milk-chocolate hair. It was common that foods were used as adjectives around the camp. Frank, like many overweight people, countered his weight issues with a sense of humor—mostly sarcastic. Dorcas enjoyed it and felt ashamedly comfortable around him. This was Frank's third time at Slimming Acres, and while each time he returned to the camp heavier than the last, this time would hopefully be different. Never before did he have the power of prayer on his side...and Dorcas had a direct line to heaven.

"Sugar and cream?"

"Yes, please," Anna said.

"And you, Mark?"

"Black is fine."

Stacy served the coffee and brought over the pie topped with swirls of whipped cream.

"How nice of you two to stop by. It's always a relief after so many children to have some post-pubescent guests."

Stacy made the comment with a straight face, but Anna couldn't hold back a chuckle—one that was followed by a ring of the doorbell.

"Speak of the devils..." Stacy said. "Excuse me, I'll be right back."

Anna and Mark eyed one another as they listened to the counterfeit enthusiasm coming from Stacy. Had they not been so tuned in to the trick-or-treaters, they might have heard a sneeze coming from outside the den window. It seemed one ghost in the neighborhood was more interested in spying than in collecting candy. It quickly ducked down when Stacy came back into the room.

"You'd think I liked Halloween by looking at the yard," she said. "I don't really enjoy the kids; I just like to decorate. Maybe if I had kids of my own—"

"Why don't you?" Mark asked.

Anna looked up from her coffee in time to see Stacy do the same.

Stacy glared at him before summoning a smile. She took a deep breath, answering on the exhale. "I guess it's not in the Lord's plan."

Anna lowered her eyes back to the coffee cup. Outside, the ghost sank back into the bushes.

"More pie, Mark?" Stacy offered.

Anna found herself pitying Stacy, and like her mother, she couldn't help but try and alleviate some of that pity in the only way she knew how. "Say, Stacy, would you like to come over for punch at my place later? We only have a few minutes left on our patrol."

"Thanks, but I can't."

"Why not?"

Stacy looked around for an excuse, but none came to her. "What the devil! I'll go."

Atchoo! Whether it was the freshly cut grass or pollen floating in the air, an antihistamine was to be first on Constance's list before her next stakeout. All three caught a glimpse of the bobbing white sheet outside the window. Stacy's eyes widened fearfully. Anna ran to the window, but only in time to see the ghost run down the street. It was too dark to notice the turquoise polyester swishing underneath the sheet.

Anna and Mark returned to the streets of Prairie Springs. Not surprisingly, all was calm. So calm, in fact, that it was reminiscent of the way life used to be before people locked their doors and hid pistols in their nightstands. As they passed Ted and Dorcas' house, Ted waved and took a final gander down the street before turning off the porch light. Anna told Mark she bought her car from them, but he, like everyone else in town, already knew that.

Ted wasn't the only one turning off their light. As they walked down the block, others were doing the same. The only illumination that soon remained came from the dim, sparse streetlights. Suddenly, the innocent streets seemed unfamiliar and daunting. Anna was aware of every sound in the darkness, including the sound of her own increasing heartbeat. She grabbed Mark's arm and walked quickly to the next street light. As they turned the corner onto Harper Valley Lane, a pickup passed. They heard it screech around the block. It passed again, intentionally close, and slowed slightly.

A pumpkin came hurtling at them. They ducked.

"What the hell?"

"The Armadillos!" Mark said, turning to see where the pumpkin had landed. The pickup stopped a few houses away. The reverse lights came on. "Run!" he yelled.

They ran towards the next house where they took shelter behind a parked car in the driveway. After a few revs of the engine, whoever it was, drove away. Anna sighed in relief.

"Who, pray tell, are the Armadillos?"

"A group of men from the town's churches. They've taken it upon themselves to keep Prairie Springs Christian. They also try to keep it white and straight. Scaring people they don't want around is one of their tactics."

"They do a helluva job," Anna remarked. "This must be what Winnie was warning us about. Were they after you or me?"

"I think they gave up on me. They sent me a letter once insisting I teach the kids gospel music instead of 'secular' music. I told my students they could learn church music at church, but in my class, they would learn about Mozart and Beethoven. It isn't just about the music, ya know, it's about why the piece was written. A composer's notes are like an artist's paintings. To understand them, you have to go behind the scenes."

Anna appreciated his passion, but it wasn't her biggest concern at the moment. "Why are they after *me*?"

"I can't be sure, but my guess is because you're a Jewish Yankee with a gay friend. I'd be careful if I were you."

"Don't scare me, Mark."

"I don't mean to. I just don't want anything to happen to you."

Rose sat on her porch swing in a whimsical daze wearing a witch's hat. Bitsy sat beside her bedecked with orange and black streamers. The Halloween punch from two hours ago had gone straight to her head. The funny thing was she didn't know she was drunk. She did know, however, she'd never had so much fun on Halloween. Every child that came on the porch was greeted with a witch's cackle and a handful of peanut butter cups.

Rose's house was the only one with the porch light still burning. She turned to see Elvira and the Scarecrow coming down the street a few houses away. "Yoo-hoo! Anna! Mark! Follow the yellow brick road!" she called, but her voice didn't carry like she had hoped; the leaves rattling in the breeze drowned her out.

When they walked up the sidewalk, Rose called, "Grab the pumpkin. Let's take it around back and put it in the garden. We can look at it while we drink some more of that punch. I'll whip up some popcorn and meet y'all there." She hurried inside. "Come on Tipsy—Bitsy...Come on."

Anna and Mark were sitting in chairs in the glow of the two jack-o'-lanterns when Rose came out the back door. "Y'all want butter on it?"

"Sure," Anna said. "Don't drown it, but a little would be nice."

"Okay."

They sipped on punch while they waited.

"Here I come," Rose announced, holding open the screen door with her foot as she waited for Bitsy. "Isn't this fun?" She took a seat and placed the popcorn bowl on the table.

Mark offered to serve her punch, which she didn't refuse.

"I haven't felt this good in a long time. It's like the good Lord has washed my worries away...What *do* you put in here, Anna? Multivitamins? I can't tell you how good I feel...Could it be a miracle? Do y'all feel good, too? Of course, y'all are probably too young to know the difference, but I'll declare, this punch has me wanting to do a jig..."

An exhausted Wonder Woman came through the lychgate. "Ooh. A party. I'll be right out—just gotta change. I know I *look* sexy in this outfit, but it's awfully uncomfortable."

"Flo is a lovely person," Rose dreamily exhaled. "I don't know why some man hasn't swept her off her feet."

"Were *you* ever married?" Anna asked.

"Me?" Rose said, flattered the conversation was about her. "Yes, once. He passed away, though. Then I was engaged a second time, but he got sent to Vietnam and never came home."

"I'm sorry, Rose," Anna said.

"Well, I'm not! If he was going to leave me for another woman, I'm glad he did it before we tied the knot."

They all laughed, then Mark interrupted the lull that followed. "When did you buy this place?"

"My husband and I bought it years ago. Let's see, I guess it was back in—yes, in the sixties—sixty-six, I believe. He died soon afterwards." Rose took a swallow of the punch. "This stuff is terrific, Anna...or did I already say that?"

"Yes, you mentioned it. Thank you."

"What's in here?"

"Fruit juices and stuff."

"You have a lovely garden, Rose," Mark commented. "Anna told me that her friend did it."

"Oh yes. What was his name?"

"Kyle," Anna answered.

"Kyle? Yes, Kyle. He was a good kid. What ever happened to him?"

"He went back to New York," Anna reminded her, finding Rose's memory lapse amusing.

"New York? What's he doing there? I was hoping he'd paint the house...I was going to let him live here for free if he did."

"Really? I'll tell him you said that, but he just got a job there."

"Well, that's too bad."

"Speaking of Kyle," Anna said, "I need to call him back. He wanted to tell me about—uh, something." She didn't want to mention anything to Rose about her sister.

Flo walked out when Anna was going inside. "Am I too late? Is the party over?"

"No, help yourself to the punch, Flo. There's more where that came from. I'll be right back."

"Punch? I was hoping for something a little—"

"Just try it," Mark ordered. "You'll like it, I promise."

Anna smiled and went inside to call Kyle. "Anna, you should've been there. There was a—"

"Kyle? Tell me later. I have company, but I want to hear about Ivory Black."

"Oh, right. You remember my friend, Marvin?"

"Uh, no. I can't say that I do."

"Remember that bar where we went to the drag show earlier this summer?"

"Yeah."

"Marvin was the guy we sat with. He was with this guy, Ken...Ring a bell? Anyway, his friend, an older lady, went on stage with the drag queen and judged the strip show, and—"

"Now I do! She sang that Reba song with the drag queen!"

"That was Ivory Black. I ran into them the other day, but it didn't click until Marvin introduced us. I couldn't believe it when he said her name. I asked her if she was from Prairie Springs and had a sister named Rose. She said she didn't, but then Marvin told her not to lie."

"What a small world! This is incredible. Should I tell Rose?"

"I guess so. Why not?"

"Or do you think we should surprise her? Maybe you could come here for Christmas and get Ivory to come with you. That would be a great gift for Rose, don't ya think? Speaking of Rose, we are sitting outside drinking punch, and she said—"

"Wait! Is Rose getting hammered?"

"She doesn't know it, but her mouth does. You'll never believe what she said. She said you were such a nice guy that she wants you to come paint her house and you could live here for free. I suppose she means in the cabin upstairs."

"Really?"

"Yep. The power of a good drink to open the mind."

"If only the entire world could drink your punch. I wonder if she'll feel the same way tomorrow."

"Only time will tell, but it seems she's coming around. You wanna say hello to her? I'll get her—hang on."

Anna went outside, but Flo and Mark were the only people there. "Rose went to the bathroom," Flo told her.

Anna went back inside to the phone. "Kyle, she's in the bathroom. But guess who's coming over? Stacy."

"Trey's wife?"

"Uh-huh."

"That's nice," he said flatly.

"Come on, Kyle. Don't get upset."

"I'm not upset."

"She was all alone, and I invited her over for some punch. We stopped by her house, and she's really quite nice. I don't think she has many friends."

"Probably too uptight...I guess your Halloween was pretty boring in Prairie Springs, huh?"

"Hardly, but I'll tell ya later. I'd better get back out to the guests. Love you."

"Love you, too, Cupcake."

Flo was waiting for Anna to come back out. "This stuff goes straight to your head. What's in here?"

"Everclear and—"

"*And!* Isn't that enough?"

Anna smiled.

"Knock-knock!" Stacy appeared at the lychgate carrying a plastic serving plate of bat-shaped cookies.

Anna hurried to lead her back to where they were sitting.

"Sorry it took me so long. I didn't want to come empty-handed, so I made these—well, heated them—they're the slice-and-bake kind. Oh my gosh! It's beautiful back here with the lights."

"Stacy, this is Flo."

"Yes. Everyone knows Flo...How are you?"

"Hiya, Stacy."

"And Rose will be right back. She just ran to the bathroom." Anna took the cookies and placed them on the table with the popcorn and the jack-o'-lantern.

"I'll get you some punch," Mark offered.

As Stacy sipped her punch, Rose's back screen door opened. It slammed in Bitsy's face, but he managed to nudge it open with his nose. Rose made her way to the table, pausing to admire the flowers and plants. "I just love it out here...and I love y'all, too." No one spoke as they watched Rose's Julie Andrews-ish performance, dancing and whirling about. At one point she lost her balance and grabbed a tree. "Yikes," she said. "I suppose I'm too old to be spinning around." She took a few crossed-over steps and waited for her inner ear to settle. "I've stopped, but everything else is still turning 'round and 'round."

Mark went to help her back to the chair.

"What was I saying?" Rose continued, searching the yard and the skies for a clue as to where she had left the conversation.

"Never mind about that," Anna said. "We have company."

Rose slowly focused on each person until she came to Stacy. "Who's that?"

Stacy, flushed, ducked her head in embarrassment.

"Rose, dear," Flo said. "That's Stacy Stewart, the mayor's wife."

Stacy grinned, giving an outward appearance of pride, but she hated that title.

Flo wondered what Anna was thinking, inviting Rose's loose tongue and Trey's wife to the same gathering. Had it been on purpose? Flo found herself looking forward to part two of the real-life soap opera unfolding at 1914 Harper Valley Lane.

"I remember what we were talking about. That boy, Kyle!" Rose exclaimed.

"Kyle? Your friend from the teachers' party?" Stacy asked Anna.

"Yes."

"He seemed like a nice guy, but I didn't get to visit with him much."

Anna grinned.

"Oh, he is," Rose insisted. "He is indeed. It's a shame he's going to hell because he chose the life of a homosesh—homoseshu—You know what I'm trying—"

"Yes, Rose. We all know what you are trying to say," Anna finished.

"He's gay?" Stacy asked, shocked.

"Sharp as a tack, this one," Flo said.

"It's just that I didn't know," Stacy politely defended. "I would hate to be gay in this town."

Anna was taken aback by Stacy's comment, expecting a more biblical, and less compassionate, reaction. "That's nice of you to say, Stacy."

"I'm less rigid than I might appear. Plus, I majored in psychology in college," she said matter-of-factly.

"You should open a practice," Mark suggested. "I'm sure you would have a ton of clients...I'd go."

Anna glanced at him and wondered what demons he was dealing with.

"You could teach people how not to be homoseshuas," Rose added, this time proud the word had rolled right off her tongue.

"That's not something you teach," Stacy remarked.

Flo chimed in, "Well, I'm very open-minded."

"Are you ishni—sinuating that I'm not?

"By all means, no, Rose. You are *very* open-minded. That's why you have so many blasted rules to live by. You are like a verbal Bible, dear. You always have been."

Rose's eyes watered. "Is that what everyone thinks?"

Flo continued, "I can't speak for everybody, but I'm tired of all these people who call themselves Christians judging people in the name of God. God is love. I haven't sat on many a church pew, but I know that. As a matter of fact, it seems that many people who are sitting on church pews every Sunday listening to someone else tell them how to live their lives are the most hateful people I know—no offense, Stacy. They are always judging and talking behind people's backs. I'm sorry, but if that's what religion does to people, I don't want to be a part of it. God and me, we have a good thing going—we talk all the time."

"You do?" Rose was shocked.

"Of course. I just don't need anyone telling me what to pray or how to say it, and I certainly don't need anyone telling me how I should live my life. Over the years I've gotten where I can pretty much tell right from wrong. I don't always do right, but that's what makes me *me*. Ain't our choices what make us unique?"

"Maybe *you* should open a practice," Stacy chirped.

"I have enough practices going on," Flo confessed.

"Like what, Flo?" Anna prodded, sloshing the ice around in her cup.

Flo pretended not to hear the question. "Did I leave my cigarettes inside?"

Mark pointed to them on the armrest of her chair.

Flo laughed. "If they'd been a snake they'd've bit me." She realized she was still wearing her Wonder Woman bracelets.

The intense conversation was followed by silence, which was interrupted by a snore from Rose's direction.

"We lost one," Mark teased.

"Poor thing, she must have been exhausted to have just fallen asleep like that," Stacy said, concerned.

Anna noticed the punch didn't seem to affect Stacy. "Can I get you a refill?"

"That would be delightful. I can't tell you the last time I had Kool-Aid."

Anna had no way of knowing Stacy kept a bottle of vodka hidden inside a spaghetti canister in the back of her pantry. Sylvia, their housekeeper, was the only person who knew about it, and she stumbled upon it by accident thinking the container was full of pasta.

"Hey, Stacy..." Flo nagged, "...would you do me a favor and ask that husband of yours when he plans on getting that pothole fixed in front of the house? I almost blew out a tire the other night."

"I'll be sure and mention that to him...Say, Anna, speaking of fixing things up, Trey told me he's looking for someone to do the landscaping around the town square. Do you think your friend would be interested? It could also lead to other things. You never know."

Like a divorce. "That would be great! I'll ask him."

After the night came to a close, Mark stayed to help clean up. Anna was on to his scheme right away. The only man who stuck around to clean was a man who wanted to get laid. Anna wasn't about to give in to that type of—"Would you like to stay over?" As soon as she said it, she regretted it. *Damn that punch!*

CHAPTER TEN

After the discovery and subsequent uproar regarding Winnie's uncustomary—not to mention, illegal—burial of Humphrey, she tried to persuade the mayor to sell her the piece of land under the tree so he could rest in undisturbed peace. This was her third visit in the past two months to resolve the situation.

"How does one dollar sound? That'll get you twenty square feet, enough for his plot."

Winnie smiled. "One other thing..."

Trey rested his pen on the desk.

"...Would it hurt ya to spruce up the square? Good grief! It's no wonder people don't wanna come here. It looks like a ghost town. I keep waitin' for a fuckin' tumbleweed to come blowin' through. Me and Maxine will be renovating the theater building. You'd think the town could at least plant a shrub."

"Y'all are going to do something to the old theater?"

"Yessir. I thought you knew."

"I saw the sign was gone, but I didn't know why. Anyway, we don't have a landscaper on staff."

"You should get that Kyle feller to do it. He sure made a nice garden over there at Flo's."

"Yeah, yeah. I've been considering it. Now, get on. I have work to do."

Winnie stood and gave him a kiss on the forehead. "Thank you for the land."

As soon as she left, Trey toyed with the familiar card from his Rolodex where he had jotted down the information Anna had given him. Offering Kyle a job meant risking his marriage, his reputation, his career...among other things. After a moment of pensive contemplation, he dialed the number.

As he counted the rings, he doodled on the back of an envelope. When the answering machine came on, Kyle's voice sent chills down his spine. *Beep*. He took a shallow breath and hung up.

Kyle was in the shower when the phone rang. Wearing a towel, he went to check for a message. He recognized the area code and dialed back.

"Trey Stewart."

"You rang?"

"Uh, yeah, I did. How are ya?"

"I'm good. Got a job...enjoying the city." A painfully loud silence followed. "Um...Have you seen Anna lately?"

"I saw her in the parking lot of the Save-All one day, but I don't think she saw me. She's easy to spot in Dorcas' old Green Machine."

Kyle chuckled. "So...what's up?"

"I'm doing fine. I, uh—You know, the thing with Stacy, I just can't risk it."

"I mean, why did you call?"

"No reason. It was a mistake, I guess."

"A mistake? Why would it be a mistake? Are my phone manners that sour?"

"No, no. It's not that. Not that at all," Trey released an

audible sigh. "It's—there's, uh—how would you like a job with the City of Prairie Springs?"

"What?"

"You see—Well, uh, we need someone to do the landscaping for the town square."

"And for one project you want to put me on salary?"

"Yeah...Well, there will be other projects. You'd be in charge of the parks and, uh, all public landscaping projects, and, uh, I'm sure other stuff will come up too."

"Are you making this up as you go along?"

"No. Seriously. I've, uh, been thinking about it, and I think it would do wonders for the town to fix things up so when people drive through, they might want to actually stop. Whadaya say?"

"I'll have to think about it, Trey. Wouldn't it be awkward with us both being in the same town?"

"Yeah," he paused. "That, or fun."

"Fun? I'm not looking for a game, buddy. I'm looking for a relationship."

Trey was quiet. "...Um, so, do you want the job?"

"Give me a day or two to think about it. I'll call you back later."

"Fine." Trey said, offended.

"Thanks for the offer, though."

"Kyle. I'm, uh—You know, I feel bad about—"

"Let's talk about it later."

"Okay," Trey agreed, softly.

"I'll call you in a couple of days."

Kyle didn't need a couple of days. He looked around his tiny East Village apartment—the miniature stove and refrigerator, the radiator that sounded like a passing marching band, the sirens outside—and he knew he wanted to leave. Of course, none of these excuses were reason enough to move halfway across the country...but Trey was.

He would give notice at Goldstein, Goldberg & Goldblatt and count on never using them as a reference, and his landlord would be glad to see him leave his rent-stabilized apartment. He couldn't wait to tell Anna the exciting news. He began dialing her number and abruptly hung up.

THURSDAY, NOVEMBER 13, 2007

Dorcas and Frank snuck out of Slimming Acres for a hedonistic trip to Taco Bell. Dorcas was halfway through a Burrito Supreme when Frank spotted a camp leader getting out of his car in the parking lot.

"They must've spotted us," Frank said. "Let's make a run for it. Come on!" He yanked Dorcas by the hand and pulled her so quickly out of the opposite side door, that she didn't have a chance to wipe a dribble of taco sauce from the corner of her mouth. "My purse!" Dorcas tried to free herself. "I've got to get my purse, Frank."

Frank stopped a woman about to enter and offered her ten dollars to retrieve Dorcas' purse. Meanwhile, Frank left a fidgety Dorcas at the door and ran to get the car. Dorcas had never been so nervous in her life. If they got caught, they would be condemned to the 'lettuce-only' group back at camp. When Frank's hired lackey opened the door to return the purse, Dorcas couldn't believe her eyes.

Frank's car pulled up.

"That was a close one," Frank belched, as they sped off.

"Close one, my hide! That camp leader wasn't after us at all. He was after the same thing we were, a Burrito Supreme. And get this—he ordered extra sour cream!"

Frank released a victory cheer and hit the steering wheel. "You realize the position we're in, Dorcas. We can blackmail him to get what we want. Food, Dorcas, food!"

"Oh, Frank. I don't think that's a very wise thing to do. It's certainly not a nice thing. I can't even believe you'd suggest that!"

"I'm hungry, Dorcas baby. I'll do anything for calories."

"I thought you were at Slimming Acres because you wanted

to lose weight. You're doing so well. I have faith in you, Frank. You can do this...you can beat it."

"I can't beat it, Dorcas. That's why I keep having to come back and start over, each time fatter than the last."

"Well, this time we're in it together."

At the next traffic light, he leaned over and kissed Dorcas on the lips before she had time to react. "I'm a married woman," she scolded...and leaned in for another one.

"You're beautiful, Dorcas. I can't help myself."

Those were words she had given up on ever hearing again. The last time someone told her she was beautiful was back in high school. Suddenly, she felt as glamorous as Rita Hayworth, even though a glance in the visor mirror brought her back to reality, and revealed the drop of dried taco sauce to the right of her lip.

Later that night, Dorcas and Frank met again by the pond, only this time Dorcas also removed her clothes, and they made love. Afterwards, as they lay on a blanket near the water, Frank ran a finger up and down her arm. Ted was the furthest thing from Dorcas' mind.

She felt attractive for the first time in years. If she went to hell for that elation, it was a risk she was willing to take. Lying next to Frank, she wondered how she could have been so wrong in picking her husband. The only thing Ted did well was elementary construction. "What do you like to do in your spare time, Frank, baby? Do you have any hobbies...like building things?

"Me? No, I'm not much of a builder, baby, although I do love a good model airplane or car. I started when I was a kid—sort of as an escape.

"An escape from what?"

"Life. Oh, and I'm a big Lucille Ball fan. She sent me an auto-graphed picture when I was a kid. I wrote to thank her for letting me laugh."

"Letting you?"

"Yes. All the kids made fun of me at school. Surprise! I was the fattest one in my class and I heard it all: blimp, blubber, fatso.

Someone even started calling me 'C.A.' and that stuck for years. I didn't know what it meant, until one day I asked. 'Clogged Ass,' Troy Lipton told me. I hated him."

"Oh, Frank. That's just horrible. Kids can be so mean."

"Well, you can imagine how relieved I was every day when the last bell rang and school let out. I'd go sit on a big rock in front of the school—that's where I waited for my mom to pick me up— and I'd eat a snack I packed the night before."

The mockery still tormented him, even after all these years. She could see the pain in his avocado eyes.

"When I got home, I'd run to the TV and turn on *I Love Lucy*. For thirty minutes, I could laugh."

"I'm glad you wrote her and she wrote back...What's the favorite model car you ever made?"

"I'd say it's probably the 18-wheeler from *B.J. & the Bear*. You'll have to come see it some time."

"I'd like that." She settled back down onto the quilt, and they watched the sky as if it were a giant movie screen. "See the Big Dipper?" she pointed.

About a hundred and twenty miles to the north, Ted was sitting on a bench in his backyard looking up at the night sky. He focused on the North Star and followed the other stars until he found the Big Dipper. He was recalling the first time he met Dorcas when a squeak from the side gate interrupted him. *She's come home!* He turned around with wide eyes.

"Ted?" a male voice said.

"Yeah. Come on back. Who's there?"

"It's Ronald—Ronald Black."

Ted stood to shake his hand. "Ronald. Well, I'll be. How're you doing?"

"Doin' fine. Thought maybe you'd want some company."

"Company? Uh, sure."

"You know, since your wife up and left you too," Ronald said.

"I'm struggling just a bit with all of it. Does it get easier?"

"What do you mean?"

"Do you still wait by the phone for Ivory to call?"

"No. Not so much anymore. At first I did. Shoot, every time I saw someone outside I thought it was Ivory coming home. I guess she never will, and I'm okay with that now."

"How'd you get over it?"

"Time."...*Rose.*

"I've done nothing for weeks except wait by the phone for Dorcas to call. The police won't investigate further after Judy Jane saw her board the bus. My only hope is Constance. And after that malicious article she wrote in the newspaper, I don't think *she'll* help me much. Do you ever wonder if Ivory met someone else? That's what I'm worried about with Dorcky."

"I guess we're the two deadbeat husbands whose wives left us," Ronald continued.

"Nah, mine didn't. I'm sure she just needed some space and went down to Houston to visit a cousin or something."

Ronald shook his head. "Whatever you say, Ted."

As the night came to an end, Frank and Dorcas gathered their belongings and snuck back to the dorms. Ted went back inside and checked to make sure the phone had a dial tone. Trey absent-mindedly watched television in the den as he fantasized what a life with Kyle might be like. And a few blocks away, hidden behind a detached garage and using the light from the night sky, a teenage boy unbuttoned his fly, opened a blue folder, and pulled out the familiar picture he had ripped from a mail-order catalog. After relieving himself sexually, he carefully placed the picture back into the folder so it wouldn't get wrinkled, dusted himself off and went back inside.

FRIDAY, NOVEMBER 14, 2007

Anna was plagued with worries about lesson plans, observations, and classroom management, and she did her best to not dwell on the fact that she lived in a one-horse town and was sleeping with a guy she only halfway cared for. Her only consolation was that Mark was better than the battery-operated alternative. To top off her worries, since the near miss with the pickup truck on Halloween, she had begun receiving hateful letters in the mail and on her car windshield, and random complaints had been reported to the principal alleging she was teaching in a much too secular manner. A recent message came in the mail on stationery with an embossed armadillo. Not only was it hateful, it was misspelled. *You ain't welcome here so leaf.*

When the bell rang after the last class, she reminded the students to drop off their homework on her desk. She walked out with Ricky Richards to have a talk with his father, who was standing, as usual, by the side of the patrol car.

"Hello, Mr. Richards. I'm Anna Aron."

"*Officer* Richards, and I know who you are. My son in some kinda trouble?"

"No. No, it's not about him."

He looked over at Ricky, "Son, wait in the car."

Anna, attempting to suppress any emotion, proceeded to explain the unwarranted harassment she was receiving.

"I don't know what to tell you, ma'am," he said with a smirk. "If you'll excuse me...I've got to get the kid home." Officer Richards tipped his hat and drove off, leaving Anna standing in the school driveway blocking the other cars.

SATURDAY, NOVEMBER 15, 2007

Anna sat in the garden and watched the leaves drift from the trees, taking in the soothing colors of autumn before going inside to face the chore that awaited her. Teaching was rewarding, but at times she wondered if it was worth it. There was nothing more frustrating than teaching children who had no interest in learning and parents who didn't see to it that they did.

She heated water on the stove and five minutes later sat at the table with a cup of hot cocoa and a red pen. One by one, she made her way through the stack of folders until she got to a blue one with a blade of grass sticking out. She took the grass and put it in the ashtray on the table. As she did, she thought about Kyle. He was the reason she had bought the ashtray, although Flo was the only one who used it as of late. She opened the blue folder with Ricky Richard's name on it, but there was no Spanish homework, just random drawings and a glossy paper in the side pocket. She picked up the phone.

"Kyle? You'll never guess what I just found..."

CHAPTER ELEVEN

In front of the bathroom mirror of Room 200 at The Roadside Palace, eyelashes were being extended, blush and lipstick applied, and hair slicked back in preparation for the jet-black Bettie Page wig. Being famous wasn't always what it was cracked up to be, and more often than not, at least for the slightly delusional, a disguise was the only way to go. At ten minutes after eleven, the infamous diva emerged from the motel room. The bright morning sun slapped her in the face. She was a model without a runway—or more accurately—a cereal box. While her face was on many a breakfast table across the United States, few knew her name...or cared to.

After phoning for a taxi, Violet prepared herself for her Prairie Springs debut, but Prairie Springs had made no such preparations.

The cab driver turned in his seat to make small talk. "Chawli Dickson, at your service."

"Face the front. I can't risk you recognizing me," Violet said, pushing up her Joan Collins sunglasses.

"Should I?"

"Should you! Well, I—I've only been on—I shan't even dignify that with an answer." It was supposed to have come out like Jane Wyman in *Falcon Crest* but had more of a Marge Simpson tone. She cleared her throat to continue. "I'm from New York and I'm famous. Let's just leave it at that." *It's almost as if they didn't know I was coming! Where's the parade, the banners...Where are the people?*

"Been in any movies?"

"I told you, no more questions. Face the front...What happened to Mr. Miller?" she asked, changing the subject and forgetting her haughty accent.

"How do you know Mr. Miller?"

"He used to be the taxi driver here and drove me on several occasions. I'm surprised he didn't mention me. He was probably too busy to notice."

"I don't think he's too busy anymore. Mr. Miller got in trouble. Come to find out he scattered nails on the road to rake up business."

Violet smiled mischievously. "That's absurd." She didn't mention that the nails had been her idea.

"It's the truth, ma'am."

"Wait! Slow down. What's that they're doing there?" Violet's accent was as random as a slot machine—this time more relaxed and Southern. "Don't tell me they're going to reopen the old theater."

"You know that old place?"

"Know it? Of course I do. I used to go there all the time with my—I had a premiere there once...one of my early pictures."

"It must've been a silent picture because I don't remember hearing anything about a premiere here in Prairie Springs."

"Drive on and stop with the inquisition."

"I just have one more for you ma'am, and I promise I'll be quiet. Where are we going?"

"I'll tell you when we get there. I haven't made up my mind

yet." She decided when they approached the Dairy Queen. A Country Basket with creamy gravy was too enticing to pass up.

It wasn't until Ricky Richards' mother ran to the grocery store, leaving him ample time to do his thing behind the garage, did he realize the devastating mistake he had made. He opened the blue folder expecting to find the underwear model, but instead found his Spanish homework!

Maybe Ms. Aron didn't see the folded catalog page? How would I explain it if she did? I'll tell her I saved the page to show my parents which underwear I want for Christmas. She'll never believe me. If only I could take back all of the mean things I said about her, maybe she wouldn't blab to the entire school. She's probably writing a note to my parents at this very moment!

He hopped on his bike and rode up to the school hoping to find the stack of folders through the window.

Kyle climbed the stairs to his East Village apartment, set the groceries on the counter except for the chicken teriyaki TV dinner, which he threw into the microwave and absentmindedly watched spin on the carousel. When the food was hot, he flipped on *Wheel of Fortune* and sat at the drop-leaf table. Most of his things were already packed for the move to Prairie Springs. He couldn't wait to surprise Anna.

The folders on Ms. Aron's desk were gone. Ricky hopped back on the bike and pedaled furiously to the field behind 1914 Harper Valley Lane. He slipped through the back gate. Flo was sitting in her recliner doing a word-find puzzle when she heard the familiar creak. A quick peruse of her appointment book showed her as free as a bird. She tightened her robe and pushed back the kitchen curtain. A figure slowly crept behind the shrubs until reaching Anna's window. Flo grabbed the phone to warn her of the prowler.

Ducking below Anna's dining room window, Ricky heard the phone ring and stood to see if she would answer it. The stack of folders was in plain sight on the table. *Had they been graded?* The curtain swayed in the cabin across the way and he knew he had been spotted. He ran as fast as he could out the back gate and jumped on his bicycle.

Anna came out just in time to see him pedaling away.

SATURDAY, NOVEMBER 22, 2007

The one person who was thrilled, or even cared, Violet White had come to town was her "chauffeur," Chawli Dickson. The two had worked out a daily rate, and she had been all over town without being recognized. She found it slightly amusing—anonymously watching people she had known her entire life. Constance still wore those awful turquoise clothes; Judy Jane Johnson still only half smiled; Roberto had gained a few pounds and still pumped gas at the service station.

Violet didn't make the long journey to be a mysterious observer in the crowd, however. She told Chawli to pull into The 36. "I'd better get myself something to eat. You can drop me off. I'll walk next door to the motel when I'm done."

"Yes, ma'am. Have a good night."

"See you bright and early tomorrow," Violet confirmed.

"At eleven, right?"

"That's right. Oh, wait—tomorrow's church. Make it ten-thirty."

Either way, Chawli hardly considered it bright and early. The roosters were already napping by that hour.

"Table for one, please."

"Follow me," Flo instructed.

"As far away from the people as possible," Violet insisted in a Bette Davis tone.

Flo cocked her eyebrows. There was only a handful of customers in the place. She gestured towards a booth, "Is this okay, your highness, or would you prefer the roof?" Flo knew people who acted rich were the worst tippers, so she was willing to risk the dollar for a dose of attitude.

"This'll be just fine."

Flo set the menu on the table and walked away.

The door opened. It was Rose—Rose and...Ronald? Violet raised the menu in front of her face. She reached for her sunglasses, but they weren't in her purse. She was in a state of panic when Flo reappeared to take her order.

"Lose somethin'?"

"My sunglasses."

"Sunglasses? It's dark out. Whadaya need sunglasses for?"

"I have sensitive eyes. These fluorescents are killers on my pupils."

"Okay, well they're on your head."

Violet reached up and heaved a sigh of relief.

"Ready to order?"

"Just bring me a vanilla shake, an order of fries and some balsamic vinegar."

Flo flashed a smile and walked away. *Big spender.*

While Violet discreetly observed the interaction between Rose and Ronald, Flo observed Violet. There was only one person she knew who put vinegar in a milkshake. *Ain't that somethin'! Right when love starts to bloom, in waltzes heartache wearing a cheap wig!*

If it had been in Flo's personality to interfere in other people's lives, she could have created a scene. Instead, she grabbed the pitcher of water and made the rounds.

"Do you have a phone I can use? I need to call my chauffeur," Violet asked as Flo refilled her water glass.

"Someone as highfalutin as you dudn't have a cell phone?"

"I do, but the batteries burned out on it, and I can't figure out what kind to buy."

Flo smiled. *Still stupid.* "You can use the phone up at the counter."

"Thank you." Violet took the business card from her purse and surreptitiously made her way to the phone, keeping her back to the other customers. Chawli answered on the second ring. After a brief discussion, she enticed him back with an extra twenty bucks. He waited in the parking lot as instructed.

When Rose and Ronald finally left, Violet was on her fourth cup of coffee and her bladder was about to explode, but she couldn't risk going to the bathroom. If she had to, she would urinate in a cup in the taxi, but she was determined to follow the pair. She left a ten and a five on the table for a seven-dollar check and hurried out the door as soon as Ronald and Rose pulled away.

"Follow that car!" Violet said, going into character as Angie Dickinson in *Policewoman*.

"Ronald Black's?"

"Yes, dang-it!"

"Whoa! No need to get vulgar."

Lying on his bed watching the ceiling fan blades spin, Ricky Richards knew he couldn't fake a cold for the rest of his life. He had been able to pull off the charade all week, but was certain his mother would insist he go to church in the morning. Church tomorrow meant school on Monday. He promised God that if Ms. Aron would die, he'd only think of women the rest of his life, and he'd never sin again...and he'd wash the dishes without being asked.

Then it hit him: *That's it!*

Finishing up her errands for the day, Anna stopped at the Save-All with a small list and a handful of coupons. She also bought some flowers for Rose. Deciding roses were too clichéd, she opted for carnations.

The flowers were to show support for what she knew most in town would condemn. Rose was falling for a married man—not to mention a married man who was also her brother-in-law. Anna couldn't resist her landlord's newfound, uncontrollable grin—the unmistakable beam of being in love.

Anna was one of a few with whom Rose could speak openly. The details didn't matter to Anna, which was probably why Rose shared them so gratuitously. During their talks, Anna winced each time Rose mentioned sinning, so she wrote in the card that accompanied the carnations:

We're all searching for the happiness that you found. Enjoy it!
Love, A.

Knowing Bitsy would be let out to do his business in the garden, Anna left the flowers by Rose's back door. After a quick shower, she put on the new Linda Eder CD while she washed and boiled the mustard greens. Using the recipe from the Cajun cookbook she'd borrowed from Flo, she added small shrimp and fish sauce. When it came time to make the red beans and rice, she took the easy way out. Kyle would have scowled when she opened a can of beans and served up minute rice, but since he wasn't there...

Also absent was Mark, who had gone whitewater rafting with his buddies. It was the first weekend they had spent apart, and honestly, she was grateful for the break.

Since leaving The 36 Diner, Violet still hadn't used the bathroom, and her bladder felt like an overfilled water balloon. After driving around for what seemed like an eternity, Rose and Ronald stopped for gas. The two lovebirds were so into each other, Jesus Christ could have run by in a Speedo and they wouldn't have seen him, so Violet braved the dash into the ladies' room without too much concern.

With a full tank of gas, Ronald and Rose returned to the ho-hum streets of Prairie Springs. Violet and her chauffeur followed at a distance.

"I'm going to have to charge you another twenty if we stay out past eight," Chawli insisted. "My wife doesn't like me staying out this late."

"Late? It's not even seven yet. I can always hire another driver, you know."

"Sure. And where do you plan on finding one? I'm the only taxi 'round here."

"They can't go too much longer. Honestly, how many times can they drive around the same blocks?" Violet leaned forward and slapped Chawli on the shoulder. "Oh, he's turning onto Rose's street. Stay back and turn off the lights!"

"You know Rose? What are we going to do now?" he asked, wanting to do nothing more than to pull into his own driveway two doors down and call it a night.

Violet noticed Chawli's humor was much more pleasant in the morning and just after lunch. "I told you I don't like questions. Park it here on the other side of the street...Isn't that Dorcas' car?"

"It *was*. She and Ted sold it to the new girl—some Jewish Yankee teacher. How do you know that car?"

Violet ignored the question.

They watched as Rose and Ronald walked inside.

Violet pushed Chawli's head down from the back seat. "Duck!" she whispered when the kitchen light came on.

"What'll we do, just sit here?"

Violet could make out the two familiar silhouettes moving inside. "I can't take this anymore. Let's go."

Behind Rose's house, Anna was enjoying her new CD and dreaming of "...Central Park in June" as she vacuumed the floor.

Flo, who had been home from work long enough to take a quick shower, heard the rear gate open. The clock above the couch said it was five after eleven. She peeked out of the curtains but didn't see anyone. As she opened the front door to look over to Anna's, a hand pushed her inside.

"You 'bout scared the petunias outta me! What's wrong with you?" Flo hissed.

The man rested his real gun on top of the bookcase inside the door and went for the water pistol in the kitchen drawer. After a long day at work, the only reason she squeezed this man in was because he offered to pay double. She could hardly scramble enough energy to play Wonder Woman.

"Can't I just be Lynda Carter tonight?"

"Not at these prices!"

Flo, defeated, disappeared into the bedroom and reappeared in costume. A stream of water came at her, but she was too slow to react with her magical bracelets and was hit right below the eye.

"Do you mind if I make some coffee first?" Flo pleaded and grabbed the kitchen towel to wipe her face. "I need a little pick-me-up."

"Aw, dammit! You're gonna make me lose my hard-on."

"Don't worry, you'll get it back, but I need some caffeine first. Wonder Woman drank coffee, too, you know. Go ahead and take your clothes off and get ready for me. Do you want a cup?"

"No. I'll pass," the man said, stripping down to his under-garment.

No sooner had the coffee pot stopped brewing did Flo hear another faint squeak at the back gate. "Shhh! Quiet. Someone's out there."

"You didn't double-book, did you?"

"I'm serious. I bet it's the same peeping Tom who was at

Anna's the other day. Turn out the lights!" With her window open a few inches, Flo had a clear view. The movement in the shrubbery stopped when the garden lights came on.

"Hurry up, Bitsy," Rose said. "Oh look, Ronald, someone left me flowers...They're from Anna. Isn't she a doll? Say, do you wanna sit outside and enjoy the night air?"

"I'd rather enjoy the air in the bedroom," Ronald responded. A click of the tongue beckoned Bitsy back inside, and with the flip of a switch, the garden was dark again.

The figure resumed skulking towards Anna's cabin.

"Aren't you going to do something? Don't just sit there, you moron."

"Why should I? That Jewish woman's nothing more than a big heap of trouble for Prairie Springs."

"Anna? Cause trouble? She wouldn't hurt a fly."

"I'm not talking about—I'm talking about perverting our kids' minds."

"Ha!" Flo rolled her eyes as she continued peering out the window. "You're worried about perversions when I'm standing here dressed up like a 1970s superhero so you can get your rocks off? I'm going to call the cops."

"I'm off-duty at the moment, and would like to keep it that way."

"Jiminy Cricket! He's got a gun! Do something!"

"A gun? You didn't tell me that!"

Carrying a flashlight and handcuffs in one hand and his real gun in the other, her client quietly tiptoed across the lawn. "Freeze! Police!"

"Dad?"

Rose, hearing the commotion, turned the garden lights back on and opened the door.

"Son! What're you doing?" Officer Richards shone the flashlight into Ricky's wide-eyed face.

Ricky's jaw dropped when Wonder Woman ran over. "What the—"

"Drop the gun, son!"

When he did, his father, wearing only a pair of lace panties, walked over and pushed him against the side of Anna's cabin.

"But Dad, you don't understand—" Ricky said as he felt the metal from the handcuffs squeeze his wrists.

"What's going on?" Ronald goggled. Rose took shelter behind him.

There was no response from anyone.

"What are you doing over here at this time of night, Ron, buddy?"

Ronald shook his head. "*That's* what you want to talk about right now?"

"Is Anna home? Is she all right?" Rose asked, concerned.

Anna stepped out the front door of her cabin. "I'm fine, Rose. What's going on?" Anna took inventory. "My God! What kind of town is this?" she blurted after absorbing the perplexingly comical scene. "What are you doing here, Ricky?"

He looked down at the ground and didn't answer.

"Does this have something to do with your homework?"

No answer.

"You got the highest grade in the class, you know."

Ricky looked up, confused.

"Mr.—*Officer* Richards, if you'll make sure he doesn't get his hands on a gun again, you can take the handcuffs off. Then you can go back over to Flo's and—"

"What are you wearing, Flo?" Rose asked from her back porch. "I thought that was your Halloween costume."

An almost naked policeman is wearing lingerie and you're questioning my *outfit?* "It's laundry day, Rose. Go enjoy whatever you were doing."

Ronald turned off the lights and followed Rose back inside. The click of the door lock echoed in the night.

"Dad, what are you wearing and what are you doing with Wonder Woman? Isn't that Flo from the diner?"

He glanced down forgetting he wasn't dressed. "These are—I, uh—She, uh. Flo and I, uh—Flo's a—"

"She moonlights, and your dad helps support her," Anna interjected. "And those look to be red lace panties."

Flo's shoulders relaxed.

"She's a prostitute?" Ricky blurted.

Flo shrugged and remained silent.

"Son, you can never say a word to anyone about this. No one. You hear me? Or so help me, I'll cut off—"

"Officer Richards! Ricky won't say anything to anyone...will you Ricky?" Anna said.

"No...I won't say a thing."

"I didn't think so."

"I'm gonna go get dressed and take you home, son," Officer Richards turned to Anna but didn't speak.

"This one's on the house," Flo told Officer Richards when he went to get his clothes.

As the father and son duo exited through the back gate, Anna could hear Officer Richards scolding Ricky. "You are grounded forever. What is wrong with you stealing one of my guns—You weren't really going to shoot her...were you?"

Anna and Flo stood in their respective doorways. Anna searched for a change of topic. "That greens recipe was great, Flo."

"You liked that, did ya?"

"Wanna come over for a nightcap? I need something to calm my nerves!"

"I'll get my robe."

"Yes, please do."

That was how the night ended at 1914 Harper Valley Lane. Flo was right: didn't we all have our secrets? It was only a matter of them becoming known that provoked judgment.

Knowing Ronald was preoccupied with Rose, Violet asked Chawli to drop her off at a humble wood-frame house. "Go on. That's all for tonight...I have a friend who lives here." He held his hand out the window, wanting payment more than he did an explanation. She gave him a five-dollar tip and told him to forget about taking her to church the next morning.

When she was certain no neighbors were watching, she took the key from her purse and stuck it into the lock. She felt like a criminal in her own home as she crossed the threshold and closed the door behind her.

Everything was remarkably unchanged. Their portrait still hung crookedly on the wall above the television. The afghan was still draped over her footstool. She walked down the hallway to their bedroom. The bed was made, and her clothes still hung in the closet, though she hardly recognized the woman who used to wear them.

She turned off the bedroom light and walked back into the kitchen. In the corner, next to the table, was a stack of *People* magazines. Ronald never canceled her subscription. Surely he wouldn't notice if she took one with her...or two or three. She pulled from the middle of the stack and stuck them in her purse. That's when she saw it—the coffee cup.

The day she left, she and Ronald had a terrible fight. She doubted his love for her because he rarely vocalized it, despite his many actions that proved otherwise—the half-built gazebo in the backyard, making her coffee each morning, killing bugs for her when she screamed.

The coffee cup was the same one she threw at him and broke against the living room wall. It was now glued back together and resting at her place at the table.

Doesn't Ronald know I can't put hot liquid in a cup that's been glued? Honestly! After removing her wig, she picked up the cup and held it with both hands as if it were a portal to the past. The fight scene played in her head. She swallowed hard, kissed the cup and placed it back onto the table.

SUNDAY, NOVEMBER 23, 2007

Golden Years: A Geriatric Playground was a one-hundred-patient residential facility for those not only in their golden years, but also for a few who were in their final golden days. Anna had taken to visiting the facility with Bitsy on Sundays, while the rest of the town was attending church. The residents' faces lit up as soon as the human/canine duo came through the door. Bitsy merely tolerated the visits; he didn't care for the smell and all of those hands patting his head. Anna enjoyed talking with the people and listening to a different perspective on life. There were a couple of residents with whom she had grown especially fond.

One of those was Dr. Waxman, a short, gray-haired man with cataracts. There was nothing particularly compelling about him, but Anna was intrigued by the pain buried behind the cloudy film covering his eyes. He was also a great storyteller. On their last visit, he left her with a cliffhanger.

She hurried down the hallway, tugging at Bitsy, and knocked on the door.

"Anna, Bitsy, come in. I've been waiting for y'all."

"You're looking well, Dr. Waxman."

"I've had a good morning."

"I'm glad to hear it. I'll also be glad to hear the rest of that story from the last time."

He gazed blankly. "What story was that, dear?"

"You know, the one about Eddie."

"Oh yes! That one. You know, you're the first person I've ever told it to. But before I get back into it, will you look over there and see if you see a box of Kleenex in my cabinet? I think someone's been stealing them. You can't trust these people 'round here."

Anna opened the cabinet. Three boxes of Kleenex sat on the shelf. "No, they're here."

"Well, I don't know how I missed 'em." He rubbed his forehead with his thumb and forefinger as if trying to massage his brain into action. "These eyes aren't what they used to be."

Anna pulled up a chair beside his bed and lifted her canine companion to his side. "Bitsy wants to tell you hello."

"That's a small one, idn't he?" He said the same thing the last time.

"Yes. He's a little one." She put Bitsy back down on the floor. He sniffed around the bed and found a place to settle. "So, what happened next? When we left off, Eddie was just about to get married."

"Right, right...Oh, let me see...Okay, yeah. He married the girl. I told him on his wedding day it was a big mistake, but he wouldn't listen. No sir! He insisted it was what the Lord wanted him to do. I told him the Lord didn't have to sleep with that bitter, lifeless girl every night. Boy howdy, was she a stick-in-the-mud! He asked me to be the best man, but I told him I wouldn't be, not after what he had done."

"What'd he do?" Anna leaned in closer.

"The unforgivable."

"What? What?"

"You see, he and this stick-in-the-mud girl of his had been going out for several years, but they waited until after high school to tie the knot and consummate their relationship—at least *she* waited. The fellow had him another girl..."

Anna nodded.

"...And the other girl was the one he *should've* married, and the one he was in love with. He even got her pregnant, and that's how I found out about everything. Shoot, I didn't even know Eddie until he and this beautiful gal came into my office one day at the hospital. Sure, I knew *of* him and his family, but I'd never met him. This gal thought she might be pregnant and sure 'nough she was...Why can't I think of her name...? Anyway, I told them I'd be happy to be their doctor, but that's when the whole mess started."

"What mess, Dr. Waxman?"

"Eddie came back into my office after they left and whispered something in my ear."

"What'd he say?"

Dr. Waxman motioned for her to lean in.

Anna gasped. "Dispose of it? You mean, an abortion?"

He shook his head and pulled her closer.

"*Agh!* Kill it after it was born?" Anna retreated.

"*Shhh!*" He slapped the air and looked towards the doorway. "I told you, no one knows about this."

"Okay, okay...Sorry. Go on..."

"You made me go and lose my thought. Oh, yes. He told me he'd pay me. He said his father had money." Dr. Waxman gazed out the window, and Anna wondered if what came next was going to explain the pain in his eyes. She took hold of his hand and squeezed it as his chin quivered.

"You're not going to understand this, dear, but times were tough, and so when it came time for her to give birth, I accepted the money."

Anna wanted to pick up Bitsy and stomp out of the room.

"I told the girl—oh, what *was* her name? I told her the baby had died shortly after birth."

Anna gasped again and let go of the doctor's hand.

"Don't go judging me just yet. I didn't kill the baby like he wanted. My wife, who was the nurse at the time, carried it home and the very next day we took it to the adoption agency in Austin."

"Did this lady—the mother. Did she get to see it? Didn't the baby cry?"

"There were complications, and we had to put her out. I remember she came to for a few seconds, but other than a quick glimpse, she never saw it. Later, I told her the baby had stopped breathing, and I wouldn't let her see it."

"Your wife was in on it, too?"

"No, absolutely not. My wife would have had me hung had she known. I'd told her the mother wanted to give it up for adoption. And as far as I know, no one else knew the baby ever existed."

"That's horrible. Poor girl."

"I know and I've regretted it every day since. Biggest mistake of my life. And there's no worse punishment than what we do to ourselves. I don't need you to punish me, too."

"What'd you do with the money?"

"Ah, the money. I never spent a nickel. I put it all into an interest-bearing account at the bank until a few years ago. I didn't want the government to get their hands on it—it was a nice chunk of dough after thirty years. I'll tell you what I did with it," he chuckled. "I stuffed it into a toy giraffe I had in the garage. I don't know and don't care what happened to it after that. I just hope my family didn't find it."

Anna sat back. "That's quite a story, Dr. Waxman."

"I guess you can call me Arthur, now."

She attempted a smile.

The cereal-box diva awoke late. It had been a long time since she had slept so well, falling right into the familiar sag in the mattress. She became Violet with the slip of the wig and called for her driver. She wanted to get out of the house before—if—Ronald came home.

CHAPTER TWELVE

A bus en route from Houston to Dallas stopped at The 36 Diner for a planned, 10-minute break. Flo was prepared for the influx and made sure the snack counter was stocked in advance. She placed her tip jar by the register, knowing people dropped their change into it. Those coins added up to the tune of about twenty dollars a week.

After enough time for snacks, sodas, and a quick bathroom break, the driver stepped inside and announced it was time to re-board. Those standing outside took a final drag on their cigarettes before following the driver back onto the bus. After a hiss of pressure from the brakes, the bus continued up Highway 36.

Flo moved the tip jar back under the counter and washed her hands in the kitchen. When she returned to the register, there was a young man in his late-twenties with caramel skin and eyes the color of seaweed.

"Where on earth did you come from? You look like you should be advertising cologne in a magazine, shoog."

"The *boos*."

"*Boos*?"

179

"The autoboos?"

"Oh, the bus! Honey, it already left."

"Uh-oh. What can I to do?"

"Where are you from? You've got quite an accent, handsome."

"Argentina."

"My word! Well, don't worry. Everything'll be okay." Flo slipped her arm in his and led him to the table nearest to the register. "What's your name?"

"Luciano."

"Nice to meet ya. I'm Flo. Sit here." After pouring two cups of coffee, she took the seat opposite him. "So, cutie pie, where were you headed?"

Luciano looked puzzled and Flo rephrased. "Where were you going?"

"Anywhere. I need to work."

"What kind of work?"

"Construction."

"Are you single?"

"Yes, ma'am."

She slapped the table. "I know of just the place."

Ted, who ate pretty much every meal at the diner since Dorcas left him, was in the corner finishing up a bowl of potato soup. "Ted," Flo called. "Soup's on me if you do me a quick favor."

When Luciano walked through the door of the Theater Café, Maxine was instantly captivated by his rugged good looks. She put her hands on her hips. "So, Flo sent you."

"I don't know her name—a waitress."

"No, I'm telling you. Flo already called and gave me a heads up. You're hired."

She immediately put him to work. Everyone was in a frenzy to get the café ready for the grand opening the day after Thanksgiving.

Later that afternoon, Anna stopped by the café to check on the progress. "It's looking great in here. I can't believe all you guys have done."

"How was your day at school?" Maxine asked.

"*Tsk*. The kids don't want to do anything if they can help it. They're too restless about the long holiday weekend coming up."

Maxine gave her a tour and showed her Winnie's new apartment in the rear of the building: a hidden loft behind a hutch that doubled as a secret door. Living at the café allowed Winnie to get out of the Roadside Palace, and at the same time keep an eye on the money, although it was doubtful anyone would look for it since most thought she didn't have a dime. Everyone in town presumed Maxine had taken Winnie under her wing with money her mother left for her.

The sunken auditorium area of the theater had been made level and was filled with enough tables and chairs to host anyone in town who might have a caffeine addiction. It had been Mark's suggestion to put in shelves for a free book exchange. He was ready to start the chain of events by donating the ones he had already read from his personal library.

The town didn't know how to react to the renovations taking place. People scrutinized the progress daily, though not all were pleased. There were some in town who weren't keen on the idea of non-churchgoing citizens owning a business that might attract gullible and susceptible youth.

Maxine tried to stay positive and focused, paying the naysayers little attention. Winnie, on the other hand, managed things a bit differently. She shot them the bird through the plate-glass windows.

"Do you think we should paint the walls white?" Maxine asked Anna.

"Seems kind of boring."

Winnie stuck her head from around a box of dishes. "You should call Kyle and ask him. The queer ones have an eye for that sort of thing."

"Mama would be happy, you know. She always told me I should have my own business."

"It looks like she was right, Maxine. It takes guts to open a place of your own."

"Anna, look at this old coffee grinder we found. Isn't it nice? It doesn't work, though, so it will just be for decoration. And check out our cash register. I still haven't learned how to work it. It's different than the ones at the Save-All."

"I told her we should just use a pencil and paper, but she insisted we get a computer machine." Winnie yelled from the rear of the café. "They always say 'don't go into business with friends.'"

When Anna turned in Winnie's direction, she noticed the handsome Latin. "Maxine, who is that? Is he Italian? God must've been in a good mood when He made him."

"Luciano," Maxine called. "Come and meet my friend, Anna."

Luciano was busy building a handrail for the ramp leading down to the seating area.

"He's from Argentina."

"Oh. *Mucho gusto,*" Anna said.

Maxine rolled her eyes. "English, *por favor.*"

"I'm sorry, Maxine. I just told Luciano it was nice to meet him."

"Nice to meet you, too. Excuse me. I need to go back to working," Luciano excused himself with a wink obviously intended for Maxine.

Anna waited until he walked away. "Um, I believe he was flirting with you."

"*Sí.* He was," Maxine answered confidently.

Since they were standing next to the recently finished pastry display case, Maxine decided to take advantage of Anna's presence. "Pretend you're a customer and order something. I could use the practice."

"I'll have a latte."

"I don't know how to make that one yet. Pick something else."

"A cappuccino?"

"Something simpler."

"Coffee—cream, no sugar."

"We don't have any cream. Refrigerator isn't here yet."

"I have some in *my* fridge," Winnie yelled.

"Ignore her. That'll be two bucks please."

"Oh, um...Let me see." Anna dug in her purse.

"You don't have to pay me, silly."

"Oh, right. I was wondering—but I don't mind."

"Do you have any plans for Thanksgiving?" Maxine asked.

"Gosh, I'm glad you said that. Rose is making dinner and she wants everyone to come. I almost forgot to mention it."

"That's kind. Do you think she'd mind if I brought Luciano?"

"Why would she? Winnie..." she called, "...you're invited, too."

"Invited where?"

"Thanksgiving at Rose's."

"What'll we bring? I don't have much of a kitchen here, but I could whip up some brownies or something."

"Winnie's brownies are good," Maxine reminded her.

"Yes, I remember. I'll tell her you guys are coming. It should be fun."

At the end of the day, after everyone had left and Winnie retreated to her rear abode, Luciano and Maxine walked over to a bench at the courthouse in the center of the square. She learned his family owned an auto parts business in Buenos Aires, where he worked delivering orders and made decent money, "...but ever since I watched *Miami Vice*, I wanted to come to the United States."

"Is it everything you hoped?"

"It wasn't until today."

"What do you mean? The job?"

"No. You. You and me sitting here. I never expect it."

"Expected. Me neither." She had been listening without facing him, but turned.

Luciano smiled and reached to touch her face. "You have some paint on your chick."

Maxine didn't correct his pronunciation, nor did she stop him from rubbing the paint off. He leaned in and kissed her next to her mouth. When she didn't resist, he pulled her closer and kissed her on the lips. After the kiss, Maxine took a deep breath and rubbed her hands on her knees. "Want to go to Dairy Queen and get something to eat?"

"Just milk?"

"They have more than that. Come on. My treat. We can walk."

A burger, the conversation, and a cool evening led Maxine to invite him over to her place. They drank a beer, listened to music, and continued talking. Later that evening, Luciano got what he had been wanting all day. With the lights off and the curtains drawn, Maxine trembled in her own skin as she came to a thunderous climax. Mothers scrambled to cover their youngsters' ears as her moans of pleasure echoed throughout Milam County.

Chapter Thirteen

Thanksgiving

"Old Theater Home to New Café—Grand Opening Tomorrow," was the headline on the front page of *The Herald*. What an exciting day for Prairie Springs! Some dreamed it would be the beginnings of bigger and better things to come for the small Texas town. Others insisted it would turn into the devil's playground for impressionable youth. Either way, it was the topic at most Thanksgiving tables as people stuffed their faces with turkey.

One turkey in town, however, never got cooked. Ted had planned all week for Thanksgiving. The bird had been defrosting on the counter since Monday evening. All Dorcas had to do was walk through the door and sit down at the table to a cooked meal. He knew it was a long shot since she hadn't written or called, but he wanted to believe she would show. He had bought a Thanksgiving card expressing his undying love to prop next to her plate of salmonella. On Wednesday afternoon, while Ted was shelling pecans for the pie, there was a knock at his door, and he was served with divorce papers.

Dorcas had impeccable timing.

"Looks like y'all are going to have quite the opening tomorrow," Rose commented. "Does everyone have potatoes?"

"Our plates are full, Rose. Don't worry about us. Serve yourself," Flo answered.

"This cool weather sure is nice," Maxine shivered for emphasis. "Makes ya wanna light a fire, dudn't it?"

Several months ago, no one, including Rose, could have imagined the hodgepodge of characters that would gather around her dinner table. To begin with, no one could have imagined Rose *hosting* a Thanksgiving dinner.

"We could get the fireplace going," Rose agreed with Maxine.

"That's not a bad idea," Winnie said. "Goodness, I haven't sat by a fire since the last blue moon. Lasagna, why don't you get it going?"

"It's *Loo-see-ah-no*." Maxine slowly sounded it out. "Nobody would name their kid after a French food?"

"Lasagna is an Italian dish," Mark corrected.

"I'd like to make a toast," Anna interrupted. "To the wonderful people here at the table, to the chef, to the grand opening tomorrow...and to our blessings."

As the glasses clinked together, Flo added, "And for Rose letting us have wine with dinner."

"What's special about that?" Luciano asked, puzzled.

"Because until recently, we weren't allowed to have any alcohol on the property. Religious nonsense," Flo explained quietly to Luciano, but returned to her normal speaking voice, "Before, I always had to sneak my booze in a flask."

"I can't believe you! You told me that was your medi—Well,

no more sneaking," Rose insisted. "I want everyone to be comfortable."

Ronald, wickedly proud, slid his socked foot gently up Rose's calf. It was also *his* first time to have wine with dinner. This new relaxed life wasn't something he was used to, but he was so enamored, he took the wrapping along with the package and pretended it was old hat.

"These greens are fuckin' disgusting," Winnie murmured to Flo.

"Anna made them."

"Made what?" Anna responded. "Oh, the greens. Yes, I did. I hope you like them. I got the recipe from one of Flo's Cajun cookbooks."

"They're lovely, dear," Winnie uttered, even though her face disagreed.

There was a knock at the front door. "Ohhh! I wonder who *that* could be?" Winnie was as giddy as a dog with a fresh bone.

All eyes followed Ronald as he stood to answer the door.

"Is, uh, Rose home?"

Anna recognized the voice. "Kyle?" She ran to the door holding a napkin with her arms outstretched. "Oh my gosh! What are you doing here?"

"Surprise! I'm moving back. You can thank Winnie there. Trey told me she was the one who kept raving about me."

Winnie sat back proudly.

"I can't believe it! Winnie, you knew about this?"

"She could hardly keep it quiet," Maxine said.

"You knew, too?"

"We all knew," Rose confessed. "Ronald's been fixing up the apartment above yours while you've been at school; it's ready with a phone and all."

"Don't just stand there, dollface. Sit down and join us. Fix yourself a fuckin' plate."

"You haven't changed a bit, Winnie," Kyle remarked.

"Would you like dark or white meat?" Rose asked, plate in hand. Anna poured him a glass of wine.

"Wine?" Kyle was shocked.

"There have been some changes around here," Anna explained.

"So how was your trip?" Ronald inquired.

Anna patted Kyle's hand. "Oh, sorry. Kyle, this is Ronald, Rose's new boyfriend. And this is Luciano, Maxine's boyfriend. And this is Mark, *my* boyfriend."

He had heard about all of them except Luciano and nodded how-do-you-do. "It was a nice trip...long, but nice. Strangest thing happened in the taxi, though. The driver laughed when we pulled up to the house. He said, 'This place again?' I asked him what he meant, and he told me he'd been driving some movie star around, and she always wanted to sit in front of this house."

"*My* house?" Rose pressed. "A movie star?"

"That's what he said."

"I'm sure he's confused," Flo calmly assured. "These houses can all look the same."

No one confused Rose's house with any other in town, but Flo figured one surprise a day was enough.

After the dining table was cleared, Luciano built the fire, and everyone sat around drinking coffee and eating Winnie's brownies, save for Ronald and Rose, who were too full from dinner.

Kyle was glad to be back home.

THANKSGIVING NIGHT

When all the guests left, Rose put on a pot of coffee to erase the lingering effects of the wine. She cleared the table and put the leftovers into containers acquired at random Tupperware Parties over the years. Ronald washed the dishes and cleaned the stove. Rose could easily fall in love with a man who helped clean...and that's exactly what she feared was happening. While he faced the sink,

Rose reached up and massaged his shoulders. He relaxed, not realizing he was so tense.

"Thank you for helping," she told him.

"Of course." He turned to kiss her on the forehead. "You wanna pour us some coffee and take it into the living room? I'll join you in just a few more minutes. You can go relax."

How nice to be told to relax. "Are you sure?"

"I got this."

Rose's gaze became lustful, and she was not unsettled about it. She carried the coffee into the living room, and when Ronald finished in the kitchen, he took a seat in the wingback chair next to hers.

"I do believe that was the nicest Thanksgiving I've ever had," she declared. "It was certainly the first one I can remember where I actually felt grateful—and thankful—for the people around the table...and for myself."

"Yourself?" Ronald lifted the mug from the lamp table separating them.

"Yes. I've always been too hard on myself, I realized. I take life too seriously, forgetting to enjoy it—put it on the coaster; it'll leave a ring—and I give you some of the credit."

"For what? What did I do?"

"It's not so much what you did, but what you caused me to do...to allow myself to be with you."

Ronald enjoyed, and even relished, the fact that he had been a catalyst for a positive change in Rose, but wasn't certain how to respond. "The dinner was delicious."

"Wasn't it? Everybody brought wonderful dishes. But I agree with Winnie about those greens! I didn't much care for 'em."

"I liked them. Different, but good...Maxine's boyfriend is a charmer, even with his broken English. Where'd she say he's from, El Salvador?"

"Argentina, I believe."

"That's right," Ronald nodded. "Today is what family is

about. A mix of people with different perspectives. It's nice not to have to worry about being perfect and just be yourself."

"I felt like I was being hugged all day—you know, validated or something. Did I tell you the pastor wants me to kick Anna out because she's Jewish? She's one of the nicest people I've ever met. There's no way I could do that. No way whatsoever."

Ronald shook his head. "Makes you think about the society we live in, doesn't it?"

"I'll say."

"Are you about finished with your coffee?"

Rose took a final gulp, "I am now."

"Give me your hand."

"Why? What are you going to do?"

He looked her in the eyes. "You have to trust me, Rose."

He pulled her to the center of the room, and they stood with their bodies touching.

Rose attempted to suck in her stomach.

"Relax, Rose. Relax."

She exhaled, releasing tension and stared into his eyes.

"Stand here. I'll be right back."

He went to the stereo and put in a Glenn Miller CD. Rose's smile melted Ronald, and he danced her straight into the bedroom.

Unfastening her dress, he gently guided it off her shoulders and let it fall to the floor.

"Ronald. The light. Please turn it off."

The moonlight glowed through the sheer curtains. He removed his belt and loosened his trousers. They dropped to the floor and he stepped out of them.

Rose looked down and smiled. "Oh, Ronald."

"What can I say? You turn me on."

He kissed each of her cheeks, the tip of her nose, above her eyebrows...her neck. Her head tilted and her eyes closed, aroused and anticipating where he would kiss her next. With each contact, she took a sharp breath and her shoulders flexed in response. It was almost too much to bear. Sensing her pleasure, he took off her brassiere and kissed her bare chest. He ran his finger down her cleavage stopping at the hem of her panties. "Take my shirt off," he instructed.

Rose unbuttoned his shirt and slid it down his arms. It got caught on his wrists. Ronald unbuttoned the cuffs and hung the shirt on the bedpost.

He held her snugly. She could feel the sparse hairs on his chest against her skin. The stubble from his beard was rough on her shoulder where he rested his head as they swayed back and forth to the music playing in the other room.

In a gentle motion, he lowered her to the bed, straddling her softly, and relaxed on top of her. The warmth of his body was a stark contrast to the chilly air in the room. The heaviness of his body enveloped her. Nobody could hurt her...every fear dissipated...every worry vanished. Ronald kissed her and ran his tongue along the roof of her mouth. He slid his tongue between her lips and teeth. Rose quivered.

Ronald rolled off her body and lay beside her, continuing to kiss her. He ran his hand down her torso, working his way inside her panties. She let out a moan, anticipating what was to follow. With his free hand he took hold of her arm, gripped it tightly, and raised it above her head.

Kyle and Anna were in the garden catching up on their months apart when they were interrupted by the moan of pleasure. A frightened raccoon climbed the fence and scurried away. "Was that Rose?" Kyle grinned knowingly.

"Sounded like it. Good for her."

"I guess you didn't mention anything about Ivory to Rose, did you?"

"It's not my place. I'm sure she left for a reason. Who am I to butt in?"

FRIDAY, NOVEMBER 28, 2007

The day after Thanksgiving, 1914 Harper Valley Lane was beginning to look a lot like Christmas. Kyle and Anna had hung lights in the trees and draped them throughout the shrubbery around the perimeter of the house. They were now assembling Rose's artificial tree, separating the color-coded metal spiraled end tips. "Don't these branches remind you of toilet brush bristles?" Kyle remarked.

While Kyle and Anna assembled the tree, Rose and Ronald rummaged through boxes in the third-floor storage room in search of more decorations. The neighbors would be in for a treat this year. Not even Rose could remember the last time lights shined in her yard and a tree graced her front window.

In town, Maxine, Winnie, and Luciano, were nervously awaiting their first customers. The doors would open in five minutes. Mark was the first in line, opting for caffeine and books, over tree-trimming or shopping.

"Shouldn't we just go ahead and open?" Maxine suggested.

"Just a second. I almost forgot my Santa hat." Winnie reached under the counter and adjusted it over her wig. "Okay! I'm ready. Open the doors and stand back!"

Instead of a stampede, it was more of a trickle—a slow start, but as Maxine pointed out, noon probably wasn't the best time for coffee.

Over the course of the day, business grew steadier. For the grand opening, customers received a free t-shirt boasting a picture of the marquee with THEATER CAFÉ in the now-playing section.

When Maxine wasn't serving coffee or tending the register, she watched her Argentine prince move about in his black jeans and one of the café's t-shirts, both of which she thought he filled out nicely.

Once the last customer left, an exhausted Maxine and Winnie exited through the hidden door to Winnie's apartment to count their first-day earnings. A tired Luciano biked to the Roadside Palace, where he rented a room by the week.

Flo's eggnog had kicked in and put everyone in the holiday spirit. Anna couldn't wait for Christmas. "It's one thing Christians celebrate better than the Jews," she said wryly as she, Flo and Kyle strolled through the garden admiring the festive ambiance.

"I'm going to have a boob job," Flo announced. "Whaday'all think?" She lifted them a tittle to demonstrate. "They're really sagging, see? I think it'd be good for business."

"Waitressing?" Kyle asked, confused.

"Flo, uh, moonlights entertaining gentleman callers."

"Really?"

"Anna makes it sound so non-trashy. I love this girl," Flo gushed.

"That explains the man I saw leaving your cabin the first night I was here—remember that, Anna?—He was a client of yours?"

"Probably. What'd he look like?"

"I couldn't see much 'cause it was dark. Could have had gray hair."

"You really narrowed it down, buddy. Most of my clients are bald or gray." She knew exactly who he was talking about but didn't volunteer names. "Let's change the subject back to my breasts. I was hoping you'd go with me to the plastic surgeon, Anna."

"Me? Really? I'd be honored."

"It should be an *uplifting* experience," Kyle joked.

A peaceful silence followed the chuckle as they took in the garden lights while enjoying the crisp night air. Anna hooked her arm through Kyle's and leaned on his shoulder.

Flo was touched by the two friends' close relationship and wished *her* contact with men wasn't so fleeting. Flo had only truly loved once, and he left her because she "wasn't good enough."

She'd lived her life in fear of trying again. It had taken years for her to accept herself. Risking it all for a man seemed too risky, but the alternative was loneliness. To not become emotional, she interrupted the silence. "Potcorn?"

"Popcorn?" Kyle clarified.

"No, *pot-corn*." She pointed to the plant. "Winnie gave me some cannabutter left over from her brownies."

Kyle nodded, "What the hell. Beats microwave."

They followed Flo into her cabin.

MONDAY, DECEMBER 1, 2007

Judging by the messages, Trey was certain the townspeople spent the Thanksgiving holiday around the dinner table making lists of complaints. There was so much to do when he went to work, he turned around and drove over to the Canine Buffet to discover Ted had called in sick. This meant, on top of Trey's mayoral duties, he had to man the extruding machinery at the plant. The production line couldn't slow with Christmas around the corner. Dog food had to be in the stores before December 25th, when thousands of kids around the country would receive puppies as gifts.

The secretary at the factory called him over the intercom. Trey motioned to one of the supervisors to operate the equipment while he went to see what she wanted.

"There's someone here to see you," she mumbled.

Trey looked around and didn't see anyone. The receptionist tilted her head towards his office.

Sitting in his office chair was Kyle. "Long time no see. How are you?" Trey's reaction was dispassionate. "As glad as I am to see you, could we meet after work at the courthouse? One of my employees called in sick, so we're short-handed, and I'm in a foul mood."

"Something I can do to help?"

"No, I just—" he paused. "Actually...it's not difficult. I could show you if you really mean it."

"Sure."

After instructing Kyle on the machinery, Trey thanked him and went to face the paperwork on his desk.

At the five o'clock whistle, Kyle stayed behind waiting for the last person to leave before he stuck his head into Trey's office.

"I've missed you," Trey said before Kyle could get a word out.

"Me too."

Trey motioned for him to take a seat. "I still don't know what to do about us."

Kyle pulled out a cigarette. "Is it okay if I smoke in here?"

Trey retrieved an ashtray from his desk drawer, but put it away. "I've got a better idea, why don't we go over to the new café? It's next to where your landscaping work will begin, and I can show you what we want done."

Kyle was hoping for some time alone with Trey, but knew it probably wasn't a good idea.

"You need a ride?"

"No. I rode a bike. Rose had one sitting in her shed. I'll meet you there."

"Oh geez," Trey hissed. "Do you mind if I take a shower first? Look at me—smell me. I reek."

Kyle wondered how *he* must smell considering he had worked more hours in the factory than Trey. "No, that's fine. Go ahead."

"I'll just be a minute." Trey locked the front door of the building, shut off the lights, and disappeared down the hall into what Kyle assumed was a locker room.

Kyle picked up a magazine from the secretary's desk and thumbed through it. Hollywood gossip didn't interest him, and he tossed it back. Not knowing what to do next, he read a plaque on the wall: Best Employer of the Year. Unable to resist any longer, he headed down the hall.

"I had a feeling you were going to do that," a lathered Trey greeted.

Kyle quickly undressed and joined him. Trey kissed Kyle's neck as he washed his back and then pushed tightly against him. Kyle turned and their lips locked. The wet hairs on Trey's chest felt rough against Kyle's smooth skin. Kyle used the soapy lather to slide one hand between Trey's butt cheeks, while the other hand stayed busy on the front side. Trey did the same and the two men clinched in ecstasy.

"That ought to cool us down a bit," Kyle said, catching his breath.

"Briefly, I'm afraid," Trey bragged as they rinsed off. "It's nice to touch you again after all this time." He reached for the towels and threw one to Kyle. "Ready for coffee?"

"I'll meet you there."

Kyle locked the bike to a signpost in front of the café and waited for Trey to get out of his truck.

As luck would have it, one of the few people in the café was Stacy. She waved them over to her table.

"Shit. Just act normal," Trey mumbled.

"It's nice to see you again, Kyle."

"You too, Stacy. I'm gonna order. Be right back."

Trey leaned and kissed his wife, hoping everyone was watching. "Whatcha readin'?" he asked.

"A psychology book I found on the shelf. You can exchange books, the sign says. I think it's a great idea...You sure are in a good mood. What gives?"

"Can't a husband be glad to see his wife?"

"I wouldn't know," she said through a smile.

"I told Kyle to meet me here so I could, uh, show him where he'll be working in the square."

"I'm sure he'll do a good job. The gay guys are good at that sort of thing."

"How did you know—I mean, he's gay? How do you know that?"

"Halloween at Anna's, remember? I told you, I went over for punch and Rose brought it up. I swear, half the time I feel like I'm talking to a wall. You don't listen to me." Onlookers would have sworn she was posing for the paparazzi the way her lips barely moved as she spoke.

"Stacy, please. Not here."

Kyle walked back over. "Can I get you guys something? Trey, you wanted a coffee, right? Stacy...anything?"

"No, I'm good. Thank you," Stacy quickly responded.

"Yeah, a coffee. Cream and sugar," Trey answered, curtly.

"Please and thank you," Stacy added. "You don't have to be so rude," she told him after Kyle walked away.

"There's Winnie," Trey pointed. "I still don't know why Maxine let her be a partner. She'll smoke away all of their profits."

"You've got to give her credit for trying...especially at *her* age."

"I'd just like to know where she got the money to open—"

"One coffee with cream and sugar," Kyle announced, causing an abrupt end to Trey's thought. "I got you a bottle of Perrier," he told Stacy.

"That's so sweet. Let me give you some money for it."

"No, it's on me. It's the least I can do."

She was touched by his generosity and snapped her purse shut and hung it back on the chair. "Tell me, Kyle. What do you think of our town's new little hotspot?"

Kyle looked around. "Pretty snazzy."

"We're proud of it," Stacy said. "Trey, tell Kyle what the plans are for the landscaping in the square."

"Right. Uh, you're the pro, but we were thinking about, um, some planters...and, you know: stuff. More lights and benches would be nice."

"Don't worry. I'll fix it up nicely."

"I'm sure Trey will approve of anything you want to do," Stacy added.

As a woman paraded up to the counter, whispered murmurs could be heard around the tables.

Stacy, again, spoke through her smile. "Holy moly! It's Ivory Black!"

Ivory had barely ordered a coffee before Constance came running through the door with her camera. Part of Ivory wished she was still Violet White. At least Violet would have appreciated the attention. Ivory would have too, in New York, but not in her hometown where other, more pressing issues were on her mind.

"Ivory! We've missed you," Constance started in. "Where have you been? What were you doing? Why did you leave?"

Ivory inhaled deeply. "Constance, I didn't miss *you*. New York. Working. And, 'cause I wanted to." Ivory turned to Maxine and ordered a low-fat cappuccino with extra cinnamon.

With Constance following closely behind, and people watching her every move, Ivory, took each step carefully. The last thing she needed was to throw humiliation on top of her nerves by causing a scene. A patron's sneeze broke her concentration. Her heel caught on the non-slip mat, twisting her ankle. The coffee cup went flying as she fell. The gasps of horror ended before the last piece of the broken coffee cup made a final clang against the wall. *Maybe Ronald could glue this one back together as well.*

Luciano was the first to assist the distraught customer.

"Do something," Stacy demanded of her husband. "Don't just sit there if you want votes the next term."

Trey stood.

"Poor Ivory," Kyle commented. "I didn't even recognize her —I mean, I thought she was still in New York."

"You knew where she was?"

"I have a friend in New York who's friends with her."

"With Ivory?"

"Yeah. I was going to ask her to come back with me, but then she disappeared."

"She's good at that," Stacy said, keeping an eye on how Trey was handling the situation.

When Ivory was back on her feet, she limped to the nearest vacant table, and Maxine carried over a fresh cup of coffee.

Ivory was good for business. People kept ordering refills and eating desserts they hadn't wanted so they could gawk and gossip. No customer wanted to leave before she did. Many of the oglers presumed that with Constance's mouth, Ronald would come running through the door at any moment. They weren't about to miss that!

Kyle excused himself, hoping his bicycle would be quicker than Constance's hijinks.

Like a child who was late to dinner, Kyle dropped his bike in the front yard and ran to the door.

"Open up! It's me, Kyle!"

Rose came to the door, disheveled. Ronald followed, tucking in his shirt.

Kyle walked inside. "You're not going to believe who I just saw."

Ronald found the arm of the chair to rest upon.

"Ivory is back! I just saw her at the Theater Café."

Rose sank down in the chair beside Ronald. "What are we going to do? Does anyone else know she's here?"

"'Fraid so. She made quite an entrance at the café. Constance was there, too."

"I should go," Ronald moaned.

"Don't leave," Rose begged. "Don't leave me. She doesn't deserve you. Oh, please don't leave me, Ronald."

Only minutes ago, Rose was safely wrapped in her lover's arms, snuggled under the sheets and dreaming of the remaining years they'd happily spend together. Now, she was questioning how life could go on? "He didn't even say goodbye. Why is God letting this happen to me?"

"I'm sorry, Rose."

"Leave me alone, Kyle. I just wanna be by myself."

"I don't think that's a good idea."

"Leave. Get out."

Kyle backed away towards the door. "Fine. I'll leave...but I'm coming back to check on you."

Dorcas and Frank had both trimmed down considerably. She had gone from a size 16 to a size 10, and he had gone from a 46-inch waist to a 42. The weight loss had also led to an increase in energy levels, and the two could be found around the camp playing table tennis, rowing in a canoe, and swimming in the pool. At night they snuck to their favorite spot by the pond. They spent most of their free time together, and Dorcas rarely thought of Ted, even though she did wonder how he had reacted when the divorce papers were served. She regretted not doing it personally, but didn't want him to see her until she had reached her weight-loss goal. Hopefully, her omnipresent sister had been around to take a snapshot of Ted's reaction for the newspaper.

The fact was, Dorcas didn't think much about anyone in Prairie Springs. Since she and Frank graduated to the second level at Slimming Acres, they were allowed off site, with permission, and opted to explore the big city of Houston. Dorcas' favorite activity was to go downtown and walk along the bayou before seeing a play. Frank allowed her to do the things Ted would have never dreamed of doing, or was too ashamed to do with his "heifer" of a wife.

This particular evening, the two lovebirds decided to eat out. Frank picked the downtown restaurant where they dined. As usual, neither ordered beyond a salad and grilled chicken breast because they had to show the receipt for their meal back at the camp. When the dessert cart rolled by, they politely declined. They didn't go completely without sweets, however; Dorcas kept two Tic Tacs in her purse.

While she was digging for the breath mints, Frank was digging in his pocket. When she looked up, he was down on one knee and all eyes were on them.

"Dorcas. Will you marry me?"

"Oh! You know I will…" Applause erupted in the restaurant. "…Just as soon as I'm divorced."

Dorcas knew how to silence a crowd! The appalled patrons abruptly ceased clapping and returned to their meals.

WEDNESDAY, DECEMBER 3, 2007

Stacy came home in the early afternoon after a quick trip to Temple, where she treated herself to a new leather coat she had been eyeing. As she pulled into the driveway, she noticed a fuzzy, gray blob by the garage door and got out of her BMW to examine it. It was a spindly kitten, so weak he couldn't stand on his own. She gently picked it up and stroked its head to soothe his plaintive cries. As his helpless eyes met hers, the two lonely souls had no way of knowing how much each one truly needed the other. Cuddling him to her chest, she barely got the car door closed before a clap of thunder heralded the imminent downpour. Raindrops bombarded them as she carried him into the house.

"It's storming," she cooed to him. "I think that's what I'll call you—Stormy. Yes. Stormy's a good name for you, don't you think, little boy? Do you like that? I know something else you'll like. I bet you'd like some baked chicken. Why don't I fix you a nice warm plate?"

She took one of the cushions from a chair at the informal dining table and placed it on the floor. "You just wait right here. Mommy's going to fix you some cuisine."

Stacy had forgotten about the expensive leather jacket in the car as she fell into her newly found maternal role.

After Stormy ate, she placed him on the couch and petted him until the soothing sound from the rain mellowed them both.

When Trey came home, Stormy was attempting to follow Stacy around the kitchen. "What's that?"

"A Doberman, Trey. What does it *look* like?"

Trey removed his jacket and hung it in the laundry room. "Ted came back to work today."

"That's nice. What was wrong with him?"

"Heartsick, I guess. Dorcas filed for divorce last week."

Stacy looked at him. Trey couldn't decipher her expression, but if he had to guess, there was a hint of envy.

"Sad, huh?" Trey uttered, probingly.

"Depends." It was a hushed, callous response.

"I'm going to change," he announced. Halfway upstairs, he stopped. "What'd you name him?"

"Stormy."

"Appropriate...Are you cooking, or do you want to order in?"

"Let's order a pizza."

"Thin crust for me."

"Thin crust for me," she mimicked to Stormy. "All these years, and he still thinks I don't know what kind of pizza he likes. Never get married, Stormy. It's just not worth it."

CHAPTER FOURTEEN

Anna took it upon herself to use any remaining decorations from the boxes Ronald pulled from the storage room. When Kyle arrived, the backyard looked like a 1970s dime store. Anna was on a ladder hanging a plastic noseless snowman from a tree branch. "Kyle! Look what I've done! Doesn't it look festive?"

"That's one word." He eyed an elf with a broken arm resting against the fountain.

"What's that supposed to mean?"

"It sort of looks like Santa vomited."

Anna, still standing on the ladder, surveyed her yard creation and laughed. "I guess it does look a tad tawdry."

"A tad," Kyle smiled. "Do you mind if I give it a go?"

"Be my guest. I'm going to finish my book."

A few hours later, every light was meticulously placed, glittery snowflakes hung from tree branches, and a personalized stocking graced the porch of each tenant. The garden bench had been turned into a sleigh, and candy canes lined the flagstone walks. The main attraction was the big, colorfully lighted Christmas tree in the center of the yard next to the fountain. Anna peeked outside and hurried to place her stereo speakers in the windows and filled the CD changer with Christmas music.

"Where did you get all of these things?"

"I bought some of it, but most is stuff the town was getting rid of. Trey told me to help myself."

"It looks like—It looks like Christmas."

When Flo came home, her jaw fell open. She ran inside and emerged with hot chocolate and a Virginia Slim.

Unfortunately, the cheerful ambiance was in direct contrast to Rose's mood. Still depressed over Ronald's sudden departure, she couldn't get into the Christmas spirit...and wishing her sister was dead didn't help matters.

THURSDAY, DECEMBER 4, 2007

After school let out, Anna stopped by the Golden Years for a quick visit with her newest friend, Ms. Mae Pearl Fisher. The lovable resident's only daughter never came to visit, so she anxiously anticipated Anna's company. Anna was appalled by the daughter's behavior and felt for the retired schoolteacher. Mae Pearl was tough, and refused to let her daughter sour her positive disposition. The matchmaker in Anna was eager to hook up Mae Pearl with Dr. Waxman. "If nothing else, you could be friends and hang out together." She gave Dr. Waxman the same encouragement. But other than the occasional encounter in the dining room where manners, not a mutual interest, were the reason for speaking, not so much as a glance was exchanged between the two residents.

Mae Pearl recognized Anna's voice as she greeted the other residents. By the time she knocked on her door, Mae Pearl was already wearing a smile. "Hello there. I brought you something."

"You did? What?"

"Papers to grade. Or how about this: I'll grade the papers if you'll keep me company. They're multiple choice, and I have the answer key."

"Great." Mae Pearl eagerly agreed and pulled her afghan up to cover her legs while she sat in the chair. "You have such pretty hair, dear."

"Thank you, Mae Pearl." Anna arranged the papers and took a red pen from her purse. "Have you heard from your daughter?"

"No, but I'm sure she'll call any day now. She's awfully busy, you know."

"I can't imagine she's too busy to call you. How long does it take to pick up the phone and dial a number?"

Mae Pearl grunted and hoped the subject would change to one less painful. Unfortunately, the next topic was not much better.

"Have you seen Dr. Waxman this week?" Anna asked.

"Who? Oh, Arthur. You say 'doctor' and I immediately think of hospitals. Yes, dear. He sat by me in the dining room the other day. Chews with his mouth open."

Anna didn't know how to respond. "Oh. Well...did you hear about the new Theater Café on the town square?"

"I did. I read all about it in the newspaper. I also read about that missing lady that came back to town. You know, I used to know her."

"Ivory Black? How'd you know *her*?"

"She, Dorcas and I played bingo together sometimes at the VFW hall. Seemed kind of crazy to me. Always talking about famous actors and actresses. When I heard she went missing, my first thought was she probably went out to Hollywood or some-wheres like that."

"New York."

"Yeah. That's what I read." Mae Pearl scratched her elbow. "Have you been to that café?"

"I have. Several times, as a matter of fact. My friend Maxine owns it."

"I read that, too. I didn't know she had that kind of money."

"Her mother died, so I guess she left her something."

"And Edwina is the other owner, I read."

"Oh, Winnie. Yes, she is. She's a character. Do you know her, too?"

"Who doesn't? She's a riot."

"Say, Mae Pearl, where's your roommate?"

"Agnes had a doctor's appointment today. She hasn't been feeling well."

"I'm sorry, Mae Pearl."

"Me too."

"How long have you known her?"

"Oh, 'bout forty years, I suppose."

"Forty! Oh, Mae Pearl, do you want me to go over to the hospital and check on her?"

"Don't trouble yourself, dear. Wouldn't help anyway. Just say a little prayer. I don't know what I'll do if I lose someone else. First my husband, and now my daughter doesn't—" Mae Pearl stopped herself and gestured to the tests Anna was grading. "Did anyone get a perfect score?"

"Not yet. They can't seem to catch on to the subjunctive."

"I can't say that I could either."

"What did *you* teach?"

"Me? Oh, I was girls' athletic coach—volleyball and basketball. We won the basketball championships three years in a row."

"You must've been a good coach."

"Oh, I was," she said proudly. Mae Pearl carried on about years gone by, awards, particular students...Anna was listening but focused on grading.

"Ninety-six!" Anna blurted. "Good for him."

"Who's the smarty pants?"

"Ricky Richards."

"I don't know why I asked. I wouldn't know any of them."

Anna grinned and capped her red pen. "Well, Mae Pearl, that's the last one. I hate to leave, but I've got to get home and see what's for dinner. My friend Kyle moved here from New York. Did I tell you that? He's a great cook, but I'm going to be as big as a house if I'm not careful."

"Give me a kiss before you leave."

"I'll see you soon." Anna pushed Mae Pearl's hair aside and kissed her on the forehead.

Rose read the sordid saga in each edition of *The Herald*. Constance followed Ronald and Ivory around like they were Bogart and Bacall. The biweekly column read like a soap opera, and Rose, who preferred her dirty laundry remain in the basket on the back porch, kept expecting to be one of the characters. Thus far, she had escaped Constance's wrath.

Rose was tormented with images of a heartwarming reunion between husband and wife. She pictured him throwing his arms around Ivory, falling to his knees and begging her for forgiveness. In reality, the reunion was entirely different...

Limping up the sidewalk to the front door of her house, Ivory stared at the doorbell. It was strange to have to wait for admittance, especially since she had a key in her purse.

What should have felt familiar seemed awkward and surreal. Was that really the porch swing she'd sat on for years? Was that doormat welcoming *her*? A deluge of feelings flooded her subconscious. Why was she seeing it all differently as Ivory than she had as Violet? Would her husband even recognize her new look? For a second, she regretted having ever left Prairie Springs and her humdrum life with Ronald.

The front door opened and Ronald squinted through the screen before pushing it open. "Ivory?"

Ivory inhaled a stuttered breath. "Yes. Yes. It's me. You recognized me."

"Recognized you? You look the same. What are you doing here?"

"Well, I've come back...for a visit."

Ronald knew this was his only chance to direct the course of what lay ahead. "Watch your step."

"I see you put the coffee cup back together."

"Yeah, I did. Did you want some?"

"Some what?"

"Coffee."

"No, I just had some...but the cup turned out nicely. You were always good at that sort of thing...And you've washed the dishes."

"Of course."

Ivory might as well have been in a room with a dachshund, the way Ronald avoided eye contact. He motioned toward the living room. "Um. Wanna sit down?"

"Sure. Is that your same ol' recliner?"

"Yeah...yeah. It's the same one."

"I see the afghan is still on the footstool. Have you washed it?"

"Yeah—No. I didn't know it was dirty."

"A little dust has probably settled on it over the past six months, don't you think, Ronald? But don't worry."

Ivory sat on the edge of the sofa. Ronald pulled up the rarely used extra dining chair from the corner.

"Was it worth it?" he asked without relaxing his focus on the odd strand of carpet standing higher than the rest.

Ivory looked to see what he was staring at and then back at him. "I had to do it."

"Where have you been? I mean—"

"New York City, Ronald. I live there now. Can you believe it? Although, I do take little side trips, ya know. I'm quite the traveler. Worldly!"

"I see."

"What about you? Aw, Ronald, you should be there. My dreams are finally—"

"You didn't ask me to be there."

"Don't be silly, Ronald. I'm trying to tell you what I've been doing. Do you want to hear it or not? Honestly! You're no different than you were when I left. If you'll be quiet for a minute —My stars, Ronald, would you look at this furniture! I can't believe this used to be mine. You should see all of the wonderful furnishings they have in New York. You wouldn't believe it. You know, I bought me a real fancy rug for my apartment. It's like walking on a big Persian cat. I try not to walk on it too much. Anyway, what was I saying? Oh right, the furniture. Would you just look at it! Ronald? Are you even listening to a word I'm saying? What's got you so interested in the carpet, anyway?"

"I'm listening. Go ahead."

"Well, look at me when I'm talking to you! For crying out loud, you haven't seen me in a month of Sundays. You'd think you'd want to look at me now and again. Wait. Now that I think about it, why would you? You never did before."

"How come you left me?"

"You wouldn't understand. Tell me about you...How've *you* been?"

While Ivory wondered how she ever lived with such wretched furniture, Ronald wondered how he ever lived with such a wretched woman. Ivory felt like sandpaper compared to Rose's gentle touch and kind, inspiring words. The anger of those wasted years boiled inside of him. He regretted answering the door, and wanted Ivory to leave—get up from the chair, go back to New York, and never return.

"Are you going to answer me or just sit there? Honestly, Ronald. I don't know what's gotten into you."

Ronald stood and this time looked straight into her eyes. "I'll tell you what's gotten into me, Ivory. But listen up, because I'm only saying it once. I loved you. I loved you since the first time I saw you way back when. But you never believed it. No matter how many ways I tried to show you, you just couldn't see it. You want proof? Go out the back door and see what's in the yard. I built that—that *gosh-dang* gazebo for you. Everything I've done in my life has been for you. And how do you show your appreciation? You leave me. You left me in a town so small even the cows felt sorry for me. Every Sunday in church everyone prayed for me. I felt like an idiot, Ivory. And now you come traipsing back like you expect everything to be just like it was between us? Is that what you're hoping? Because let me tell you something, lady. It ain't gonna be just like it was. It ain't even gonna be *near* like it was. For your information, I am in love with another woman. That's right. I am in love with another woman, and I don't want our marriage anymore. You can have your...your...*damn* gazebo. You can have this horrible furniture. You can have the coffee cup I glued back together. And you can have everything I own, but you can't have me—And stop crying! If you can't take the bucking, then you shouldn't have ridden the horse."

Ronald stuck his hands in his pockets and went to the front porch.

After a few minutes, the screen door opened and Ivory emerged to join him. "Who is she?"

Ronald turned to face her. "It's Rose."

Ivory gently pulled Ronald's hand from his pocket. She pulled him down to sit beside her on the porch swing. "Ronald, thank you for the gazebo. Thank you for all you've done for me. I knew about you and Rose; I just wanted to hear you say it. All I ask is that we stay friends, because I do love you, Ronald."

"Why, Ivory? Why did you leave?"

Ivory gently wiped a tear from Ronald's face.

"I had to. I felt so trapped in this small good-for-nothing town, and I had to get out. I had to see the world. And I didn't want *you*, or *anyone*, to get in the way."

"I hate you for that," he replied, softly.

"I don't blame you, but I don't regret what I did."

Ronald stared into the night sky.

"Would it be okay if I stayed here for a while? I'll sleep on the couch."

Ronald shrugged his shoulders, "I guess. We're still married... aren't we?"

"Yes. We're still married."

Later that night, she slipped some bedding over the sofa and went to sleep. When Ronald woke to relieve his bladder, Ivory's bare feet hung uncovered. "Take the bed, Ivory. I'll sleep on the couch."

FRIDAY, DECEMBER 5, 2007

"I know my apartment doesn't look like a home yet, but it's getting there," Kyle said to Anna and Rose as he put the finishing touches on the chicken cordon bleu he was preparing for dinner.

"Rose, you've got to cheer up," Kyle told her. "There's always plenty of fish in the sea."

"At this age, most of the fish in my sea are floaters. I'm not young anymore, in case you haven't noticed."

Anna interjected, "I know! We can try finding someone for you on the Internet."

"That's a good idea," Kyle agreed.

"Nobody'd want me. Plus, I'm too old to know about the Internet. I can barely work the TV remote."

"How about some wine, Rose? It might cheer you up," Kyle offered, reaching for a glass.

"Go ahead, pour me some. What's it gonna hurt?"

Anna handed the glass to Rose. "Have you seen the yard from up here? Look out the window. Didn't Kyle do a nice job?"

"What? Oh yeah. It's real nice."

"Come on, Rose. Sulking's not going to help. Cheer up. You don't know for sure Ronald's going back to Ivory," Anna encouraged.

"He didn't even kiss me goodbye. That's what hurt the most. I should've never gotten involved with a married man. It's a sin, you know. If anyone were to find out—"

"Please, Rose, don't start with the sinning stuff," Kyle insisted. "If Ronald walked through that door right now and planted a big smackeroo on your lips, I guarantee you, you wouldn't be talking about sinning."

"It's just God's way of putting an end to things that aren't right."

"We must pray to different gods."

"Can we change the subject please?" Anna pleaded in her schoolteacher tone. After no volunteers for a new topic, she said, "You know, I've been going up to the nursing home and visiting people. And one old—one woman I've been talking to used to be a schoolteacher, and she has a daughter who never goes to visit her. Isn't that sad?"

"What's her name?" Rose asked.

"Um, Mae Pearl."

"Mae Pearl Fisher?"

"Yeah, you know her?"

"That's Judy Jane Johnson's mother."

"Judy Jane Johnson from next door? The one whose face only half works?"

"That's the one."

"Well, why on earth doesn't she go visit her own mother?"

Rose took a small sip of wine. "It's a long story."

"Perfect timing," Kyle said, bringing the food to the table. "We needed a dinner conversation."

Rose left around eleven in the evening. Anna stayed upstairs with Kyle and they finished off the bottle of wine and made a batch of slice-and-bake chocolate chip cookies. Kyle was putting on a pot of coffee when Anna said, "I just can't believe the way Judy Jane is behaving in the name of religion. Of all the—I have half a mind to go next door and give that woman a piece of me."

Kyle reached for the ashtray.

"Doesn't it bother you?" she asked.

"Of course it does, but ask if it surprises me."

"What I don't get is that Mae Pearl probably only has a couple of years left. How can Judy Jane Johnson live with herself knowing that her mother is only a mile away, and she doesn't give enough of a damn to go see her? That's what I'd like to know."

"Yeah. I can understand being shocked at first, but you'd think she'd have come to terms with it by now."

"Oh, Kyle, I feel so stupid. I was trying to set her up with Dr.

Waxman, the other resident I told you about. She kept telling me she wasn't interested, but I kept pushing for it. God, I'm so blind! I should have put the pieces together when she said she was a PE teacher."

"Not all PE teachers are lesbians," Kyle reminded before taking a sip of coffee. "You know what the good thing is? She shares a room with the woman she loves, even if it *is* in a nursing home."

As the night came to an end in Prairie Springs, only God knew the trials and tribulations weighing on the hearts of the population. Trey and Stacy went to bed facing opposite walls, trying to forget about the person lying next to them. Mae Pearl fell asleep with her arm extended towards Agnes' bed. Ricky Richards went to bed with tears in his eyes after succumbing to the natural urges he felt. Ted fell asleep with his heart in shambles and his head on Dorcas' pillow. Rose never slept at all. And one liberated soul in Prairie Springs would never wake.

Chapter Fifteen

Saturday, December 6, 2007

I vory thought it best to visit her sister alone, and Ronald, figuring he would complicate matters, agreed. She grabbed the car keys from the hook by the front door. "Wish me luck."

Ivory found the town to be listless. She needed her New York friends who took her for herbal tea, on shopping expeditions, to the occasional drag show, and surprised her with makeovers.

She parked in the driveway behind Rose's car. She chose to wear a knee-length wool skirt the color of Dijon mustard, a black blouse, and her favorite black cardigan that extended beyond her hips.

The objective was not to show Rose up, but to exude confidence—something she would need if she were to pull this off. The slightest slip and she was liable to slap her sister and run back to Ronald out of spite. She took a deep breath and rang the bell.

The Westminster chime echoed throughout the house. Rose sat at the kitchen table in her robe, absentmindedly twisting the corner of a paper napkin. She'd forgotten to turn off the coffee pot, but didn't care. Using the table for support, she hoisted herself into a standing position and went to the door. "Ivory. What are you—? Come in out of the cool."

"Hello, Rose dah-ling." Ivory planted a kiss on her cheek and made a model-like spin in the foyer. "It is just *grand* to see you. You look wonderful."

Rose patted her disheveled hair.

"And look at this place! I love what you've done to the front yard."

"What? Oh that. Yeah. Um—" Rose retied her robe. "Do you want some coffee? And there's banana bread."

"None for me, sweetness. Why don't you just come over here and relax? We need to talk."

Rose knew what her uninvited sibling wanted to chat about. She hoped Anna, Flo—anyone—would drop by to interrupt.

"Come on. Sit down over here with me," Ivory insisted. "Do you mind if I turn on this lamp?" She didn't wait for a reply. Rose took a seat, attempting to overlook that Ivory had taken over her usual chair. "I know you've been sleeping with my husband."

"But—"

"Just let me get this out, Rose. Just listen for a minute. I know y'all have been sleeping together, and I want you to know that I don't blame you for it."

"You don't?"

"Silly Rose, it takes two to tango, but I don't blame either of you. I don't blame anyone but myself for what's happened to my marriage. What I'm trying to say is that I couldn't be happier for the two of you."

Rose did a double take. "Really?"

"Yes. Honestly. Like I told him, if he's going to be with another woman, I'm glad it's you and not some two-bit floozy."

"Well, no, I'm not a—"

"I won't say I wasn't surprised by the whole thing. Shoot, when I saw y'all together I have to admit I was mad as hell." She picked up the *Southern Living* from the lamp table and set it back down.

"I've never heard you cuss, Ivory."

"Being in show business and such, you hear it all. I'm not the woman you knew before. Would you believe I'm famous?"

"What do you mean, *famous*?"

"I'm surprised no one's recognized me...especially you, my own flesh and blood. I'm on the Rise & Shine cereal box."

"Wait a minute. I've got a box of that in the kitchen." She pulled it from the shelf. "It *is* you. I eat this every day and never paid any attention. What happened to your wrinkles?"

"Photography tricks—Makeup—You know."

"Well, Ivory. You should be proud of yourself. That's quite an accomplishment."

"I am. I am."

"You always *did* want to be famous. It looks like your dreams have come true."

"One of them, anyway."

"Is everything else alright?"

Ivory paused long enough to look out of the window. "I suppose so—" She caught herself. "Of course everything is all right," she amended. "Busy, busy, but other than that...I do miss you, you know? The way we used to sit on the porch and drink lemonade."

"Those were the days, huh? You should try my new lemonade, Ivory. Anna gave me a recipe that's quite tasty."

"What does it have in it beside lemons...and who's Anna?"

"White wine," Rose blabbed, "but don't tell the preacher."

"You don't have to worry about that. I quit the church. Hardly anyone goes to church up in New York City."

"You quit the church? You'd practically worn a spot on the pew, you went so often before."

"Not anymore...But I still pray and read my Bible."

"I'm scared to go back to church here," Rose defended. "I haven't been in so long, and now everyone probably hates me since I'm letting to a Jewish girl and her homosexual friend. That's who Anna is, by the way."

Ivory slapped her knee. "You rented the places out back?"

"Yep. And I couldn't be happier about it."

"That's wonderful! Is Flo still here?"

"Last I checked."

Ivory relaxed. "Rose, dear. I think I *will* have some coffee and banana bread, if you don't mind. You'll have to tell me all about what's going on. A gay boy, a Jew, *and* white wine? I've got to know more! Maybe I left Prairie Springs too soon."

"I guess you did what you had to do. I wish you would have confided in me. I can't tell you how worried I have—we all have been. I'd convinced myself that if you ever came back, I was never going to speak to you again. But at the same time, I prayed you were safe."

"I'm sorry. You're right. I should've told you."

Ivory reached to grab Rose's hand and patted it with the other. "Don't be nervous," Rose said. "I can feel your hand shaking."

Ivory gently smiled at her sister.

Rose was relieved. Was it a coincidence the siblings had found enlightenment at the same period of their lives, or was it fate? Whatever it was, each was equally grateful.

FRIDAY, DECEMBER 19, 2007

It was the last day of school before the holiday break, and the teachers were as anxious as the students for the final bell.

When it rang, Anna held Ricky back.

"Take a seat. I want to ask you a question." Anna walked to the front of her desk. "Do you think your parents would mind if you came over for dinner tomorrow night? There's someone I'd like you to meet."

"Uh, I don't know. I guess it'd be okay."

"Then, I'll expect you around seven tomorrow evening?"

"Yeah, sure." Ricky stood. "Is it okay if I go? There's something I have to do tonight."

"Go. Get out of here. See you tomorrow."

After the teachers were dismissed thirty minutes later, Anna stopped by the nursing home to drop off a couple of small gifts she'd picked up for her two favorite residents.

As she entered, she heard the usual yammering. *Take me outta here!...Girl! They're holding me here!...Where're my kids?...Push me!...Help me!* Judging from the cries, it sounded more like a torture chamber than a place where care was given in the final days. One woman sat smiling, while fiercely popping bubble wrap. Another had persuaded Anna to push her outside where she needed to wait for her husband. Anna obliged and the nurse came running to inform Anna she wasn't allowed to take them beyond the front doors. "But she said she always waits for her husband outside."

"Honey, her husband's been dead for fifteen years."

Gifts in hand, Anna stopped by the nurses' station to officially announce her arrival and the rooms she was visiting.

"Anna," the head nurse pulled her aside. "I'm sorry. I thought you knew, but Dr. Waxman passed away a couple of weeks ago."

"Oh—God...How?"

"He was old, dear."

Anna looked at the bag of gifts she was carrying. "And Mae Pearl? Is she still with us?"

The nurse smiled. "I'm sure she'll be thrilled to see you."

Anna walked down the hallway, passing Dr. Waxman's room without looking in. Death always seemed premature. If only she'd stopped by sooner. "Mae Pearl?" Anna knocked.

"Anna! What a surprise."

"How are you?" Anna whispered, after noticing that Mae Pearl's roommate was asleep.

"I'm fine, dear. I guess you heard the news about Arthur."

"Yeah. They just told me. I'm still in shock."

Mae Pearl was noticeably less shocked than Anna.

"How's school? It let out today, didn't it?"

"Yes. Yes, it did. And I'm ready for a break, I tell you." She reached into her bag. "I brought you guys a little something for your room and then another little surprise to open on Christmas. I'll put it under the tree on the way out."

"Anna, you shouldn't have. Look at the pretty wrapping paper with the colorful doughnuts."

"No, Mae Pearl, they're wreaths."

Mae Pearl laughed at herself. "I see that now."

Anna watched as her stiff fingers struggled with the paper. "Want me to help you with that?"

"Would you?"

Anna broke the tape and pulled back a piece of the paper. "It's a stupid gift, really. You'll probably just laugh at it."

Mae Pearl held up The Grabber.

"When you can't reach something, you can use this." Anna demonstrated by lifting a box of tissues.

"That's pretty clever. Thank you, Anna." Mae Pearl squeezed it a couple of times to practice. "Speaking of gifts—Arthur, uh, Dr. Waxman, wanted me to give you this." Inside the nightstand drawer, she retrieved an unsealed envelope. Next to it was a sandwich baggie of pills.

"Should you be taking those pills, Mae Pearl?"

"That's pain medicine. The nurses give them to me, but I rarely need them. They might come in handy one day." She offered a coy, reticent smile in Anna's direction. "Anyway, Arthur must've known it was his time to go because he gave me the envelope in the cafeteria the day before he passed."

Anna read her name on the front and pulled out an old, faded picture of a diapered, newborn baby with its legs in the air.

"Is that a birthmark on the bottom of his tiny heel?"

Anna looked more closely. "Oh yeah."

"Looks like a fingernail moon."

"Either you have super eyesight, or you've already taken a peek."

"I couldn't help myself. Why would he give you a picture of a baby?"

Anna furrowed her brow and placed the photograph back in the envelope.

Stacy took Stormy all over town, thanks to his very own custom Coach leather pet purse, and had conversations with him while running errands. "Don't you think this blouse would look good on me?" "Should we get chocolate or rocky road ice cream?" The people who usually greeted her paused, assuming she was talking to herself, before silently strolling along. Why hadn't she thought of a portable companion before? Without the needless and utterly boring chitchat up and down every aisle, she made it through the supermarket in record time.

Stacy chose the rearmost table at the Theater Café to read yet another psychology book from the shelves.

"Still haven't opened your practice?"

Stacy was puzzled at first, not placing him.

"Mark...the music teacher...Halloween?"

"Oh gosh, Mark. Forgive me. How are you?"

"Fine. Another wild Friday night getting high on caffeine."

Stacy guffawed. "Right. This is about as wild as things get around here, I suppose."

"I just wanted to say hello. I'll let you return to your book—it's a good one." He stepped back towards his table.

Stacy blushed and glanced down at the page. Then, in an impulsive move, she turned. "Mark? Would you care to join me?"

He cautiously looked around.

"I don't bite."

"Thank you. I'd like that," he grinned and took the chair opposite hers.

Watching from the counter, Winnie wasn't missing a beat of the action.

"Did you hear that? Sounds like a cat," Mark commented.

"No. I didn't hear anything."

"There it is again."

Stacy looked around. "Must be coming from outside," she covered.

Stormy poked his head out of the tote. Mark smiled. "What's wrong, don't wanna let the cat outta the bag?"

She nervously giggled and pushed Stormy back inside. "What's Anna up to these days?"

"Who knows? Since Kyle came back into town she doesn't have a lot of time for me."

"Gosh. I know the feeling."

"Are you and your husband having problems?"

Stacy fiddled with the spoon on her saucer. "That's awfully direct. You caught me a bit off guard."

"I didn't mean to—"

"No, no. It's fine. Almost refreshing." She bent the page corner, closed the book, and inhaled sharply. "We have our ups and downs."

Mark listened.

"He's uh...I uh. Gosh, how do I say this without being crass? Let's see. We haven't had sex in years..."

Mark didn't react.

"...We barely speak, and when we do, we argue. It's like he's acting, you know? He's certainly not the same person I married. I've done everything I know to try and get him to love me, but I've nothing left. And keeping up appearances is stressful. Everyone thinks we're the happy couple—"

"Stacy, uh. Maybe we should talk about this somewhere else? There are a lot of ears around us."

"I know the perfect place." She stood. "We can take my car. You'll love it."

"What about Trey? Won't he be worried?"

"Trey, worried? Ha! Anyway, he's in Austin visiting at the 'hospital.'"

Ricky Richards pulled the scouting handbook from his backpack and turned to "Basic Scouting Knots." He grabbed the rope from the closet to practice.

In his younger years he was able to cope. A few years into puberty, the urges grew stronger, and so was the need to satisfy it. His years of pleas for God to change him went unheard. He couldn't see a way out, believing the rest of the world was just like Prairie Springs.

He wrote a note to his parents and stuck it in his pocket. It was easy to sneak out of the house when his parents tuned in to *Focus on the Family*. He left wearing his backpack and hopped on his bike.

Kyle knocked on Anna's door and let himself in. "What's up?"

"Nothing much," Anna answered. "Getting ready to wash clothes."

"Does that mean you're staying home?"

"I guess. Why?"

"I was wondering if I could borrow your car."

"Sure. How come?"

"I've got a date."

"A date? Trey?"

"Yep."

"You won't be too embarrassed to be seen in my green boat?"

"It's not that bad," he said. "I'm getting used to it."

"The keys are hanging on the kitchen cabinet." She went back to separating the coloreds from the whites, fighting back tears. "Where're you going to meet?"

"At the Roadside Palace, but if you need the car, you can just drop me off. I don't know where we're going after that."

"No, I won't need it until tomorrow, but could you put some gas in it? I think it's almost empty."

"Okay. Thanks, Anna. Are you alright?"

"Yeah," she said, but not convincingly. "Dr. Waxman, the man I visited in the nursing home, passed away. I just found out today."

Kyle walked over and hugged her from behind. "Geez, Anna. That's too bad. How old was he?"

"I dunno. He was old. I just wasn't prepared for it is all."

"Are we ever?"

"I suppose not."

"Are you sure you don't want to drop me off? We could talk more in the car."

"Please. Go on. Enjoy. Some alone time will be good for me."

"What about Mark? Why don't you call him?"

"We broke up."

"You what? When did that happen?"

"He doesn't know it yet, but I don't want to see him anymore —as lovers, anyway. I'll still see him at school."

"What changed your mind?"

"He's just not the one. There wasn't that connection, you know."

"Are you sure you don't want me to stay? I will if you want me to."

"No, I told you, go on. Have fun. I might stop by and visit with Rose later."

"If you're sure."

"Go!"

Kyle left and ran through the yard.

"Hot date?"

"Oh, Flo! You startled me...and yes."

"Give him my love." She waved and took a puff on her slender cigarette.

Kyle smiled and ran along.

On what would have been Humphrey's 76th birthday, Winnie went to visit his gravesite at The Springs. Fearing she would fall in a hole if she walked through the tall grass, she drove beyond the gravel parking lot to get closer to the tree. As she approached, she couldn't believe what she was seeing. She threw the gear into park and hopped out.

"What the heck are you doin' on my Humphrey, sonny?"

There was no answer.

She spotted the noose dangling from the branch when she approached. "Sonny boy?"

He turned. "I'll shoot you if you come any closer. Leave me alone."

"The hell you will, you idgit!" Winnie reached into her jacket pocket, pulled out a pistol and shot the ground next to the boy. "Oh, crap! Look at what you made me do! I done shot my dead Humphrey!"

Winnie kept her aim as she approached, but when she realized his gun was only a stick, she dropped her guard.

"Is that you, Ricky? I've known you since you was in diapers. What in the world are you doing with that rope in the tree like that?"

"You wouldn't understand."

"Try me. You might be surprised what I understand. Come on, kiddo. Sit down with me. I've got just the thing for you."

She pulled a lighter from her pocket and dug under her wig.

"What's that?"

"Ha! There's the proof you don't know what you're doin'. If you don't know what *this* is, that means you don't know what a lot of stuff is. And hell, sonny, you might just find somethin' you think is worth living for."

Winnie lit the joint and passed it to Ricky. "No thanks, I don't smoke."

"Why? You concerned with your health? You's gonna hang yourself a minute ago. Just take a drag."

He sucked on the joint but didn't inhale. "Ah now! You're awastin' it. You gotta breathe it in. Try again." Winnie watched. "I guess it wudn't for nothin' I didn't win the mother of the year award," she chuckled and elbowed Ricky.

He took another drag, inhaled, and coughed. Winnie laughed. "Takes some getting used to."

"How did you know I was here?" he asked.

"How did I—? Ah hell! I didn't know you was here. I came to visit my Humphrey. You're sittin' on him, ya know."

Ricky jumped up, "I'm sorry—I didn't know."

"Settle down. Whadaya think he's gonna do, reach up and tickle your ass?" She grabbed his arm and pulled him back to her side. "Tell me. What's got you so down you think that rope is gonna do the trick?"

"I'm not sure what's wrong with me."

"You sick?"

"No—I mean—Maybe I am. I dunno."

"Uh...Give me that. You've had enough," she said, yanking the joint from between his fingers. "You got pains or something?"

"No. I don't feel bad, it's just I'm not sure what's wrong with my mind."

"Welcome to the fuckin' club!" she laughed. "I'm sorry. Go ahead and tell Ms. Winnie all your troubles."

After dropping Stormy off at home, Mark drove Stacy's car the thirty-mile trip up the highway with Stacy talking nonstop.

Downtown Temple was lifeless except for one small, dimly lit café where the cheesecake was to die for, and the coffee was even better.

They parked and walked inside. Stacy was poised and graceful and maintained impeccable posture. Her presence demanded attention. "It's so cozy in here. Shall we ask for the non-smoking section?"

"Fine with me," Mark agreed.

"Sit wherever there's a spot," a curly-haired teenage girl instructed. Stacy noticed she had a pimple on the tip of her nose that she'd tried to cover with concealer and too much powder.

"It's strange, Mark. I know I've really just met you and all, but I feel like I've known you my entire life..."

He smiled.

"...Maybe it's because Trey and I never talk anymore."

They took a table for two next to the wall.

"Was it better before, when you were just dating?"

"Before we married it was fine—wonderful, to be honest—but I swear, sometimes I feel like the last thing he said to me was 'I do.' After that, I'm not sure we've ever communicated like two human beings."

"I'm sorry, Stacy. Have you ever thought, you know, that maybe you aren't—you weren't—giving him something he needs?"

Stacy pulled her head back in shock. "Like what? I'm not sure I follow you."

"You know...sexually."

She quickly adjusted her posture. "Are you saying I might not be attractive enough?"

"Hell no! I think you're—"

"What? Say it."

"I think you're hot."

She giggled, and blood rushed from the tips of her toes to the top of her head. *Hot...hot!* She'd heard other more sophisticated adjectives, but 'hot?' "Really?...So, go on..."

"Maybe he has other needs."

"Trey? Oh, come now. I don't think—"

The door to the café opened. Mark, seeing who had just stepped inside, reached supportively for Stacy's forearm.

She was unsure whether to shrug it away and pretend she didn't notice the tingle in her spine or see where the physical contact led, disregarding completely the fact that she was a married woman. She opted to play the role of wife. "Mark, I don't mean to—It's just, I *am* married."

"Trey."

"Yes, Trey. As much as I'd like to—"

"No. Trey just walked in with Kyle."

Like an animatronic mannequin in a store window, Stacy slowly turned to see them out of the corner of her eye. "He's supposed to be in...We've got to hide!"

"Hide from what, Stacy?"

"Really, Mark. I can't have my husband see me on a date with another man."

"Why not? Isn't *he* on a date with another man?"

"Huh? What are you saying?"

She grabbed a coffee-stained newspaper from a nearby table and held it up as a shield as she observed from a distance.

"You silly boy," Winnie said. "You see? I told you, you didn't have no problems."

"Oh yeah? What am I supposed to do about my parents?"

"Ricky, the last piece of advice I'm gonna give ya, and you'd better remember this—is that this is *your* life—it ain't theirs. Change is always just around the corner. Survive the rest of high school, get good grades, pick a college a long ways away. You don't have to ever come back here. I know you think the rest of the world is like this town, but there's a reason it ain't even on most maps. There's bigger and better places where you can be whoever you are, or whoever you want to be. The last place you'd wanna kill yourself is in Prairie Springs, for cryin' out loud. Hell, sonny, you wouldn't even have a good story to tell in Heaven. And what kind of an idiot would wanna kill himself before Christmas? What's today? Oh right, it's the eighteenth, Humphrey's birthday. You just got—what—another week before opening your presents?"

"Less than a week. Today's the nineteenth," Ricky corrected her.

Winnie refigured her mental calendar and shook her head. "You know, you're right. God *does* work in his little quirky ways, don't he? That's just proof it ain't your time to go."

Ricky turned and observed Winnie squinting up at the stars. "Thanks."

"Don't thank *me*." She pointed towards the sky. "Help this old lady up, young man."

He offered his hand. She dusted off her dress and blew a kiss to the ground where Humphrey lay.

Ricky, pushing his bike, walked alongside Winnie. "I hear you're invited to Anna's—uh, Ms. Aron's—party tomorrow, Ricky?"

"Yeah. She told me there was someone she wanted me to meet. She's probably going to have a shrink there or something."

Winnie smiled. God did have his tricks and his special servants, but not all of them warmed the pews on Sundays.

Trey lit a cigarette. He exhaled the smoke away from the table. Stacy peeked around an upside-down newspaper with her mouth agape. Kyle followed Trey's startled gaze.

"Oh shit! What's she doing here?"

"I don't know, but I'm supposed to be in Austin." He spoke without moving his lips, a trick he'd learned from the wide-eyed woman across the room.

Trey stubbed out his cigarette. Kyle waved as if that might ease the fact that he was dating her husband.

Stacy took a deep breath. "Everything is fine...Espresso, Mark?"

Her dismissal of the situation frightened Trey to the point that he walked over to their table.

"Should I, uh—" Mark pulled the napkin from his lap.

"No, Mark. Stay seated," Stacy instructed. "Trey, we will discuss this at home behind closed doors like adults, keeping our voices at levels inaudible to the neighbors. Now, if you don't mind, I'm on a date."

"A date?"

"Yes, dear, a date."

"Okay...Have you been seeing him for a while?"

"You smoke?"

Seeing things heat up, Mark offered his chair to Trey a second time.

"Keep your seat. I'd hate to interrupt here," Trey said, and walked back over to Kyle.

"I had no idea he was going to be here. He said he was going to Austin, the son of a bitch...Coffee, please!" she waggled her fingers to no one in particular.

"I think it's self-serve," Mark said.

"That would explain the horrible service, wouldn't it?"

Trey and Kyle exited as quickly as they'd come in. As soon as the door closed behind them, Stacy's shoulders fell limp, as if someone had cut the strings of a marionette. "Mark, be a dear and order me a slice of that chocolate cheesecake."

Saturday, December 20, 2007

Ronald called Rose regularly, but to keep the rumors in check, and more importantly, to keep their business away from Constance and the printing press, personal visits were out of the question for the time being.

Ivory's return ticket was for Christmas Day. She and Ronald had managed to reconcile their differences without any bitterness, and a welcome peace settled over the house. Each morning, Ivory took her coffee to drink in the gazebo, which was above and beyond anything she had dreamed; she was amazed, but not surprised, at its perfection.

She smiled warmly as her husband walked out the back door to join her. "It's funny, huh? Now that our marriage is over, I sure have been enjoying us."

He took a seat on the wooden bench across from her.

"Wonder why that is? Maybe it's 'cause the pressure's off, or because we don't have to pretend? I don't know." She took a sip of coffee. "Do you think we should file for divorce?"

Ronald looked up from the coffee cup he was clutching for warmth. "I don't think that's necessary. I ain't never planning on remarrying."

"You and Rose wouldn't ever want to—"

"What on earth for? You just said it yourself—marriage ruined it for us. Why would I risk it with Rose?"

"Just asking."

Ivory rested her mug beside her and watched a bird fly from the bare peach tree to the fence post.

At the Midway Motel and Truck Stop off I-35 in Temple, Trey lay in bed tracing Kyle's chest with his finger and knew he was falling hard. He would have preferred if Stacy had found out differently, but the fact was, it didn't matter how it happened. She knew. And with his life no longer a secret, for the first time he could acknowledge his true feelings for Kyle. The dreaded sunlight seeped beneath the thick motel curtains. Trey blew into Kyle's ear until he slowly opened his eyes.

"Good morning," Kyle uttered through tight lips so as not to unleash his morning breath.

"Did you sleep well?"

"Like a queen," he said as he stretched.

"We have to get back."

"Yeah...I know."

Kyle got up and ran buck-naked to the bathroom and turned

on the shower. "I'll be out in a minute," he yelled. After he flushed the toilet, he opened the bathroom door. "Would you like to join me?"

Trey wrapped himself in the sheet and ran over.

"Aren't *we* modest," Kyle said, ripping away the sheet.

That same morning, back in Prairie Springs, Stacy wasn't in quite as jovial of a mood. The night had been restless and there was still no sign of her husband. She forwent her usual morning routine and moped around in her pajamas instead. As she downed her second helping of Trey's empty-calorie fruity rice cereal, she contemplated the dregs of her marriage: *Has he cheated before? Have there been other women? Certainly not. Wait. Did he ever even go to Austin? What was he doing on those overnight trips? Is Kyle his first guy? Oh my gosh. What if he didn't use protection! Was it wrong to have retaliatory sex with Mark? What will everyone in town think?* One thing was for sure—she was in no mood to go to Anna's get-together that evening.

Stacy abandoned her cereal and tuned the radio to 104.1 FM, cranked up the volume and danced around the living room before baking two-dozen peanut butter cookies. While those were in the oven, she cleaned the kitchen sink. As they were cooling, she cleaned the downstairs bathroom. Then she pulled out the vacuum cleaner and vacuumed the rugs while devouring six of the cookies. Stormy attempted to ride the rug sweeper attachment but kept falling off. Dusting followed. With the music still playing, she sat on the couch and looked around the house. Immaculate! Without warning, she broke down and bawled. Life as she knew it was over. Stormy, having never seen her cry before, tilted his head, blinking occasionally, as he watched. When most of the tears stopped, she went into the kitchen and took another peanut butter cookie from the sheet, reached for the secret spaghetti container and poured herself a drink. Stormy circled her ankles as Stacy ate her seventh cookie. The radio deejay was starting the weather report when Stacy cupped her mouth, heaved, and tossed her cookies.

Three blocks over, Ricky Richards turned down the radio in the middle of the weather report when his mother came into his room.

"What's wrong? Why do you look like that? Did someone die?" Ricky asked.

"No, no one died. We have to talk."

Officer Richards appeared and joined his wife, Vivian.

"You're grounded, son," his mom said.

Ricky furrowed his brow. "What for? What did I do?"

"Ricky, dear. It's come to our attention that you are—Well, that you are—We found—Let me put it this way: Are you listening to Satan?"

"On the radio?"

"You know what your mother means, son."

Ricky didn't answer, and didn't want to hear what his parents had to say. When he tried to leave, his father grabbed his arm.

"Let go of me!"

"Don't you talk to your father that way. He has been nothing but good to us and I won't have you—"

"So help me, Dad, if you don't let go of me—"

Officer Richards reluctantly released Ricky, who grabbed his backpack and rushed out of the house.

Vivian reprimanded her husband. "What'd you go and do that for?"

Anna was running herself ragged getting ready for her holiday soirée. Her to-do list wasn't getting any shorter and with almost everyone she knew invited, she could have used Kyle's help.

When she lent him her car, she expected him to be back long before now. If she hadn't been dying to hear the gossipy details of his evening, she would have been furious, but she tended to other duties as she waited. Rose came over trying to balance a gold plastic star she'd bobby-pinned to the top of her head. "Do you like it? It's the star that I used to put on top of the tree."

"It's, uh—festive."

Rose beamed.

"You sure are in a chipper mood," Anna said.

"Why shouldn't I be? Ivory leaves soon, and I'll get Ronald back. I have wonderful new friends, and I'm three pounds lighter."

"Are you sure Ronald is coming back? And, aren't you still upset with him? I mean, he just left you without so much as an *adiós*."

"Oh, Anna. I'm too old to hold a grudge. I've been thinking about it, and it's a tough situation for all three of us. And since Ivory gave me her blessing, I'm certain Ronald and I can get back on track. Can you tell I've lost three pounds?"

Anna looked up from the Velveeta she was cutting into chunks to make nacho cheese. "See what a romp in the sheets does for you?"

Rose giggled.

"They say it's a great way to stay in shape." Anna read the back of the picante sauce jar again to make sure she was following the three-step recipe correctly. "Maybe that would explain *my* sagging figure."

"Don't be silly Anna, you look great. Enjoy your body while it's young. I don't know what Ronald sees in me, to be honest. My entire body needs starching."

Anna laughed.

"Can I help you with something, dear?"

"I've got to make Christmas cookies...Winnie's bringing some of her brownies."

"Can't she make anything else?"

"I'm not complaining. And let's see...Maxine and Luciano are bringing over Spanish rice. Stacy said she'd bring shredded beef for the taco meat. She says it's good, so let's just hope it is. Roberto, from the gas station, is bringing homemade tortillas, and his family—remember those ladies that went to the hospital and to Maxine's mom's memorial? Well, they're bringing tamales."

"Is the mayor coming?"

"The last I heard he was, but if he and Kyle don't hurry and get..."

"If he and Kyle don't hurry and get what, dear?"

"Nothing. Could you hand me that jar of jalapeños?"

"Say, Anna. You don't find it odd giving a Christmas party being you're Jewish?" Rose handed her the jar.

"It's all in good holiday fun. Christmas, Hanukkah: tomato, to-mah-to."

"Well, I've never been more in the spirit, I tell you. It's like a winter wonderland outside. Aside from the fifty-degree temperatures and sunny skies, I feel like it could snow any minute. Kyle did an excellent job with the yard—and now this party! Last night when I was watching television, I was remembering the day y'all came and how mean I was. I hope y'all don't hold it against me. For all I know, you and Kyle probably sit around telling stories of the old lady stuck in the Renaissance era, and talk bad behind my back."

"No we don't. Kyle and I are both very fond of you."

"You young 'uns have it easy. By the time y'all grew up, things were more accepted. But for the old fogies like me, it's hard. You didn't have boys sleeping with boys and such. Those kinds of things didn't happen, so you have to understand it's a lot to swallow."

"Rose. It's not that boys didn't sleep with boys. It's that people didn't talk about it. How many jalapeños should I put in?"

"Ten or twelve, but chop 'em up first."

"Won't that be a bit spicy?"

"For four pounds of cheese? I don't think so. But my word! Are you expecting the cavalry?"

Anna and Rose were interrupted by the sound of footsteps running up the outdoor stairs.

"Sounds like Kyle's home," Rose said.

"Yeah. He must have to go to the bathroom. Thank God he's back with my car."

"Should I leave?" Rose questioned.

"Why would you need to leave?"

"I thought maybe you two wanted to talk."

"Well, I'm sure we will—" Anna stirred the cheese over low heat. "But is there anything we can't talk about in front of you? We all have our secrets, remember?"

Rose's deadpan expression turned into a grin. "Yes, I suppose we do...I have a crock pot I should've let you use. It would've been much easier. And it's a little early to be melting the cheese, don't you think?"

"Oh well, it's too late now. Did you want a soda or something?"

"No, I'm good, but thank you."

A moment of silence was interrupted by a woman's voice in the backyard, "Rose...Rose...Rose? Are you here?"

Rose stood and opened the door to Anna's cabin.

"There you are," the voice said. "Can I borrow a couple of eggs?"

"Who is it?" Anna asked.

Rose turned from the doorway, "Judy Jane Johnson—wants to borrow some eggs."

Anna wiped her hands on the side of her apron and walked to the door. "Hi, Mrs. Johnson. I'm Anna. How are you?"

Judy Jane half-smiled. "Fine. Just ran short on eggs. I was sure I had another dozen but—"

"I'm so glad you came over," Anna interrupted. "I was

meaning to invite you and your husband to the little get-together we're having this evening."

"Well, Jerry's on a fishing trip, but I would love to. What time?"

"Seven-thirty."

"Should I bring anything? I've got to bring something."

"Christmas cookies," Anna said. "That would be a great help."

"Fine. No problem. See you at seven-thirty then," she enthusiastically responded and turned to go. "Oh, Rose, now I'll need a few more eggs for the cookies."

"The back door is open. Help yourself."

Anna went back to stirring the cheese and Rose took a seat at the dining table. "That was awfully neighborly of you, Anna."

"Wasn't it?"

"I thought you were bitter with her about her mother."

The sly expression on Anna's face said it all.

"Oh, Anna. You're not going to—"

"Aren't I?"

Kyle knocked once and opened the door. "Sorry I'm late. Hi, Rose." He kissed both women on the cheek. "You'll never believe what happened."

"My car keys?"

He hung them on the hook at the end of the kitchen cabinet. "We went up to Temple last night and—"

"Who's 'we?'" Rose asked.

Kyle hesitated and glanced at Anna who gave him the go-ahead. "Trey and I. Anyway, everything was fine. He took me to this quaint café downtown, and we took a seat by the front window."

"What was he wearing?" Anna asked.

"Um. Khakis and a striped button-down. Casual and sexy."

"Pleated?"

"Uh...no. Flat front."

"Good. Okay, go on."

"Yeah, go on," Rose cheered.

"Well, when we looked around the place, staring at him from across the café was none other than—Any guesses?"

"No. Who?"

"What about you, Rose?"

"Constance?"

"No, thank God. It was Stacy!"

"Get out of here!" Anna slapped the counter, moved the pot to an unlit burner, and removed her apron. "You're kidding me!"

"Can you believe it?"

"And then what happened?" Anna asked anxiously.

"We left. Trey went over and tried to explain but—Anna, you'll never believe who Stacy was with! Any guesses?"

"No, we don't know, Kyle," Rose barked. "Who? Who was she with?"

He looked back at Anna and flinched. "She was with Mark."

Anna, pretending the news hadn't phased her, tied her apron back on. "I'm going to add another jalapeño. That'd be all right wouldn't it, Rose?"

"Anna, Cupcake," Kyle walked into the kitchen and rubbed her shoulders as she chopped up another pepper. "Weren't you going to break it off with him anyway?"

"Yes, Kyle, I was. But *I* was going to do it. He wasn't supposed to cheat on me."

"What do you think, Rose...Rose?" Kyle snapped his fingers to get her attention.

"Stacy Stewart was cheating on Trey? I always thought they made such a happy couple. I guess you don't really know people."

"Uh, Rose. Do I need to remind you that I'm sleeping with Trey?"

Rose paused. "That's different."

Kyle glanced at a bewildered Anna. "How is that different?"

"Kyle, please. Uh, could you help me open these chips?"

"You think Mark will show up tonight?" Rose asked.

"Forget Mark. What about Stacy? She's bringing the meat!"

Anna reached for the cordless phone and asked Kyle for the number.

"Please, girl. When are you going to get a cellular phone?"

"Says the boy who just got one last month," Anna quipped.

"Stacy? Hi. It's Anna—Anna Aron. Listen, I just wanted to confirm you are coming to the party this evening. If you don't, we're not going to have anything to put in the tortillas. I'm already making the nacho cheese and we're all getting ready—"

"We call it *queso* here. And why wouldn't I come?" Stacy asked gleefully.

"Great. Can't wait to see you. And there's someone very special I want you to meet tonight."

"Someone for me to meet? What does that mean?"

"Not what you think. He's a student of mine. I think you might be able to help him."

"What makes you think that?"

"Just a hunch. I'll see you around seven-ish."

"Of course, Anna."

Anna gave a thumbs-up to Kyle and Rose. "Fine. Bye now." She hung up the phone. "That's weird, she sounded strangely normal...Who wants to run to the grocery store with me?"

In the kitchen, Stacy looked down at Stormy and turned to Trey. "We're *going* to the party. Get the pressure cooker out for me, dear sweet, betraying husband of mine," she ordered, pointing to the cabinet. He ran his fingers through the tips of her hair. "Don't you touch me, you son of a bitch!"

He backed off and retrieved the pressure cooker from the cabinet above the microwave.

Stacy took the beef from the refrigerator. "I should poison it and kill everyone."

"I don't think that'd do any good."

"What do you suggest we do then, Trey? Are we supposed to

keep up this charade we're playing...go on like everything is hunky-dory? Is that the answer? Or should we just go ahead and call Constance and let her do an up-close-and-personal interview? Let her into our bedroom to see how the happiest couple in Prairie Springs *really* lives. Is that what you want? Huh?" She slammed the meat onto the cutting board. "What I don't under-stand, Trey, is how you can—How could *I* have been so stupid? Why didn't you tell me, for God's sake? What did you think I was going to do to you? I've *always* told you your happiness meant the world to me. All I've ever wanted was for you—for us—to be happy. I can't help but think that I've done something wrong that made you not want to confide in me."

"It wasn't you, Stacy. Don't blame who I am, or what's happening, on yourself. You've been the perfect wife. It's me who's failed us. I've been deceitful, and you finally caught me. It's all me. It's my fault."

Stacy yanked the Tupperware spaghetti holder from the cabi-net, poured a shot of vodka, and trimmed the fat off the meat.

"I didn't know you drank."

"Apparently there's a lot we don't know about each other," Stacy whimpered.

"Are you crying?"

"Surely you're not surprised I'm showing some emotion. I do have feelings, you know. So basically, I've wasted all of my life loving you. You were just using me. You used me so no one in this town would ever suspect. Did you *ever* love me?"

"How can you say that? Of course I loved you—I still do. But before you go on accusing me of betrayal, remember I wasn't the only one on a date last night. If I remember correctly, you also had another man across from you at that table."

"Oh, Trey," she laughed. "What I had was an innocent cup of coffee, smart-ass." She conveniently left out what happened *after* coffee...in their house...in their bed.

"Where is this mouth coming from?"

"I'm out of character for the moment...And it feels divine! So don't tempt me or you will see the true flip side. And believe me, you don't want to go there."

"I'm going upstairs for a while."

"Yeah, you do that."

With all the apprehension in Prairie Springs, one thing was certain: Anna's holiday dinner party was sure to be a smash.

Chapter Sixteen

D orcas was afraid Frank would soon be in a hospital if he didn't watch what he ate. She was having second thoughts about her life-altering decision to leave Ted. Frank had regained eleven pounds four ounces of his former weight, which meant only one thing: he was cheating on her. There might not have been another woman, but somewhere, somehow, he was getting his hands on high-calorie snacks. If he ate behind her back, what else was he capable of? Without trust, relationship failure was guaranteed.

At least when Ted cheated on her, she knew who it was with. If Dorcas could have given one word of advice to Flo, it would be to not wear the same cheap White Diamettes perfume while waitressing as she did while whoring. Many a night, Ted came home smelling of the foul fragrance, but Dorcas never said a word; instead, she went to her most unwavering friend, the Pillsbury Doughboy, for consolation.

When Dorcas and Frank first dated, they did other things besides eat and dream of eating, and those were the things she missed. They'd go to plays at the Alley Theater, and afterwards walk around the corner to a cozy café and drink black coffee until the place closed. However, since they no longer lived at the camp and only had to attend weekly meetings, their relationship had devolved into dinner partners, one of whom was ordering heavy cream sauces and asking the waiter for more garlic breadsticks.

"Frank, sweetie. Do you really think you need any more of that bread? Careful with the calories and fat."

"Dammit, Dorcky! One little piece of bread ain't gonna hurt anything. This is a special occasion."

"Why? What are we celebrating?"

"Our love."

"Oh, give me a break," Dorcas responded. "You've been celebrating *our love* a lot lately. Are you trying to measure *our love* in inches?"

"You need to stop with the comments right now, Dorcky."

"I'm just trying to make a point."

"Well, do it quieter so the table behind you doesn't hear."

Dorcas turned and gasped...

Earlier that morning at the Third Baptist Church, members and non-members alike arrived ready for the annual trip to The Galleria shopping mall in Houston. These ladies were determined to show the cityfolk what fashion was really about. The only man present, aside from the bus driver and the young boys accompanying their mothers, sat in the rear of the bus in a daze as he stared out the window.

Constance was sporting a turquoise outfit, including matching gloves, scarf, and nylon coat.

"You going shopping or skiing?" someone quipped.

Constance overlooked the snide comment, and responded, "I'm surprised Stacy isn't here—she never misses this trip."

No sooner had they pulled onto the highway did the fun

begin. The most anticipated challenge was the Bible Drill. Crystal Stewart called out, "Galatians 5:12!"

Armed with red-letter editions of the King James Bible, the travelers hurried to find the verse. Bessy Mae yelled, "I got it: *I would that they were even cut off which trouble you.*"

"One point for Bessy Mae." Crystal Stewart made a mark in her notebook.

Having an unexpected day off was not a feeling Flo knew well. Always covering for others at work, she decided it was time to call in a favor. She started her day at Henna's getting her hair done. While she was under the hair dryer, she took advantage of the myriad beauty and fashion magazines to search for the ideal breasts. By the time the dryer cut off, she circled a couple of pictures and stuck the magazine in her purse.

At home, Tammy Wynette kept Flo company as she cleaned. Over the years, she had accumulated an abundance of tchotchke. Everywhere she looked—wall shelves, bookshelves, any free surface—she was reminded how much she despised dusting. After vacuuming, she leaned back on the blue vinyl sofa with her feet propped and woke an hour later. She shot up to make the guacamole for the party.

After an exhausting day at the Houston Galleria, the Prairie Springs church group, laden with shopping bags, crammed back onto the bus for dinner.

A painstaking poll to choose the restaurant was fruitless and resulted in asking the winner of the Bible drill: "Ted, what are you in the mood for?"

Little did he know his answer would seal the fate of not only the other passengers on the bus, but his own as well. "I-talian."

"Huh?"

"What? I didn't say anything," Anna replied.

"Oh my. I've reached the point of hearing things. I could've sworn you called my name."

"*Rose?*"

"Okay, now I *know* someone is calling me." She opened Anna's door to find Ivory and Ronald standing at the back of her house. "We're over here." Rose was delighted to see them both, but curtailed her exuberance. "Would you let Bitsy out for me?"

"Sure," Ivory answered.

Bitsy made a straight shot from Rose's back door to Anna's front door to slide between his mistress' feet.

"What did y'all bring?" Rose asked as they walked over.

"Ivory made her pecan pralines."

Rose wasn't prepared for the rapport that redeveloped between the old married couple. Unsure how to greet them, she hugged her sister and patted Ronald on the back.

"Ivory," Rose gestured. "This is Anna, my tenant from New York."

"That's right!" She quickly set the dish of pralines on the counter. "I'm from New York, too!"

"You are not," Ronald reminded her.

"Well, I practically am. I've lived there for half a year."

Anna looked intensely at Ivory. "I *do* remember you. It was at that bar near Christopher Street."

"What are you talking about?"

"That's where we saw you—Kyle and I. You got up on stage and sang with the drag queen."

"You were there? Well, for heaven's sake! What a small world. I had so much fun that night."

"What's a drag queen?" Rose queried.

"Honestly, Rose. You need to live a little—get out more. I thought everyone knew what a drag queen was," Ivory laughed.

A freshly showered Kyle came running down the outside stairs and barged into Anna's apartment smelling of shampoo and bath soap. "Sorry. Didn't know anyone had already arrived."

"Kyle," Anna said, "This is Ivory."

"Yes, we've met. The infamous Ivory Black—"

"I wouldn't say '*in*famous,'" she corrected. "You say we've met?"

"He was with me at the bar, Ivory."

"...And I also ran into you on the corner of Park and Twenty-third. I was coming out of Walgreens—?"

"Oh, that's right. Well, my stars! What are you doing here in this town?"

"Long, complicated story. Short version is I came down with Anna to help her move and ended up getting a job."

"Well, I just can't believe—Leaving the Big Apple for this place," Ivory commented.

"Give me a break, Ivory. You lived here your whole life," Rose replied.

"That's why I know what I'm talking about."

"I heard a car door," Anna announced.

"Bet it's Winnie." Rose went to the doorway and watched the gate. "Nope. Not her."

Stacy strutted through the yard with Trey by her side. "Look at what y'all've done to the place. It's absolutely lovely, Rose."

"It's the mayor and his wife," Rose whispered to the others. "How exciting is this!"

Stacy was a master at composing herself and appeared as though she hadn't a care in the world. Living in denial was a terrific gift she'd perfected during her years of matrimony.

"Hello, everyone..." Stacy greeted while searching for a place to rest the Pyrex dish of shredded beef. "Ivory. How *are* you doing? I hope you didn't hurt yourself when you fell."

"I'm fine now. Oh, that was so embarrassing. I shouldn't have worn Manilows to a simple cafe!"

Stacy looked puzzled. "Manilows?"

"I thought *you* would know, of all people. They're high heels, of course."

Stacy disguised her grin with a pucker. "I see. Well, down here in the South we're always the last to receive the latest fashions. But I'm glad you're back safely in town where you belong. I'm sure Ronald is thrilled to have you back."

"She's not staying," Ronald clarified.

Stacy frowned. "Not staying?"

"No, I go back to New York the day after Christmas."

"You don't say. Well, I'm sorry to hear that." Stacy darted glances at Ronald, hoping to figure out what was going on.

"May I take your coats?" Kyle offered.

"I hope the meat turned out to your liking, Anna," she said while removing her new leather coat.

"I'm sure it's great, Stacy, but I could really use your help. I should've started yesterday."

"Say no more." Stacy rolled up her sleeves and walked into the kitchen. Trey took a seat on the couch next to Kyle.

At precisely seven-thirty, a knock on the door signaled Judy Jane Johnson's arrival. She wore a green sweatshirt with a painted Christmas tree topped with a small bell, and a green skirt spangled with sequined presents. "I made it myself," she shamelessly admitted. "I brought three dozen Christmas cookies. I hope we'll have enough. I didn't know there would be so many people."

"It should be plenty," Anna assured her. "Thank you so much." She wiped her hands and signaled Kyle, who then reached for the car keys and excused himself.

"Where's he off to?" Rose asked.

"Don't worry. He'll be right back—Let's have something to drink."

Flo arrived in time to help with the drinks, sporting a Santa hat bobby-pinned over her bouffant hairdo and holding a frighteningly small bowl of guacamole.

While Anna's party was getting started, in Houston, after a short wait for a large table, the hungry Prairie Springs church group descended upon the Olive Grove Restaurant. Constance sat at the head of the table to keep an eye out for anything newsworthy. It didn't take long for her to overhear bickering from the table behind her.

She partially turned to have a better earshot of the goings-on and immediately recognized the voice. "Dorcas!" Her outburst silenced the loquacious group of Baptist women.

Ted was shocked by his new, thinner wife. "Honey?"

"You're going to have to excuse me," Dorcas told Frank.

"I assume that's Ted?"

She nodded. "What are the odds!"

Constance frantically searched for her feathery pen. There was nothing like being in the right place at the right time.

"Just sit tight while I grab the wheelchair from the trunk," Kyle said.

"This is too much trouble. Y'all are real sweethearts for doing this for me—including me in your festivities."

"Yeah, Anna's a good person." Kyle retrieved the wheelchair from the trunk with a final yank. He helped Mae Pearl into it. "It's gonna be a bumpy ride—hold on tight."

When Kyle backed Mae Pearl into Anna's apartment, Judy Jane Johnson was in deep conversation with Trey, hoping to persuade him to redo the city-owned piece of property next to the bank so she would have a prettier view from the teller window. As Kyle wheeled her across the floor, Judy Jane Johnson's mouth fell open...to the extent it could.

Anna casually introduced her to the guests, "This is my friend, Mae Pearl Fisher. I visit with her at Golden Years quite often."

"I told her it was too much trouble, but she insisted." In the commotion, Mae Pearl hadn't noticed her daughter stood only feet away.

"Mother?"

"JJ?"

Judy Jane glared at Anna. "You set this up, didn't you?"

"Set what up?" Anna replied in her most innocent voice.

Her calmness only added fuel to Judy Jane Johnson's fire. "That woman is a lesbian!"

Winnie barged through the door with Maxine and Luciano a step behind. "Merry fuckin' Christmas, everyone!"

After some time alone together outside, Ted and Dorcas returned to the dining room holding hands. The others were well into their meals as the couple released hands to sit at their corresponding tables.

Constance gave her sister's new svelte body the evil eye as she reached for her pen and pad and turned to Ted. "Tell me, Ted...Did you have any idea Dorcas would be here? Is that why you picked Italian food? Was Dorcas glad to see you? Are you getting back together with your wife? Is the divorce off...?"

Ted ignored Constance's interrogation and ate a slice of cold pizza.

Seeing she was getting nowhere with him, the unstoppable reporter turned to her sister. "Did you know Ted would be here? Did you set this meeting up? Who are you with this evening? What was said when you and Ted—"

"Get a life!" Dorcas snapped as she shifted in her chair. "And a new dress, for heaven's sake. Turquoise isn't your color."

"I guess this means we're over?" Frank commented.

"Oh, Frank, I'm sorry. I had no idea I missed him so much. I hope you understand."

Frank grabbed another breadstick and signaled the waiter. "Can I see the dessert cart?"

As fun as it had been, Dorcas knew her emotions regarding Frank were shallow. Suddenly it was all very clear: her running away to Houston...allowing herself to be with Frank was all an attempt to make Ted jealous and appreciative of her.

The church group's table was empty, save for a few to-go boxes. Ted informed Crystal Stewart, the preacher's wife, that he would be staying behind with Dorcas. "I won't hear of it. There's room on the bus for Dorcas."

Dorcas left Frank where he was happiest: sitting in front of an infinite supply of breadsticks.

The last guests to arrive were Ricky Richards and Roberto and his family, who brought tortillas and tamales. Anna hadn't taken into account the limited capacity of her small apartment when making the guest list, and moved the party outside. Ronald and Trey set up folding chairs next to the garden benches.

Kyle put on holiday music, and Rose offered refills of Anna's delicious punch. Stacy, searching for a place to sit, approached the chair next to Ricky Richards.

"Hi, Ricky. Do you mind if I sit here?"

"No ma'am."

"Isn't this a lovely party? Are you having a nice time?"

"I guess."

"It's a shame there aren't others here your age."

"I don't mind. I like older people. People my age don't understand me."

"Do you have a girlfriend?"

"No ma'am."

"Well, Ricky, I'm surprised to hear that. Someone as handsome as you are—"

"Girls don't understand me either."

"You don't have much in common with the other kids?"

"No...not really."

Stacy took a bite of her taco. "I'm so hungry I could eat the plate. I don't think I've ever *been* so hungry. It's like I'm completely empty inside."

"Everything okay over here?" Trey innocently asked as he made his way around to greet everyone.

Stacy glared at him. "Why would you ask that? Ricky and I are just talking."

"Trey, bring me a chair, would ya?" Winnie asked as she approached the trio. "I'm gonna sit here next to Stacy and my friend, Ricky...Who was it Anna wanted you to meet?"

"I dunno. I know everyone here."

Trey brought over a chair and excused himself. "Thank you, doll," Winnie told him.

"Did y'all close the café this evening?" Stacy asked Winnie.

"We opened this morning but closed early. With half the flippin' town on the shopping trip and the other half here, we didn't think it was worth staying open for."

"Prairie Springs isn't *that* small," Stacy defended.

"Yes it is," Ricky retorted.

"Ricky is having a hard time with his sexuality and feels trapped."

Ricky scowled at Winnie. "Stop telling people. How could you tell her that?"

"'Cause it's the truth and—What do you mean? Stacy here is the first person I've told, and I'm only telling her 'cause she can help you."

"You can make me well?"

"Well—I, uh..." Stacy inhaled a breath of confidence. "You aren't sick, Ricky dear."

"Hah!" Winnie interrupted. "He ain't all well, though. Yesterday I found him ready to dangle himself from a tree limb."

Stacy gasped. "Is that true, Ricky?"

Ricky lowered his head.

"Do your parents know?"

Winnie snapped. "What kind of fuckin' question is that? Oh,

sorry. What kind of *question* is that? You think he walked in and said, 'Mommy, Daddy, I was just about to hang myself when some old lady stopped me?'"

"I was just asking. Don't you think they should know?"

"That I was going to kill myself? I'm going to get another Coke."

Winnie waited until Ricky walked to the ice chest. "Here's your chance to do something good for someone, woman. Don't go and blow it!"

Stacy proudly straightened her posture with a premature sense of accomplishment.

Kyle met Ricky at the drink table.

"Hey, Ricky. How's it going?"

"Fine, I guess."

"You having a good time?"

"Not really."

Kyle scooped out a refill of punch for himself. "You know something, Ricky? I was wondering if you'd be interested in helping me out with some landscaping jobs. I could use someone strong like you to help with moving dirt and stuff like that. Would you be interested?"

"Sure, I guess." Ricky's eyes danced. He couldn't believe he was being asked to work with this handsome man who could've easily been one of the models from his catalog. It was a dream come true. He remembered what Winnie had told him, *Change is always around the corner.*

"Don't sound *too* excited."

Ricky smiled. "I mean—that'd be great."

"Good. I'll be glad to have some help."

Even though he didn't want to leave Kyle's company, Ricky excused himself back to his plate of food where Winnie and Stacy were sitting. When he returned, Stacy stood and hugged him, "It's going to be okay, Ricky. You are in a safe place here. Being with people who won't judge you is everything. We all love you exactly as you are, and know this: There is a world waiting for you."

"I'll leave you two alone. I'm going to go pay my respects to Louise." Winnie walked over and picked some leaves from the plant growing on the fertile soil when Maxine joined her. "Oh nuts, child! You scared me!"

"*Weed*ing the garden?"

"I guess you could say that," Winnie giggled.

"Hi, Mama."

Winnie wrapped her arm around Maxine's waist.

"I'm glad she's scattered here," Maxine said. "At least she's not lying in a cemetery, huh?"

"I got Humphrey under a tree. When I go, I hope someone doesn't put me in some frickin' cemetery in the blazing sun next to someone I don't know and probably didn't want to."

Anna walked over. "You guys having a nice time? Can I get you anything?"

"Oh, honey. It's a real nice party."

Thanks Winnie.

"Thanks. But what a shame Judy Jane Johnson didn't stay long enough to loosen up. She hardly spoke to Mae Pearl."

"I don't know what's wrong with people. Fuckin' nut-jobs, I tell ya."

"Winnie, how did *you* turn out so different than everyone else?" Maxine asked.

"Oh, child, I decided living my own life was much more fun than living everyone else's." Winnie pointed her head. "Looks like Ricky and Stacy are getting close. Poor boy."

"I think it might help them both. They're each going through a difficult time." Anna bit at a fingernail and excused herself.

Flo, who had connected a space heater outside, was sitting on the single step to her cabin keeping Mae Pearl company when Anna passed. Flo casually pointed to her breasts. "Hey shoog, don't forget we have our appointment the day after New Year's."

"No, beautiful, I haven't forgotten."

Judy Jane Johnson paced back and forth in her living room, fuming. *How dare she bring my mother? The nerve! And at this holy time of year! I can't let this go on right next door!* She picked up the phone and called the police. "I'd like to report an out-of-control party next door. The music is so loud I can't hear myself think. What kind of town has this turned into?...I don't know. Sounds like gangster music, ya know, rap, or whatever it's called...And hurry!"

She climbed the stairs to her bedroom where she had a great view of the action from her window.

In ten minutes, Officer Richards showed up at the lychgate. Stacy, certain he'd come for his son, squeezed Ricky's hand in support.

"We got a call that y'all are disturbing the neighbors."

"And what's *your* take on the situation? Flo asked. The *crickets* are louder than we are."

"Ricky? What's going on here? Why are you with all of these adults?"

"Ms. Aron invited me."

"She did, did she? Well, you're coming home with me."

"No, I'm not."

"Yes, you are, and don't talk to me like that."

"I'm not going anywhere. Why would I go home?"

"Listen to me, you little faggot! What you need is a good whupping!"

"What's the problem, Officer Richards?" Trey interrupted.

"What's the problem? I'll tell you what the problem is—my son is a queer. Did everyone hear that? My boy is a queer faggot! Why don't we ask these people what should happen to you, Ricky? I'm sure they'd agree the devil's got a hold on you, son, and that hold has to be broken, even if I have to beat it out of you."

Rose, Ivory, and Ronald sat silently by the fountain. Mae Pearl and Flo huddled near the space heater. Maxine and Winnie watched from the rear of the yard, while Trey and Kyle stood near

Anna. Roberto, his family, and Luciano, most of whom were undocumented, stood as far out of sight as possible.

All eyes were on Officer Richards as "Silent Night" played on the speakers.

"This is all y'all's fault," he said, pointing to Anna and Kyle. "This town was a respectable place before you Yankees strolled in. Y'all probably think this is funny...or...or cute or something." He faced his son. "Did these Yankees touch you?"

Ricky shook his head.

"I'm going to arrest them anyway for disturbing the peace."

Officer Richards reached for his handcuffs. He winked at his fellow Armadillo, Trey, as he cuffed Kyle's right hand. Stacy suddenly wasn't the only victim of Trey's double life.

"If my homosexual husband isn't going to say anything," Stacy spoke up, "then I will."

Officer Richards looked at Trey in shock. "Is that true?"

"No, of course it's not true," Trey scoffed with a chuckle.

Officer Richards continued with Kyle's left hand. "I should hope not!"

Trey watched as the officer snapped the cuffs tightly around his boyfriend's wrists.

"Wait! It *is* true. If you're going to arrest anyone, arrest me."

Stacy gasped. "How dare you say such a thing, dear! Being gay isn't a crime—it's perfectly natural. What's not natural is for you to marry a woman, lie to her for years, and end up breaking her heart. But that's beside the point."

Officer Richards eyed Trey up and down. "I can't believe what I'm hearing! Does Brother Stewart know about—? You people are all *sick!*"

Flo stomped out her cigarette in anger and stood. "Of all the —Get the hell out of here you two-bit hypocrite! If you want to discuss *sick* then we can discuss how you pay me to dress up like a superhero so you can poke me with your petite penis while you shoot me with a water gun."

Ricky couldn't restrain a snicker and quickly covered his mouth.

Officer Richards turned redder than his lace panties.

"What?" Rose said, stunned.

"Yes. It's true. I'm a whore—a lowlife tramp!"

"Don't talk like that, dammit! You're a fuckin' princess!" Winnie yelled. "I won't hear of this nonsense anymore!" She jammed the fresh cannabis leaves into her sweater pocket and stepped nearer to the action. "You get the hell outta here!" she told Officer Richards while waving a crooked finger. "You've gone and messed with the wrong people! And so help me, if you cause any problems it will be the last thing you do."

Outnumbered, Officer Richards exited through the lychgate. Judy Jane Johnson flung open the window and yelled, "What's wrong with you, you yellow-belly!"

"Lord have mercy." Stacy squeezed Ricky's hand. "You're going to stay here with us."

"My stars! This place is more entertaining than New York City," Ivory noted to Ronald.

As the others talked amongst themselves, Trey comforted an exhausted Winnie by putting his arm around her in a private, intimate moment.

"I'm proud of you, boy," Winnie told him softly.

Trey leaned and kissed her on the cheek.

"It doesn't bother you about me being gay?"

"I'm staring death at the door and you're asking me if I'm upset that my grandbaby is happy? Do you think there's anything more on this earth I would want for you...or for anyone?"

"You're something else, you know that, Winn —Grandmother?" Trey couldn't defend, or erase, how bitterly he'd treated his own flesh and blood in the past by attempting to ignore her existence, but he knew he had to change. It was high time he formed his own opinion about his grandmother instead of abiding by his parents' negative innuendos.

Winnie smiled. "So fuckin' formal? Whadaya think about Granny, or Grams?"

"I like Grams...*Grams*."

Winnie burst into a smile. Trey pulled her close and gave his grandmother a long overdue hug.

"Pralines, anyone?" Kyle announced, holding up a small platter, one handcuff dangling from his wrist. "I don't suppose anyone has a key?"

"I do!" Flo shouted. "I've got it in my nightstand drawer."

"Well," Anna said to Maxine, "I think everyone's having a nice time. Don't you?"

Chapter Seventeen

E arly the next morning, a noise outside provoked Anna to investigate. She stepped out in her robe to find Rose picking up cups and collecting trash from the party. "Thank you, Rose. But you don't have to do that."

"I don't mind, angel. Put on some coffee. We've got to talk."

Anna scratched her forehead. "I have a pot brewing now." She stuck two slices of bread in the toaster and opened a jar of the dewberry preserves Rose had given her. Anna had two clean cups on the counter when Rose came inside.

"What's up?" Anna asked.

"Nothing, dear. Is the coffee ready?"

"Almost."

Rose took a seat at the dining table. "So did, uh—did you know about Flo?"

"Is that what you wanted to talk about?"

"I just wondered if you knew, is all."

"I just recently found out."

"But you knew?"

"Yes, I knew."

Rose wiped the table with her hand as if sweeping away imaginary crumbs. "I just can't figure out why she would keep it from me. I thought we were friends."

Anna took the coffee to the table along with the sugar bowl and the carton of milk. "I don't know, Rose. But you need to keep in mind that only until recently, you were—How should I say this?—You've changed a lot in the past few months. Flo probably didn't feel comfortable—I'd bet she didn't want to upset you."

"You think so?"

"I'm sure of it." She returned with the toast and preserves.

"What do you think about the whole thing? Were you surprised when *you* found out?"

"Sure I was surprised, but Kyle had seen men coming and going and, well, I put the pieces together. I'm surprised you didn't put two and two together that night you saw her dressed as Wonder Woman when Ricky Richards was trying to kill me. Remember...? And Officer Richards was wearing lingerie...Ring a bell?"

"She said it was laundry day. I didn't know what to make of it all. It may be too much for me to be comfortable with. What do you think I should do? You're more experienced in these things than I am."

"What does that mean? I'm not a prostitute nor have I ever—"

"Oh no, dear. I didn't mean *that*. I just mean you have more experience with different people and different...things."

"I don't think you should worry yourself with what someone else does. She's still the same Flo she was before you found out. The only difference is now it's out in the open."

"I guess you're right. I hope it doesn't make any problems for us with the police and all."

"I don't think you have to worry about that either. It's not like Officer Richards is going to say anything since he's—or he was—one of her clients."

"Yeah, I reckon not." Rose took a sip of coffee. "I see you've barely touched the preserves. Don't you like them?"

"Too much. I'm rationing so I don't run out."

"Please. There are more where those came from."

"I would love another jar. I'd be happy to pay you."

"You will do no such thing! So what time did, uh, Ricky leave? I hope he didn't get a beating."

Anna looked down at her toast. "He never left. He stayed with Kyle."

"With Kyle!"

"Don't even think it, Rose. It was just for one night and only to keep him safe. Winnie is coming to get him while his parents are at church. That way he can swing by his house and pick up a few things."

"He's gonna stay with Winnie?"

"Yep. That's who he said he wanted to stay with."

"Huh! How do you like that?"

Anna spread a knife full of preserves across her toast.

For the first time in many weeks, Dorcas slept in her own familiar, cozy bed. When she awoke, she expected Ted to greet her with a thousand kisses. He wasn't even in the room. Disappointed, a deluge of doubts assailed her. Unwilling to accept the absent celebration for her return, she crawled out of bed hoping for banners, balloons, and other expressions of her husband's undying love to be scattered about the house.

To her dismay, there was nothing out of the ordinary. She found him in the garage cleaning up one of his messes. "Good morning. I hope you shower before church," a gloomy Dorcas admonished.

"Good morning, sweetheart. I'll bathe, don't worry."

Dorcas mustered a smile. "Did you want something for breakfast?"

"Sure could use *something* in my stomach."

She went back inside and fried up two eggs and three strips of bacon, and made oatmeal for herself.

The smell of bacon lured Ted inside. He hung his favorite denim baseball cap by the door. "Dorcas, I was wondering what you'd think about getting away this Christmas instead of exchanging gifts? I thought we might go someplace you've always wanted to go." He wrapped his arms around her as she cooked.

"Do you mean it, Ted? Really? San Francisco?"

He took a seat at the table. "Uh...I was thinking more along the lines of Galveston."

"Galveston? Why on earth would I wanna go there? If you love me, you'll take me to San Francisco."

He took a tissue from his pocket and blew his nose. "Fine. San Francisco it is."

Dorcas, still holding the spatula, jumped up and down and sent a piece of bacon flying across the room. "This is great, Teddy. An airplane and all?"

"Yep."

"I can hardly wait!" Concocted images of San Francisco filled her head. Her eyes danced back and forth as if reading the air. Suddenly, reality sobered her enthusiasm and robbed her dreamy expression. "Won't it be too expensive?" She bent down and picked the bacon up off the floor, rinsed it, and put it on the plate.

"No doubt about that. That's why I was thinking about someplace closer."

"I guess we could go somewhere closer, but not Galveston. Please not Galveston. What about Corpus Christi...or San Antonio?"

"No, if you wanna go to San Francisco, then that's where we'll go."

"I can't wait to tell everyone at church."

His forced grin vanished when he looked down at his breakfast plate. "What happened?"

"Happened? Oh, the bacon. Sorry, but crispier is better for you. They taught us at camp to burn it."

He nibbled a piece. "Tastes like those fake bacon bits. Maybe next time we can try sausage?"

Life was full of lessons to be learned, much more profound than fully cooked bacon. Anna learned that a lengthy guest list wasn't always ideal, nor were unannounced family reunions. Ivory learned that her happiness depended on no one other than herself and was counting the days until her return to New York. Ricky Richards learned the family he was born into might not be the one that loved him the most. But not everyone was ripe for the teaching. Officer Richards knew exactly what he had to do to stop his son from embarrassing him. He mulled over his plan as he sat on his porch polishing his gun. Behind the secret hutch at the Theater Café, Winnie was less concerned with sheen and more concerned with purpose. Bullet by bullet, she loaded the chamber.

Anna's party, as controversial as it turned out to be, had one positive result: Trey and Stacy could converse without yelling at one another. The turbulent couple skipped church and spent the morning extracting emotions so deep they had to pause to maintain their composure. It upset her more that she had been lied to than it did that her husband was gay...or that he smoked on occasion. After a long silence, Trey said, "I need some air." Stacy, with Stormy at her feet, followed him outside and watched him light a cigarette.

"I slept with Mark. I just want you to know."

"What?" He chuckled. "You did not."

"Why would you say that? I'm telling you I did."

"You're just trying to get back at me."

"Trey, dear, I slept with him...in *our* bed."

Trey had years to come to grips with what he was doing and the surreptitious way he snuck out of town to do it, but he thought Stacy dropping this bombshell was tactless. "Trollop!"

"Fag!"

The only sound for a while was a steady purr coming from an unfazed Stormy.

Trey walked over to the pool and stared at the water. "You know what we need?"

"A divorce?"

"No. To go skinny-dipping."

"I'm hardly in the mood, Trey."

"Come on. It'll be good for us. We've got to find a way to enjoy each other."

She sat petting Stormy and watched as Trey unbuttoned and took off his shirt. She pretended not to look when his khakis fell to his ankles. "It'll be more fun if we both do it, Stace." He stepped out of his pants and walked over, took Stormy from her lap, and helped her up.

"It's too cold," she whined.

"The pool is heated. Once we get in, you'll be fine."

He undressed her and took off his underwear. They both stood naked on the pool deck. "This is who we are," he said. "Look at us. Call me a fag now."

"I can't," she murmured.

He pulled her close. "Stacy, I wished to God I could love you the way you deserve to be loved, but it's not—"

She held up a finger to his mouth to shush him.

He tenderly ran his finger down her shoulder blade. "You have to forgive me for the hurt I've caused. I couldn't live with myself if you don't. I'm sorry. Can you forgive me?"

She could only offer a slight nod of the head. It was enough of a confirmation for him to hug her.

When he released his embrace, she looked down and grinned. "Looks like I'm not the only one who's cold."

Trey cringed at his shrinking manhood, grabbed her, and jumped into the pool.

"Missing Woman Reunites with Husband on Church Shopping Trip." It was such a heartwarming story, Constance considered not printing it. But when she added a line about Dorcas' weight loss and a statistic on how many people regain the weight, she sent it to the press. After all, there were too many witnesses to not mention Dorcas' return to Prairie Springs. News was news, after all. As it played out, Constance's petty concern had been in vain. A tornado pegged a nearby county, topping the news and depriving her sister of any front-page publicity.

Dorcas was somewhat compensated when the preacher at the Third Baptist Church invited both her and Ted to stand before the congregation to give thanks to the Lord Almighty for their reunion.

Brother Stewart couldn't let this opportunity slip by without asking for money. "Look what the Lord did for Ted and Dorcas—twice! If you give at least forty-eight dollars—That's the number the Lord is showing me—you will meet your mate. I'm sure of it."

The preacher forcefully patted Ted on the shoulder. "Ted, would you mind leading us in prayer?"

Gently pushing Ted aside, Dorcas took the microphone, "I'll say the prayer."

"That is reserved for deacons. You are welcome to make the announcements for the Third Base Ladies League."

Brother Stewart took the microphone from Dorcas and handed it back to Ted.

"Let us pray," Ted announced.

Empowered by her weight loss, Dorcas snatched the microphone from Ted and said, "What you're saying is that God doesn't want to hear women pray? Or are you just saying, Brother

Stewart, that it's okay for us to drop our money in the offering plate as long as we don't open our mouths?"

"Calm down, Dorcas," Ted said under his breath, which was broadcast as a loud whisper over the PA system.

"I will not calm down—And furthermore..." she turned to the congregation, "I know most of y'all are wondering who the other man was. Well, y'all can just keep wondering. But before you cast your sanctimonious glances at me, you'd better find a mirror...and I mean real quick. In Jesus' name, Amen."

Dorcas Bledsoe held the distinction of being the first and only woman to preach at the Third Baptist Church.

Monday, December 22, 2007

Maxine was taking Spanish lessons twice a week in hopes of a possible trip to Argentina. It was a slow process, and she barely advanced past *me llamo Maxine, gracias,* and *por favor.* Since the party, Roberto and Luciano had become good buddies, and while Maxine couldn't understand what they were talking about, the one word that stuck out in the mumbo-jumbo was "*linda.*" She was convinced Luciano was cheating on her.

It was during one of her lessons when Anna and Rose happened to drop by the café.

"Where's Maxine?" Anna asked Winnie, who was working the register.

Winnie pointed to a table. Maxine sat studying a book with Roberto's aunt, who was tickled pink at the idea of earning ten dollars an hour plus free drinks and desserts for her services.

"What can I get you two lovely young ladies?"

Rose was taken aback by Winnie's compliment, although she had spent the last hour poking at her hair, powdering her face and changing skirts three times. Anna, on the other hand, threw on some jeans and a sweatshirt and pulled her hair into a ponytail.

"I'll have a latte," Anna ordered, but continued perusing the pastries. "Go ahead, Rose. I haven't decided what I want to eat."

"Let me have a hot chocolate and three donut holes."

"Oh. That sounds good. I always forget about hot chocolate. I'll have the same, but I'll take a slice of the pecan pie. You know what? Go ahead and add on the chicken salad sandwich and a glass of water."

Rose reached in her wallet but Anna stopped her. "My treat, Rose...to thank you for helping clean up."

While Winnie prepared their orders, Rose asked about Ricky. Winnie quickly hushed her. "Not now. He's with someone."

"*With* someone?"

Winnie hushed her again. "That'll be nine seventy-eight," She hurried them along when another customer approached.

"Let's sit by Maxine and see what she's up to," Rose suggested.

"How about let's sit over here and let everyone wonder what *we're* up to. Anyway, if she wanted to learn Spanish, why didn't she ask me? I would've taught her for free."

Anna directed Rose's attention to the hutch just as Stacy emerged. Stacy caught them eyeing her. She winked and joined them.

"I think he's going to be fine," Stacy reported. "He's such a dear boy, and our sessions will be good for both of us."

"I'm so glad," Anna said.

"Oh, about him being a..." Rose lowered her voice, "...a homosexual?"

Anna nodded and took Rose's hand in a sympathetic gesture.

Stacy wiped a pie crust crumb from Anna's chin. "You know what I was thinking, Anna? Since everybody and his dog seems to all of a sudden be gay in this town—it makes me wonder how many more people are scared out of their wits to wake up each morning. How willing would you be—I know this is risky—but how willing would you be to head up a group for teens at the school? Before you answer, I've been thinking about it, and I'm sure Maxine and Winnie would let us meet here. I mean even if only one person came, it'd be worth it, don't you think? I don't want you to risk your job by handing out fliers or anything like that. But maybe you could, you know, just leave a stack of them somewhere, and they could get passed around on their own."

"I dunno, Stacy. I think it's a great idea. I really do. It's just that—"

"I think it's a swell idea, Anna," Rose added.

"You do?"

"Of course. And Kyle could help out like a counselor or something. It'd be interesting to see who comes."

"Yes, it would," Stacy agreed. "And I want these kids to know they have a place to turn, instead of a tree branch or pill bottles."

"I'll think about it," Anna said.

"What's there to think about?" Rose pressed.

Anna could not believe Rose was the same person who had forbidden Kyle to stay at her place for fear of what the neighbors might think.

"Fine. I'll do it."

"Great." Stacy stood. "Wish I could stay and talk some more, but I've got to get going. I need to finish planning the Christmas parade. I'll be in touch." On her way out, she passed Maxine by the counter. *"¡Hola!"*

"¡Hola!" A sense of achievement overcame Maxine. Her lessons were paying off. She was practically bilingual!

CHAPTER EIGHTEEN

CHRISTMAS EVE

"I'm glad we stopped so I could get a Diet Coke. I'd bet they are expensive inside the airport—Look at how big it is, Ted. To think that all of these people are going somewhere exciting...Do we go in any door? Let me see what the ticket—" Dorcas collided with a woman exiting; her Diet Coke sloshed onto the stranger's jacket. "Oh my gosh! I'm so sorry! It's a good thing it's diet. At least it won't be sticky."

"Dammit! You should watch where you're going."

"There's no need for cussing, especially on Christmas Eve. It's just a drop. It'll wash right out." She hurried Ted along. "Go on, honey. We have to catch our flight!"

"I knew you were going to spill that."

"It's not my fault. She should watch where she's going! With those big ol' sunglasses she probably didn't even see me—Oh, this is so exciting! Don't you think, Ted? How does everyone know where to go, for goodness' sake? It's a good thing we got here early. What time is it anyhow?"

"Ten-thirty."

"Good. Then we've got three hours. With the lines and all, it might take us two of those just to get to the counter. We'd better get a move on."

"Did you pack my hemorrhoid cream?"

"Ted, don't say that out loud. Yes, I packed it."

"What about my Geritol?"

"Good grief, honey! How old *are* you? Can't you think of something besides your medication? People might think we escaped from a nursing home."

"I just don't want to forget anything."

"Well, if we have, I'm sure there'll be pharmacies in San Francisco for all your ailments—anal and otherwise."

The line moved quickly. A mere ten minutes passed before a perky lady in a navy-blue polyester suit welcomed them. "Where are you flying today?"

"Well, believe it or not, I used to be fat. Big as a house—or a heifer—as my husband, Ted, used to say. And then, well, I checked myself into Slimming Acres. Ya know, a camp where they teach you what foods to eat and stuff, make you exercise and do activities. Anyway…Well, to make a long story short—"

"I'm sorry, ma'am. I'd love to hear the story, but since there are other people who have flights to catch, if I could just have your photo IDs?"

Dorcas continued, "We've never flown before. There are a lot of people. Is it always this busy? I've never seen so many suitcases in my life. My, my. This'll be our first Christmas we haven't spent in Prairie Springs. I suppose they celebrate Christmas in San Francisco. Don't you, Ted? I hope there's a Christmas tree or at least some colorful lights on our hotel. You did bring the reservation with you, didn't you, dear…? Ted? Yoo-hoo? Do you have the hotel reservation number or whatever they gave you?"

"Yes, yes," Ted said abruptly as he strained to hear the ticket agent.

"A gate still hasn't been assigned since it's a bit early. Make sure to check the monitors."

"Okay. Thank you...Come on, Dorcas."

They walked away with their carry-ons.

"What monitors, Ted? What's she talking about? Go back and ask her. I told you we were getting here too early. What are we going to do for the next—What time is it?"

"Ten forty-five."

"Shoot! That was fast. We've *still* got nearly three hours. Did you bring a book or something to read? Word finds? Oh, look, a McDonald's! We could get breakfast."

"They stopped serving it at ten-thirty."

"That's right, I shouldn't eat there anyway. Do you know how much fat is in those biscuits?"

Ted paused. "There's a TV screen. You think that's what the lady was talking about?"

"Yeah. I'd spect so. Is our flight up there yet?"

"I'm looking, Dorcas, I'm looking!" he snapped.

"Well you don't have to bark at me."

"I'm not barking, I'm just—I can't concentrate with you yapping like that. What's wrong with you?"

"I'm just nervous, is all. I've never flown before, much less gone to a different state. We don't even know what kind of people might be there. What if they don't like us?"

"I told you we should have just gone down to Galveston. It would've been less stressful."

"I've got to find a bathroom. Come on, Ted."

Anna and Kyle walked in the door to Anna's apartment and both headed for the sofa. "I can't wait to get out of these shoes! That was one boring Christmas parade." Anna untied her ankle boots and used her feet to kick them off.

"Yes it was, but Stacy and Trey certainly played the part, didn't they? I don't think anyone suspected a thing." Kyle walked over to the kitchen. "What are you doing?"

"Getting us some entertainment." He pulled the joint from a plastic zip bag, lit it, and took a drag. He passed it to Anna as he sat back down on the couch. She coughed on the first puff, exhaling like a car with an exhaust issue, but found the second try easier. They sat quietly.

"Gosh, Kyle, the silence is nice, right? I hate those *Feliz Navidad* singing floats."

"At least I will never forget how to say Merry Christmas in Spanish."

"That's for sure. I hope it doesn't play in my head all day." Anna giggled, "That poor elf on top of the DeLorean when it overheated. Did you ever see a kid run so fast?"

"And what about Ed Stewart's car? That was a little extravagant for a preacher and his wife."

"What's her name? Do you know?"

"Crystal."

"Oh, right. I knew that...Speaking of cars, my favorite was the pink Lincoln. Did you get any of those lotion samples she was throwing out?"

Trey pulled one from his back pocket and handed it to Anna. "You can have mine." Printed on the small foil packet was her information. "Wait. Her name is Mary Kay and she sells makeup? What are the chances?"

"Do you miss New York?" Anna asked.

"Dang, that came out of nowhere. I miss being in New York and seeing all the different cultures. But I like it here for other reasons. It's much easier to get around and I can sing in the work truck and nobody can hear me."

"Yeah...I know what you're saying...What are we talking about?"

Kyle stared blankly at Anna. "*Feliz Navidad.*"

Anna laughed. "*Feliz Navidad* to you, too. This is nice."

A knock on the door had them scrambling to hide the evidence, but even that produced more giggles than results. "Just a minute!" Kyle shouted.

After disposing of the joint in a potted plant, he opened the door.

"Who is it?" Anna asked.

Kyle stood silently.

Anna staggered her way to the door. "Mom?"

Abigail Aron pivoted her big, black sunglasses to the top of her head. "Season's greetings!...What's that smell?"

Mae Pearl and Agnes settled in for their mid-afternoon nap. The nurse had closed the curtain that separated them. "I love you," Mae Pearl said as Agnes drifted to sleep.

"Love you, too," she mumbled.

Mae Pearl picked up The Grabber and pulled open the dividing curtain. She loved watching Agnes sleep, and spent hours gazing at her partner. Agnes slept more and more, but that didn't matter to Mae Pearl. Her presence in the room was reason enough to continue living.

Mae Pearl also drifted off, but woke with a start. She instinctively knew she was hearing Agnes' final breath.

She propped herself on her elbows and used The Grabber to nudge her. "Agnes, baby! Not on Christmas Eve!" Mae Pearl sat alone with her partner until she ran out of tears. She blew her nose and buzzed the nurses.

They quickly pulled the sheet over Agnes' head as if hiding her would make the pain go away. Mae Pearl watched as they pushed her out on a gurney, covered from head to toe. *Where are they taking her? God, please not into a dark room. Agnes hates the dark.*

Mae Pearl had waited many years to be with Agnes in a place where they could love freely, roam in the gardens, lie next to streams, and mingle with the angels. That evening, after writing a note, she prayed as she had never prayed before. "Take me home. Take me home. Take me home. Sweet Jesus, take me home."

It's been said one cannot die from a broken heart, but Mae Pearl proved that old adage wrong. Clutching the note, her heart slowly came to a rest, and her soul was set free.

CHAPTER NINETEEN

CHRISTMAS DAY

Ricky Richards' absence had his mother, Vivian, pacing the floor. It was one thing that her son had been gone the week leading up to December 25ᵗʰ, but seeing the unopened gifts under the tree was too much. She wondered if he even missed them. Neglecting her tradition of making a coconut pie and dressing up for the posed Christmas pictures, she moped around the house in her robe, pleading with God to send her son home. Her husband, on the other hand, didn't appear to be bothered in the least by his missing son.

"I've half a mind to go over to Rose's and demand she tell me where he is," Vivian told her husband.

"Let him be. He's made his decision. He's chosen to follow the Devil, and as painful as it is, we can't have him...*contaminating* our lives."

"Don't say that!" she cried.

"Just because you don't want to hear it doesn't mean it

shouldn't be said. We did the best we could, Viv, but from here on out he's on his own, and we'll have nothing more to do with him."

"Don't you care where he is? What if he's hungry? I don't even want to think what those—those Yankees are doing to him."

"You hit the nail on the head. This would have never happened if those Yankees hadn't come to town. We should've done more to scare them away. I've got to do something before they indoctrinate someone else's kid." He stood and reached for his jacket behind the door.

"Oh, honey, what are you going to do? Don't go and do anything stupid."

Officer Richards put on his cowboy hat. "I'll be back."

Anna awoke and looked around her bedroom, confused. She had no memory of getting in bed. The last thing she recalled was lighting up a joint with Kyle.

She followed the enticing aroma of bacon. "Mom!"

"Good morning, angel. I'm preparing us a nice kosher breakfast," she said flippantly. "Did you sleep well?"

"What? Huh? Yeah. Why are you here?"

"What kind of a question is that? Aren't you glad I'm here? If not, I'll just pack up my suitcase, ride that horrible bus back to Austin and make the nearly four-hour flight to New York."

"Was the trip that bad?"

"I wasn't going to mention it, but if you don't love me and don't want me here, there's a number of ways I could've better spent my time and money."

Anna let out an exasperated sigh. "Of course I want you here...I just wished you would've called first. Honestly, how on earth did you find your way?"

"I'm not completely senseless, you know. I had your address, and once I arrived, I went into that highway diner where the bus stops, and a nice waitress helped me. She said she lives here, too. Do you know her? Quite a character. We're going to have dinner here this evening. Would you like to join us?"

"Dinner with Flo? Here?"

"So, you *do* know her—And your landlady is sweet. She could use some fashion tips but—Speaking of fashion, don't you own a comb?"

Anna ran her fingers through her disheveled hair in an attempt to tame it. "I just woke up."

"You aren't using cheap shampoos are you? There's a lot of ways to cut corners, but shampoo isn't one of them...Sit down. I've made us a heart attack for breakfast since I couldn't find the bagels."

"They're hard to come by. The only ones they have sit on the shelves for weeks, and they're as tough as leather."

"You should ask them to special order, dear. I'd bet they'd do something as simple as that if you spoke up."

"Why didn't Dad come? Or is he here too, somewhere?"

"No, he's on that ridiculous fishing trip he takes every year down in Florida. He's determined to convince me we should get a place in Boca. He keeps reminding me, 'They get more—'"

"'—expensive every year,'" Anna chimed in. "Yeah, I can hear him saying it."

"How's your job? Do you have a boyfriend yet?"

"In this town? I've yet to meet my match," she said with noted dejection. "But Kyle is good company. Why are you so hung up on me getting married anyway?"

"I just don't want you to be a spinster. You're not getting any younger, you know. What happens when Kyle meets the man of his dreams? Where will that leave you?"

"I think he already has."

"He met someone *here*? Well, Anna, if *he* can meet—Do you want some coffee?"

"Fine."

Despite her mother pointing out all of the negatives in her

life, Anna had to admit it was nice waking up to breakfast, coffee, and companionship. The silence outside was deafening. She always felt left out on Christmas morning. While all of the other kids were ripping open presents, she played Monopoly with her family and agonized over the fact that the majority of stores and restaurants were closed. She was looking forward to spending the morning at the nursing home with Mae Pearl.

"I know you told me on the phone about your students, but what are the other *teachers* like? Have you made friends with any of them?"

"No—well, one. We dated for a while, but then Kyle caught him cheating."

"Who was he cheating with?"

"The mayor's wife."

"Really? Does he like older women?"

"No, the mayor and his wife are both around my age."

"Did the mayor find out?"

"Trey—that's the mayor—knows all about it. He was with Kyle when he caught them together."

Anna's mother took a swig from her coffee cup and placed it back on the table. "Are you saying that Kyle was *with* the mayor? That's who you were talking about when you said he found the love of his life?"

Anna nodded. "Yep."

"Maybe we should look into a place here instead of Boca. The real estate is probably much more affordable."

"Dad couldn't fish."

"You don't want us here, do you?"

"I'm not saying that. I'm just saying—You and Dad wouldn't be happy. I can guarantee it."

"Well, if you don't want me living near you, I hope you will at least have dinner with us tonight."

"Sure."

"Who's 'us?'"

"You, me, Flo, Rose—I met her because I knocked on her door first—and Kyle, too, of course."

"You've been here a few hours and already you have dinner plans with most of the people I know? You're really something, Mom, you know that?"

"I've always been very sociable. You can help me get everything ready. I told everyone around seven. Does that sound good?"

"Yeah, whatever."

After they finished their breakfast and cleared the table, Anna said, "I'm going to visit a friend in the nursing home. Mae Pearl—that's my friend—and her partner live in the same room. Isn't that sweet? No one knows, though. Well, a few do."

"Don't make me *verklempt*." Abigail teared up. "That's so sad."

Anna handed her a tissue.

"Those ladies...It must be hard on them."

"Why don't you come with me? Oh, and if you really want to cry? Her daughter lives next door and won't even visit her."

"That's preposterous! Why not?"

"Religious reasons, I guess. Thinks she's a sinner."

"Since when is love a sin?"

"That's what *I* said. Anyway, I'm going to take a quick shower. Do you need anything?"

"No, sweetheart, I've found everything I've needed so far. I'll go change my clothes after I clean up here. Take your time."

After showering, Anna found her mother dressing in the bedroom. "Dress casually, please."

"Do you have a jacket you can lend me? Some clumsy woman at the airport spilled her soda on mine."

Anna pointed to the open closet door, "Yeah, they're to the left."

On the way to the car, they walked slowly through the garden so her mom could admire Kyle's handiwork. "You can't imagine what it looked like when we first moved in."

"Did you do the Christmas decorations?"

"That was also Kyle. Follow me. I'm parked in front."

"Good grief! Who would have a car *that* color? I saw that watermelon on wheels when I arrived and thought—"

"Get in."

"It's yours?"

"Yeah, and I like it. I think it's pretty."

Her mom caressed the velour seats. "Well, it *is* soft. I didn't mean to offend you, dear. I had no idea it was yours. You *should* be proud."

"I am—Now, buckle up."

Anna and Abigail walked through the doors of the Golden Years Nursing Home just as the Christmas celebration was ending.

The gift she left for Mae Pearl was sitting unopened under the tree. "I don't see her, Mom. Let's check her room."

The only noise was the echo of their footsteps in the long hallway. She raised her arm to knock, but the room was empty. She took a step backwards to check the room number. "That's weird."

The head nurse met them on their return to the nurses' station. "I'm sorry," she said, "Mae Pearl passed away last night."

"Oh." Anna swallowed. "H-how?"

"It was just her time, I suppose." The nurse handed Anna a letter. "She must've written it just before she died."

"How's Agnes doing?"

"She passed a little while before Mae Pearl."

Anna fought back the tears. "Is it me? Everyone I visit dies."

The nurse shook her head. "Most of the people here could go at any time. You offer them what they most want: you erase the loneliness. I *do* think when someone cares, it gives them an internal peace to be able to make the transition."

Anna dabbed at her tears. "That's kind of you to say...Would it be okay if I went to her room once more?"

"Of course."

Both beds were stripped down to the thin, gray mattresses.

The energy of the room had died along with its occupants; it might as well have been a storage closet.

Anna searched for the The Grabber and spotted it leaning against the nightstand. On top was a pen and a notepad matching the paper in her hand. Underneath was an empty sandwich baggie.

Walking past the Christmas tree in the lobby, Anna took Mae Pearl's gift, removed the tag and handed it to a dejected man sitting alone. His face lit up. "Merry Christmas," she whispered as she leaned over and kissed him on the forehead.

Abigail wrapped her arm around her daughter's shoulder as they walked to the car. "You make a mother proud."

Anna didn't respond. She placed the The Grabber on the floorboard, stuck the keys into the ignition, opened the letter and read silently:

Anna:
Agnes has left me, and I don't want to be here without her. Thanks for the love. Don't be sad for me, and don't hate my daughter. I'll take care of her from above.
All will be sorted out in the end—or should I say the beginning? I'm asking the Good Lord to take me home. If He loves me, He'll hear my prayers. I think He will.
—Mae Pearl—

Anna placed the letter on top of the dashboard and backed out.

"What'd it say?"

Anna shook her head, knowing if she spoke she would break down.

Abigail rested her hand on her daughter's leg. When they arrived home, Anna took the letter next door to Judy Jane Johnson's house. Her husband Jerry opened the door.

"Give this to your wife," she said, unable to look him in the eye. "And tell her, '*He* heard.'"

Kyle sat alone downtown on a bench holding the Anne Tyler book Anna had finished. Even the Theater Café was dark and lifeless, except for a crack of light emanating from around the rear hutch. The entire square was quiet. He warmed up on the bike ride over, but the longer he sat, the colder it grew. The decorations he'd hung graced the light posts; the Santa sleigh he was facing looked joyful. But festive was the last thing Kyle was feeling with no plans on Christmas Day.

A hand on his shoulder startled him. "Mind if I sit down?"

"Déjà vu," Kyle said.

"'Déjà' who?"

"Nothing." He scooted over.

"What are you doing out here in the cold? I done seen you from inside."

"I didn't have any plans and didn't want to sit home alone."

"Where's the girl?"

"Her mom came into town."

"Family! They're always raining on *my* parade, I tell you."

"You have family here?"

"Of course I do. Like I said before, I wouldn't be here if it wudn't for them. Someone's gotta watch after 'em," she giggled and nudged Kyle in the ribs. "Say, you wanna come inside where it's warm. I can fix us something hot to drink, and I know someone else who'll be glad to see you. Poor thing's been cooped up in my little apartment, scared to come out. I told him we could put curtains up in the front windows so he could at least walk around, but he wouldn't hear of it—said some shit about curtains not going with the décor. He's queer all right! Parents must've been blind not to see that one bloomin'."

Kyle laughed. They walked across the street and were about to enter the café when a patrol car passed. It was Officer Richards. He stared, but continued on and turned the corner. As soon as the car was out of sight, Winnie thrust up her middle finger.

"He done saw us. Maybe it'd be safer for Ricky if you *didn't* come in. I'll make you some coffee and bring it out to the bench. How's that sound?"

"Fine, Winnie. Thanks."

Kyle returned to his seat; the wood was still warm. Winnie came out not five minutes later with a big paper cup of coffee. "Merry Christmas, sonny."

"Merry Christmas, Winnie."

Winnie sat with him for a spell before complaining the weather was too cold for her fragile bones. She returned to the café and lingered by the register, arranging cups and hoping Officer Richards would drive by again and see she was alone.

Stacy, driving her BMW, was returning from delivering a German chocolate cake and a bag of toys to a less fortunate family when she spotted Kyle sitting outside on the square. She pulled into the parking space closest to him and got out. "What are you doing out here? Aren't you cold?"

"Winnie just brought some coffee out. I'm fine."

Stacy looked towards the café and then back at Kyle.

"You don't *look* fine. A little nostalgic, are we?"

"You're good...Maybe a tad."

"Hop in. Trey's got the barbecue grill going. Come join us."

"Are you sure?"

"Of course, I'm sure. Why not? Ride with me and you can get your bike later. It's too cold to be riding around."

He dusted his pants and waved to Winnie before he got into her car.

A block down, Officer Richards pulled out from behind a bush at the post office, flashed his lights and tailed Stacy. She pulled over.

"What could *he* want?" Kyle asked.

"I'm sure just to wish us a happy holiday." She waited for him to approach before lowering the car window.

Officer Richards, still in plain clothes, approached. "Where's my son?"

"How would I know? Isn't he at your house?" Stacy replied.

"That Yankee you've got with you knows where he is."

"Is that true, Kyle?" she asked with a discreet wink.

"I don't know where he is. Haven't seen him since the party."

"There you have it. We don't know, but I will be praying for his safe return. I'll tell Trey you sent your regards." She raised the window, ending their conversation, and drove away.

Trey was in the kitchen peeling carrots when Stacy walked in. "I brought you a Christmas present," she chirped.

"Another one?" Trey shook the clingy strips of peel from his hands.

She reached into the laundry room and pulled Kyle inside. "Merry Christmas!"

Trey looked at him, then at his wife, and back at Kyle.

"I found him homesick in the cold. You know me and strays."

"Are you sure? I mean—Thank you."

"I'll finish peeling the carrots," she offered. "Anything else?"

"Onions. We'll be at the grill."

Stacy watched as the two walked across the living room and out the patio door. "They *do* make a cute couple," she said aloud to herself.

While all was merry at the mayor's house, things weren't so cheery at Ivory and Ronald Black's humble abode. For one last time, Ivory turned on the Christmas lights Ronald had draped around the gazebo and admired them from the window in the back door. "Believe it or not, I'm a little sad to go back. I don't know what I was thinking, leaving on Christmas Day. The good thing is the fewer people on the plane, the fewer autographs I'll have to sign."

Ronald rolled his eyes. "You've signed so many since you've been here," he mumbled.

"Did you say something?"

"I said, 'You'd better take a fresh pen.'"

"You're right!" Ivory ambled aimlessly through the house. "I hope I haven't forgotten to pack anything. I know I didn't bring much. Do you use the skillet? Or, what about my pillow? I could squeeze those in my suitcase. You don't think I could take apart the recliner, do you? I'd bet it's still too big—"

"Ivory, be reasonable."

"I suppose you're right. New York spaces are small anyway. Oh, and you can cancel my *People* magazine subscription," she said, staring at the foot-high stack near the kitchen table.

Ronald stood as a spectator at the edge of the kitchen, picking at the loose corner of the Formica countertop. His wife was leaving him for the second time. "You sure you don't want me to drive you to the airport?"

"To Houston? Don't be silly. I already have a bus ticket."

"Yeah, alright...I thought you were flying out of Austin. Houston is too far." He stuck his hands in his pockets. "So...this is it?" His voice involuntarily raised to suppress his emotions.

"I guess so. Well, I hope you'll come and see me in New York sometime. I'll show you around."

A horn honked outside. "That must be my chauffeur."

"Oh, I was going to drive you to the bus stop at least."

"This'll be easier, Ronald...for us both."

He reached down to help with the bags. "Ivory, I—"

She held up her hand to stop him. "I know. I do, too."

The men loaded the bags into the trunk while Ivory sat in the back seat. She put on her movie-star sunglasses and hat and waved out the window as she rode off. She never looked back.

Ronald stood lost in his own front yard until a gentle voice called his name. He turned towards it; his eyes crinkled as a smile appeared. "Where'd *you* come from?"

"I've been waiting in my car all morning. The Stones always go to Oklahoma for Christmas, so I borrowed their driveway."

"She's gone, Rose."

"I know." Rose took his hand, "...At least she told *you* goodbye."

While most of the town was celebrating with friends and family, at The 36 Diner, Flo served up hot coffee and breakfast dishes to hungry truckers and the occasional traveler.

In an attempt to be festive, she sported the same Santa hat she wore to Anna's party. She was sucking hard on the cigarette she'd just lit when she noticed the unmistakable green Bonneville pulling in. She greeted Anna and Abigail at the door. "Hi y'all. What brings you here, today of all days?"

"The wonderful waitstaff," Anna said as she kissed Flo on the cheek. "My mom tells me you've already met."

"Hiya, Flo."

"Hi, Mrs. Aron."

"Call me Abigail."

"Y'all can sit anywhere you'd like."

"Which is your section?" Abigail asked.

"It's *all* my section today, honey."

Abigail chose a booth in front so Flo could visit when she had a minute.

"This is where Kyle and I sat when we first arrived to town," Anna said.

"Are y'all having a nice Christmas?" Flo asked, leaving two menus on the table.

"We're Jewish, remember?"

"Oh Christ, Anna, I forgot. So, what'll I get y'all?"

"Just coffee since we're going to have dinner later. We're still on, right?" Abigail confirmed.

"I've been looking forward to it all day. Anna, babe, you okay? You look a little down in the dumps."

Anna looked up. "Mae Pearl died."

Flo lowered her order pad, "Oh, precious! Are you alright?"

"She'll be okay," Abigail answered.

Flo quickly conceded. "Well, at least you have your mother

with you. I'm sure that makes it easier. I'll go get that coffee, ladies."

"She's a nice woman, Anna. You're lucky you have such good neighbors. You know you can't trust everyone, but—Oh, what am I saying, you're not a kid anymore. Have you any friends your own age?"

"Yes. Maxine. She's near my age, but now she has a boyfriend and is busy with the café she opened. It's really nice, we'll have to go."

Flo returned. "Two coffees. Y'all wanna nibble on some pie? We have chocolate, pumpkin and pecan."

"We'll pass," Abigail said.

Flo left them alone again.

"Why don't you invite Maxine to dinner tonight? I'd like to meet her while I'm here."

"How long are you staying, by the way?"

"Maybe we *should* get some pie...Pecan?"

"Anyway, it's your dinner. *You* invite her."

"I wish you wouldn't look at it that way. I am just trying to be friendly."

"I know...I'm sorry. I'll call her when we get home. But don't count on her since she's probably busy with Luciano—that's her boyfriend."

"He can come, too. I always say, 'the more the merrier.'"

The loud swish of the air brakes announced the arrival of the Greyhound bus.

Flo called to Ivory sitting alone near the rear of the dining room, "The bus is here."

A few passengers got off to use the facilities and grab some snacks. Ivory approached to pay for the soda she'd enjoyed.

"No charge, sugar. And I had the kitchen fix you up a ham sandwich, chips and an apple. It's the *biggest apple* I could find." Flo handed her the brown paper sack.

Ivory's feet would not do her bidding.

"Go on. The bus driver is honking...and Merry Christmas!" Flo shooed her along.

Lugging suitcases, and with the lunch sack clutched in her mouth, she walked out the door. Anna looked up and caught a glimpse of her departure.

"Flo, was that Ivory Black?"

She nodded and watched Ivory step onto the bus. "Yep. That was her. The one and only."

Later that afternoon, Abigail phoned Maxine. "We'd love to," she said. It was the perfect timing to accept an invitation. All of the gifts had been exchanged, the stockings emptied, and the post-celebratory blues were quickly setting in. Maxine suggested having it at the Theater Café, so Winnie and Ricky Richards could join in on the fun.

"I always say, 'the more the merrier.'"

It was settled. "Now, what on earth are we going to prepare in two hours for eight people—possibly nine, if Kyle comes? How much tomato sauce do you have, Anna?"

"A ton. Save-All had it on sale last week, and I had coupons."

"Spaghetti and Bolognese it is."

Abigail was busy boiling pasta in the kitchen and Anna was resting on the couch with her eyes closed when a painful sound in the distance frightened them both.

"Is someone having a baby?" her mom asked.

"I don't think so." Anna stepped outside and followed the moan. It was coming from the second story of Judy Jane Johnson's house.

Kyle came through the lychgate pushing his bike. "Who's crying?"

"Judy Jane Johnson. Her mother passed away."

"Mae Pearl? Oh God, Anna. I'm sorry. Are you okay?"

She nodded.

"How's your mom? Are you guys having a nice time?"

"It's all right. Go and say hello. She's going to invite you to dinner tonight, just so you know."

"Nice. Just the three of us?"

"More like three hundred."

"Who else is coming?"

"You know, the usual gang," Anna said with a sigh.

"I can tell you're not doing as well as you're letting on." Kyle wrapped Anna in a hug. "At least Mae Pearl had you to confide in. That counts for a lot. You did all you could...Hey, did you get your gift?"

"What gift?"

"I left it in your stocking."

Anna rushed over to the stocking hanging by her door and eagerly stuck her hand inside. She retrieved a small brass apple-shaped bell.

"...since you're a teacher."

Anna merrily jingled her present. "Aww. It's so nice. Thank you, Kyle."

"Reach back in."

"There's more?" Anna pulled out two tickets. "What're these?"

"Juice Newton will be in Temple. I got us tickets!"

"Get out! Thank you...thank you." She kissed him on the cheek with multiple pecks while hoping Trey's stocking wasn't stuffed with the same tickets.

Having the dinner at the Theater Café had been a good idea as far as the extra room was concerned. Unfortunately, it created too much action in the parking lot to go unnoticed.

During the passing of the garlic bread, there was a desperate knock at the front door. It was Vivian.

"Isn't someone going to let the woman in?" Abigail asked. "I always say, the more the—" Anna shushed her.

Ricky rested his fork, stood and walked to the doorway. As soon as he opened the door, his mother embraced him. "I've been worried sick! Where have you been? Where's your jacket? I'm taking you home. Your father said he had something real special planned for you tonight—just the two of you. Praise God, you are okay! Come on. Let's go."

All eyes were on Ricky as they awaited his decision. "I guess I'd better try and go home."

Kyle stood. "If you have any trouble, you know where to come." He watched as Ricky and his mother walked out and got into the car.

"Kyle, sweetheart, I was hoping you'd bring the new beau," Abigail said when he returned to the table. "Anna's told me so much about him, and I am dying to meet him."

"He had, uh, family plans. He's going to his parents' house."

"I see...And Maxine, how long have you and Luciano been dating? Are there wedding bells in the future?"

"Mom!"

"What? What's wrong with asking that? How am I to get to know these people if I don't ask any questions?"

"None just yet, Mrs. Aron," Maxine said.

Luciano squeezed Maxine's thigh under the table.

Vivian Richards paced the linoleum living room floor as she waited for her husband and son to return from their planned outing. It seemed only yesterday an innocent Ricky used to sit in her lap and look up to her for all the answers. Where had she gone wrong? Despite all of her misgivings, she couldn't have been more relieved to have him at home again.

At just after midnight, Officer Richards came home, but there was no Ricky.

"Where is he? Where's Ricky?"

Officer Richards walked to the laundry room where he took off his muddy boots.

"What happened to your boots? Where's Ricky? Is he all right?"

"He's fine. I dropped him off where he wanted to be."

"Where? You mean you dropped him back off with those Yankees? Why on earth would you—"

"It's what he wanted."

"But it's not what *I* wanted? How are we going to control his behavior if he's not even at home?"

"I don't wanna talk about it. Ricky explained everything and I dropped him off. End of discussion."

Vivian was in hysterics. "I can't believe you gave in to him like that! What kind of parents are we if we let him manipulate us? This is on you. If those loons do something to him, I'll never forgive you. We have to go get him out of there."

"I *said* I don't want to talk about it, Viv." Officer Richards, in a noticeably forced effort to amend his mood, stood in front of his wife, ran his hands down her arms and calmly stated, "There's nothing more we can do. He's made his decision. Let's just get some rest. It's Christmas after all."

Vivian watched as her husband retreated into the bedroom.

December 25th had come to an end. Another year would roll around before kids would begin voluntarily washing the dishes with the hope that Santa Claus would be good to them.

CHAPTER TWENTY

The next day was considerably warmer, and Winnie did what she put off doing on Christmas Day: visiting her dearly departed Humphrey. There wasn't a cloud in sight, and the temperature was just right for a light jacket. She threw on a scarf to keep her throat warm and slipped a pair of gloves in her pocket.

She parked the car in her usual spot and grabbed the cloth placemat she brought to sit on.

"Merry Christmas, Humph. How you doing? Was Santa good to you?" she snickered. "It's a shame you died just when Prairie Springs was getting exciting. Are you watching from upstairs? Is the Good Lord seeing all that's going on here? Things are a-changin'. I'm happy it happened before it was *my* time. I think soon, Humph, everything's gonna be out in the open and people can live without secrets and lies. Wouldn't that be a fuckin' blessin'? The best news is Trey now calls me Grams. Can you believe it? What's heaven like, honey? Is it as good as it's cracked up to be?"

A breeze rustled the branches of the pecan tree causing a few dead leaves to flutter onto Winnie's jacket. "It's windier than I thought, Humph." She brushed the leaves away and watched as the wind ushered them into the creek. The water glistened and shimmered in the sunlight as if it were full of diamonds. A dead tree limb floating downstream stole her attention; it rounded the bend and hung on something yellow. She stood to get a better look. It was a yellow t-shirt.

"No-o-o!" Being beaten by the gentle but steady current was Ricky. "What have you done?" she yelled. "You stupid fool!"

She placed one foot into the chilly water and braced the other on an exposed tree root. In an exhausting effort, she pulled the body onto the grass. She collapsed into a sitting position beside him and wept.

As quickly as she could, Winnie made it to town, picked up Kyle, and went back to The Springs. Kyle loaded the cold, waterlogged corpse into the back seat and drove directly to the Richards' house.

Kyle turned off the motor. "I'll go tell them."

"No. I think they like you less than they like me. I'll do it."

Winnie crossed her arms to keep her hands warm. She scuttered to the door and knocked. Vivian answered, wearing a white apron.

"We have your son, ma'am," Winnie spoke calmly.

"They've brought him home, honey...Where is he?" Vivian said as she ran to the car. Officer Richards following behind.

Kyle got out to try and stop her.

"Why is he wet?" She peered into the back seat. "What's wrong with him? What have you done to my baby!" she said, wailing.

Winnie kept her distance on the opposite side of the car. "I found him dead."

"Y'all killed him...Y'all killed my boy!" With one hand clutching the rear door handle, Vivian fell to her knees and sobbed.

Stone-faced, Officer Richards went inside the house and returned with a pair of handcuffs.

"You are under arrest for the murder of my son. You have *no* rights." He forcefully cuffed Kyle and banged his face into the top of Winnie's car.

"Kyle didn't do it!" Winnie hollered. "He did it to himself."

The way Officer Richards held Kyle's head down, Kyle had a good view of the muddy boots embedded with pecan tree leaves and prairie grass. "No, Winnie, it looks like he had some help."

"Shut your mouth!" the officer snapped. "*You* drowned my son, you damn faggot Yankee!"

"How do you know he drowned?" Vivian slowly stood, using the car as a brace. "Tell me you didn't do this to our son! Tell me you didn't!"

"You know it wasn't me. It was this—this fairy here," he spat, pointing at Kyle. "I've been telling you all along they were trouble. You've gotta believe—"

"You came home last night tracking mud in our house, and you told me you left Ricky at the café."

"Ricky didn't come back to the café last night," Winnie countered. "I stayed up most of the night worried about him, but I ain't never seen him since he left with you at dinner last night, ma'am."

"No!" Vivian screamed and ran inside, as if trying to outrun the truth.

"I should shoot you both right here and now," Officer Richards said quietly.

"Why'd you do it?" an emotional Winnie asked.

"I had to do something. Y'all filled him with Satan. All I did was—All I did—I had to do it. I baptized him to cleanse him...I didn't mean to—'In the name of the Father, the Son, and the

Holy Spirit...'" As he spoke, he released his grip on Kyle and held up his hands in the open air as if he were choking it, reliving the moment. "It was the only way."

The gunshot rang out like thunder in the still, morning air.

Feathers floated down on the somber scene as a lifeless sparrow, an unintentional victim of Vivian's outrage, spiraled into the street behind them.

"Un-cuff that man, you piece of shit!" Vivian approached.

"I'll do no such thing."

"You *will* let him go," she growled, pointing the gun at him.

He glared at his wife, and un-cuffed Kyle.

"You two, get out of here," she told Kyle and Winnie.

"What'll we do with your boy?" Winnie asked.

"Please take him out of here! I can't see him like that."

Officer Richards should have known when the sparrow fell from the sky that God was turning a blind eye to what was about to happen.

Vivian waited until Winnie and Kyle pulled away. Her overwrought husband retreated inside. Vivian closed the front door behind him and fired once into the side of his head. She took the gun and put it in his hand.

The kitchen radio was set to her favorite "Simply Beautiful" station, playing instrumental versions of the classics. Vivian washed up in the kitchen sink, and casually picked up the phone. "Connie? It's Viv...Can you come over?"

She took the dough she had been working on before the interruption, sprinkled the countertop with flour and rolled out the pie crust.

. . .

Kyle and Winnie sat in the alley behind the café. "What're we going to do with Ricky?" Kyle asked.

"There's room for him under the tree with Humphrey, but I guess we'd better leave that to his mama." Winnie glanced into the back seat. "Poor boy...He was such a sweetheart. This is going to devastate Stacy...The hell with it. What's his mama gonna do, dig him up and put him in the cemetery?"

Constance, carrying a turquoise umbrella, arrived before the pie went into the oven.

"The door's open," Vivian called out from the kitchen.

Constance didn't comment on the body splayed out on the living room floor. "Are you okay?"

"Yeah. Sure. Why do you ask?"

"Uh...no reason. Um...whatcha making?"

"Pecan pie...Want some?"

"I think I'll pass."

"Is it raining? I saw you brought an umbrella."

Constance didn't respond.

"Can I get you something to drink? Coffee? There's still some left in the pot."

"No, I'm good."

"Suit yourself."

"Viv, dear, are you alright?"

"I'm fine, Connie."

Constance looked towards where Officer Richards lay. "Do we need to talk about the elephant in the room? Surely you didn't invite me for dessert."

Vivian joined Constance at the round dining table. As soon as she did, she bawled. "Ricky is gone! My baby is gone!"

"Where'd he go?"

Vivian hit the table with her fist. "That bastard killed him. He took my baby from me."

"Hold on! Let me get my pen."

Once Vivian was able to continue, she told Constance the entire story ending with, "...and I told him, I said, 'I will never forgive you for this—ever!' And then he took his gun and shot himself in the head. See? He's got it in his hand...I didn't know who to call."

"Where were you when he did it?"

"I, uh, ran to the bedroom. I couldn't even look at him. You understand, don't you, Connie?"

"This is what you're going to do. You're going to change clothes, and don't forget the apron—it's covered in blood splatter —and give everything to me. Then you're going to take a shower and call the police...Go on, now, hurry."

"But what about the pie?"

"Forget the damn pie, Viv!"

Constance Faye Barker's front-page story disclosed every-thing, culminating with how Officer Dick Richards came inside, pried the gun from his wife's hand and shot himself in the head.

There would never be any more questions asked. It would be declared a suicide with no further investigation by anyone in town. The national media, however, would be a tad more persis-tent and bothersome...downright irritating at times. But even under pressure, Vivian never cracked.

SATURDAY, DECEMBER 27, 2007

A blanket of grief covered Prairie Springs. Two days after Christmas, people from all around gathered at The Springs for the burial of the young, athletic, and intelligent boy whom most had known since his diaper days.

After the service, Winnie offered her condolences privately to Vivian.

"Thank you, Winnie...Do you think I could be buried here with Ricky...you know, when the time comes."

"Abso-fuckin'-lutely, honey." Winnie consoled Vivian with

the answer she wanted to hear even if she didn't have the power to make that call.

Constance, standing within earshot, scribbled away in her notebook.

While the memorial for Ricky was taking place at The Springs, Officer Richards was being buried in the local cemetery. Not only had no one gone to pay a final farewell, but the birds flew from the trees, the cows in the nearby pasture looked away, and the ants took shelter deep within their beds.

The Armadillos were so shaken and consumed with guilt that only three members showed up to the next meeting. Two of them doused the shack with gasoline, and the third dropped the match.

"Prairie Springs: Creek or Cemetery?" emblazoned the top of Constance's page two article.

Coincidentally, the day the story came out was the same day Anna and her mother scattered the remains of Mae Pearl and Agnes at The Springs. They stood silently as they watched the ashes meld together and disappear into the stream. "This is the first time they can touch without worry. Isn't that sad? What kind of world is this we live in?"

"It's what you make of it, honey," her mom told her. "You've got to kiss its butt and kick it in the butt at the same time. No two ways about it." She nudged her daughter closer. "You can't change the world, Anna."

"I'm not trying to change the world, Mom—I'm just trying to make it better."

Abigail proudly kissed her daughter on the head.

WEDNESDAY, DECEMBER 31, 2007

New Year's Eve in Rose's garden was bittersweet. It was filled with champagne and obligatory kisses, but the sadness of the recent deaths, coupled with Abigail's departure in two days, kept emotions subdued. Shortly after midnight, the drinks and kisses ceased, and the small gathering of friends went back to their corresponding residences. There were a few bangs and bursts of fireworks in the distance to remind everyone a new year was upon them, and everyone hoped it would be less painful than the one that had just expired.

CHAPTER TWENTY-ONE

A s usual, Constance, expecting the latest delivery of *The National Enquirer*, stood on the front porch and waited for the postman. When the truck made the corner, she ran to the curb with her hands out.

"Happy New Year, Ms. Barker." The mailman handed her a postcard.

"Happy New Year!" Constance examined the picture of the Golden Gate Bridge and turned it over.

Dear Constance,
We're having a wonderful time. Glad you're not here. Not because I don't like you, but because you'd realize we don't really have any news in Prairie Springs.
Love, Dorcas (and Ted)

Constance let out a thunderous laugh as she went inside and slipped on the new dress she picked up at Sears in the Temple Mall. It was the most beautiful shade of turquoise she'd ever seen! She topped it off with turquoise pantyhose and shoes, and preened in front of the mirror. She was ready to start the day with her new title of CHIEF REPORTER for *The Herald*, nameplate and all.

The position entitled her to snoop around even more than she already did, but the owner of the newspaper didn't care. His concern was with the subscription numbers, and since Constance started reporting two years ago, not one person had canceled who didn't die or move.

Dr. Kimball's plastic surgery skills were better known for concealing scars or for minor reconstructive surgery than they were for cosmetic vanity. It was almost unheard of that someone would trust him with a bosom, as Flo was about to do.

"What time is your appointment?" Anna asked.

"One. What time is it?"

"One-fifteen." Anna pointed to the huge clock on the waiting room wall.

"I didn't notice. I guess I'm too excited."

"I still don't know why you're so concerned, Flo. Your boobs look great to me."

"I'm wearing a bra, sugar. The bra comes off and my tits become knees. You'll find out for yourself in a few years."

"Yeah, that's what Mom says."

"Speaking of your mom, did she get off okay?"

"I hope so. Her flight leaves Austin at—oh, about now, I guess. I'll call her tonight and make sure she made it back safely. Getting back to your boobs...I heard a story about a woman who had a bunch of cosmetic surgery and was later in a life or death situation. The person prayed and prayed for God to save her, but he didn't. When she got to heaven, she asked him why not. He said, 'Oh, I'm sorry. I didn't recognize you.'"

Flo laughed. "I'm just getting a boob job, though. I'm not

messing with my face. I just think I'll feel prettier with some enhancements."

Anna leaned towards Flo and kissed her on the cheek. "You're like a butterfly: you have no idea how beautiful you are."

"Florence Junek?" the doctor called.

"What is that, Czech?" Anna asked.

"Sure is, hun," she answered while draping her white, faux leather purse on her shoulder. Anna had yet to stand. "Well, don't think I just wanted you to keep me company in the waiting room."

The doctor handed Flo a gown. "You can change behind that screen and then take a seat up here," he instructed, patting the examination table.

"I know just what I want. I brought pictures," Flo announced as she was changing and exited with the magazine opened to where a grocery receipt marked the page.

The doctor glanced quickly. "Let's have a look and see what we've got to work with."

Flo lowered her gown and Anna chimed in, "They don't look like knees. They look fine, Flo. I don't know why you want to mess with them at all."

"I have to agree with your friend, Florence. I don't see anything wrong with them."

"Well, this ain't about the two of you, is it? I want 'em lifted and fuller. I've already made up my mind."

"Why mess with perfection?" Dr. Kimball said.

"Aren't you sweet?" Flo winked.

"Oh, you had a C-section?" He noted the scar on her lower abdomen.

Flo glanced down. "That? Oh, heavens no! That was when, uh, they, uh, took out my liver."

"They took it out?" the doctor questioned.

"Yeah. That's not a problem is it? You can still operate on my tits, right?"

"Flo," Anna explained, "you can't live without a liver, silly. You'd be dead in a second."

"Besides, that's not where your liver is," the doctor continued.

"Maybe this was a bad idea after all. I'm gonna think about it a bit longer. Y'all are right; they really don't look that bad in here. Maybe I just need new lights in my bathroom. How much do I owe you for the appointment, Doctor?"

"This one's on me."

"Well, thank you. Come by The 36 and I'll give you some coffee—no charge."

Flo went to dress.

"I'll wait in the hall," Anna said as she opened the door. When she did, Constance nearly fell inside.

"I will call you in when we're finished, Constance," the doctor said, annoyed.

"I didn't know if you had anyone in here or not."

Anna and Flo left, leaving Constance to discuss her cosmetic needs with Dr. Kimball. "Where on earth did she find turquoise nylons?" Flo wondered aloud.

When Anna returned home, she curled up on her sofa with a heating pad. She attempted to read the Alice Hoffman novel she held in her hands, but couldn't stay focused. She tossed the book aside and was sitting up when Kyle knocked and opened the door.

"Hi, Cupcake. You sick?"

"Eh. Don't mind me. How was your day?"

"Fine. Got all of the town's Christmas decorations down and stored away. I wish Ricky were still around to have helped— would've made it more fun. Did you go with Flo to her appointment?"

"Yes. It was interesting. I'll put on some coffee."

"Caffeine sounds nice." Kyle took a seat at in the living room.

"I guess my mom got off okay. I haven't heard from her." Anna filled the carafe. "Remind me to call her later, will ya?"

"Sure. Say, school starts Monday, doesn't it?"

"Yes, dammit."

"That bad?"

"Not really. But it sure is easy to get used to doing nothing. In a way, I'll be glad to get back to a routine. And the kids really aren't that bad, but I'll sure miss Ricky. Speaking of teaching, don't you think it's weird Maxine didn't ask me to teach her Spanish? Rose and I saw her taking lessons—"

"Yeah, Luciano told me."

"Well, I still think she should've asked me."

Kyle wasn't up for the whining. "*Pssh.* Don't worry about it. Did you really want to teach all day, and then again at night and on weekends? Be glad she didn't ask."

"You're right. Wonder why that's bothering me so much?"

Anna joined Kyle in the living room as they waited for the coffee. "I feel like I've hardly seen you lately with everything going on. First my mom, then Trey...the holidays."

"I know. The past two weeks just flew by. Trey and I have been having a good time together at least. Stacy's been great. It's like a whole other side of her has emerged. She's completely torn up over Ricky. I think he helped her as much as she was helping him. You know they were having counseling sessions at the café?"

"Yeah, Rose and I spotted her coming out from behind that secret hutch. Why doesn't Winnie want anyone to know she lives there?"

"Got me. She's so quiet about her life. She keeps you entertained with a bunch of nothing so you don't ask too many questions."

"What'd you get Trey for Christmas?"

"I got him the cutest little stuffed dog. When you squeeze it, it says, 'I ruff you.'"

Anna stood, hearing the coffee pot gurgle. "You're already at the 'I love you' stage? That's pretty fast don't you think?"

"I didn't say it. The dog does," Kyle defended, sitting up from his slouch. "Why do I feel like you're judging me?"

Anna shook her head. "I'm sorry. I shouldn't have said anything. I'm a bit down about life...Aren't you? I mean the whole Ricky thing is sickening. There's been a lot of death for me lately."

"It's a lot, but it's also an inevitable part of life. The Ricky thing is fucked up, but we did all we could. It's important we see each day as a new beginning. I'm healthy, have a job, I'm in *ruff*, and you live right below me. What more could I ask for?"

"A town that doesn't kill people for being themselves? I'm sorry. I'm just in a funk."

"What's really going on?"

"I'm PMSing and have horrible cramps. Can you believe my timing? What a way to ring in the New Year."

"God shouldn't allow menstruation during the holidays," Kyle added jokingly. "Or why not just do away with menstruation completely!"

"Here's your coffee—Wouldn't that be nice! I'd save a fortune on tampons."

"What were you going to tell me that needed to wait for coffee?"

"Oh, right...First of all, wait here." Anna ran to the closet, and when she came back, she handed him a shopping bag.

"What's this?"

"Your gift. I completely forgot with Mom here."

"You didn't have to get me a Christmas present."

"I didn't. It's a Hanukkah present."

Kyle opened the bag and removed a midnight-blue cotton sweater. "A new sweater to start the new year. Do you like the color?"

"It's great, Anna. Thank you!" He stood to kiss her on the cheek. "I wasn't expecting anything."

"Yeah, right."

"Hey! Don't forget the Juice Newton concert is next weekend."

"Are you kidding? I won't. You can wear the sweater to the concert."

Kyle folded it and tucked it back into the bag.

"What I was going to tell you was about the plastic surgeon visit."

"Right. How was it?"

"Interesting. *Very* interesting..."

That evening, Ted and Dorcas spent their last night strolling through the gay Castro district in San Francisco. Anna called her mom, after a reminder from Kyle, and was relieved to hear the trip was uneventful. Across the garden, Flo rocked in her recliner as she clutched a fleecy baby blanket. Four blocks away, a titillated Constance, dressed in a satin turquoise nightgown, settled in her chair and flipped on the Tiffany-style desk lamp. While nibbling on a piece of holiday fudge, she thumbed through Florence Junek's medical record that she swiped when the doctor's back was turned.

MONDAY, JANUARY 5, 2008

Many of the letters to the editor in *The Herald* continued to address the death of Ricky Richards. Most emphasized the need for acceptance and understanding. A few, however, blamed the boy for a life of sin.

When Kyle came home from work, he showered and warmed leftovers to eat while he read the newspaper. When he finished, he carried it over to Flo's. "Did you read this?"

As the pastor of Prairie Springs Church of the Lord, I'd like to personally invite everyone to attend our small little church. To you white folks, you'll have to cross the tracks, but once you do, you'll find a place where our Lord embraces you and squeezes you and fills you with His spirit. We accept all colors and varieties of peoples, as does Jesus Christ. Come and worship!
—Peggy Thomas, Pastor—

"I saw that. I know Ms. Peggy. She comes to The 36 sometimes. Funny as a clown."

"We should go," Kyle urged.

"To her church?"

"Sure. Why not? Sounds interesting."

"What about my shift?"

"Not a problem. They have an early service."

"Damn. What the hell, I'll go."

"Anna and I are going to a concert in Temple on Saturday night, but we should be back early. I'll meet you Sunday morning. I'm going to ask Trey and Stacy too. We can all go in Anna's boat-car."

"Fine by me, shoog."

While the holiday break passed too quickly, Anna was glad to be back teaching. At the very least, it got her out of bed each morning. Before the start of the second day, she placed a stack of flyers outside her classroom door. LGBT ACCEPTANCE MEETING, JANUARY 8TH, 7:00 PM AT THE THEATER CAFÉ. Many of the flyers ended up on the floor, stuck to kids' backs and maliciously taped to lockers.

TUESDAY, JANUARY 6, 2008

When Flo's phone rang Tuesday evening, she was deep into a *Hart to Hart* rerun. "Hello?"

"I know about the baby."

"Who is this?" She muted the TV.

"I'm not telling you that! What matters is—"

"Constance?"

"No."

"I have caller ID, you lamebrain."

"Darnit. Okay, well I've done some investigating, and I have a story that could turn this town upside down. I don't *want* to print it, but I will if you don't pay me ten thousand dollars."

"Constance, I can barely pay my rent, for heaven's sake. Where do you think I'm going to come up with ten thousand dollars? Plus, I don't know who you think you can blackmail with a story about a dead baby."

"You...or the father."

"Good luck finding out who that is. Do what you have to do."

She hung up the phone and clicked the volume back on the television, but could no longer pay attention to the Harts' predicament when she had her own. Why would Constance bring this up after all this time? Why did she care? And how did she find out? Tears welled up in Flo's eyes as painful memories flooded her mind. She reached for the phone again and dialed, dabbing at her eyes. "Winnie?"

While Flo was weeping tears of sadness, a shout of elation echoed throughout the garden. It scared Rose so badly she dropped the towel she had just pulled from the dryer. The crows in Judy Jane Johnson's yard unanimously abandoned the trees and made their way further south. The energy in the air was uplifting—a miracle had just occurred.

It didn't take long for God to smile when hate was replaced with love. No sooner had Judy Jane uttered *Forgive me!* while down on her knees at the foot of her bed, did she feel the frozen side of her face come to life. Though she couldn't turn back time, her regret and heartfelt plea finally gave her something to smile about. Now, she needed to prove she meant what she said.

Thursday, January 8, 2008

The day of the support group, Stacy spent all morning making tasty treats, chip dips, and cinnamon rolls. Maxine was perturbed at Stacy for bringing food, hoping to sell more of their menu items. Nevertheless, most ordered something to drink when they entered, not wanting to appear too eager to participate in the official meeting. The teenage guests lingered around the serving area until a very pretty blonde took a seat at the group's designated table. The others followed her lead.

Anna, Kyle and Stacy were thrilled at the turnout. Thirteen kids initially showed, mostly nervous gigglers, but that number decreased by two after a couple of parents forcefully removed their children.

A handful of disgruntled townspeople protested in front of the café.

When the meeting got underway, Winnie kept an eye out for Constance, who was sure to slither her way inside. The first teen to stand and introduce herself was the pretty blonde, Linda.

Maxine watched Luciano's reaction. Was *she* the one? Luciano's response was certainly subtle, but it was enough for Maxine. She charged towards the group. "You tramp! You bleached-blond floozy! You, Liiinda—you got the hots for my boyfriend?" Maxine yelled as she reached for the frightened girl.

Luciano rushed from the table he was wiping, grabbed Maxine and pulled her aside.

As Stacy struggled to bring order back to the meeting and calm the confused Linda, Luciano explained to Maxine that *linda* in Spanish means pretty. "I have been saying how pretty you are. There's no other girl."

Maxine felt like a fool and offered a chagrined, but heartfelt apology to Linda and the group.

"Besides," Linda said, nervously taking in a deep breath, "I like girls, anyway."

The growing crowd of apoplectic protestors was getting louder and more violent, thanks in part to a report on the local AM radio station about the meeting.

Winnie, sensing the tension, slipped behind the hutch while Stacy worked to maintain the attendees' attention. "Does anyone else have anything to add? What are some things the school could do—or even the town?...Anyone?"

Judy Jane Johnson had been quietly listening a few tables away. She stood, "I'd like to say something."

"Oh...Judy Jane...Um, as long as it's supportive, that should be fine." Stacy was caught so off guard, she didn't notice her fully functioning face.

"Many of you know me, or at least your parents do. I work at the bank. Someone showed me the announcement about the meeting and, well, I—I lost my mother recently. She was a terrific woman. All I can say is how much she loved me, and made sure I never lacked anything. My heavens, she would've walked across broken glass to've made sure I had school supplies and food on the table." She swallowed and glanced around, not accustomed to speaking in front of a group. "I'm a Christian woman, as most of you know. I mainly go to Second Baptist, but occasionally I pop into First or Third. Anyway, I've been doing a lot of thinking— more thinking than you know—and sometimes it's hard for us to accept things we don't understand. My mother was..." she could barely get the words out, "...in love with another woman. And I wouldn't have anything to do with her because of it, and now— now she's gone."

After a sip of water and a deep breath, she continued. "What I've learned is—my, they're loud, aren't they?—What I've learned is that whether something is right or wrong it's not up to us to decide. What matters is that we, as human beings and children of our Lord Almighty, give other humans a peaceful place to live. I asked the Lord to forgive me for pretending my mother didn't exist and letting her die alone. Not only was I hurting the person I should've been loving, I was destroying myself. If there's a sin in all of this, that is it. Thank you." A loving and complete smile filled her face.

Before Judy Jane could retake her seat, the café's front plate-glass window came crashing in from the pounding. A woman fell through and landed on the shattered tempered glass.

The mob filled the café and stormed towards the group when Winnie emerged waving an unloaded rifle.

"Get the fuck outta here. Get! Get on!" She managed to scare the protestors back outside, but by this time the students had left the premises. Amidst the commotion, Winnie noticed a turquoise paparazzo standing across the street snapping pictures. She handed her rifle to Kyle and stepped gingerly through the broken glass to confront her.

"This was quite an event," Constance commented.

"Un-fuckin'-fortunate is what it was. But that's not what I want to talk to you about."

"Oh?"

"Flo called and told me you're trying to blackmail her about the baby. How did you find out?"

"It's all in a day's work."

"I see. Well, let me show you what's in an old lady's day." Winnie unzipped her jacket and pulled out the pistol. "That baby was a long time ago, and Flo's done cried enough tears over it, and she don't need you bringing it all back. So buzz off!"

"I think there's something you should know. I've been doing some investigating and I think the baby might still be alive."

Winnie stuck the gun back into the inside pocket of her jacket. "What are you saying? You tell me what you know, you snoop! If I have a—"

"You'll find out when everyone else does: when the article

comes out on the front page of *The Herald.* And what do you mean, 'If I have a—'...If you have a *what*?"

"None of your business. Now, get out of here. And don't you dare put a picture with any schoolkids in it. You can show the adult fools, but we don't need another Dick in this town."

"I would never do that, Winnie. I'm not as evil as people make me out to be."

SATURDAY, JANUARY 10, 2008

Heading to the Juice Newton concert, Anna and Kyle drove north on Highway 36.

"You look dapper in your new sweater. Is it comfortable?"

"Very...Change of subject, but do you think the town was this eventful before we got here? It almost feels like we set off some chain of events."

"Don't be silly. We're not that powerful...are we?"

"I didn't think we were. Hopefully this year will be less tragic," Kyle commented as he opened the glove box for his cigarettes. "What's this?"

"Oh. That's the picture Dr. Waxman left for me at the nursing home."

"Right. You told me about it but never showed it to me." Kyle silently studied the picture and returned it. "How about some music?" He reached in the back seat for his boombox and put on Juice Newton's *Greatest Hits* CD.

Anna laughed.

"I came prepared."

Their seats were twenty rows from the stage. Anna found her view blocked by a large ten-gallon Stetson. "Look at this yutz, Kyle, wearing a hat indoors. I can't see a thing."

The cowboy to her right overheard her complaint and took it upon himself to remedy the situation. He reached and removed the other man's hat. "The woman can't see."

Anna was taken aback and hoped her complaint wouldn't

start a brawl. She smiled at the kind man sporting crispy Wranglers. She recognized the scent he was wearing as the original Polo cologne. "Thank you. That's much better."

"I'm Wilbur, attorney-at-law."

Wilbur?

"Anna Aron. Schoolteacher."

The two visited between songs. When the concert ended, Anna asked if she could have his number.

"Sure. You got a pen?"

Anna dug in her purse. "Here you go."

Wilbur wrote his number on the back of the ticket stub. Anna did the same and waved coyly as she walked away.

"He's an attorney, Kyle—a good-looking attorney who likes Juice Newton. Could this be my Trey?"

"Let's hope." Kyle was suspicious of a lawyer who didn't carry business cards. He wasn't keen on him, but that was nothing new. There wasn't a man out there good enough for his Cupcake. "Is attorney-at-law his last name?"

"Maybe he's just proud of it. Or, maybe he went ahead and answered my second question? Don't you always ask what someone does after you ask their name?"

"That, or 'My place, or yours?'" Kyle took Anna's arm and they walked to the car.

"That was an awesome Christmas gift. Wasn't she great?"

"Glad you enjoyed, Cupcake...Are we going to check out that Church of the Lord tomorrow morning?"

"I'm game."

They pulled up to the house just shy of eleven. Walking to their cabins, Anna pulled the ticket stub from her pocket and glanced at the back. "A five-five-five prefix? That's the number they use in movies!"

Kyle took the ticket from her hand. "You don't want to date anyone named Wilbur anyway. Give me a hug."

SUNDAY, JANUARY 11, 2008

"Praise Jesus! Look at these people. Good morning and hallelujah! How y'all doin' this morning?" Pastor Peggy rhythmically exclaimed as she proudly admired the congregants filling the worn wooden pews. A runner of raggedy, faded red carpet decorated the aisle between. "Stand on your feet. Come on! We got some praisin' to do. Take hold of the person's hand next to you, and raise 'em in the air. Amen. Let me see them hands glorifying our Lord Jesus Christ."

The all-black choir, robed in green, interjected with, "Higher...higher...higher...and higherrrrr." The congregation followed the lead of the choir. When the choir members released hands, clapped to the music, and sang, "I Stand Amazed in the Presence," so did everyone else. Save for the group of stiff, white observers sitting in the back pew.

When the song ended, Pastor Peggy said, "I think I see some visitors this morning. Hold on, let me put on my sunglasses. Y'all's blinding me! Amen? It's so good to see some variety here this glorious day. Is that the mayor and his wife I see back there? Quick, brothers, pass the offerin' plate. Does your daddy know y'all's over here? Nah, I'm just messin' with ya. We's so glad y'all've come to praise the Lord with us today and hope you come back next Sunday...and the Sunday after that. Amen? I said 'Amen?'"

Amen!

"For those of you who don't know," Peggy continued, "we spend the service praisin' our Lord in song and prayer. Hallelujah! We celebrate Him, yes we do. We worship Him, yes we do. We sing praises, yes we do. Our book is the Bible, so let's open 'em up. Open it to Psalms one-thirty-nine, verses thirteen and fourteen, and let's get this party started...

For you created my inmost being; you knit me together in my mother's womb. I praise you because I am fearfully and wonderfully made; your works are wonderful, I know that full well.

"Now ain't that somethin'? Seems like every time I open up the newspaper lately, I have to read an article 'bout someone gettin' killed. And that just don't make no kind of sense. What's going on here? We're not smart enough to look at one another and see we're all different? Look around you. Look at Brother Roger there. Why, he's got freckles on his nose. And Sister Effie's got one leg longer than the other. And Sister Flo back there's got big ol' poofy hair. All these things we can see, but I'm not going to get me a gun and shoot ya, or get a stick and beat ya. I'm going to praise Jesus we don't all look alike...and think alike...and sound alike. Imagine how the choir would sound if everybody could only sing one note? The problem comes when we go beneath the skin, beneath the 'pearances. That's when we freak out, ya know what I'm sayin'? We think, for some crazy reason, we have to comment on what's going on in the insides of peoples. We all got our secrets—our demons. We all gone and done things we're sorry for. Ain't none of us perfect. So why is it, you tell me, we can't accept people on the inside the same way we do on the outside? The Good Bible, hallelujah, says it all. Tells me right there—look at it—says, 'I'm fearfully and wonderfully made.'...Bow your heads. Let's pray to Jesus before we sing Him some more praises. 'Dear Lord, help me. And help everyone here this morning to leave here with their heads held high. Help us to be confident and proud of the way You's made us. Help us, sweet, Lord Jesus, to remember You don't make mistakes. And to *not* like the way You made us breaks Your heart. There are no mistakes in this audience today. Not one! Help us love ourselves and others. Amen.'"

Amen! proclaimed the congregation.

"Now's the time to come forward if you haven't accepted Jesus as your Lord and Savior. Or, if you want to join the church...or, maybe you just need to renew your relationship with God. The choir's gonna sing, so come on down. Don't be shy." Several people made their way to the front, including Flo.

"Here. Take this." Flo handed Peggy ten dollars. "I don't know what's going on, but are you telling me Jesus still likes me?"

"Shoot, girl. He don't just *like* you. Come here, give me a hug."

Like Flo, Stacy was so moved that she pulled out her check-book and wrote on the PAY TO THE ORDER OF line: *This month's utilities and new carpet. Send us the bill.*

After the service, Anna, Kyle, Trey, Stacy and Flo piled into the green Bonneville, and Anna drove Flo over to The 36 Diner.

"*That's* what I call a church," Flo commented as she stowed her Bible in Anna's glove box. "I'll get it from you later—Oh, who's this?" she pulled out the picture of the baby.

"I wish someone would tell *me*. A man I visited at the nursing home left it for me when he died."

"Can I see?" Stacy asked.

Flo, mouth agape, her breath frozen, passed the picture over her shoulder.

"You all right, Flo?" Anna asked, concerned.

"What? Yeah...I'm fine."

"You don't look fine," Trey countered. "Anna, stop the car."

Flo opened the car door and vomited alongside the road. Stacy dug in her purse for a tissue and passed it up front. "I'm okay. I guess the Lord's cleaning me out."

Across town at the Third Baptist Church, the parking lot was slower than usual to fill up for the 11 AM service. Apparently, many of the congregants didn't take to attending the same church as a murderer.

When Ed Stewart took his throne-like seat in front of the choir at the beginning of the service, he couldn't help but notice the empty pews in the auditorium and the absence of women, primarily mothers, as well as his own family.

Had Brother Stewart known, he would have played the apocalypse card sooner. As it stood, he wasn't hopeful when the offering plates were passed. Little did he know, attendance and revenue would only get worse.

Vivian spent most of her days under the tree at The Springs knitting scarves and doll clothes as she talked to Ricky.

Almost daily, women, mostly mothers, stopped by to keep her company or bring her something to eat. Winnie hadn't planned on seeing her, but ran into her when she went to visit Humphrey. She took a seat next to Vivian under the tree.

"Fancy running into you here. I brought a bag of pretzels."

"Hi, Winnie."

"How ya holdin' up?"

"I don't think I am."

Winnie offered her the open bag, but Vivian shook her head and continued knitting.

"Ya know, Ricky and me had a conversation at this very tree one day."

Vivian stopped knitting. "Really?"

"Yes, ma'am. It was *serendipous,* as they say. I came to visit Humphrey and ran into Ricky—"

"*Serendipitous?*"

"That's what I said, ain't it? The only reason I came on that day was because I was confused on the dates. Humphrey's birthday was on the eighteenth, and I came on the nineteenth. Ricky was in a bad place—talkin' about killin' himself."

"I don't want to hear this."

"Yes, you do. Because this meeting is also *seren—sernip*—Say it again."

"*Serendipitous.*"

"Vocabulary ain't my strong suit. Anyway, Ricky was a good kid. Had a lot going for him. Did you know he wanted to be an architect?"

"An *architect*? I thought he wanted to play football. That's what he always told us."

"Nah. He wanted to design arenas. You know, where they have concerts and play sports and such. He talked about going to Rome to see the Colosseum. We were—Maxine, Stacy and me— we were going to give him a trip for his graduation."

"He never mentioned Rome to us."

"I'm not sure y'all kept an open line for communicatin', did ya?"

"It seems we didn't, but we only did what we thought was right."

"Y'all had one job to do as parents: love your kid."

"I should have stepped in earlier. If I had, my Ricky might still be here."

"Ain't life funny. When it's too late, it always seems so easy, dudn't it? I bet you're thinkin' it don't really matter if he liked a boy or a girl, ain't ya?"

"It does seem unimportant now. Why were we so angry when we found out?"

"How *did* you find out? Ricky thought I blabbed but it wudn't me."

Vivian knitted a few stitches.

"I knew something was going on because he'd lock himself in his room and preferred being alone. And almost every night he'd say he was going to go look at the stars and would disappear for a while."

"That's how you knew?"

"That's when I *started* to suspect, but I wasn't certain until I watched to see where he went and found the underwear catalog behind the garage. I never said a word. I thought if I didn't mention it, it would go away."

"Then you knew all along those kids from New York weren't doin' anything to Ricky? Why would you let his father carry on like that?"

"We had to blame someone. We certainly didn't make him that way!"

Winnie wiped her nose with her sleeve. "Are you dense? He was born that way."

Vivian whimpered. "I don't know how to move on."

"What do you think would make Ricky happy?"

"Probably making sure this never happens again to someone else."

"There ya go, doll. That's your answer...You feelin' better?"

Vivian let out a short breath. "I really do."

"See, I told you this was serenpi—"

"Serendipitous."

"Want me to leave the pretzels?"

Vivian looked around the field and at the creek. "No. I think I'll head home."

When the Church of the Lord group took Flo to the The 36 Diner, they stayed for lunch.

"Flo's a bit off today," Stacy remarked.

"She does seem distracted to say the least." Kyle waved his hand to get her attention. "Flo, this is mustard. I asked for ketchup."

During her break, they watched as she held a lighter in the air attempting to light a cigarette that wasn't in her mouth.

After lunch, Anna reminded Flo she'd pick her up later.

That afternoon, when Anna pulled up to the diner, Flo was standing outside smoking. Anna honked to get her attention.

"I couldn't help but notice you seemed a little distracted today, Flo. Is everything all right?" Anna asked while they sat at the traffic light.

"Yeah, I'll be fine. Getting old, I guess. No matter how much I try to fight it, I suppose it's inevitable."

"Are you sure that's all it is?"

When Flo didn't answer, Anna glanced over. Tears streamed down her face. "That's my—That's my baby in the picture."

"What? Are you sure? I mean, how can you tell?"

"The birthmark on his heel."

"Well, I'm sure he's not the only person with a birthmark on his heel. It could be common—"

"In the shape of a crescent moon?"

"I see your point, but I'm sure there's a logical—"

"I just don't know how it's possible. When I woke up, the doctor told me my baby had died. But I saw him! I came to for a few seconds. I saw that moon on his heel. That's the only thing I remember."

Sunday afternoon, Ted and Dorcas drove up to Temple to have the pictures from their trip developed at the one-hour photo lab at Wal-Mart. While they waited, they grabbed supper at Luby's cafeteria. Dorcas couldn't bear to pass down the buffet line, or as she called it, "temptation with a sneeze guard."

"Ted, I just can't. I'd order one of everything. Just get me a salad, and I'll go get us a table."

"This is the last time we can afford to eat out for a while, Dorcas. Are you sure?"

"Okay, then the chicken-fried steak, fried okra, mashed potatoes and a pecan pie. No, get me green beans instead of okra and pudding instead of pie. Wait. No, I can't. Just a salad. That's all."

"Suit yourself."

At the table, Dorcas grazed on her salad. "You could have got me some dressing, for Pete's sake. It's like eating grass. Your liver and onions looks yummy. Is that garlic bread?"

"It is."

He could ask if I want a bite. "Where are we going to travel next? What about France?"

"They say Kansas is nice," Ted remarked.

"Who's 'they?' I don't even know what's in Kansas. I've never heard anyone talk about it."

The man pushing the drink cart interrupted. "Can I get y'all some more iced tea?"

"Unsweetened for both of us." Dorcas looked at the name tag pinned on his shirt pocket. "Thank you, Wilbur."

MONDAY, JANUARY 19, 2008

Monday's *Herald* would not only be the second highest selling edition in the newspaper's history, reaching readers as far away as El Paso, but it would also make Constance Faye Barker almost a household name. The second of the two-part series would eclipse the first in sales and cement her name across Texas.

People throughout Prairie Springs were devouring every word of the front-page news. Rose pushed Ronald away as she carefully read the revealing article. Dorcas couldn't believe her sister had finally written something worth reading and went so far as to call and congratulate her. Anna was so engrossed in the article that several students in her first period class pulled out their textbooks and blatantly cheated on their Spanish tests, and she was none the wiser.

Flo was understandably infuriated when she barged into Constance's house and found her mulling over the purloined medical chart. "So, this is how you get your information? You steal it?"

"A reporter's gotta do what a reporter's—"

"Save it, Constance." Flo took the chair across from her at the dining table. "Have you no decency whatsoever? This is my life, dammit! It's not to be splattered across the front pages of the newspaper, for God's sake! What's wrong with you? I have half a mind to—"

"I thought you'd be thrilled to know your baby is still alive...or at least it could be."

"Oh, I'm thrilled all right," Flo said sardonically. "I'm thrilled to know that, according to your article, it looks like I wanted to have my baby murdered. I wanted nothing of the sort, and had I known then what I know now, I would've killed the father first."

"Then you know who the father is?"

"Of course I know who the father is, you twit."

"Well, I don't know how you could *possibly* know. There've been so many men."

"I haven't always been a whore, you dumb cluck. I want you to find my baby. Now that you have the resources, use them for something good." Flo stood, took hold of her purse, and stormed out the door.

Not two steps from the porch, she froze, turned, and pushed the door back open. "Do *you* know who the father is?"

Constance grinned deviously.

While Flo was paying a visit to Constance, another rendezvous was concluding in Austin.

"How much is this gonna cost?"

"The going rate is twenty grand plus expenses."

"Fine. But it has to be done by Wednesday."

"That's less than two days!"

"Is that a problem?"

"No. I'll get it done."

That night, the Roadside Palace would have one less vacant room. Paid in full. In cash.

The windows at the Theater Café had been repaired, and Maxine was trying to conduct business as usual. Winnie was a nervous wreck. She'd already broken three coffee cups, and when she wasn't breaking things, she was pacing back and forth.

"You're going to wear out your shoes, Winnie. What gives?" Maxine asked.

"Oh, it's all this news about Flo. I feel like I should do something." She nervously bit at her nails. "I can't just do nothing. I'm going to visit Trey across the way."

As she walked inside the mayor's office, she waved to Kyle who was planting a plum tree by the courthouse steps. "Is my grandson here?" she asked the secretary.

"I'm sorry. I don't know—"

"Cut the act! You know I'm his grandmother! Is he here or not?"

"Hold one second." She picked up the telephone, "Winnie's here to see you, sir." She hung up the phone. "It's right down this hall—"

"I know where the friggin' office is, missy."

"Hi, Grams." Trey greeted his grandma with a kiss on the cheek.

"Well, ain't that gentlemanly of ya."

"I've only got a few minutes. I've got to get over to the dog food plant."

"I won't keep ya, sonny. Ain't you fixed up your office right nice. Is that a new chair?"

"Thanks. It is, but I suspect you want to do more than talk about the décor of my office."

"You're right about that. You've got to do something. This town is a mess."

"I am doing something, Winn—Grams. We hired a new police officer this morning, Officer Chuck Dickson. He's been a policeman for years up in Texarkana. Lots of experience. Moved down here to be closer to his family. He's Wilma and Chawli Dickson's kid."

"Wilma? Ain't that the woman who fell through the window at the café?"

"Yeah. Anyway, Chuck was down visiting his parents and wondered about the lack of police force at the protest. He guessed we might be hiring."

"*He* wudn't at the protest, was he?"

"No."

"Well, he can't be worse than Officer Richards," Winnie commented as she picked at her nails. "I need you to designate the tree at The Springs a cemetery. I told Vivian she could be buried with her son...and you know I'm a woman of my word."

"I'll bring it up at the City Council meeting."

"Thank you...Now, whadaya think about this whole Flo thing?"

"Pretty weird. I can't believe Flo wanted to murder—"

"She didn't. It ain't at all like what Constance wrote, ya know. I know for a fact that Flo wanted that baby. It was the father who didn't want it."

"Who's the father, anyway?"

"I dunno." It broke her heart to lie to her grandson, but it would hurt a lot less than the truth.

Kyle arrived home from work at four-thirty and pulled the lawnmower from the shed. The grass needed a slight trim, and as Head of the Parks Department, he felt his own yard should reflect his title.

Anna was inside when the mower stopped abruptly, followed by Kyle yelling. She hurried to the window to find him dancing in panic. Running out the door, she was certain he had cut off a toe. "What's wrong? What happened?"

"Fire ants!" he howled. "Get the hose! Quick!" He tried to brush them from his legs but they crawled on his hands and up his arms. Most hovered around the elastic in his socks, but several managed to find their way inside. "Hurry, Anna!" He kicked off his shoes and both socks.

"I'm hurrying...I'm hurrying." Anna turned on the spigot, but the hose remained dry. She searched desperately for the kink. When she found it and straightened the hose, a soothing jet of water shot onto Kyle's legs. Anna sprayed him from head to toe.

"You poor thing," she said, seeing the white-and-red welts. "Come inside. I might have some lotion."

Anna sat him down on the couch and ran to the bathroom. She returned with a bottle of calamine lotion that was in the apartment when she moved in. "It's all dried up! Oh, it's from nineteen ninety-eight." She grabbed a banana from the kitchen, took the peel and left the fruit on the counter.

"What are you doing?"

"Banana peel is soothing for insect bites. I read it somewhere." She rubbed his left leg with the banana peel. "I can't believe how many bites you have. This is horrible." When she reached his foot, she stopped. "What's this?"

"Nothing." Kyle tried to hide his foot.

Anna grabbed it. "Kyle?"

"I'm sorry I didn't say anything...When I saw that picture in your glove box, it took everything I had not to cry, but I didn't want to spoil the concert. I was going to tell you. I was just waiting for the right time."

"Obviously the universe decided the time was now."

"Did it have to be so dramatic? Son-of-a-bitch! These little shits pack a punch."

"In all our years of being friends, you never thought to tell me you were adopted?"

"I thought about it. I just never said anything."

"Surely, there's something *you* haven't told me about your life?"

Anna didn't answer. "Wait. So...Oh, my god! You're Flo's kid!"

"Huh? Flo? What are you talking about?"

Anna ran and pulled the rolled-up newspaper from her purse. "Kyle, it's all right here."

The articled noted his birth weight, length, and mentioned the crescent-shaped birthmark on the bottom of his left heel. As he read the details of his birth, he felt real for the first time in his life.

After numerous attempts to track down his adoption history, followed by the subsequent letter of disappointment: *We regret to inform you...* He really *did* exist.

His elation quickly faded. "She wanted to kill me?"

"Kyle, remember this is sensationalist, hyperbolic Constance. Get it from the horse's mouth. Talk to Flo."

"You're right. She doesn't seem like the baby murdering type...Does she?"

"Of course not. Flo's the sweetest soul around."

"She's also a hooker waitress. I never pictured my mom as—It just can't be her!"

Anna ran her fingers through his hair to comfort him. "You could've done a lot worse, you know? She's the quintessential hooker with a heart of gold!"

Kyle smiled a bit in spite of himself. "It's just weird how I made up all these images of what my mom would look like and how she'd walk and talk. It's just weird, you know?"

"What are you going to do? You have to tell her."

"Do I?"

"Of course you do, Kyle. She deserves to know—I'll call her."

"No! She's working, remember. I'll talk to her later this evening."

"Just don't do to her what you don't want people doing to you."

"What do you mean?"

"Judging. Everything was okay with Flo being a prostitute before you found out she was your mother."

"Yeah, you're right," he said softly. "I'm going to finish mowing."

As Stacy tossed a box of Rise & Shine cereal into her cart, she noticed him at the end of the aisle. She hoped he hadn't seen her and quickly made a U-turn. When she thought she was in the clear, she hurried to the checkout lane.

He pulled in behind her.

"Stacy?"

"Mark! It's so good to see you."

"How's Stormy?" he asked, expecting to find him poking his head from her Coach bag.

"Oh, he's fine," she responded dismissively.

"Read any good books lately?"

"No."

Stacy placed the separator bar between her items and Mark's and moved along with the conveyor belt. "Plastic or paper?"

"How's married life?"

"Paper...Mark, you *know* how my marriage is. Look, it's good to see you—really. But if you think you can ask me out again in the express lane, then you're completely mistaken. As far as I'm concerned, that night we slept together was a mistake, and I'd appreciate it if you'd never mention it again." She handed the cashier her credit card.

"Whoa, Stacy. I wasn't going to ask you out. I was just being polite. I'm sorry if I upset you."

Driving home, Stacy was ashamed by her overreactive outburst and hoped to forget about the entire event. Unfortunately, six minutes after leaving the Save-All parking lot, Constance walked through the door and up to the same cashier. With a smile and a twenty-dollar bill, she asked, "Heard any good gossip lately?"

"Uh, like yeah..."

"Yoo-hoo! Constance, dear," Dorcas leaned out the car window and called across the parking lot. She was so excited to see her sister that when she opened her door, she hit the shiny black sedan parked adjacent. As she was straining to see through the tinted windows, a man with greasy hair carelessly parted to one side emerged.

Dorcas recoiled, "I'm so sorry! I didn't mean to—It's just that I used to be fat. I forget I don't have to open the door as wide."

The man walked around to inspect the damage. "Barely see it. Don't worry."

"Oh, thank you!" Dorcas breathed a sigh of relief. "I hear a phone ringing, and I don't have one," she told the man. "...Constance! Constance! It's me. Wait up a minute, will ya?"

The man got back in the sedan to answer his cell phone. "I told you not to call me. I'll call you. Anyway, I've yet to get her alone. Now she's with some other lady...Don't worry, we still have another day and a half."

While Kyle waited for Flo to arrive home, he attempted to call his adoptive parents, although there was nothing nurturing about them. They divorced years ago. His mother didn't answer, so he rang his father, who was home with his girlfriend. To make matters worse, Kyle phoned during *Wheel of Fortune*. Each time he tried to speak, he could hear his father yelling at the TV, "Buy a vowel!" Exasperated, he hung up and went outside for air.

Halfway through a cigarette, he spotted Flo coming through the lychgate. He watched as she went inside. He gave her a few minutes to get settled and walked over. The door was ajar, so he knocked and let himself in.

"You decent?"

"Kyle? I'll be out in a second. Make yourself comfortable."

Kyle sat on the sofa. It was the first time he'd noticed the crescent moons decorating her walls, on her shelf of knick-knacks and on her vinyl tablecloth.

Flo appeared sticking a bobby pin in her hair and wearing a robe covered with crescent moons. "Getting out of your work clothes is always a relief."

"I like your robe."

"Thank you, doll. I saw it in a mail-order catalog and just had to have it. I guess you can tell I like moons. And, well, after

Constance's article, I guess the whole world knows why. Is that why you came over? To ask me if I'm a murderer?"

"No."

"Well, you're the first. Can I get you a beer?"

"That would be nice."

She grabbed two beers from the fridge, popped the tops and handed one to him. She sat beside him on the couch. "I could just kill that Constance for writing that lie. She only knew the half of it. Apparently for her, two and two equal whatever-the-hell she wants. She just made stuff up. Can you believe someone threw eggs at me today?"

"I, uh—"

"Kyle, boy, if you knew how many nights I lay awake stroking that soft baby blanket I bought...When Dr. Waxman told me my baby was gone, *I* almost died. You've got to believe me. I didn't do it." She took a swig of her beer. "I don't know why it matters so much to me that you believe me, but you've just got to. And you have to convince Anna, too...and Rose. What we've got here is too special for this to ruin it. Please, Kyle."

"I do believe you, Flo. I do. And Anna doesn't need convincing because she got her information from Dr. Waxman." He leaned over and kissed her on the cheek.

Flo pulled a frayed tissue from her pocket to wipe her eyes and blow her nose. "You know, I don't know where my baby is, or if I'll ever see him again, or even if he's still alive. But if he were, I'd hope he's a lot like you."

Kyle's eyes grew bright, and he glanced again at the crescent moons. "I've got to go. I'll call you later."

Flo didn't get up as she watched him walk out.

An hour later, the sun had set completely on Harper Valley Lane. The chirping of the birds had given way to crickets, and the morning glories were resting for the night. Barefoot, Kyle turned off the garden lights, went to the bench by the fountain and lit a candle. He crossed his leg so the birthmark was illuminated by the flame and signaled Anna to call Flo.

He could hear the phone ringing inside Flo's apartment. Seconds later she emerged. "Who's there? Kyle is that you? What are you doing out here in the dark?"

All he could see was her silhouette in the doorway. "Come closer."

Anna peered out the open window.

"What's this all about?"

"Come over here. I want to show you something."

Flo approached until she was about a yard away. Her eyes were drawn to the light of the candle. When they focused on the distinctive mark on his left foot, her lips quivered.

"I'm your baby boy."

Flo clutched him and cried like she'd never cried before. As the two embraced, she looked up at the sky and there it was: the crescent moon smiling down upon them.

Chapter Twenty-Two

Tuesday night, Officer Chuck Dickson was dispatched to his first call in Prairie Springs: a car wreck in the same intersection where Winnie had collided with Ronald Black. This time, Winnie was rammed from behind by a shiny black sedan. The man driving flew through the windshield, over Winnie's car, and landed on the pavement.

Unlike the first wreck, Winnie held tightly to her wig and continued doing so as she got out of the car. She loosened her grip as she watched paramedics tend to the injured man, but when Officer Dickson approached her to discuss the wreck, his strong aftershave provoked a hearty sneeze. Her wig went flying, and the joints landed on the ground between them.

For the few hours she spent behind bars, she giggled about how she'd slammed on the brakes and purposely caused the collision. No unwelcome visitors stayed overnight in Prairie Springs without Winnie finding out.

Like most women, Winnie thought ahead, considering all possibilities, even the most unlikely ones. While everyone else in town was caught up in part one of Constance's story, Winnie was knee-deep in part two: if the father had been willing to have the baby murdered, how far would he go to keep his secret dead and buried?

Winnie first became suspicious when Luciano happened to mention that the motel guest staying next to him drove a black car, dressed in black and wore dark sunglasses. Since she knew the manager of the Roadside Palace on a first-name basis, she convinced him to give her the housekeeping passkey so she could investigate.

After making sure the mystery car was nowhere to be found, she casually entered Room 202. The only luggage was a black overnight bag sitting in the chair next to the window. On the table was a clipping of Constance's byline photo with her address written next to it. She quietly exited. As she turned to walk away, a black sedan pulled into the parking lot.

Winnie's heart skipped a beat. She hurried to hide in the housekeeping closet until he passed.

"Next time you're at the café, dessert's on me," she told the manager when she returned the key. When the driver was back in his room, Winnie walked to the parking lot, got in her car and waited.

Just after sundown, the man left his hotel room and sped off.

With the black sedan safely out of sight, Winnie buckled her seatbelt, revved up the motor and took off down the road. She passed him just before the traffic light, held onto her wig, and slammed on the brakes.

Constance's police scanner droned the details of the accident from her oak nightstand. She listened, but went back to darning a snag in her turquoise cardigan. Traffic accidents were beneath her now.

WEDNESDAY, JANUARY 21, 2008

With the hitman in the ICU, Kyle's biological father was taking matters into his own hands. Part Two of Constance's article would be published tomorrow, and he was determined to put a stop to it by ridding the town, once and for all, of the turquoise obsessed gossip queen.

The clock in the rental car read 9:32 PM. He parked so he could observe Constance through her sheer curtains. When she sank into a chair, he made his move.

He snuck around to the side of her house. While crouching, he stuck a piece of Doublemint gum in his mouth and placed the foil in his shirt pocket.

At the patio door, he peered through the glass and could see the back of a swivel rocker in the living room.

Knowing the sound would be muffled by the blaring television, he slowly turned the doorknob. With a gentle push, the door opened. Never taking his eyes off the chair, he slipped inside.

Step by step, he crept towards the living room. His footsteps falling silently on the bright turquoise carpet. As he neared the rocker, he raised his hands to ensure a tight snare.

The chair violently swiveled around.

"What are *you* doing here?" he exclaimed.

"Let me ask that *my* way: 'What the fuck are *you* doing here,' Eddie? But I think that tie in your hand tells me all I need to know. I've been watching your reflection in the tea kettle since you stepped foot in the hallway, and not once did you even hesitate."

"That woman deserves to be punished for writing all of those lies."

"Lies? Oh, my dear son, I want to believe you, I really do. But instead of just *praying* for the old and sick, maybe you should've visited them on occasion. While you were behind your fuckin' pulpit, Anna Aron was at the nursing home visiting Dr. Waxman in his last days. He told her *everything*. He even gave her a picture of the baby...who, you'll be happy to know, was just reunited with his mother."

"What? That's impossible!"

"No it ain't. Lucky for you, the doctor was a compassionate

man. He didn't kill the baby; he dropped it off at an adoption agency in Austin the next day."

"This is absurd. You don't know what you're talking about. You've always been crazy...I've never slept with that whore."

"Come now. Even *I* don't believe that. Flo is like my child—more than *you* ever were. At least *she* talks to me. Oh, and ya know what else? The money you paid for the murder—guess what happened to it?"

"I'm sure you're going to tell me."

That was enough of an admission. Winnie knew her son was guilty, but this acknowledgment broke her heart.

Flo stormed out of the coat closet. "You son of a bitch!—no offense, Winnie. You wanted to murder our child to protect your holier-than-thou ambitions! Scum of the earth! Had I known, I would've killed you—you nutless scrotum."

"Drop your weapon!" Officer Dickson ordered, as he barged through the front door. "You're under arrest for conspiracy and the attempted murder of Constance Faye Baker."

"Barker," Winnie corrected.

Officer Dickson handcuffed Ed Stewart and took him to the back seat of his patrol car.

Flo nervously lit a cigarette. "I'm glad that's over...Where's Constance? Is she still hiding?"

Winnie chuckled. "I forgot about her...Constance! Coast is clear. You can come out now."

Constance cautiously opened the pantry door and peeked through the crevice.

Winnie waved. "Get on out here, you ding-dong."

Constance emerged as white as a ghost and shaking profusely.

"Oh my Lord, you wet yourself," Flo noticed.

"No...I knocked over the vinegar." Constance's voice vibrated as if she were talking into a fan. "...Are you smoking in my house?"

"Coping mechanism. Get over it."

Constance made her way to the sofa. "Thank you, Winnie. I won't forget this."

"All in a fuckin' day's work, honey."

The wind picked up, warning people of the upcoming rain, and the night skies came alive with electrified webs of lightning and ovations of thunder.

THURSDAY, JANUARY 22, 2008

By dawn the skies were clear. The bark of the storm had been worse than its bite. The only damage was a few fallen tree limbs. Still, the paperboys had to wake half an hour earlier to stuff Thursday's edition into plastic bags. Had they known that most newspapers would barely touch the ground, they probably wouldn't have bothered. Eager folks waited quietly inside their houses listening for the *thud* in the yard. The first paper was thrown at 4:17 that morning and by five, there was hardly a kitchen light in town that wasn't on. Circuits were busy as neighbors phoned one another, friends called their enemies, and several irate residents harassed Constance to the point she had to turn on the answering machine. At the landscaped mansion on the farm-to-market road, everything breakable was being smashed by a hysterical wife who'd discovered her husband wasn't the man she thought he was.

Wearing a robe, with Stormy at her feet, Stacy practically intercepted the newspaper, excited to find out the identity of Kyle's father. She read it and began laughing hysterically. She continued laughing as she walked down the hall to the guest room. Both Trey and Kyle were still asleep. She sat on the edge of the bed, waking Trey, and handed him the newspaper.

"What's going on?" Trey muttered.

"Read it."

"Holy shit!"

Kyle woke. "What? What's happening? Hi, Stacy. Oh, the article! What's it say? Who's my father?"

Trey lowered the newspaper. "The same as mine."

Kyle grabbed the paper. "It can't be."

"Say hello to your half-brother," Stacy grinned and walked out.

It is true for anyone who plays with fire—karma. It's all a matter of time.

Brother Edward Stewart should have known all too well: when building a house, a foundation of solid rock is better than sinking sand. Irrefutable wisdom that would go on to be the topic of Pastor Peggy Thomas' sermon the following Sunday, preached to a packed house at Prairie Springs' Church of the Lord. By summer, the crowds would become so large, Peggy would have to find a larger building.

The weekend of May 31, 2008

On Saturday, the final renovations were being completed at the former Third Baptist Church. After finishing the installation of a new runner of red carpet (courtesy of Stacy), there was only one thing left to do: replace the current sign with Church of the Lord. On Sunday, after an opening prayer, the sermon began.

"Praise the Lord! And welcome to the new, Church of the Lord. Whoa, it's bright in here! Let's get started..."

Saturday, June 7, 2008

The Cotton Festival

The roads leading to Prairie Springs were lined with "summer snow." Trucks from all over the county poured into town carrying fluffy white balls of cotton. Despite trailers designed to contain it, some inevitably flew off in transport and collected on the sides of the road. Aside from religion, cotton was the biggest business around. It was so big that every June it was celebrated with a festival on the town square.

A small display of fireworks kicked off the event. Mayor Trey Stewart took the stage to welcome everyone to the celebration. The first country and western song enticed a few two-steppers to make their way around the makeshift plywood dance floor. More couples joined in for the second song, and by the third, they were bumping into one another. Stacy and Anna danced together, and Stacy was glad she wore her boots since Anna did more *toe*-stepping than two-stepping. Winnie, Rose and Ronald stood watching. Ronald eventually coerced Rose to dance a waltz. It had been so long she feared she wouldn't remember how, but as soon as she stepped onto the dance floor, she swung from side to side as she had at her high school prom.

Standing alone, Winnie admired the metamorphosis occurring in the town she never thought capable of change. She caught a glimpse of a falling star in the distance and waved to her daddy.

Maxine grabbed Winnie's arm, interrupting her thoughts. "We're going to Argentina!"

"Who's 'we?'"

"Me and Luciano."

"That's great...I think."

Maxine tugged Luciano back onto the dance floor.

Winnie, alone again, spotted Dorcas at the nacho stand. She walked over. "How's Ted treatin' you these days?"

"Hiya, Winnie—Extra cheese, please—I can't win."

"Sorry 'bout that, doll."

Dorcas whimpered, "He told me my extra skin looks like curtains—I'm trying to open 'em back up by stuffing myself."

"Wait just a fuckin' minute, honey! He didn't want you when you were fat, and he don't want you now? Screw him! Some men you just can't please. You ever thought about tryin' to please yourself?"

Dorcas paid for her nachos and handed them to Winnie. "You know, you're right. Maybe Ivory Black wasn't so crazy after all. I'm going to leave the SOB if he can't love me like I am."

Trey and Kyle, who were managing the cotton-filled dunking booth, called to Winnie, "Grams!" She waved to her grandsons, heart aflutter. When she turned back around, Dorcas had gone.

Anna decided to sit out a few songs and spare Stacy what was left of her toes. Kyle spotted her on the bench.

"Enjoying yourself, Cupcake?"

"I am, believe it or not."

Kyle took a seat on the bench next to her.

"Have you seen your mom? Is she here?" Anna asked.

"I don't think I'm ever going to get used to calling her *Mom*. But no, she said she was going to celebrate cotton by sleeping on cotton sheets." Anna grinned. "Sounds like a good idea."

"Why, are you ready to leave?"

"I think I am."

Kyle knew she wasn't nearly as tired as she made out to be. He recognized the look of loneliness. "A dance before we go?" he asked.

Anna looked down at his toes. "Are you sure you want to risk it?"

"Absolutely, Cupcake."

The stories will continue...

www.ingramcontent.com/pod-product-compliance
Lightning Source LLC
Chambersburg PA
CBHW030242120726
47903CB00005B/1582